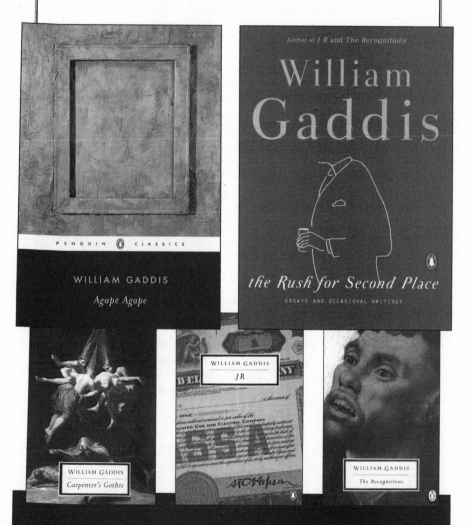

CONJUNCTIONS

Bi-Annual Volumes of New Writing

Edited by
Bradford Morrow

published by Bard College

EDITOR: Bradford Morrow
MANAGING EDITOR: Michael Bergstein
SENIOR EDITORS: Robert Antoni, Martine Bellen, Peter Constantine, Brian
    Evenson, Pat Sims
WEBMASTER: Brian Evenson
ASSOCIATE EDITORS: Jedediah Berry, Micaela Morrissette, Eric Olson, Alan
    Tinkler, Patrizia Villani
ART EDITOR: Norton Batkin
PUBLICITY: Mark R. Primoff
EDITORIAL ASSISTANTS: Tayt Harlin, Katherine Marino, J. W. McCormack

CONJUNCTIONS is published in the Spring and Fall of
each year by Bard College, Annandale-on-Hudson, NY
12504. This issue is made possible in part with the generous funding of the National Endowment for the Arts, and
with public funds from the New York State Council on the
Arts, a State Agency. Special thanks to Sarah and Matthew
Gaddis, Chatham Ewing and Sonya McDonald of the Department of Special
Collections at Washington University in St. Louis, Jane Shore, Benjamin Swett,
Christchurch Press, Andrew Klein, and Nielsen Gallery, Boston.

SUBSCRIPTIONS: Send subscription orders to CONJUNCTIONS, Bard College,
Annandale-on-Hudson, NY 12504. Single year (two volumes): $18.00 for individ-
uals; $25.00 for institutions and overseas. Two years (four volumes): $32.00 for
individuals; $45.00 for institutions and overseas. Patron subscription (lifetime):
$500.00. Overseas subscribers please make payment by International Money
Order. For information about subscriptions, back issues, and advertising, call
Michael Bergstein at (845) 758-1539 or fax (845) 758-2660.

All editorial communications should be sent to Bradford Morrow, Conjunctions,
21 East 10th Street, New York, NY 10003. Unsolicited manuscripts cannot be
returned unless accompanied by a stamped, self-addressed envelope. Electronic
submissions will not be considered.

Conjunctions is listed and indexed in the American Humanities Index.

Visit the Conjunctions Web site at www.conjunctions.com.

Original cover art by Jake Berthot, The Return, 1999, oil on panel, 16⅛ x 14⅜
inches; Woods (Cherry Hill), 1999, oil on panel, 15 x 14³⁄₁₆ inches. Reproduced by
kind permission of the artist and Nielsen Gallery, Boston. Cover design by Jerry
Kelly.

Available through D.A.P./Distributed Art Publishers, Inc., 155 Sixth Avenue,
New York, NY 10013. Telephone: (212) 627-1999. Fax: (212) 627-9484.

Printers: Edwards Brothers

Typesetter: Bill White, Typeworks

ISSN 0278-2324
ISBN 0-941964-57-4

Manufactured in the United States of America.

TABLE OF CONTENTS

TWO KINGDOMS
Guest-Edited by Howard Norman

GUEST EDITOR'S NOTE

"WHAT GOOD IS INTELLIGENCE," said Ryonosuke Akutagawa, "if you can't discover a useful melancholy?" One afternoon on Prince Edward Island, the province of Nova Scotia, I stood with an ornithologist friend exactly where the rain ended. It has to end somewhere, of course, but there we were, looking into the rain, from a dry place a few yards away. It is difficult to articulate, but, just then, I felt for the first time the actual physical sensation, rather eerie, of being situated on a planet, a strange place where the inchoate "beginnings" of things such as weather, all the first experiments of the gods, were reenacted, constantly, somewhere, at any given moment. Surely this feeling was childlike. I was giddy and terrified in equal measure. I simply shook my head back and forth and uttered, "Imagine that." However, I didn't have to imagine it, because it—this exact circumstance—was right in front of me. But already it was past being just the thing itself; it had become the construction of memory in sentences. My companion took in our situation somewhat matter-of-factly, reserving awe for things other than happenstance. I, on the other hand, wished I could stand at this borderline for a long time. One end of the beach was draped in gray filaments, the other end bright pale white-brown. Sandpipers or some other shore birds were stitching along the froth, the border between land and sea.

What good is intelligence if you can't discover a useful melancholy? Melancholy, at times, seems the absolute perfect response to the human condition. This issue of *Conjunctions* is called "Two Kingdoms," a title derived from a wistful passage in a letter by Edward Lear: "The misalignment of emotions before sailing to Corfu. The eternal battle of two kingdoms: staying, departing; home, casting memory back to home." Lear also said of himself, "I am fixed in my melancholy, yet I am restless within it." One of the most peripatetic of men on record, Lear was also a wonderful painter of birds and landscapes. He once referred to homesickness as a "possibly fatal malady."

In my cover letter to potential contributors to this issue of *Conjunctions*, I suggested the subject of "duality," or "dualism" in our lives. Based on some of my own favorite works of literature, I

7

could imagine all sorts of scenarios, all sorts of dualistic structures, all sorts of bifurcations. A fictional account of someone who, like the narrator in Thomas Bernhard's *Wittgenstein's Nephew*, is only at home when in transit; Aharon Appelfeld's *The Iron Tracks*, whose narrator basically seesaws between his past in a concentration camp and his present, which is spent largely on trains; Martella Fizzi's novella "By and Large," in which a schizophrenic young woman communicates with her lover only via Morse code; Junichiro Tanizaki's novel *The Key*, which is composed of competing diaries of husband and wife, which is also an epistolary novel, because each purposely leaves his or her diary for the other to read. As is the case with such broad themes, in conversations with and letters between writers I soon became inundated with examples. Until, finally, Michael Palmer aptly wrote on a postcard, "Of course, duality is what all writing's about. It's the inevitable subject." I suspect it is more often than not an annoyance for a writer to have a subject "suggested," when subjects naturally insist on themselves day and night and won't leave us alone. The idea with "Two Kingdoms" was to see if writers might attend to a particular idea, and if not, send good work anyway. Both things happened. I cannot pretend to ever fully comprehend the duet of the conscious and unconscious minds as they work in a poem—or prose—but I can say each and every one of the splendid contributions to this hodgepodge anthology contains the resonant duality of (as Lear said of a Greek landscape) "the blessedly clear light—and the blessedly mysterious darkness."

My own writing is largely set in the Canadian Maritimes and the Arctic, and no matter where I live, those landscapes and histories are right in front of me. For nearly a decade, I worked and traveled in the Arctic reaches of Canada and Greenland. In a remote—remote for even the Arctic—village, one evening an elderly woman, suffering the last throes of cancer, gathered all twenty-seven Inuit citizens of that village, plus myself and another visitor, a Norwegian linguist, into a small, cluttered house of the makeshift sort you find in such villages. She was seventy-three. She proceeded to distribute small gifts and say goodbye. Her nephew handed her a bottle of whiskey. It was between minus forty and minus forty-five degrees Fahrenheit. Then she "walked out," as they said in those parts. I looked through the door's window until she disappeared. It was snowing heavily. I was told that she would simply walk as far as she could, sit or lie down, remove her clothes, drink as much whiskey as possible, and wait. And that she would not have to wait long before (rough translation) "she would travel to the land of the dead." At the time, I was bewildered at how she could be allowed to do such a thing. Years hence, I am fairly amazed at how she comported herself—as did her family and friends—with the utmost dignity. I don't mean to traffic in anthropological sentimentality; I only mean to report that after we observed her walk through blowing snow out of this kingdom, later that night a dozen or so stories about the land of the dead and what goes on there were told. If stories are a kind of eternity, then in those northern villages, eternity surely resides in the past. While this issue of *Conjunctions* was being completed, one of the contributors, Reetika Vazirani, took the life of her two-and-a-half-year-old son and then her own life. Whatever exhaustions, diminishments plagued her, whatever dark cloud choked her mind, I wish she had had enough remaining clarity to have left her son in this kingdom. Convenient psychological theory dealing with the relationship between depression and creativity suggests that writers embrace, in their craft, the "melancholy dilemma" (to quote Julia Kristeva). That is, given the "melancholy dilemma," writers resort to language, to the symbolic order. From this it would follow that people who are depressed no longer have this recourse. For the seriously depressed person, language is dead—the symbolic order fails him or her. Whichever demon she succumbed to, this notion could not have been entirely true for Reetika Vazirani, at least not up until the final shattering of her mind, the dark night of the soul, or however one attempts to describe some unfathomable, desperate rage and excruciating narrowness of purpose. Because she was writing fine poetry merely weeks before the end. For all anyone knows, language— poetry—may have been the last thing she held on to. The deepest horror: one can imagine the twisted logic of a mother doing such a thing to not leave a child motherless; one cannot fathom a mother doing such a thing. She should have plummeted alone; yet she did not. Two kingdoms: hope and hopelessness; nightmares; nightmares you can't wake from. Ad infinitum.

The prose and poetry in this issue of *Conjunctions* dignify language, and each piece is of itself a bold act of the imagination, "not allowing convenient notions of existence" (Lear), painstakingly shaping experience for posterity, even if posterity takes the form of someone years hence just rummaging through a bin in a used bookstore, who happens upon this bound gathering of work. I am grateful to the writers who allowed me to be associated with their work as guest editor, to Brad Morrow for suggesting our collaboration. I am grateful to Jerome Rothenberg, friend and mentor for thirty years, for being the first to contribute. I'd like to acknowledge my admiration for Rick Moody's Gaddis portfolio and for those writers who contributed to it. I especially wish to thank Jake Berthot for his trees, because—again I quote Lear—"the mind's eye is sometimes least patronized by a picture dedicated to the more haunting configurations." That is what I feel about so many of the pieces in this issue of *Conjunctions:* haunting configurations. And there's precise joy—and useful melancholy—throughout these pages as well.

—Howard Norman
East Calais, Vermont

In Memoriam
GEORGE PLIMPTON
1927–2003
Colleague and Friend

Zed Lake

Steve Erickson

Every passing day, Kristin could see the lake rise. The edge of the water continued to rot a little more the front porch of her little house until one morning she expected to find she finally had been swept away. With every honeymoon twilight the drunken bride of the **2009** lake was then carried across the threshold of Kristin's house by the lesbian groom of the moon, with a bridal train of small dead animals, palm fronds ripped from their trees, the trash of the recently submerged: pages of paperbacks, gin bottles, old tickets from the drowned Cathode Flower nightclub that used to be right below her on the Sunset Strip at the foot of a hillside now under water. Step out her front door at dawn into the puddles that seeped up through the decking, sunlight from the lake's surface cutting a gash across her eyes, and Kristin saw the glub glub glub of rising bubbles and wondered from what sinking building or body.

Finally the lake stopped. This was what everyone had been waiting for—once it became clear the lake wasn't going to stop until it reached the ocean; once that became clear, there was no reason not to wish the lake would just get it over with, so the horizon could finally stop shifting, so everyone could stop moving to higher ground. It felt to Kristin like the foundation of the house gave way a little more every night, and it woke her in the dark, when the walls didn't.

Back before she lost her son, as one of the several odd part-time jobs she held to support both of them, Kristin had worked as an assistant for a doctor who diagnosed the dying buildings and houses of L.A. after the lake came. Consumptive houses, malaria houses, alzheimer houses, heart-attack houses. Houses with tumors growing out the attic or the bedroom windows or the family rooms. All dying faster than Doc could pronounce them terminal —and when the sun went down, when night slipped across the city, in the hills and skyline were black patches where once were lights: an urbanological mourning, a city bound and gagged in the black memorial armbands of lightless windows and doors.

Although Kristin had never known Doc well, the older woman had been a kind of mother figure to the younger woman with her young son, the young mother who had never known her own mother. Kristin had always believed there was a sadness about Doc that she brought with her to L.A. when she fled New York, where just after the turn of the century she could hear in the walls of its tallest buildings the oncoming roar of chaos's age. It was about then that the lake had appeared in the middle of Los Angeles, coming up out of a small hole at the bottom in a way that no one could explain: first a small, inconspicuous pond on Crescent Heights a couple of blocks above Sunset, then a larger body of water that one could walk around in ten minutes, then a lagoon that swallowed up the low hills, the shops and small homes, waves splashing against the walls of the Chateau X, the old Hollywood hotel that stood where the Strip began. Sometime in that first year of the lake, when the city would send boats out to the center and divers would swim to the bottom trying to figure out where it was coming from, it was referred to in the newspapers and on the radio as "lake zero," as in "ground zero," and then at some point it got shortened to Lake Z or, sometimes, Lake Zed.

The last time Kristin saw Doc, her face had been pressed against a wall, eyes closed, listening to the fading life of an old Laurel Avenue apartment building—female voices inside the walls singing songs of . . . the madness of motherhood, Kristin would realize only years later. That particular afternoon, from the window of that apartment, from up over the hills in the far west, Kristin could see the first wave of the owls that had invaded the city ever since the lake appeared, still far enough away that their shadows on her back skittered up her spine like small black spiders. For a while Doc seemed frozen where she stood. With a kind of hesitation Kristin had never seen in her, Doc laid her hands on the walls and moved through the apartment slowly from the far doorway that was already darkening with night into the part of the room that was blood red with sunset, as though she was melting into the decomposed smear of the dead day, hands spread out away from her until it was as though they were scorched to the wall, as though her face was burned in the plaster. She didn't make any sound at all for a moment. Then Kristin heard this cry—at first

12

she thought it was coming from the room itself—and Doc had dropped to the floor, the grief on her face as though outrunning the face's own features, eyes and mouth stricken incapable of tears or sound. God only knew what terrible song Doc heard coming from the walls of that room. As a woman in need of a mother of her own, Kristin wished she hadn't seen it, because some last shred of trust in her was shattered, some small capacity for faith she didn't know she still had, until this moment when she knew she didn't have it anymore.

Now five years later, on the edge of the lake, Kristin could hear the wooden walls of her own house screaming. Nothing indicated the existence of the Sunset Strip beneath the lake's surface but the burning night torches that formed a winding watery corridor. In the distance, about half the top floor of the old hotel where Kristin had lived with her son could still be seen above water; once she had thought about taking her silver gondola out there. But there was no point to that, unless it was to slip herself into the water for good—so then why keep moving to higher land at all? Let some watery night take her. Five years, two months later, night after night and hour after hour, moment after moment Kristin still saw in her mind his small smile, still heard his voice that used to call from the other bedroom, "Mama, where are you?"

When she lost him, the lake had already been there nearly three years—since just before Kirk was born—and had already taken over most of the city. The realization had come to her one night as though in a dream; but it wasn't a dream: an amniotic fog filled the room where she slept. The smell of birth and the lake had been overpowering that night, and she had moved through the vapor to his crib where he slept, picked him up, his face glistening; she had taken him from his room and closed his door behind her, taken him to her bed and put him on the pillow next to hers where he went on sleeping, and the rest of the night she sat up in the bed placing her body like a barrier between him and the window with the lake beyond it. She had watched the center of the lake, waiting, her heart pounding: *the lake is coming for my boy.* The lake was coming for her boy, and she had come to know in a way she couldn't explain even to herself that it didn't matter where they went, it didn't matter how far they tried to get away, the lake would keep coming for him. Down in the hole of the lake, down in the

13

opening of the birth canal where the world broke its water, lurked her son's doom and she had to stop it; she had to shake herself loose of the love for Kirk that paralyzed her, find inside her the love that would save him. She had to go to war with the womb of the century that would reclaim him.

I used to be fucking fearless, you should know that about me. None of this terror of all the world's chaos that Kirk's birth unleashed in me means anything if you don't know that. Ran away from home at sixteen, traveling with this suicide-religious cult for a while, moving down to L.A. and getting into all kinds of situations just blindly, sometimes out of desperation, sometimes because I didn't have enough sense to be afraid. Lived by wits and recklessness. I was the most fearless person I've ever known but then her son was born and she was paralyzed by her love for him. In her heart he opened the door to a vast lake of fear, stretching out beyond her young years when mortality was supposed to be so inconceivable. For weeks, months, years after he was born, she had a knot in the pit of her stomach where he had been: *what is it?* she wondered, *what is this dread?* that seemed attached to nothing she could name; and then one day she knew it was the dread of his loss—although nothing she could name threatened him. It didn't matter. She dreaded just the possibility of his loss in a world where everything and anything could be lost . . . and then she dreaded the dreading itself, dreaded the idea that the dreading itself would make something dreadful come to pass.

When and how did he make me so tender? she wondered bitterly. It wasn't when he was inside her, she could remember when he was inside her . . . he just took her over at some point. He just snuck up on her. And it wasn't as though all mothers were the same; her mother certainly wasn't, whoever she was, and truthfully Kristin never believed she would be either. Certainly she always thought she would be *adequate* as a mother; just on general principle she was going to be *adequate.* But when did he get to her? Tenderness, that was a new one. She didn't like it, no not much. She had wanted to be a tough chick again. She would read him a book called *I Am a Little Monkey* and ask him, "Are you a monkey?" and he would answer, "No, I'm not a monkey!" and she would ask, "Are you a mommy?" and he would answer in exasperated disbelief, "No, I'm not a mommy!" until finally she would say, "Are you a boy?" and then he would exclaim, "Yes, I'm a boy!"—except the last time. The last time she had asked, "Are you a boy?" he had said "No!" and, puzzled, she said, "Then what are you?" and he answered, "I'm a Bright Light," and she wondered to herself, What are the odds? Whole populations unleashed in a stream of semen, whole Indias exploding in the womb . . . so what are the odds what kind of kid a mother will wind up with? How many millions of sperm are there in the white whisper of a cock? and if one happens to meet up with the waiting egg, it's one kind of kid, and if another, then it's another. Conceive at ten o'clock and you get a psycho. Conceive at 10:01 and you get a Bright Light.

So when she knew the lake was coming for him and would keep coming, and that she couldn't be paralyzed anymore, she sailed him out to the center in their silver gondola that shone in the sunlight like a bullet. Now she could still remember how Kirk, sitting at the end of his gondola as twilight fell around them, explained to her in his all-knowing three-year-old way how the clouds above were flying igloos and how the lights in the hills were the night robots that came out when the day robots went back into their cage in the sun. Even then, looking at him at the other end of the gondola, Kristin despised herself, despised the danger she subjected him to, the danger she had given birth to that lapped at their boat; she had almost turned the boat back to the peninsula behind them—but she knew what she knew, and she had to do what she had to do. When they reached the lake's center, with the hole at the bottom somewhere right below them, she had tried to explain it to him, as she lowered herself over the side of the gondola into the water. She promised she would return right away. She promised she wouldn't leave him alone for long. She told him it was so the lake couldn't hurt him anymore. I'll be gone just a minute, she told him, as he watched her silently, not crying, looking around at the lake around him and the sky above him in that preternatural way of his. She knew she had only minutes before the sky filled with owls that could hear the sound of a human heartbeat, and at that moment she could hear his heart herself. She had reached over and taken Kirk's hand in her own and pressed it, and before he could cry or try and grab her, she slipped into the lake. Looking up through the water, Kristin could see him leaning over the edge of the gondola peering down at her. Sinking, she could still hear his heart.

15

Five years, two months later, in her small wooden house at the edge of the rising lake, the dream began coming to her through the hinge where day hung onto night, coming up with the bubbles from the lake's bottom. Five years, two months after she last saw her son leaning over the edge of the gondola peering down at her through the water, after she resurfaced minutes later swimming desperately up up up until she broke the surface to gasp back her life at the last possible second, only for the devastating emptiness of the gondola to leave her cursing for the rest of her life that last second God gave her just so she could forever remember that last vision of her son looking down at her, she now sat on the porch of the house staring out at the lake vaguely aware of the boats that drifted by and the way the people in them looked at her and muttered to each other. Every night the foundation of the house gave way a little more, every night the sounds in the walls that Doc used to listen to woke Kristin in the dark when the dream didn't.

But then almost always it was the dream that did. She dreamed it so often sometimes she was almost uncertain that it really happened, that it was ever anything *but* a dream: she broke the lake's surface gasping, grabbing the side of the gondola; and her soul imploded at the horror of its emptiness—something so banal that could be so awful, an emptiness, a horror for what wasn't there rather than what was. For a minute she just stared into the bottom of the gondola like he was there and she just wasn't seeing him. Like there was some place he could be hiding. But instead it was as if he was never there at all. She dove beneath the water again as if to catch him on his way to the bottom, but there was no one to catch, and she rose to grab the gondola once more and look frantically around her; it was only then she heard something, and looked up. Looked up to see him in the distance, high in the sky. Heard his voice as it got farther away—"Mama, where are you?"—like he used to call from his crib, and the owl that had him in its clutches actually seemed to falter a bit, confused by the burden and sound, finding Kirk bigger and noisier than the usual prey. Sometimes in the dream the owl let go, and Kirk plummeted to earth. Other times the owl kept flying, until the bird and the boy were just a single black dot disappearing over a black hill, before an ever-blackening sky. . . .

One morning Kristin got up from the toilet to stare down at the blood in the bowl. She was so fascinated by the pattern that she sat on the bathroom floor studying it, circling to see it from every angle. It was the same pattern the next month and the month after that. She kept trying to decipher this menstrual Rorschach; slit between her legs was the stigmata of the full moon from which her womb telegraphed a message. Kristin even tried copying it down on paper before it dissolved into streaks down the white porcelain. Sometimes she lay in bed at night and saw the pattern in the dark above her, and watched baffled for hours until its mystery lulled her back to sleep.

Lately, in a city where sooner or later any kind of cult behavior became a fashion statement, everyone wore the blue of the lake. Everyone camouflaged herself and slipped alongside the water like a spy of the shoreline, disguised as a splash: blue hat, blue shirt, coat blue except for dark shadows rippling across the buttons like riptides, or flashes of white on the thigh of the pants like the glare of the sun on the water's surface. When Kristin rowed her silver gondola on the lake wearing a brilliant red dress, the lake around her suddenly cleared of all other boats, taking cover, as if the young woman was an incoming fireball from space, as if she was a drop of blood—but was the lake bleeding, or did blood rain from the sky? She could see it in everyone's eyes, the red provocation of her, the defiant affront of her red to the blue of the lake, daring it to rise higher and seep deeper into the land. *If the lake sends back my boy, I'll wear whatever it wants, the blue garb of its Order, I'll wear blue until the day I die. If it wants I'll wear nothing and dip my naked body into its blue embrace whenever it wants me, lie nude in my gondola and drift wherever it drifts me. If the lake will just send me back my boy.*

She would have the sort of conversation with God that seems trite until there's reason to have one. *You Sick Fuck. Having had your little joke with Abraham, hissing your little amusement in his ear and finding what cowards fathers are when he didn't spit in your face, when he didn't clutch his son close to him and say I'll go to hell first, when for all his supposed righteousness he couldn't even be a man when it came to protecting his child, then you moved onto mothers, didn't you, because mothers were more your match, beginning with Mary. Now that was fun. Tortured her boy in the grisliest, most twisted way possible before her very eyes and then had the sadistic wit to call it the Salvation of the World.*

God tries to hurt my kid, he has to go through me first. God tells me what he told Abraham, then he isn't any god that means anything to me, he isn't any god I owe anything. I kill anyone who tries to hurt my kid, any man, any woman, any god, any lake. . . .

But what about *herself*, was the part she couldn't say. What about the woman who deserts her son in the middle of a lake because she has this insane idea she has to stop it from taking him. Now Kristin believed she didn't deserve to live anymore, that when she found that boat empty she should have just sunk back down to the bottom where she belonged, and left her son to some better mother with better wings. For five years she sat on the front porch of her house at the water's edge in her red dress while blue citizens drifted by in their blue boats and whispered among themselves *the Madwoman in Red, whose son was abducted by owls;* early on, some took pity on her, rowing close enough to leave on the porch near her feet fruit and bread and fresh water. After some unmarked period of time she didn't so much wake from the trance of her tragedy as slip into a different trance, or a different phase of the same trance.

When you become a mom you develop this new instinct for danger. You develop this instinct for every possible disaster that awaits your kid around every corner. She didn't know if five years ago her danger instinct failed or overwhelmed all reason so that she led her son *to* danger instead of from it, swimming down into the lake's uterus to stop the unending flow of fear's afterbirth. *When your kid is born you think he must be some variation of yourself, your own genes realigning themselves into a new arrangement with those of the father, whoever he might have been: and then you find out that isn't right either. Then you find out there are things about your kid and who he is that have nothing to do with you or anything around him, things that are his own from the beginning, from the minute he's born, maybe from before he's born, maybe from before he's conceived . . . although there's no point getting into all that since no one knows anyway. Anyway that's when you're stuck with the Soul. That's when your own kid becomes inescapable evidence of the cosmos, a membrane-map of the spirit, that's when God becomes a Piercing Hope or a Dark Suspicion or both. That's when the limits of your imagination are no longer defined by your own death but by your child's, that's when a new instinct displaces the survival instinct or any other you once thought couldn't be displaced. Because there's nothing a mother fears more than the chaos of the world.*

And then danger has won. Then your fear takes a form. Detaches itself from all the things you were afraid of, the reasonable things and the stupid, and becomes its own thing, bigger than either the reasonable things or the stupid things. Grows in your pregnant heart until it's born ... and then you've stopped being a person, you've become fear's walking womb. Then you don't realize it at first but your fear is bigger than your motherhood. Fear has metamorphosed into the danger it feared

    and it's called a lake.

One night Kristin woke from the dream, as usual, to the sounds in her walls, as usual, to find a young woman sitting in the corner of her bedroom. Kristin had caught glimpses of this woman before, the last time flitting around the corner of her door before Kristin fell back to sleep. Because this other woman looked and spoke just like her, Kristin finally had to admit to herself that the other woman was the Kristin that Kristin had been sometime ... before. Perhaps the Kristin she had been before she left Kirk on the lake. Perhaps the Kristin she had been before the lake appeared, or before Kirk was even born. But whichever self of hers she had been before, now this other Kristin sat in the corner of the bedroom naked and wet, dripping the lake off her: why did you leave me? she asked; and Kristin answered, I couldn't stand to be you anymore. I couldn't stand to be who we were, or are ... you left him in the fucking boat in the middle of the lake. Why did you do that, or ... why did we do that—leave him there like that?

Doesn't matter anymore why, the other woman in the dark corner answered.

I don't care about you or me anymore, Kristin said.

Me neither.

All I care about is him. (She began to cry.)

Then go find him, the other woman said. That afternoon Kristin pushed the gondola out to Port Justine, from time to time putting down the pole or oars and unwrapping a telescope, searching the sky for him. A western fog came in from the sea through the Wilshire Straits to the west. Once, from Kristin's house one would have driven to it in ten, fifteen minutes; now by boat it was half an hour to Justine, a billboard on what once had been La Cienega Boulevard, advertising—year after year—a big blonde who wasn't famous for anything except being blonde and famous and bigger than anything in L.A. except her breasts, which were bigger than she was. There wasn't much of Justine left anymore, most of the billboard having floated away long ago. From one upper corner, the top of Justine's blonde hair still blew in the wind off the water. Over the years since the lake rose to the billboard's bottom edge, Port Justine had spread out into a lily pad of small shops and food stands and a pay phone; a couple of petrol pumps offered the last chance for gas between the Hollywood Hills and the ghetto that had taken over the top floors of the shopping center that rose from the water like a massive gray whale half a mile away. Docking the boat, Kristin stuck the telescope under her arm, clutched the rope rail, and followed a footbridge that rocked and swayed with the water. When she reached more stable scaffolding, she stuck the telescope in back of her red dress where it tied and started up the side of the billboard; looking down at some point, for a moment she almost lost her grip.

At the top of Justine, at the eye of the city's panorama, with the flooded skyscrapers of Wilshire Boulevard rising to the south and the mansion-islands of West Hollywood and Hancock Park to the north and east, and the domes of Baghdadville to the west, the wind was much stronger. There wasn't really all that much to hang on to—just a narrow walkway running the length of the billboard with a small handrail. As Kristin turned to where the fog came in from the sea, now lit red by the setting sun meeting the red lake in a bloody swirl, there, splashed across the horizon, she saw it, the same dark red advertisement of her subsconscious she had seen the first morning of every monthly cycle, hovering over the city.

Overwhelmed by the menstrual vortex of water and fog, rocked by the red wind trying to rip her from the billboard where she clung to the flimsy rail of the walkway, she suddenly flashed back on the moment five years *ago when I reached the hole at the lake's bottom, the gondola above my head, where at that moment Kirk was being kidnapped by an owl. I remember I was already wondering how I was going to get back up to the surface before my lungs burst . . . I was trying not to panic. I could feel the pull of a riptide and the push of a current, the hole drawing me in and turning me back, and even now I'm not really certain whether going into the hole was my idea or its idea . . . but I distinctly remember the loss of control and then I* did *panic: the opening didn't seem nearly big enough. But I slipped through suddenly in a dilated rush, and on the other side I was ... I was ... well, I mean: I was back in the lake. I mean, I swam down into the hole and, on the other side, found myself coming back up out of the hole, swimming up toward the gondola.*

At the time, and all the time since, I thought I must have just gotten confused. I mean, I assumed I just got turned around, what with currents and tides coming and going. But now up here on top of Justine, hanging on to the rail in this red wind with my menstrual blood splattered across the sky, I suddenly know something I didn't until now: that I wasn't confused. That I wasn't turned around. That I was pulled through the opening from one lake into another just like it, just like it in every way, every way except one, and that one difference was that on this other lake there was another silver gondola just like on the first lake ... except that this was a gondola without my son.

In the thrall of the wind and the red sky, there at the top of the billboard she felt hysteria lapping at her mind, first a small swell, then rocking her harder. She understood that the lake had led her here to this vantage point at this place in this moment beneath this sky so that, beneath the red heavens above, she could have this revelation of another lake and, on it, her son, still waiting there even now. Understanding this with more clarity than she had ever understood anything, she felt the coming hysteria and an irresistible urgency to get off the billboard; but when she moved to climb down, the red wind threatened to blow her off, and finally all she could do was lie flat and wait. Lying flat on her back, she slipped off her red dress and tied herself to the rail with it, although this was more instinctive than any kind of cool collected action: she was in a trance because, lying there flat on her back staring up at the sky and the wind, all she could think was that back through that hole at the bottom of the lake, back on the other side of that opening, on the Other Lake that she left behind five years ago, her boy was still there sitting in the gondola looking around, still waiting for his mother to come back. He had been waiting what had been five years on this side of the hole, on this lake, although who knew how long it was on his side, five minutes or five seconds; he might be sitting there even now, waiting as it got darker and darker, calling, "Mama?" and gazing over the gondola's side. The more Kristin thought about this up there on top of the billboard, the more she knew it to be true. Lying there in the wind

21

beneath the endometrial sky, hysteria finally began to recede. But the realization of what happened five years before didn't recede with it.

That night the red storm blew across the lake while Kristin stood on her front porch staring east to where she left her son five years before, promising she would be right back. She waited for the storm to pass but it blew all night, and so she lashed herself to the porch's post with sheets from her bed as she had lashed herself to Justine that afternoon with her dress; she couldn't bear to abandon him again. In the morning she woke chilled and soaked, still bound to the porch and having slept through the rain in a blizzard of dreams. She couldn't be certain whether the fever that racked her was the fever of dreams or the fever of rains, and finally she undid all the wet saturated knots of the sheets to stumble into the house and fall on the bed. As she took off her wet clothes and wrapped her nude body in several blankets and slept again, in her sleep she saw him still waiting for her in the gondola, calling to her, "Mama?"

She woke drenched in fever. She smelled the dreams like wet ash on the mattress. She sniffed the mattress up and down from the foot of the bed to the head and sometimes caught a whiff of the lake at the juncture where the fresh water met the sea, sometimes a whiff of the wet wood of oars—and there at the mattress's northeastern quadrant was the smell of him. It was there. She had forgotten how he smelled but now in the sweat of her dreams she remembered, because the wet stain of memory was there on the mattress; the mattress had become a map of her dreams and their remorse, longing, rage, desolation. For the rest of the afternoon, she lay naked on the bed with her head in that one spot, one side of her face to the mattress so she could smell him, and when she fell asleep again, the smell of him was all she dreamed. She woke to a call—"Mama?"—and heard it so distinctly for a moment that she believed he was there in the house. She believed he was asleep in his bed in another room and was calling out to her like he used to. She sat up with a start in the dark and listened, but the call didn't come again until she fell back to sleep.

Her fever passed but it had exhausted her. She lay back down but every time she fell asleep on the map of dreams she woke to his call, until even in her fatigue there was nothing she could do but pull on some clothes, stumble out to the porch of the house, loosen the line of the gondola and get in, slowly, wearily pushing herself with the pole east along the coastline of the Hollywood Hills to that place on the lake she last went five years before. Although it wasn't much more than a mile from where she lived, she had avoided that part of the lake all these years and dreaded it now. The shoreline had changed since then, the lake having risen farther down what was once the Strip; rowing along the Hollywood cliffs she saw newly abandoned patches of the hills, empty houses, and what were once chic little lanes that now disappeared into water. Several members of a tribe of nomads, identifiable by their lack of either blue attire or Kristin's subversive red, ran alongside the water following the gondola for a while before they gave up and turned back. Around a bend in the coast she saw the spires of the old Chateau X Hotel. As dusk fell she could see lit candles darting in the castle's top windows; from the top of the hill above the Chateau, a skytram erected just a few years before launched itself out over the water, the Nichols Canyon Line that ran to the Fairfax station in the east and then to the Old Cahuenga station beyond. Plunging south into the lake in the distance was the Port Justine Line that was begun but never finished. Not far from the coast there still bobbed on the lake's surface the remnants of a skytram shuttle that plummeted into the water ten months before when the line broke, drowning nine people, including two children.

Forty-five minutes later, the terrain became familiar to her in the twilight. She rowed to the spot; these were the watery coordinates of her loss and shame, and now her failure of nerve. Fearing she couldn't go through with this, she hoped this vision was madness, that down through the dark water there was no Other Lake on the Other Side attached to this one by a common birth canal. She drifted on the spot pulling up the oars, and for a moment stopped to lean her tired self over the side of the gondola and put her ear as close to the water's surface as the gondola would allow.

She listened for his voice.

Listened for him calling from the Other Lake on the Other Side. For a while she almost convinced herself she heard nothing, and was appalled how momentarily relieved she was, as if she would rather not have to go through whatever she had to go through to have him back; and then, confronted with her relief and guilt, and confronted with his loss all over again, she felt a despair more unnameable than she had ever felt at any moment in these five years, which she wouldn't have thought possible. Leaning over the side of the gondola, her face very close to the water so that the ends of her hair were wet, she began to cry, tears dropping onto the surface of the lake until: "Mama?" It was unmistakable. Oh dear God, she said to herself, and then heard it again—"Mama?"— and recoiled; she stared as his call to her floated up through the black water like a fish. She could see it down below, silvery and fluttery light, with the scales of a child's sobbing. With the waver of his voice, his call to her flashed in and out of view; when she lunged her hand down into the lake, she felt it brush against her fingertips before slipping away. She called back. For a moment it stuck in her throat—"Kirk?"—and then she watched it fall from her mouth and sink into the lake blue and porcelain and breathless. There was a moment's silence before his answer floated back up to her, and then she began rowing away. Maybe it was that she couldn't bring herself to believe. Maybe it was that she was afraid reaching him was beyond her; maybe it was that, for the moment, her long-held fear of the lake, into which she would have to plunge herself once more, overcame her desperation to save him, and that was the most unbearable prospect of all, because she always had been convinced she would do anything for him. She always had been convinced she would hurl herself in any harm's way for him. When he was born, every instinct of self-interest seemed to give way to an instinct she never knew she had before she had him: the love of something bigger than the love of one's own life; and now in this moment she failed that love.

She began rowing very quickly from the spot, one "Mama?" after another floating up to the surface of the lake behind her, a school of his cries desperately swimming after her. Glancing over her shoulder she could see them. She began weeping in time with her rowing, until she rounded the bend of the Chateau X and couldn't see the spot anymore behind her. She cried all the way back across the lake to her house.

That night her uterus exploded in a tantrum of blood. Hunched over the toilet she felt the presence of the other Kristin, whom she so rejected for abandoning their son: you're no better, she heard her whisper from the hallway. I left him in the gondola that night because I was afraid for him; now he waits on the Other Side (the century's uterus exploding in a tantrum of water), and you leave him there again, afraid for yourself. Kristin sobbed no, her womb answered a red yes, she crawled back to the mattress to paint the dreams mapped there with the scarlet of her thighs.

In her sleep, she smelled the smoke, felt the heat. Maybe because some part of her brain knew that a dream rarely has a scent and rarely a touch, she woke; she sat up in bed slowly at first, then was startled to complete consciousness by the smoke that began to choke her. Seeing the fire, she saw herself as others had seen her, in her arrogant red dress against the blue of the lake, a red flame floating on the water. By then the fire was in the hallway. For what seemed to her an absurdly long moment, she sat on her red dreamsoaked mattress looking at the flames just beyond the door, then shook herself from her inertia and leapt to the floor, only to realize it was too late.

Did she leave a candle burning? Did someone sail by and toss in a torch, because it was time to burn the heretic Madwoman in Red from the hills? What's that phenomenon, she thought to herself, where people burst into flames? Had the house spontaneously combusted, its fuse lit at the end that curled into a house's subconscious? Was the house committing suicide in a symphony of self-immolation—an act of protest, like a Buddhist monk? Kristin could imagine nothing to be protested unless, of course, it was her own presence, unless the house meant to burn away the human mark of its disgrace. She was beset by more responses than she could sort through in the moments the fire allowed her, but somewhere in the ember-blizzard of these responses was calm; she felt it somewhere beyond the heat, before the daze of her sleep finally succumbed to adrenaline. She went to the window of her bedroom only for the sill to fracture into flame, and then the curtains went up. She leapt back. The inferno dropped to the floor on a parachute of fire, then the floor went up in flames, then the bed. Smoke dropped Kristin to her knees, and for a thoughtless moment she reached to one of the bed's blankets, itself engulfed, so as to cover herself, before she scampered to retreat. But there was nowhere to retreat.

Perhaps this accounted for it: perhaps it was her abject helplessness, perhaps it was that she finally had nowhere to go and so surrendered to the end. Or perhaps it had nothing to do with her, perhaps it was a fluke of nature

but the lake began to rise. It rose suddenly and visibly, by inches.

At first she thought the house must be sinking. As if somewhere nearby a dam had burst; but there was no dam: it was a tide as mysterious as the intricate flow of her womb or the menstrual sky that manifested itself to her at Port Justine the afternoon before. Perhaps the lake had come so that it might claim Kristin before the fire could—so it was nothing to do with rescue, everything to do with possessiveness . . . but for whatever reason, the lake came up over the edge of the front porch, came through the front door into the front room, came into the hallway and into the bedroom and rose *up around my feet then my ankles* lapping at the flaming walls around her. It brought with it a spray, Kristin's private rain. It was now her private lake, beneath her private sky.

The lake that was her enemy. *The lake that was my fear.* The lake that was the afterbirth of her dreams. *The lake that preyed on my son.* Now came as ally, confessor, co-conspirator, savior.

It stopped at her waist. She didn't move, partly caught in the shock between the heat of the fire that had given way to the cold of the water. She kept throwing water in her face to get the stinging of the smoke out of her eyes; she didn't move, so as not to tempt either the lake or the house of ashes around her, until a wall suddenly gave way behind her, falling away from her—and it was then she saw the lake had dropped to her thighs. It liked her thighs and stayed a while. Peering off in the dark where the wall had collapsed, Kristin could see bobbing flashlights on the hillside that abutted what once was her house, and she finally dared to move toward the dark, walking up out of the water onto the new beach.

There would be no convincing any of them, she knew, that she wasn't who she had always been in their eyes, the Madwoman in Red. Even the next morning, when she would drop her red dress and stand naked in the mud of the new shore, she would know they believed she had started the fire, she would know they thought she meant to go up in flames with the house. *Are we sisters now, the lake and I? Lover and lover, wife and wife, wife and mistress, mistress and slave? Weary of all her years of drunken brides, had the lake saved me . . . for what? Does it have a conscience? I thought it came for my son five years ago . . . did it really take me instead, and I'm just now realizing it? Is it the same lake at all? or was the lake that came for my son the twin sister of the lake whose*

26

shores I've known the five years since, the lake that saved me tonight, this lake that covets me? Saving me so I could have one more chance . . . and go back. The next morning the sky would be ablaze with blood. All along the road, down the embankment that led to the lake, people would stand in their blue clothes looking up at the clotted clouds; for a moment Kristin would look up herself, before walking naked to the water, astounded witnesses diverted by her from the astounding sky. Someone reached out as if to help or stop her. The crowd parted for her as she moved through it, to a tree where the gondola was tied.

She pushed the gondola out into the water, through the embers of the house floating on the surface, charred and still smoking from the night before. She got in the boat and took the pole. Receding in the distance, with all the other people on the shore, the other Kristin raised her hand in farewell.

The woman in the gondola nodded in farewell back. She continued to push herself out into the water with the pole; as she did, people ran alongside the lake's edge. The farther Kristin sailed, the bigger the crowd grew, mesmerized by the spectacle of the nude woman guiding the silver boat. After a while she had pushed herself beneath the inverted arc of the fallen line of the skytram, then around the bend where the Chateau X rose up out of the water; she felt calm unlike the afternoon before when she took this same trip. Accompanying her were the women's voices loosed the night before from the walls of her house by the fire. Kristin could hear them as they brushed past her in the water, crossing her path as if daring her to cut them in two—all the voices she had heard for five years, darting back and forth across her passage as if to either clear the way or stop her, because they couldn't stand to lose her, not to the lake that was now her sister or lover, or mother.

The crowd on land grew. Stragglers along the shore were caught up by the others following her until, by the time she rounded the Chateau and approached the lake's origin, there were several hundred onlookers. No one called or heckled. Everyone was quiet. Soon Kristin put down the pole and took the oars to row, and as she approached the spot she dropped the oars and allowed her boat to drift to the spot, as if trusting the boat's precision more than her own; she peered over the side. Zed was blacker and emptier than it had ever been. Kristin looked up for a moment at the shore of the northern Laurel Bay now lined with

27

people; no one called to stop her. In the red glare from the sky, she could just make out people holding their hands over their eyes. It was perfectly quiet, and "Kirk?" she said, leaning over the gondola; she didn't shout it. She let it fall from her mouth and watched it sink. It vanished into the pitch black of the lake and she waited; seconds passed. A minute. Another minute and another, and then, in the pitch black where she watched her question disappear, she saw the approach of its answer. Slowly it grew before her eyes, floating up to her until it broke the surface— "Mama"—and she scooped it up in her hands. She cupped it in her hands and sat in the gondola looking at it, as if it was a prayer and the gondola was a floating pew. She splashed her face with it and felt his voice run down her cheeks. For a moment she covered her eyes. She felt his voice dry on her face. As she slipped her naked body, pink with the light of the red sky, over the gondola's side, she thought maybe she heard someone on the shore finally break the silence of the lake and shout out No! but she wasn't sure about that, *that may be in my own head. I sink. I don't swim to the hole below, I let it pull me. I didn't even get a good gulp of air first, I'm calm in my chest and my descent, and feel the peace that maybe comes with drowning, once the panic is over . . . I don't know why I don't panic. I look up and see the gondola above me like I saw it above me the last time I went this way, five years ago, but this time without his small head looking over the side. As I sink, there rise around me the small canyon houses that went under when the lake first appeared, I can see below me the sidewalks that once lined the boulevard below me too, and through the water's murk, coming up at me, I also see rising up to me the opening of the lake's birth canal, here it comes. Here it comes. Too small, it seems, for anyone to slip through, and yet I slip through anyway, or rather I feel myself drawn beyond any resistance, pushed through in a new birth, continuing down in a passage without time, from somewhere that was a minute ago or a hundred years ago, a passage*

In her mind Doc has been on this journey a long time. The exact
hour of its beginning is nameless but certainly she's been riding
in this silver goldola since that one afternoon years before when
she and her young assistant   sailed out to an apartment
building on what once   **2017**   had been called Laurel
Avenue, so that she might   diagnose all its mysteries.
Doc healed them all in those days—consumptive houses, malaria
houses, alzheimer houses, heart-attack houses, houses with tumors
growing out the attic or the bedroom windows or the family rooms
—or consoled them when they couldn't be healed.

She had fled from New York to Los Angeles, a city
congenitally incapable of a tragic sense, expressly to leave all
sense of tragedy behind. But the afternoon Kristin sailed her out to
the flooded building, in the falls of an abandoned apartment Doc
heard the sound of the sorrow that can't be surmounted or endured,
the sorrow that life's passages can't pass away. She's been in the
silver gondola ever since. She lies in the bottom staring up at the
black sea of the sky rolling by overhead, at the white waves of
clouds; but while she escaped in the gondola, in the years
afterward she couldn't escape the gondola itself. Sometime in the
night that began thirteen years ago she set sail back to the sorrow
because she needs to face it again before she dies, although
why she has no idea. It isn't a matter of conquering anything. She
now knows this sorrow is beyond conquest. It isn't a matter of
understanding anything; she knows this sorrow is beyond
understanding.

As Doc lies in the bottom of the gondola in the night of her
mind, with the cool night breeze blowing in her face, the lake is

from my own unique chaos maybe to my own unique god, and as I slip down

going down its own drain. At the other end of the gondola, a
strange teenage boy she barely knows, who calls himself Kuul—a
name half the language of childhood memory and half the
language of owl—rows them toward the center of a black
whirlpool, having left his owls far behind on land. As the boy and
the old woman near the whirlpool, they feel the churning of the
black water broken by white foam; bubbles rise at the center, and
finally the gondola is caught in the current of the vortex and begins
the long journey down into the whirlpool. Manning the pole and
oars, the boy guides them down the whirlstream as the sunken

city of Los Angeles flows by behind the lake's dark-glass curtains that rise around them—sunken palm trees and boulevards until, in the distance, at the center of the whirlpool she sees the Hotel of the Thirteen Losses. It's nothing like any hotel that she's ever seen before; it's much bigger, extending as far as she can see, with glistening ebony walls, huge deserted atriums, grand forsaken lobbies looming as the gondola speeds through the big open doors
into the foyer,
up cascading
stairways and
down the long
blue corridors
into the first
room which is
the Room of the Lost Home. This is an unostentatious room. It's plain, almost barren except for purely functional furniture; but as the silver gondola slowly glides through, Doc and the boy will note—as they'll note with the twelve other rooms to come—how from different perspectives the room takes on a different appearance. In the natural course of things, loss of home is the easiest to bear, particularly if it's the voluntary loss that comes with growing up. Only from the far corner of the room

through the birth canal of the lake, am I still sinking? am I still drowning?

does the room's loneliness give way to desolation and the terror, not only the walls and beams of the room but all light and warmth falling away, when the loss is an act of catastrophe or when the room suddenly opens up into the adjoining room that

33

is the Room of Lost Livelihood. This includes a small Sitting Room of Lost Fortune, not as impressive as the Room of Lost Livelihood that's more spacious because it must encompass the loss of not only past fortune but prospective fortune as well. The Sitting Room of Lost Fortune, however, does have a nice big window for jumping purposes. The Room of Lost Livelihood is plush with overstuffed sofas and high-armed chairs to remind those who pass through of a graciousness of living they'll never attain. From the gondola Doc notes, however, that there's nothing practical about this room, there aren't even bare necessities, just promises that shimmer enticingly before disappearing, like the vanishing walls and light and warmth of the Room of the Lost Home.

These are the first and last rooms that will manifest themselves so materially, as is this corridor down which the gondola now sails. As terrible as

am I still descending? or am I rising? and now I feel my first real panic,

these rooms can be, their dimensions remain very concrete; from here on, the rooms into

which   Doc
and   the   boy
sail   in   their
gondola   have
no truly fixed
dimensions.
Their terror is,
in   varying
degrees,   as
profound as it
sometimes   is
illusory.   The
most   shape-
changing of all
is the Room of Lost Love. Here in the Hotel of the
Thirteen Losses this is the most chameleon of
rooms. It reflects more the nature of the guest
passing through than the nature of the loss itself,
because this loss has no true nature of its own. This
room is a bombardment of hallucinations, which
isn't to say the hallucinations aren't truly
devastating, because they're revelations of the self,
a rave of the id: when Doc first sails into this room
it's nothing but a massive fireplace, with a roaring
fire; suddenly the fire is gone and the hearth

that I've gotten turned around and am returning to the wrong side, and I

becomes the cold slab of a grave. The Room of
Lost Love is never stationary. It isn't to be found in
any one permanent location of the hotel; it moves
from floor to floor, from the beginning of one
hallway to the end of another, from the penthouse to
the basement. As the gondola sails through, the
room may tend to settle, its mercurial torments

exhausted; when one has sailed far and deep enough
into the room's recesses, it may lose all
ephemerality and transform to a different space
altogether that's both the same room but a different
room, which is the Room of the Lost Mate, utterly
uninhabitable for some and a way station of sorts
for others. As the gondola leaves the Room of Lost
Love, it remains to be seen whether it will sail out
the same door it sailed in or an altogether different
exit. Something melancholy grips Doc on her
voyage through this room, and she realizes that this
is the only loss that someone might envy if she's
never known it; there is, then, perfectly contained
within the Room of Lost Love another room with
no walls at all that's the Room of the Loss of Lost
Love—the loss of never having had the experience
of losing love. Leaving the Room of Lost Love,
                    Doc's gondola
                    sails   into   a
                    huge ballroom
or, in fact, three ballrooms that are conjoined as one. These are
the Ballroom of Lost Faith, the Ballroom of Lost Dignity, and
the Ballroom of the Lost Soul. It would be difficult to tell where
one finishes and one starts; the conjoined ballrooms are mirrored
from one end to the other and the chandeliers that hang from

almost turn back, but I go on rising as something that's once more being

the ballroom ceiling glitter not only in the mirrors and the mirrors'
reflections of each other but off the water and off Doc's
silver gondola, so that the cumulative light is blinding.
Thus all perceptions are refracted, dazzled, suspect. What seems
to be lost faith may be a failure of will or nerve. What seems
to be lost dignity may be wounded pride or ego. And at the
far end of the ballroom, where tides flow in from all other rooms

of the hotel and collide, and it's all the boy can do to right the gondola's course, it's often impossible to know which transgressions of behavior, integrity, and conscience will drag the soul down into the undertow of the irredeemable.

So from out of the Three Ballrooms, Doc's silver gondola is drawn into two small, transitional rooms linked together that, from here, provide the only passage on to the rest of the hotel. The first transitional room is the Room of Lost Youth and the second is the Room of the Lost Parent. Because both are rooms in which the traveler learns her earliest,

born to the lake that thinks it miscarried me, to reclaim my place in its

most significant lessons in mortality, at first they appear to Doc to be the same. In both, all the furniture has been covered with sheets as on moving day — but the sheets are black rather than white, and gauzy and transparent, so the outline of the furniture beneath them can always be seen. There are two differences between the rooms: in the Room of Lost Youth there's a crack in the corner of one wall through which a gale blows, disheveling the sheets on the furniture so that sometimes the Room of Lost Youth might take the form of the Room of Lost Health, for instance, or the Room of Lost Promise — which is to say one might enter the Room of Lost Youth early in life or late, age isn't a factor, no one checks for identification at the door. It's the same with the Room of the Lost Parent, which may also be either one of the first or last rooms in

womb, and far above me I see it, a small flash on the surface of the water, I

the hotel one passes through; it's even possible to be born in the Room of the Lost Parent. The other difference between the two rooms is that in the Room of Lost Youth, a pillar stands in the center from floor to ceiling, while in

the Room of the Lost Parent
the pillar is gone, although its
shadow remains both night
and day cast by no apparent
light across the length of
the room and always leaving
the exit on the other side
in darkness. But there is
a navigable exit, after all;
a guest adjusts to her stay in
these rooms and sooner or
later leaves, the losses
endured if always felt.
Having sailed through these transitional rooms, then Doc's
gondola emerges in the hotel's lavish mezzanine. All this time,
sailing through the Hotel of the Thirteen Losses, Doc and the boy
navigating the boat have followed a very distant melody made only
more obscure by the oceanic symphony that plays it. Doc
recognizes it. Even faint as it is she can barely stand to hear it
again, even as she knows that it's for this melody she's come here.
Now in the hotel's lavish mezzanine the song is louder; other than a
single small door at the far end of the mezzanine that leads to
either some sort of closet or pantry, before the gondola are three
sets of double doors to three separate suites and Doc knows it's
from one of these suites the song comes. She knows she's closer

know that the silver flash above me is the gondola waiting, but since I've

now to the end of her search. She knows that behind one
of these three double doors is the suite of the most unendurable
loss of all, the loss she felt that day with Kristin in
the other woman's apartment. She assumes such a room and
such a loss must be at once splendid and terrible. They sail
through the first set of double doors

into the Suite of Lost Freedom. She might expect this suite to look like a dungeon, chains hanging from the walls, shackles close to the floor, mechanisms of torture in place of a bed or chair. She would expect no windows. In fact the suite is well appointed. It's comfortable. It's secure: the lock is on the inside of the doors, not outside. The Suite of Lost Freedom has a huge bed and love seat, and a window opens from an alcove through which blows a fresh breeze. A grand light fixture hangs from the ceiling which makes the room very bright, even happy. It not only doesn't seem such a terrible room, it's an inviting room. There's maid service, room service. Someone could very well choose to live here, particularly with someone else; behind the bed there's a secret panel although it must not be very secret if Doc knows it's there, and from the Suite of Lost Freedom to the Room of Lost Love there's a secret passage; many of the hotel's guests spend a lot of time wandering back and forth in this passage. In fact the room is filled with secret panels and secret passages to other rooms of loss, to which this suite seems eminently preferable. It isn't until Doc and the boy sit floating in the gondola for some time that she notices something: the walls are closing in. Almost imperceptibly the suite is growing

gotten confused in my way and can no longer be sure to which lake I've

smaller. Then she notices something else: the light above is growing dimmer. Almost imperceptibly the room grows darker. In the early moments of the suite becoming smaller and darker, the guest still has the capacity, with a word and the will, to stop the walls, to turn back up the light, if that's what she wants to do. It's almost impossible to say at exactly what point this

suite goes from being a room where one would choose
to live to a room that one must escape at all cost; and
to that end, even when the room has become very
small and dark, the far window still glows slightly, so
that even as the walls become so close as to crush
anyone between them, the possiblity of escape,
however increasingly difficult, remains, and may even
become a distant promise that gives life a meaning it
never had before. For all these reasons, because there
are times when the Suite of Lost Freedom is
hospitable, even apparently civilized, where one's stay
is content, even apparently fulfilling, and because even
when the suite is at its least human, when one is
desperately trying to hold back the walls with her
hands, there's still a faint hope of escape, and it seems
clear to Doc that this isn't the most unendurable of
losses, that it can be not only endured in its
smallest measure but reversed at its greatest extreme,
that it's a loss that can bring out the best and noblest
and most inspiring in people, even to the point
where they would choose over the Suite of Lost
Freedom the very next suite over, to which Doc's
gondola now
sails, back out
into the great mezzanine and then slowly and with more difficulty

returned, therefore as well I can no longer be sure to which gondola, or

through the next set of double doors
into the Suite of Lost Life. Well, Doc thinks to herself,
certainly this has to be the most unendurable loss: what
loss could be greater than the loss of one's life? Isn't,
she thinks to herself, every other loss in life measured
against this one? Isn't every other loss ultimately
endured in order to avoid this one? The gondola sails

into the middle of the Suite of Lost Life—which suddenly vanishes: the walls, the ceiling, the floors all gone in the blink of an eye, leaving the gondola suspended in a void of black. Then the suite suddenly reappears, as a rounded blue chamber. Of all the suites this is the most capricious in form and nature; and as with the Suite of Lost Freedom and its secret passage to the Room of Lost Love, populated by nomads wandering between the two, the Suite of Lost Life is riddled with secret passages to other rooms in the hotel such as the Ballroom of Lost Faith or the Ballroom of the Lost Soul, all with their own wandering exiles. Whereas Doc could feel in the other rooms the presence of hurt, walls faintly throbbing with pain, here in the Suite of Lost Life there's nothing to be felt at all except, when the suite assumes the incarnation of the blue chamber, a kind of peace. And Doc realizes that in fact the loss of one's life isn't the most unendurable of losses, that in fact whether life's end is a blue chamber or black void, there's nothing to be endured at all—that in some ways this suite shouldn't even be in the Hotel of the Thirteen Losses, that the loss of one's life is really endured by others, who are guests of the hotel in other rooms, such as the Room of the Lost Parent or the Room of the Lost Mate.

whether there truly is another gondola, or ever was, or whether there was

So this then leaves to Doc and her pursuit of the
unendurable loss only one remaining possibility,
and that's the final suite next to this one;
and so the
silver gondola
sails back out into the grand mezzanine toward the final set of
double doors. Doc braces herself. Lying in the bottom of the

gondola, remembering that afternoon in the apartment of the other hotel with Kristin, she becomes afraid as the boy rows them through the last set of double doors

into a suite of nothing but doors, each with a mirror, much like the mirrors of the Three Ballrooms, except that, as the gondola passes, each mirror loses its reflection and turns into a window, with strange faces on the other side peering in. This is the Suite of Lost Memory. Beyond the doors with the mirrors that turn into windows are corridors that run to every single other room in the hotel, because the Suite of Lost Memory may also be the Suite of the Lost Self, although that remains to be known. It's uncertain, what with corridors running to the Ballroom of Lost Dignity or the Suite of Lost Freedom, what constitutes the self, and what of the self still exists when self-consciousness is gone. This is why the Suite of Lost Memory and the Ballroom of the Lost Soul aren't the same room although they might seem the same to those outside the windows gazing in. And it's partly because of this unanswerable mystery that Doc, braced for the great wave of anguish she expected from this final suite, realizes this isn't the most unendurable loss either, that it's a kind of death, in some ways more profound than the body's death, and as a kind of death

ever even Another Side at all except in my red hysteria, or whether it's the

it's something to be endured not by the one who has lost her memory but by those around her who watch her recede into life's horizon in the gondola of amnesia. Now Doc is perplexed. Lying in the bottom of the gondola adrift in this last suite, having taken this long voyage on the lake of her mind down to the Hotel of the Thirteen Losses at the bottom of the whirlpool so

as to face what she couldn't face all those years before, she tries to remember all the suites and all the ballrooms and all the guest rooms and sitting rooms she's been through but can't, and then realizes of course she can't remember because, after all, she's in the Suite of Lost ... well, now she can't even remember what suite she's in, but she still has enough presence of mind to lift her arm and point the way out. For a moment the boy can't remember the way, but circling the windowed doors around the perimeter of the room he finally finds the exit and rows them out of ...
now it comes
back to her, the Suite of Lost Memory, yes ... and out into the mezzanine, bobbing above its flooded marble floors in the whirlpool's current, where it all comes back to her and she counts the losses to herself: home, fortune, livelihood, love, faith, dignity, the soul, health, parent, freedom, life, memory ... that's twelve. Feebly she holds up her fingers and counts them again, and wonders where in their voyage they missed a room. Bobbing there in the water, puzzled she can hear the song clearly, the song that was coming from none of the three suites, and lies there listening —"Can you hear it?" she cries out to the boy—when the boy picks up the oars and begins to row, and rows them to the far end of the mezzanine and the small single pantry door, or perhaps it's a

same chaos, the same god, the same lake, the same empty gondola I left

simple door to a janitor's closet that earlier they not so much ignored as dismissed. And as they grow closer to the door, the song becomes louder. As they reach the plain unadorned door it's so distinct now it frightens her, and she's about to cry out to the boy and tell him to stop when he takes the door knob in his hand and opens it. Out of it roars a music that's more than pain, more than anguish, more than desolation, more than sorrow, more than grief. Out of it roars the greatest of all losses, the loss that can't be endured. It's not a loss that one truly survives let alone surmounts, it's not a loss that one out-exists let alone outlives; it's the loss that breaks your heart and it never mends. It never mends. It calls into question everything, so that it entails in some way all the other losses: home is lost; fortune and livelihood have no more meaning; love not only has no more meaning but becomes a kind of emotional treason; faith becomes a kind of spiritual treason; dignity becomes a joke; the soul is forever in the terminal grip of a psychic cancer; health is an affront; the loss of a parent is the perverse twin of this loss, like the reflection in the mirror of a funhouse; freedom is a curse; life is torture. Memory is worst of all. From the doorway of this tiny closet or pantry one would almost gladly flee, if possible, to the Suite of Lost Memory or, failing to reach that, perhaps even the Suite of Lost Life. This is the Unendurable Loss because it involves the one thing that one loves more than one's own life; and no meaning that one strives to give her own life, however great or good, can ever truly compensate for what's been lost, will ever be truly convincing in any scheme of things that in the heart of hearts one believes. This loss is the essence of the universe's impossibility, it's the one thing for which a benevolent God never has a persuasive answer, and which a malevolent God holds over the head of humanity. Although she wants the boy to row far away from this door as fast as he can, in the wave of music that roars out of the tiny closet

just a minute ago, and I don't know but that as I rise to break the surface

Doc, weeping, takes hold of the sides of the gondola and summons all her strength and courage to rise from the bottom so she can look inside and face it at last. Inside the closet is nothing but a hole, the birth canal down through which rushes the lake back to wherever it came, and inside this hole Doc sees a vision of a young boy unknown to her, growing up in the apartment Doc visited with Kristin that one afternoon thirteen years ago, suddenly swept under

45

by the lake and reaching for a hand too far from him, and Doc can hear the mother crying for him frantic, disbelieving, but the boy descends; and out of the hole in his place Doc sees rise the Unendurable Loss like a bubble of black air

this

i s   t h e

l o s s   o f

o n e ' s

child

At some point past Coldwater Canyon, gliding westward into the lengthening shadows of the hills, Kuul looks down at her lying in the bottom of the gondola and knows she's gone.

He's never seen death in a person before, only in owls, but the stillness is the same; it's not like sleep. The cheeks of her face are wet—from the lake, he supposes; or some astonishing dream maybe? He's close enough to shore that now he uses the pole to push the boat into the mist off Beverly Glen, trying to think what he'll do with her. Don't people put their dead in the ground? Or do they burn them? Do they eat them? But he has nothing with which to dig out the ground except his hands, or to start a fire, which doesn't seem a good idea anyway, and the owls leave their

of the water whether, even if I make it, I have the courage, because I won't

dead where they die, which seems more sensible than anything else. So beaching the gondola on the banks of the glen, he steps out into the mud and turns and pushes the silver boat with the old woman's body back into the water and watches it disappear back into the mist, floating back out into the western part of the lake where it will eventually become caught in the current that leads to the sea.

Except now, of course, he has no boat anymore. He'll have to get another. He looks around him at the trees and the rising hillside throttled with fog, and calls to the owls for direction. When he receives no answer, he calls again. He still receives no answer, and begins to make his way up the hillside. For an hour as he makes his way up the hillside he calls again and again to the owls, and again and again receives no answer until he finally understands that, having crossed the experiential threshold of human death, he's now on his own.

be able to bear the possibility that the boat is empty again, and now in this new fear all I can do is go on, all I can do is keep swimming, up up up to

Seeing

Martine Bellen

Some have mirrors hidden in them,
           When you look, you see a familiar.
Some are whiskered, mewl.
Some spend their days like change.

If the canvas is deeper, more cavernous, than eyes can perceive,
           If the ear alleges beyond night, which lands do you visit?
Master of weather and water—

How a raindrop, an exhale, sculpt the earth
Remove mountains, oceans, anger.
Compose a person, then erase. Pentimento.

Enough moisture inside that hollyhocks grow pink blossoms
Up through her mouth, appearing as supple lips.
A field mouse nestling near her heart
Where it gathers seeds dropped by messy goldfinch who flies
In and out her throat. No wonder she wants to meditate,
Visit the space that space inhabits.

Dozed off and disappeared.
Two histories exist simultaneously.

Some track weather systems, warn ships of gales.
Some want to want; some to be wanted.

Who she was when she sat in the space
At a time other than this moment. She looks in the mirror
To see if she looks
As she remembered
Her looking.

Martine Bellen

When security relies on the status quo (false concept
Security guard).

Some are nightwalkers.

The face past forty that fills her mirror,
Which half does she see?
She shares her space with a room that includes a chair, portico,
Support. Can she know the space around that space?
Russian doll insight?

The security guard has a trust issue or fund.

Today she visits the rock and river elders at a brookside,
Notes their wisdom, winsome, opens her heart gate
And discusses with them the human element,
What makes us carbon, what makes us care.

Some modify in time different from yours
Inhabited during the same instant.

One espies the body beyond an atom, beyond a bite of cloud.

Her cat stretching its length across the sky,
Two feet from mounds of dust.

A cumulus conscious.

The Navigators
Reginald Shepherd

—For Robert Philen

1. THOMPSON'S BAYOU

weathered nature walk sign warns
"you may encounter poisonous snakes
and alligators"

the largest assemblage of venoms
on the continent, cottonmouth moccasins,
copperheads, and coral snakes, at least three kinds
of rattlesnakes (eastern diamondback, timber, pygmy)

no sign of the poison-bearing alligators

*

Spanish moss dangles from myrtle oak
branches, smooth waxy leaves I took for magnolia
but smaller, until I saw the acorns, green,
sweet, fast-maturing, so many
have fallen to the wayside: we crush
dozens underfoot

not moss at all, an epiphyte
doing no harm to the tree

*

saw palmetto sprouting
in the crook of a water oak
twenty feet up or more,
green-fronded water spout

*

oaks divided into red oaks and white
oaks: live oaks are members of the white oak
group, usually though not always
with unlobed leaves, evergreen
and durable wood

southern live oaks rarely found
north of the Georgia Coastal Plain

*

black fish with translucent blue tails and fins
bream or other cichlids
can't see them when the sun is on their water

catfish, larger, gray-bodied, churning
the bottom muds

*

oneself as snapping turtle, half
-submerged, drifting slowly
neck extended, taking in any scrap
of potential sustenance
afloat on or just beneath the surface

it's turtles all the way down

2. Big Lagoon

the mockingbirds can't make up their minds
what song they want to sing, go through them all
in hectic sequence

*

men wading out into the Gulf
Intra-Coastal Waterway
with small mesh nets for mullet and bait
fish, fishing poles to catch mackerel,
sheepshead, white trout, flounder, bluegill

just leave the damned fish alone

*

"Long Pond is not a naturally formed
waterbody but a man-made
borrow pit; the pond is fed by groundwater
seepage and by rainfall."

the dirt dug out to build some other place

*

southern live oaks reduced to gnarled
shrubs (they stay saplings
for years, scrub oak with tiny
green acorns), sand pines
stunted by the wind, the salt
wind brings in, and salt water
leaching into white sandy soils
composed of quartz, the barren coast
coated in nutrient-poor glitter

*

oaks more likely to lose their limbs
in high winds, pines just shed straw
and splayed-open cones

*

cotton balls of deer moss, pastel
green pillows of reindeer moss
(actually a lichen)

*

mourning doves in late afternoon, evening
doves in their small tuxedos
take their places in the desiccated branching
(heavy, strong, once used for shipbuilding)

redheaded woodpeckers test blond deadwood
a great blue heron guards a shredded pine

*

late wind still incomplete, full
of gaps and empty spaces

The Pound Project
Jerome Rothenberg

Swollen-eyed, rested,
*   lids sinking, darkness unconscious*
. . . .

And before hell mouth; dry plain
and two mountains

1.

head down,
screwed into the swill

I am led into a home
where no one
—not a dog or cat—
drops by.

The body of a
strangled child
stares out
& spooks me.

Warriors & children
fill my eyes.

2.

A lady asks me.
I speak in season.

With my old
suburban voice
my prejudice
grows ripe.

I am not empty
but without a taste
for differences
I atrophy.

The dance gets harder
as the mud gets high.

3.

I mate with my free kind
upon the crags.

I neither wait for you
nor need you,
feel the pressure of your tongue
that calls me down.

I know extremis
better than the cackling
of my fellows,
gaunt & green with pain.

In my hand a flower
blossoms, does it not?

4.

I let down the crystal curtain
& watch the moon.

Men & animals surround me,
I am led by these
into a hole, brown-colored
like my arm.

I wait for words the night
once brought me,
luminous, the sky a changing
field of light.

While here below,
        their sightless eyes
confound me.

5.

Nor can I shift my pains
to other,

Much less my words—like yours
that face me down
high on my wall—an afterthought
to careless speech.

We teach forgiveness
to the idle only.
For the rest the suffering
leaves its own mark.

You back away from mine,
old face like yours.

6.

I am the help of the aged;
I pay men to talk peace.

With my hands I raise
a sagging body. I am keen
& run before them,
meaning to escape.

I pay a price for
bounty. Deaf
I hear a call
to war.

Somewhere within me
armies clash.

7.

I have weathered the storm,
I have beaten out my exile.

I have made a pact with someone
& have botched it. Freed from time
my fingers have grown frail,
my pen lies helpless on the floor.

I have desires that my flesh
still harbors. Little help or gratitude
will come from those
my turnings have betrayed.

I watch the dead file by
& feel a stirring.

8.

singing: O sweet and lovely
o Lady be good

the song is traveling
from my time into yours,
like Ella's song, is
wordless.

Hear me sing it   see me
dance on water.
I coast down the street
the while my eyes

like everyman's eyes
          fill with apparitions
a *dead bullock.*

9.

Blown around the feet of
the God,

58

the landscape hides from us,
the little castle
shows its face at night
& shamans walk the streets

communing with the dead
the terror of the folk
in agony   the cries
of those who fled to open water

gathered into caves
who took their lives.

Okinawa 1945/2000

10.

Where the dead walked
    And the living were made of cardboard
their shadows disappeared.

I lost track of eternity
that makes things new.

Nothing here improves
while time is lost.

Clean as any whistle
I come forth.

But still I can't shake off
the memory of mud.

In meiner heimat.

11.

"I am noman,
my name is noman"

I wait where road
crosses road,
where hunters fly from
their quarry.

Not me but those
that I point to!
Not those but the dead
fed with blood!

Their hands rise in fury.
They hammer us down.

12.

The yidd is a stimulant
and the goyim are cattle

& the words once written
stay writ   all his words
coming back to the speaker
laying him flat.

What a downfall I had
& what havens I reached for
too late. None remained
to embrace me, but

jews, real jews, not shades
in my head but avengers.

13.

First must thou go
the road to hell

must see the millions
thou hast smitten
with thy thoughts   must cry
the cry of killers.

If thy hands are clean
as mine are
why then the swelling in thy throat
the smells of vomit?

Blinded as the dead are blind
the kings of hell.

14.

Time is the evil.
Evil.

Is what is always lost,
what takes me by the throat
& leaves me, shrunken
begging with the other thieves

then drops me in the pit
called bolgia, where a
rhyme I can't erase
repeats forever.

For others other pits
shadow their lives.

15.

the soil living pus, full of vermin,
dead maggots begetting live maggots

fascists at banquets,
pandars to authority,
jackboots,
skinheads with iron teeth

sucking hard at our flesh,
shoving old men
like books in their fires,
outcroppings of shit

too raw for feeling,
the flux in the corpse
turns to stone

16.

And I am not a demigod,
I cannot make it cohere.

Nor bring it, at a dare,
into my focus,
where the sunlight even now
turns ashen,

heavy with burnt matter,
stinking, where the century
has turned a corner,
like a swollen foetus

it has pulled me down,
        old vanity
has pulled me down.

NOTE. "The Pound Project" was commissioned by Francesco Conz for a verbal-visual project in conjunction with Mary de Rachewiltz & the Pound estate at Schloss Brunneburg in the Tirol. The various artists & poets in the project were each responsible for a suite of sixteen works responsive to aspects of Pound's own life & writings. In my case the sixteen poems included appropriations of lines from Pound—shown here in italics—& a sense of his voice & mine mingling without (so to speak) rime or reason. There was also a visual component, a photo image of Pound's face, variously collaged & colored, but I will save that for another context.—J.R.

Bed Brought out of Scotland
Susan Howe

1

Three out of five good-

byes with a serpent

wreathed round able to

slide evenly into what

is is what was taught

Quieter than one sent

emissary I send mine

after you but you have

pilfered silk for flesh

It was an age quieter

Susan Howe

2

Not pedagogic but able to

slide easily in the medium

of embroidery the Queen's

embroiderer works a little

hat for Mary a salamander

in flames three out of five

goodbyes with a serpent

3

Once against night once

black silk though silk has

perished so any heraldic

impromptu verbal feint

you envy and you mirror

Netting an insect spectre

on the same spare quilt

4

Not Scotland's lion rampant

24 flowers in erudite *petit-*

point some cut some uncut

in her own emblem book a

lion she chose to embroider

There is a *lough* which in

your language is a lake

5

Mary could have taught

from the Old Testament

Words three alphabets a

tree flanked by peacocks

Some of the game birds

must have been known

It is a small step to flaunt

a paradox

6

To do grays in running PAUL

SAYING TO TEMOTHE

She would have known

horror of empty spaces

Though she goes softly softly

Softly she goes

7

At evening pity pity

New beds were constantly

being made up

A whimsical Narcissus

with nothing to do

8

Mary late Q of Scots

we see you sinking

In regicide even the wind

is inclined to be cross

9

Until her execution in 1587

she had forced leisure to

embroider

Her cipher can still be seen

on one or two cushions

at Hardwick

10

So the Gordian knot is

cut some trick of state

Few iconoclasts deny

the Magi saw a star

11

"Seven pseudo Maries lie

before me five or six who

never were Mary Stuart

'A crayon sketch will be

enough,' wrote Catherine

de Medici"

12

Buffeted about the world

always in deep mourning

she wears jet ornaments

and Catholic emblems

Mrs. Anstruther Duncan's

miniature but is that reality

—Mary? or a copy

13

All mixed usurpers ob-

fuscatory arcana familiar

to amateurs of enamel—

Reader had I but time

Historical Pyrrhonism the full

unassuaged force of it

14

She arrived at Leith on Tuesday

August 19, 1561, in sea-fog

Even John Knox found her

face "pleasing"

Being a Man

Siri Hustvedt

IN MY WAKING LIFE I'm a woman but sometimes in my dreams I'm a man. My masculinity is rarely a question of simple anatomy. I don't discover that I've sprouted a penis and am growing a beard, but rather I realize that I'm a man in the same moment I am troubled by the vague memory that I was once a woman. My sex becomes important in the dream only when it's called into doubt. It is doubt, not certainty, that produces first the question of my sexual identity and second, the need to be one thing or the other, man or woman. Although it is now fashionable to dismiss dreams as meaningless neurological chatter, I've discovered too much in my own sleep to believe that. It is obvious that my dreams of manliness, which turn on a moment of confusion, illuminate recesses of my own muddled psyche, but I also think they can be used as a key to understanding the larger cultural terrain where the boundary between femininity and masculinity is articulated.

Most of us accept the biological realities of our sex and live with them more or less comfortably, but there are times when the body feels like a limitation. For a woman it may come when she hears a note of condescension in a man's voice and she must confront the fact that it isn't what she has said that has produced this tone, it's her sex. Of course, such a moment isn't easy to analyze because every social encounter is laden with the unsaid and the unseen. Two people inevitably create a third realm between them in which sex is only one of the myriad forces at work, and yet, like envy, resentment, class snobbery, or racism, sexual prejudice can be detected like an odor in the room, and if the smell gets too strong, it prompts a fantasy of escape: what would he have said had he seen me as a man? I'm sure that my dreams of maleness are at least partly about escaping the cultural expectations that burden femininity, but I also think they are something more complex, that the dreams recognize a truth that there is a man in me as well as a woman and that this duality is in fact part of being human, but not one that is always easy to reconcile.

71

In my dreams, my real body doesn't restrain me. I fly and have powers of telekinesis. I've grown fur, suffered gaping wounds, lost my teeth, and shed enough blood to drown in. When I write fiction, I also leave my real body behind and become someone else, another woman or a man if I wish. For me making art has always been a kind of conscious dreaming. The material for a story comes not from what I know but from what I don't know, from impulses and images that often seem to happen without my directives, a strange business altogether and one that is put in play when I become another person in my work. And yet the act of writing consists of one thing only—putting words on a page to be read by someone else. In the end, the words are everything, and strictly speaking, they are sexless. In English, unlike many other languages, our nouns don't even have gender, but it's interesting to ask whether a text can be male or female and what would make it one or the other.

Every parent and anyone who's spent time with very young children knows that sexual identity takes a while to fix itself and that toddlers rarely know if they are boys or girls. When my daughter was three, she asked my husband whether she would get a penis when she grew up. She posed this question during a period in her life I call the tutu-party-shoe phase, an era of glitter and gold, rhinestone tiaras and plastic high heels. While the little boys were puffing out their chests and playing superheroes, my daughter was tripping around the house like a mad, rather smudged version of Titania. At the same age, the daughter of a friend of mine donned a platinum Marilyn Monroe wig and refused to take it off. She ate, played, went to the park, the toilet, and to bed under the increasingly ratty white peruke, which, according to her mother, made her look more like Rumpelstiltskin than a blonde bombshell. However comic they may look to adults, children play hard at finding out what they are—boys or girls—and they live the difference through an often furious imaginary drama of sex roles. Despite the optimism of some researchers, where biology ends and culture begins is probably a question beyond science. Even infants, whose borderless existence makes the question of sexual identity seem absurd from the inside, have been born into a world in which the boy/girl question is crucial from the outside, is the first question asked after birth: "Is it a boy or a girl?" In other words, before they know, we know. And what we know is part of a vast symbolic landscape in which the lines are drawn between one thing and another in the linguistic act of naming. Once children feel sure of themselves as either boys or girls, the Zorro capes, Superman outfits, crowns, and princess costumes are replaced by more androgynous clothing. The external trappings of femininity and masculinity can be discarded at the moment the knowledge of sexual identity becomes internal, and part of that inner certainty happens in language. A six-year-old can usually state with confidence that he or she is a boy or girl, will grow up to be a man or a woman, and, barring an operation, will not change sex along the way. At the same time, the wider meanings of femininity and masculinity are far more ambiguous. *Male* and *female* are words that carry associations so dense, so old, so public but also so private, drawing a clear line between the two is riddled with difficulty. It must be said, however, that the categories male and female are very much alive in the language and are laden with our own deep cultural and personal histories that continue to evolve and change, and that it is wildly naive to suppose that dropping "chairman" for "chairperson," for example, will purge language of its sexual connotations.

We were four daughters in my family. My parents had the name "Lars" ready before each birth, but as it turned out, they had to wait a generation for him. My sister's oldest son was named Lars in honor of our grandfather and the phantom Hustvedt boy who was never born. I have often thought it was easier that we were all girls. Had there been a boy, we might have been compared and opposed to him, and the differences might have confined all of us. We were born in pairs. I was first. Then nineteen months later, my sister Liv was born. A gap of five years followed before Asti appeared and only fifteen months later, Ingrid arrived. The four of us were very close and loyal to one another as children and remain devoted friends as adults, something we have more or less taken for granted. My husband, on the other hand, has always regarded our harmony as both remarkable and somewhat puzzling. Why are there so few conflicts among us? When Liv and I were very young, we liked disaster games—shipwreck, tornado, flood, and war. Liv was always John and I was always Mary, which usually meant that John got to save Mary. I liked being rescued, and the truth was that in life as well as in play, my sister was the brave one, not I, and on several occasions she defended me from the assaults of other children, even though I was her older sister. The two youngest girls were similarly cast. Asti generally preferred the role of girl when playing, and Ingrid liked to be the boy. Liv and Ingrid took up horsemanship and both became amateur rodeo champions. Later, Liv went into business. Ingrid became an

73

architect. Asti and I both ended up in graduate school, she in French, I in English.

Although not nearly full enough, this brief sketch helps to explain why ten years into our marriage, my husband sat up in bed one morning and said to me, "I've understood everything. You're the woman. Liv's the man. Asti's the girl and Ingrid is the boy." We are all grown up now, are all married and all have children, but my sisters and I recognized in that statement a truth about our family that had never been articulated by anyone before. Despite the fact that we were all girls, we established a pattern of alternating feminine and masculine qualities among the sisters. It's notable that it was the younger girl in each pair who adopted the more masculine role, which helped compensate for the deficit in age. The effect was simple. Within each pair, the rivalry typical between siblings of the same sex who are nearly the same age was greatly diminished. It's impossible to compete if you're not playing the same game.

A number of years after that succinct assessment of me and my sisters, I was reading a book of collected papers by D. W. Winnicott, the English pediatrician and psychoanalyst, and came across a lecture called "On the Split-off Male and Female Elements," which he delivered to the British Psycho-Analytical Society in 1966. He introduces the subject by saying, "As a basis for the idea that I wish to give here I suggest that creativity is one of the common denominators of men and women. In another language, however, creativity is the prerogative of women, and in yet another language, it is a masculine feature. It is the last of the three that concerns me here." Winnicott goes on to explain that one day during a conversation with a male patient, he felt that he was hearing a girl and said: "I am listening to a girl. I know perfectly well that you are a man but I am listening to a girl. . . ." The patient replied, "If I were to tell someone about this girl, I would be called mad." Winnicott took the next step. "It was not that *you* told this to anyone; it is *I* who see the girl and hear the girl talking, when actually there is a man on my couch. The mad person is *myself*." The patient answered, "I myself could never say (knowing myself to be a man), 'I am a girl.' I am not mad in that way. But you said it, and you have spoken to both parts of me."

Winnicott's interpretation of this extraordinary dialogue (which he emphasizes has nothing to do with homosexuality) hinges on the understanding that the man's late mother, who already had an older son when she gave birth to her second child, had wanted a girl, and had insisted on seeing the second baby as the wrong sex. The reversal belonged to the mother's "madness," not the son's. The mother's wish was a lie, which in turn created a painful ghost in the son—the desired daughter. My sisters and I didn't suffer from the roles we played in our family the way Winnicott's patient did, and it's probably because my mother wasn't deluded. She loved her babies as girls. I am inclined to think that what happened with us came later and is connected to my father. We four still laugh about the fact that when my father wanted help in the garage, he usually asked for Liv or Ingrid.

I spent six years writing a book in which the narrator is a seventy-year-old man named Leo Hertzberg. When I first began the novel, I felt some anxiety about embodying a man and speaking as him. After a short time, that nervousness fell away, but it became clear to me that I was doing something different, that this speaker lived inside himself in a different way from me, and yet to *be* him, I was drawing on a masculine part of myself. I've played with sexual ambiguity in my work before. The heroine of my first novel, *The Blindfold*—a book also written in the first person—cuts her hair, takes on the name of a boy in a story she has translated, and wanders the streets of New York dressed in a man's suit. While I was writing that book, I knew Iris had to put on the suit, but I never knew why except that her cross-dressing was connected to her translation of the German novella *The Brutal Boy*, a movement from one language into another, and that by pretending to be a man, she loses some vulnerability and gains some power, which she desperately needs. It has never occurred to me until now that taking on a masculine position as a survival technique has roots in my own family, that in the suit Iris lives out the duality and uncertainty of my dreams, and that when she reinvents herself as a male character, she is finally able to imagine her own rescue. As "Klaus" she also speaks differently, uses profanity, and adopts a confident swagger she associates with men. Not long ago, I met a psychiatrist who told me that she had given *The Blindfold* to a number of her female patients. "It doesn't make them worse?" I asked her, only half-joking. "No," she said. "It helps them to see that the boundaries are important." Iris's cross-dressing is defensive, an escape from the openness, fragility, and boundlessness she connects to her femininity.

Being Leo was not an act of translation. After a while, I began to hear him. I heard a man. It's probably impossible to explain where he came from, but I'm convinced that I drew from the experience of listening to the men I have loved, my father and my husband, in particular, but also from others who have been crucial to my intellectual life—those disembodied male voices inside the innumerable books I have read over the years. Their words are in me, but then so are the words of women writers. Jane Austen, Emily and Charlotte Brontë, George Eliot, Emily Dickinson, Gertrude Stein, Djuna Barnes have also altered my imagination, and yet I'm not talking about sexual difference in terms of real bodies, but am reiterating Winnicott, ". . . I was now no longer thinking of boys and girls or men and women," he writes, "but I was thinking in terms of the male and female elements that belong to each." After years of experience, Winnicott learned to listen to his patients in a way that transcended anatomy. Reading means not seeing the writer. Marian Evans became George Eliot to hide her sex, and it worked for a while. Flaubert's declaration "Madame Bovary *c'est moi*" is as earnest as anything he ever said.

As a reader of books, I'm convinced that words have an almost magical power to generate not only more words, but fleeting images, emotions, and memories. Certain novels and poems have had a power to unearth raw and unknown parts of myself, have been like mirrors I never knew existed. In every book, the writer's body is missing, and this absence turns the page into a place where we are truly free to listen to the man or woman who is speaking. When I write a book, I am also listening. I hear the characters talk as if they were outside me rather than inside me. In one book, I heard a young woman who played at being a man; in another, I heard a man. In my dreams, I find myself pulled between the two sexes, wondering which one I am. Not knowing bothers me, but when I write, that same ambivalence becomes my liberation, and I am free to inhabit both men and women and to tell their stories.

From The Head Cornerstone
Madison Smartt Bell

I.

AT EVENING THE CLOUDS were scraped in thin mare's tails around
the setting sun, and the sea, flowing smoothly from the west beneath
the hulls of the French ships, was burnished copper. Placide
Louverture stood in the bow of *La Sirène*, rocking with the easy
swells, watching the red sky in the west toward which they sailed,
watching for birds. There were no birds. They were three weeks out
from Brest, somewhere in the Atlantic Ocean. Sixty ships of the
great fleet strung out as far as the eye could see, as far as the curved
knife edge of the horizon.

Placide's hands just grazed the railing; knees slightly flexed, he
held himself balanced on the smoothly shifting deck. Now and then
he tasted a burst of spray as the ship plowed forward. The Army captain Cyprien stood a few yards back of him, propped against a mast;
Placide was aware of his presence but paid it no heed. Presently his
younger brother, Isaac, came out to join him, walking a little un-
steadily and clutching the rail as he went. On their first voyage, from
Saint Domingue to France, they both had suffered considerably from
seasickness. That had been six years ago. Since then, Placide had
made another voyage, intended to go all the way to Egypt, but Isaac
had not accompanied him then.

The nausea scarcely troubled Placide this time out, not after the
first day. Isaac was making a slower adjustment, though he looked a
little better now than the day before, favoring Placide with a weak
smile as he stopped beside him.

"*Ki jan ou yé!*" Placide asked him. "*W byen!*"

"*Pa pi mal.*" Isaac drew himself a little straighter. "*M'ap kenbe.*"
He rocked back on his heels, catching his weight against his hand-
grip on the rail. *No worse; I'm hanging on.* . . . During their years in
France they'd spoken Creole seldom, even among themselves. The
patois was frowned upon at the Collège de la Marche, though many
of the other students had it as their mother tongue.

A flying fish came out of a billow, whirred toward them, then

77

drilled into another wave. Isaac's breath caught, and Placide turned
to smile at him again. Ill below decks for so many days, Isaac had till
now missed most of the wonders the sea had to display.

The first fish was followed by another, and another, then dozens
all at once were in the air, glittering, wet, and iridescent red in the
light of the setting sun. Placide wondered what the appearance of the
fish might augur. This thought too had the taste of home, where
every natural manifestation had its meaning if one could know it. He
and Isaac had been children when they left Saint Domingue. Now
they had the age of men. When he'd summoned them to that audience before their departure, the first consul had presented them each
a splendid uniform, brace of pistols, and a sword. But they had little
knowledge of the use of these arms.

Nor did they know what awaited them in Saint Domingue.
Placide's memories of that land were fractured; his brother's still less
clear. Placide had been tantalized with the prospect once before, for
when that other fleet had sailed to Egypt, Saint Domingue had been
the declared destination—his own presence meant only to lend cre-
dence to that deception. When the real mission was revealed to him
(at the same time as to most of the rest of the passengers), Placide
had soothed his disappointment with the thought that he might look
upon the Pyramids, and especially the Great Sphinx, which he had
seen in pictures. But the English Navy, undeceived by the ruse,
had intercepted them and turned them back to a French port.

Monsieur Coisnon, their tutor, now appeared beside Isaac, the
skirt of his dark cassock snapping in the wind. The flying fish were
still exploding from the waves, and Coisnon began to speak of them
in terms of natural history. Placide's mind drifted. He recalled that,
on his return from that aborted voyage to Egypt, M. Coisnon had told
him how in reality the Great Sphinx was somewhat diminished from
what he'd seen in the engravings, the vast sad features of her face
blown to flinders by Bonaparte's artillerymen, practicing their aim.
Coisnon had meant that tale for consolation, Placide thought, but he
had not been much consoled.

Amidships, a brass bell clanged.

"Mess call," Coisnon said. Isaac and Placide looked at each other
grimly. Coisnon shaded his eyes to peer up at the sky.

"You will remember," he said, "that when Columbus first undertook this voyage, his men thought to mutiny when he would not
turn back, sick as they were of salt meat spoiled in the cask, and fearful they'd sail off the edge of the world altogether. It was the birds

78

flying out from the islands that saved him then, restoring the confidence of the crew. As the dove saved Noah from the failing faith of his companions, returning with the olive branch."

Placide followed his tutor's expansive gesture. For a moment it seemed to him he caught the scent of flowers. He looked again; there were no birds.

"Come," said M. Coisnon. "Let us to table."

Isaac gulped. They did not eat as poorly as Columbus's men in the last days of that first voyage, and there was plenty of fresh water for them still. But after these few weeks at sea the last of any fresh food had been exhausted. Each meal was labor more than pleasure, and the tot of rum served out beforehand seemed meant to give one courage to face it.

Placide, then Isaac, clumped down to the officers' mess, M. Coisnon bringing up their rear. They found their places at the table. Certainly there was no one aboard enjoying better victuals. They ate not at the first table, with the ship's captain and his mates, but at the second, in the company of four young Army officers and a lone naval ensign whom everyone seemed to ignore. The Army captains were Cyprien, Paltre, Daspir, and Guizot. No one seemed to be able to recall the ensign's name, not even M. Coisnon, who was armed with tricks for memorizing his ever-changing pupils.

"Thanks be to God," Coisnon muttered, and inhaled a blast of rum from his cup. Placide and Isaac bowed their heads momentarily; the Army captains avoided each other's eyes. Tonight it was salt cod, as opposed to salt beef.

"One might try a hand at fishing," Captain Guizot proposed.

"If one had line and a hook," said Paltre.

Daspir lifted his plank of salt cod and held it dangling. He squinted at it comically. It was an unappealing ocher shade, with a rank smell that struck at a considerable distance. The shifting light of the swinging lantern made its surface seem to crawl.

Placide looked away. He chewed mechanically, ignoring the sour flavor. There was a mess of boiled beans and meal to complement the fish. Isaac nibbled at the corner of the chunk of hardtack he'd tried to soften in his rum. Placide nudged him to encourage him to eat; the younger boy dutifully poked a spoonful of the bean mash into his mouth and struggled to swallow it down.

"Now, what shall we find delectable in Saint Domingue?" Daspir inquired.

Both Placide and Isaac looked up. Conversation at these meals was restricted to this sort of innocuous question. Or else there might be disquisitions from Coisnon on topics which had suggested themselves to him during the day. The Army men were hard put to conceal their boredom with his lectures, yet their talk among themselves was constrained by the presence of the boys and their tutor. Placide remembered something of the same sort from his Egyptian voyage, the same hesitancy, same sense of withholding.

"*Maïs moulin,*" he said. It was the bean mash that prompted him. *Maïs moulin* stood in the relation of pure Platonic form to the sludge they were trying to eat now.

"*C'est quoi ça,*" Daspir said. *What's that?* He was a plump young man, with round cheeks and shining olive skin; he loved good food and felt privation more keenly than the others. Placide described: stewed cornmeal mixed with highly seasoned beans, with onions, peppers, perhaps a dash of syrup whose sweetness worked against the spice.

"What else?" Daspir's eyes were shining. "What for meat?"

Placide shrugged. "Goat. Fresh pork. Roasted on the *boucan* it is very good. There are many kinds of fish."

"*Lambi,*" Isaac put in. "*Lambi* with green cashew sauce." With a rapture rising to Daspir's own, he told how the meat of the conch was tenderized with papaya juice, served with a sauce of tomatoes and fresh cashews, the soft consistency of mushrooms. Then to follow there might be fruit: oranges certainly, guava, mango, soursop, several different kinds of banana—*banane figue, banane loupgarou,* and Isaac's own favorite, the tiny sweet *banane Ti Malice.*

Inspired by these recollections, Isaac managed to empty most of his plate, as Placide noticed with some relief; his brother had not succeeded in taking much nourishment since he had been laid low by *mal de mer.* And thus another dinner hour had passed more agreeably than some. With Coisnon, the two boys climbed up to take their evening constitutional on the deck. There was no moon, and the night was marvelously clear, starlight blazing down on them from a black velvet sky. The swell seemed just a little stronger than before.

Raising his arm to the constellations, Coisnon began to recount the myths of Cepheus and Cassiopeia. But he had to interrupt himself when Isaac, without warning, doubled over the rail and spewed his recent meal into the sea. Placide balanced his head while he retched and coughed; Coisnon anchored him with a hand's grip in his waistband.

"Excuse me," Isaac said, when he'd regained that much control. "I am very sorry."

"It's nothing, dear boy," Coisnon told him. "I'll take you down to your berth. No, no," he said, as Placide moved to assist. "You should stay here, and profit from the air."

Placide remained, turning again to face the ocean. At the Collège de la Marche he'd had the reputation of a solitary, especially when compared to the much more gregarious Isaac, and he was glad of a taste of solitude now. Even a partial taste. From the corner of his eye he could see the faces of Cyprien and Guizot by the hatchway, lit by the intermittent red glow of their cheroots. Somehow or other at least one of these officers was always nearby. Placide understood that the four of them were assigned to him and his brother as guardians, if not guards, though he had not discussed it with Isaac.

He raised his head to find the Northern Cross, and near it, picked out in dimmer stars, the compact form of the Dolphin. The stars went dark where the water met the sky, but the running lights of the French ships came stringing back to where he stood in the bow of *La Sirène*. One of those other vessels (Placide was not sure which) carried a flock of his father's most significant surviving enemies, notably the mulatto rebels: Villatte, Pétion, Rigaud. The thought made him uncomfortable. He felt eyes burning at his back, and turned to face them. Cyprien and Guizot looked away from him, stepped out of his path as he entered the hatchway and went below to find his berth.

Since their embarkation, the four officers detailed to the sons of Toussaint Louverture had run a nightly game of *vingt-et-un*, and when Cyprien and Guizot had finished their smoke they went below to join this night's session. They'd set up a packing case for a card table in the officers' quarters, in the bow a deck below the captain's cabin. A thin partition divided the card parlor from the four berths in the narrowest part of the bow, which were occupied by Placide, Isaac, their tutor, and the young ensign whose name no one could recall.

Daspir, who was rich, served as the bank. Night after night, the bank was irritatingly prosperous. Cyprien and Paltre, who were marginally more seasoned soldiers than the other two, had at first assumed they'd fleece him easily. But Daspir played with a quiet acuity belied by his fatuous manner. Or less, as Cyprien sometimes bitterly put to himself or to Paltre, he was just damned lucky.

Daspir was shuffling now, smiling at the other three. Above the packing case an oil lamp swung on its chain with the steady movement of the waves. Daspir's smile evaporated as he dealt the cards. His own hand showed a ten face-up. Cyprien glanced at his hole card and folded. Paltre did the same, but Guizot drew to a six, then groaned.

Expressionless now, Daspir raked in the money and dealt again. Nine up. Cyprien checked his hole card and tossed in his hand. Daspir covered bets from Paltre and Guizot and then took money from them both.

When he had won a few more hands, Daspir squared the deck and rose from his seat, leaving the cards on the table, then crossed to his bunk and stooped to drag his chest from beneath it. After shifting the contents around for a minute or two, he produced a bottle of very decent brandy. It was not the first he had discovered during the voyage, though now he squinted at the level through the glass, as if to suggest that his supply was not completely inexhaustible.

"Permettez-moi," he said, smiling again as he came back to the packing case. *Allow me.* Despite the roll of the ship, his step was steady and his hand too as he poured—he smiled with his mouth but his eyes remained cool. Again, Cyprien thought that the man was not the idle voluptuary he might seem. He pushed his cup forward for the splash of brandy, grunted his thanks.

Daspir sat down and dealt the cards. Cyprien and Paltre folded three times in succession, while Guizot bet heavily and lost. Guizot said nothing, but Cyprien could sense his rising anger; he had a weak head for liquor as well as for cards. Perhaps Daspir was aware of the strained mood also, for he squared the deck again and poured another dose of brandy all around.

"Your health, gentlemen," he said, and when they'd drunk, "How long do you suppose we'll be about this business?"

"Judging by tonight's progress," Paltre said, "you'll have parted us from the remains of our substance in another week's time."

"In Saint Domingue, I mean," said Daspir, with one of his fey giggles.

"Oh," Paltre said, raising his eyebrows in mock surprise, "in *Saint Domingue.*"

"How long can it possibly take to put down a nigger insurrection?" Guizot burst out. But Daspir kept looking quietly at Cyprien, who picked up his cup of brandy and drank. Guizot was already drunk, that was plain, and angry over his losses at the table.

"One rag-headed monkey at the head of a band of brigands," Guizot grumbled. "Why, the four of us might go out and arrest him and put an end to the whole affair in a week."

"*Quiet*," Cyprien snapped, glancing pointedly at the partition in the bow. "You know that we have no such orders."

"Nonsense." Guizot belched. "They are sleeping. And if they heard, what would they understand. . . ."

Daspir had begun to shuffle the cards again. His soft olive hands, with the neatly trimmed fingernails, moved smoothly over the deck. Cyprien exchanged a glance with Paltre. This *nigger insurrection* had been going on for ten years, though the two of them had thought no more of it on their first trip out than Guizot did now. During that earlier mission there had been some idle chatter of the same sort: a mere handful of men might arrest Toussaint, and never mind all Hédouville's tedious temporizing. A couple of those chatterers, young officers with whom Cyprien and Paltre had struck up a short-term friendship, had been found dead on the road outside Gonaives, victims of an ambush which had never been explained or punished.

"Ours is a peaceful mission," Cyprien said, reciting the official line. "As Toussaint Louverture professes loyalty to France, he must certainly bow to the authority of the Captain General Leclerc."

"Oh, to be sure," Guizot snorted. "And for that one requires twenty-five thousand troops of the line. No, you speak of Hédouville and *his* style of diplomacy—and Hédouville ran home with his tail between his legs."

Cyprien flattened his hands on the splintery surface of the packing case. For a long moment there was no sound audible above the ocean's rhythm except the fluttering of the cards. A ship's rat ran along the groove of the wall and deck and squeezed through a crack in the bow partition.

"I am sure you do not mean to insult me," Cyprien said.

"Certainly not." Daspir had spoken; he put down the cards. "Nor you nor Captain Paltre, I am sure." Daspir looked at Guizot, his eyes grown chill.

"Not in the least, my friends." Guizot, who was seated between Paltre and Cyprien, looked quickly from one to the other. "No, you are both men of courage and honor." He hiccuped. "Enough word-mincing, is all I mean to say. Are we to be outfaced by some gilt nigger in a general's suit? Are we not soldiers?"

Guizot reached for Cyprien's and Paltre's hands. Cyprien let his own be taken. At once he felt a surge of confused emotion, as if

Guizot had communicated it with his touch. Daspir joined hands with them to close the circle.

"Come, shall we make a pact?" Guizot said. This time it was he who gave a meaningful look at the bow partition. "We may be placed to have some special opportunity—and there'd be glory in it. Let it be the four of us who bring the rebel in."

Cyprien thought of his comrades dead by the roadside, of Hédouville's abrupt departure, which did have the taste of ignominy. For a second he caught Paltre's eye. Shadows stroked across their faces with the swinging of the lamp. After all, there was something here to be avenged.

"So be it, then," he said. "I'll drink to that."

There was a squeeze of all their hands, and all at once they cheered. Then Daspir broke the circled handclasp, reaching one more time for his brandy bottle.

Placide woke with such a start he knocked his head against the wall. It was a minute or two before the movement of the sea reminded him where he was. There was that, and Coisnon's snoring, and the muttering of that young ensign, who often talked unhappily in his sleep. A ship's rat scuttled in the bilges beneath his plank berth. Through the partition he could hear the muffled, unintelligible voices of the four Army officers at their cards and liquor.

What had he dreamed? Billows, above which were billows, rolling one into the next like ocean waves, but these were waves of sand. A searing light over golden dunes, and then rising from the sand the august scarred face of the Sphinx, looming over him with her wounds, the weight of all that stone—it was then that he'd begun to be afraid (his heart still thumping even now) under the weight, fear of the Sphinx and her terrible stony voice, but then it was night, the sand was sea, and there in the place of the Sphinx (but still enormous) was the mermaid spirit Lasirène, glowing blue-green like phosphorescence or like stars, the dark pull of her gravity bearing Placide down beneath the waters.

He put his hand against the curving boards, feeling the pulse of the ocean. The rush of the water outside helped to calm him. He listened to the breathing of the other three in his compartment, to the persistent scrabbling of the rat. What was it they were sailing toward this time?

He needed to relieve himself, but he did not want to walk out to the jakes abovedecks; he didn't care for the way the four captains looked at him, so late, when they'd been drinking—nor the way they avoided looking at him sometimes. He found a bottle he'd laid by for such situations, unstopped it, and directed his stream so that it ran soundlessly against the glass wall. When he was done he corked the bottle and wedged it back in the same place. Isaac coughed and shifted in his sleep, and Placide stepped across the narrow space and leaned over him, listening, till his younger brother's breath grew regular. Then he lay down again on the hard boards of his bunk.

Drowsiness carried him back toward the fearful immanence of the great *loa*. Lasirène, Erzulie of the waters! Placide had been a long time out of his own country; he had remembered the beauty of this mystery, but not her weight. Coisnon had taught them of Odysseus, how he stopped his crewmen's ears and ordered himself bound to the mast, that he might hear the siren song without being carried down by it to his own drowning. But that was only an old Greek story.

Placide worked his shoulders against the plank bed. This berth was a privilege of a sort, and yet he would have slept more easily in a hammock such as the ordinary sailors used. But in his discomfort he had pulled away from the dream vortex and the fish-tailed goddess waiting at the bottom. He was thinking with his mind. Surely it must be no accident that this ship itself was called *La Sirène*. No accident either that she had not yet sailed ahead of the main fleet.

"*Your father,*" the first consul had told them when he summoned them to his cabinet at the Tuileries, "*is a great man; he has rendered eminent services to France. You will tell him that I, the first magistrate of the French people, I promise him protection, glory, and honor. Do not suppose that France has any intention to bring war to Saint Domingue: the army which she sends there is not intended to fight the troops of the country but to augment their force. Here is General Leclerc, my brother-in-law, whom I have named captain general, and who will command this army. Orders are given that you will be fifteen days ahead in Saint Domingue, to announce to your father the coming of the expedition.*"

Following this reassuring address, Placide and Isaac had been guests of honor at a grand dinner, attended by the captain general Leclerc himself, with his seductive wife, Pauline, sister of the first consul. Also the vice admiral Bougainville was there, with state counselors and many other persons of distinction, even Vincent, the colonel of engineers, whom Placide knew to be a close and trusted friend of his father. Yet Vincent had seemed unusually silent and withdrawn that evening, though he was always friendly to the boys. The two of them appeared in the gorgeous dress uniforms they had just been given, and Pauline Leclerc, world famous for her coquetry as much as for her beauty, made much of Isaac's fine appearance, while her husband (himself only twenty-nine years of age) pretended to growl at the flirtation.

In the event, however, their ship had remained moored for a very long time at Brest, while soldiers and supplies were assembled and embarked. *La Sirène* had put out in the midst of the entire fleet. For many days, Placide and Isaac believed that somewhere in the mid-Atlantic their ship would simply put on more sail and speed out ahead of the others, bearing the two of them, and the first consul's letter, to their father. Isaac, at least, had believed wholeheartedly that such a thing must happen, while Placide, experienced in voyages of disguised destination and in being used himself as a decoy, had privately been a little doubtful from the start. And now they must be less than fifteen days from their landfall in Saint Domingue. What if a different ship had sailed ahead—the one that carried Rigaud and his cohorts, or some other?

It might be for that that Lasirène seemed angry: she had been deceived, ill served. *Mais ce n'est pas de ma faute!* Placide cried mentally, *I couldn't help it!* A spirit might pardon your failure if it was plain you could not have prevented it. Placide thought he remembered that much, though Toussaint had been very firm in directing his sons away from the *hounfors* and into the Catholic Church. Still, with his father's long campaigns and frequent absences, there were times when both he and Isaac had followed the drums. Placide had seen the gods come down, seen the people who bore them totter with the shock of their descent.

This was the mystery into which he sailed, and he was helpless to change his course. Let it be, then. Let it come to him, to them all. He closed his eyes and made his breathing slow and even, though he no longer had the least desire to sleep.

II.

"You were uneasy in the night," Michel Arnaud remarked to his wife.

"Oh?" said Claudine Arnaud, pausing with her coffee cup in mid-air. "I regret to have disturbed your rest."

"It is nothing," Arnaud said. He looked at her sidelong. The suspended coffee cup showed no hint of a tremor. In fact, Claudine had appeared to gain strength these last few months. She was lean, certainly, but no longer looked frail. Her face, once pallid, had broken out in freckles, since lately she took no care against the sun. She sipped from her cup and set it down precisely in the saucer, then reached across the table to curl her fingers over his wrist.

"Don't concern yourself," Claudine said, with a transparent smile. "I have no trouble." Behind her chair, the mulattress Cléo shifted her feet, staring mistrustfully down at Arnaud, who raised his eyes to meet hers briefly.

"Encore du café, s'il vous plaît."

Cléo moved around the table, lifted the pot, and poured. The pot was silver, newly acquired—lately they'd begun to replace some of the amenities lost or destroyed when the rebel slaves burned this plantation in 1791. Household service was improving too, though it came wrapped in what Arnaud was wont to regard as an excess of mutual politeness. And Cléo's attachment to his wife was a strange thing!—though he got an indirect benefit from it. In the old days, when Cléo had been his mistress as well as his housekeeper, the two women had hated each other cordially.

He turned his palm up to give his wife's fingers a little squeeze, then disengaged his hand and stirred sugar into his coffee. White sugar, of his own manufacture. There was that additional sweetness—very few cane planters on the Northern Plain had recovered their operations to the point of producing white sugar rather than the less laborious brown.

Marie-Noelle came out onto the long porch to serve a platter of bananas and fried eggs. Arnaud helped himself generously, and covertly studied the black girl's hips, moving deliciously under the thin cotton of her gown as she walked away. In the old days, he'd have had her before breakfast, and never mind who heard or knew. But now—he felt Cléo's eyes were drilling him and looked away, from everyone; he hardly knew where to rest his gaze.

Down below the low hill where the big house stood, the small cabins and *ajoupas* of the field hands he'd been able to regather spread out around the tiny chapel Claudine had insisted that he build. The blacks were now taking their own morning nourishment and marshaling themselves for a day in the cane plantings or at the mill; soon the iron bell would be rung. Claudine and Arnaud were breakfasting on the porch, for the hypothetical cool, but there was none. The air was heavy, oppressively damp; drifts of soggy blue cloud cut off the sun.

Arnaud looked at his wife again, more carefully. It was true that she appeared quite well. There was no palsy, no mad glitter in her eye. Last night they had made love, an uncommon thing for them, and it had been uncommonly successful. They fell away from each other into a deep black slumber, but sometime later in the night Arnaud had been roused by her spasmodic kicking. She thrashed her head in a tangle of hair and out of her mouth rose a long high silvery ululation. Then her voice broke and went deep and rasping, as her whole body became rigid, trembling as she uttered the words in Creole: *Aba blan! Tuyé moun-yo!* Then she'd convulsed, knees drawing to her chest, the cords of her neck all standing out taut as speechlessly she strangled. Arnaud had been ready to run for help, but then Claudine relaxed, went limp, and presently began to snore.

He himself had slept but lightly for what remained of the night. And now he thought that Cléo, who slept in the next room, beyond the flimsiest possible partition, must have heard it all. *Down with the whites. Kill those people!*

Down below the iron bell clanged, releasing him. Arnaud pushed back his chair and stood. When he bent down to peck at his wife's cheek, Claudine turned her face upward so that he received her lips instead.

A hummingbird whirred before a hyacinth bloom, and Claudine felt her mind go out of her body, into the invisible blur of those wings. She had gone down the steps from the porch to watch her husband descend the trail to his day's work. Behind her she heard Cléo and Marie-Noelle muttering as they cleared the table.

"Té gegne lespri nan têt li, wi. . . ."

True for them, and Claudine felt no resentment of the comment. *There was a spirit in her head. . . .* She was so visited sometimes when she slept, as well as when the drums beat in the *hounfor.* To others, a spirit might bring counsel, knowledge of the future even, but Claudine never remembered anything at all. Unless someone perhaps could tell her what words had been uttered through her lips—but she would not ask Arnaud. Afterward she normally felt clean and free, but today she was only more agitated. Perhaps it was the heavy weather. Her hands opened and closed at her hips. She could not tell which way to turn.

At this hour she might normally have convened the little school she operated for the smaller children of the plantation (though

Arnaud thought it a frivolity and would have stopped it if he could). But in the heavy atmosphere today the children would be indisposed. And though her teaching often soothed her own disquiet, she thought today that it would not. She turned from the descending path and walked around the back of the house, swinging her arms lightly to dry the dampness of her palms.

Here another trail went zigzag up the cliff, and Claudine grew more damp and clammy as she climbed. A turn of the trail brought her to a flat pocket, partly sheltered by a great boulder the height of her own shoulders. The trail ended in this spot. She stopped to breathe. This lassitude! She was weary from whatever had passed in the night, the thing that she could not recall. She waited till her breath was even, till her pulse no longer throbbed, then, standing tiptoe, reached across the boulder to wet her fingers in the trickle of spring water that ran down the wrinkles of the black rock. The water was sharply cold, a grateful shock. She sipped a mouthful from the leaking cup of her hand, then pressed her dampened fingertips against her throat and temples.

"*M'ap bay w dlo,*" a child's voice called from behind and above her. "*Kite'm fe sa!*"

Claudine settled back on her heels. In fact the runnel of the spring was just barely within her longest reach. Etienne, a black child probably five years old, bare-legged and clothed only in the ragged remnant of a cotton shirt, scampered down toward her, his whole face alight. *I'll give you water—let me do it.* There was no trail where he descended, and the slope was just a few degrees off the vertical, but a few spotted goats were grazing the scrub there among the rocks and Etienne moved as easily as they. He bounced down onto the level ground beside her, and immediately turned to fish out a gourd cup that lay atop a barrel of meal in a crevice of the cliff—Arnaud having furnished this spot as an emergency retreat. Grinning, Etienne scrambled to the top of the boulder and stretched the gourd out toward the spring, careless of the sixty-foot drop on which he teetered.

"*Ai,*" Claudine gasped. "*Attention, cheri.*" She took hold of his shirttail. But Etienne's balance was flawless; he put no weight against her grip. In a moment he had slipped down to the boulder and was raising the brimming gourd to her.

"*W'ap bwe sa, wi,*" he said. *You'll drink this.*

"Yes," Claudine said, accepting the gourd with a certain ceremony. The water was very cool and sweet. She swallowed and returned the gourd to him half full and when he'd drunk his share, she curtsied with a smile. Etienne giggled. Claudine smoothed her skirts and sat down on a stone, looking out.

Below, the cabins of the field hands fanned out randomly from the little white-washed chapel. They'd overbuilt the site of the old *grand'case* which had been burned in the risings of 1791—the house that had been the theater of her misery when Arnaud first brought her out to Saint Domingue from France. More distant, two dark threads of smoke were rising from the cane mill and distillery, and further still, two teams of men with ox-drawn wagons were cutting and loading cane from the wide *carrés* marked out by citrus hedges.

The higher ground where Arnaud had built the new *grand'case* was a better spot, less plagued by insects, more secure. On any height, however modest, one had a better chance to catch a breeze. Claudine realized she had hoped for a breath of wind when she climbed here, but there was none, only the heavy air and the lowering sky, the dull weight of anticipation. Something was coming— she didn't know what. She might, perhaps, ask Cléo what she had shouted in her sleep. . . .

A cold touch startled her. She turned her head; the smiling Etienne was dabbling water around the neckline of her dress. After the first jolt the sensation was pleasant. She felt a drop purl down the joints of her spine.

"*Ou pa apprann nou jodi-a,*" he said. *You are not teaching us today.* A statement, not a question.

"*Non,*" said Claudine, and as she thought, "It is Saturday."

Etienne leaned against her back, draping an arm across her shoulder. His slack hand lay at the top of her breast, his cheek against her hair. In the heat his warm weight might have been disagreeable, but she felt herself wonderfully comforted.

Idly her gaze drifted toward the west. Along the *allée* which ran to the main road, about two-thirds of the royal palms still stood. The rest had been destroyed in the insurrection, so that the whole looked like a row of broken teeth. It seemed that the high palms shivered slightly, though where she sat Claudine could feel no breeze. Beyond, the green plain curved toward the horizon and the blue haze above the sea. Midway, a point of dust moved spiderlike in her direction.

She shifted her position when she noticed this, and felt that Etienne's attention had focused too, though neither of them spoke. They watched the dot of dust until it grew into a plume, pushing its way toward them through the silence. Then Claudine saw the silver

90

flashing of the white horse in full gallop, and the small, tight-knit figure of the leading rider. The men of his escort carried pennants on long staves.

"Come!" she said, jumping up from her stone. "We must go down quickly."

It seemed unlikely that Etienne would have recognized the horseman, but he ran down the path ahead of her in a state of high excitement, his velocity attracting other small children into his wake. Claudine went more slowly, careful of the grade. As she passed the house, Cléo came out onto the long porch, shading her eyes to look into the west, and Marie-Noelle joined her, wiping her hands on her apron.

Claudine stopped at the edge of the compound, looking down the long *allée* to the point where Arnaud had recently hung a wooden gate to the stone posts from which the original ironwork had been torn. She watched; for a time there was no movement. Nearby a green shoot had sprung four feet high from the trunk of a severed palm, and a blue butterfly hovered over its new fronds. Etienne and the playmates he'd gathered went hurtling down the *allée,* scattering a couple of goats who'd wandered there. The children braked to a sudden halt at the skirl of a *lambi* shell. Immediately the wooden gates swung inward. Flanked by the pennants of his escort, Toussaint Louverture rode toward her at a brisk trot, astride his great white charger, Bel Argent.

Claudine drew herself a little straighter, and crossed her hands below her waistline. She was conscious of how she must appear, fixed in the long perspective of the green *allée.* There was a hollow under her heels where once had been a gallows post. She took a step forward onto surer ground, and recomposed herself for the reception.

Spooked by the advancing horsemen, the children turned tail and came running back toward her. Etienne and Marie-Noelle's oldest boy, Dieufait, took hold of her skirts on either side and peeped out from behind her. Toussaint had slowed his horse to a walk several yards short of her, so as not to coat her with his dust. He slipped down from the saddle, and walked toward her, leading Bel Argent by the reins. As always, she was a little surprised to see that he was no taller than she was herself once he had dismounted. Shaking the children free of her skirt, she curtsied to his bow.

"You are welcome, General," she said, "to Habitation Arnaud."

"*Merci.*" Toussaint took her hand in his oddly pressureless grip and bowed his head over it. Claudine felt a tingle that sprang upward

from the arches of her feet—when she'd thought herself long im-
mune to such a blush. There was a pack of rumors lately, that Toussaint received the *amours* of many white women of the highest
standing, attracted by the thrill of his power if they were not simply
angling for gain. He did not kiss her hand, however, but only
breathed upon her knuckles, and now he raised his eyes to meet her
own. His hat was in his other hand, his head bound up in a yellow
madras cloth. The gaze was assaying, somehow. Toussaint broke it
with a click of his tongue, as if he'd seen what he'd been looking for.

"You'll stay the night," Claudine said. "I trust—I hope."

"Oh no, Madame," Toussaint told her, and covered his mouth
with his long fingers, as if it pained him to disappoint her. "Your pardon, but we are pressed—we stop for water only, for our horses and
ourselves."

Behind him, Guiaou and Riau had ridden up, Guiaou still bran-
dishing the rosy conch shell he'd used to trumpet their arrival.
Claudine pressed her hand to the flat bone between her breasts.

"But—tomorrow we will celebrate the mass."

"Is it so?" said Toussaint, smiling slightly, with the same auto-
matic movement to cover his mouth. "Well then. Of course."

Claudine fluttered at the little boys who still stood round-eyed at
her back. "Did you not hear?" she hissed at them. "Go find something for these men to drink—and take their horses to water."

Michel Arnaud received the news of Toussaint's arrival with mixed
emotions. The word that horsemen were on the way came to him
shouted from man to man across the cane fields, and by the time he
stepped to the door of the mill he had the comical view of tiny
Dieufait leading the huge white warhorse toward the water trough.
Toussaint was here, Arnaud thought, in part to reassure himself—to
touch the proofs that his government had restored conditions where-
in a planter might refine white sugar. For sugar was money, and
money was guns. . . . Arnaud chopped off that sequence of ideas.
Also of course there was the issue of inspection, and enforcement of
the new and strict labor code for the free blacks.

Arnaud had benefited from these rules, although his workers
found them very harsh. But at any rate it was better to be inspected
by Toussaint than Dessalines. The whip had been long since abandoned, but if Dessalines got hold of a laggard or a truant he might
order the culprit flogged with a bundle of thorny vines, which tore

the skin and laid the flesh open to infection, so that the man might afterward die. It was true that the others would work that much harder, for a few days at least, after Dessalines had passed. Toussaint had a different style—if he had not been terribly provoked, he punished only with a glare, whereupon the suspect would apply himself to his cane knife or hoe with tripled diligence, pursued by his own imagination of what might follow if he did not.

But somehow Arnaud was not eager for this meeting. Let Claudine play hostess if she would; he knew she'd press Toussaint and his men to dine with them that night. If he accepted, they'd be in for a display of his famous piety on the morrow morn. . . . He pulled down the brim of the wide straw hat he wore against the sun and walked behind the mill down the crooked path which led through the bush to his distillery. Arnaud did not drink strong spirits as carelessly as he once had, but it seemed to him now advisable to test the quality of the morning run.

There, about twenty minutes later, Toussaint came down with his companions: Captain Riau of the Second Regiment and Guiaou, a cavalryman from Toussaint's honor guard. At once Arnaud, bowing and smiling, proffered a sample of his first-run rum, but the governor general refused it, though he saw it dripped directly from the coil. Riau and Guiaou accepted their measure, and drank with evident enthusiasm.

"What news have you from the Collège de la Marche?" Toussaint inquired.

"I beg your pardon?" Arnaud stuttered.

Toussaint did not bother to repeat the question. Arnaud's brain ratcheted backward. A couple of Cléo's sons, whom he had fathered, had indeed been recently shipped off to that same school in France where Toussaint's brats were stabled. They were actually Arnaud's only sons so far as he knew, as Claudine was barren, but he had never meant to acknowledge them. He had sold all Cléo's children off the plantation when they were quite small, but a couple of them had reappeared, a little after Cléo did. Faced with Cléo's importuning, Arnaud had seen the wisdom of sending those boys overseas to school—which got them off the property at least. In his present situation he was not able to pay the whole of their expenses, but it seemed that Cléo had a brother who'd prospered quite wonderfully under the new regime. . . .

How the devil had Toussaint known about it? He made it his business to know many unlikely things. At least he had not put the question in Claudine's presence; there was that to be grateful for.

"No, no, we have heard nothing yet," he said, with a rather sickly smile. "The boys are remiss!—they do not write their mother."

There the subject rested. The four of them set out on the obligatory tour: cane fields, provision grounds, the cane mill, and refinery. . . . At the end, Toussaint intruded into Arnaud's books, pursing his lips or raising his eyebrows over the figures of his exports and his income.

Claudine, with the aid of Marie-Noelle and Cléo, had organized a midday meal featuring grilled freshwater fish, with a sauce of hot peppers, tomato, and onion. Toussaint took none of this, but only a piece of bread, a glass of water, and an uncut mango. Arnaud knew or at least suspected that his well-known abstemiousness was rooted in a fear of poison. But Riau and Guiaou ate heartily, and Riau, the more articulate of the pair, was ready enough with his compliments. Then, finally, at the peak of the afternoon's heat, it was time for the siesta.

The mattress was soggy under her back. Claudine could feel sweat pooling before the padding could absorb it. She could not sleep, could hardly rest, tired as she felt from the night before. The heat was still more smothering than it had been this morning. Toussaint's arrival partly explained her mood, she thought; it was the thing she had felt coming, but it was not yet complete, and so her restlessness was not assuaged. Through the slats of the jalousies she could hear Cléo's murmuring voice as she gossiped with one of Toussaint's men on the porch.

At her side, Arnaud released a snore. Claudine felt a flash of resentment, that he could rest when she could not. But he'd taken a strong measure of rum with his lunch, which was no longer his usual practice. When he lay down, Arnaud had taken her left hand in his and dozed off caressing, with the ball of his thumb, the wrinkled stump of the finger where she'd once worn her wedding ring. He did this often, almost always, but there was nothing erotic in it, and hardly any tenderness; it was more like the superstitious fondling of a fetish. Now she carefully disengaged her hand, slid quietly to the edge of the bed, and stood.

Cléo sat on the edge of a stool, in a pose which showed the graceful line of her back as she bent her attention on Captain Riau, who stood below the porch railing, looking up at her. "Where are you going with Papa Toussaint?" she asked him. Claudine heard a flirtatious lilt in her voice.

"To Santo Domingo," Riau said. "Across the border, at Ouanaminthe—" It seemed as if he would have continued, but he saw Claudine in the doorway and stopped.

"*Bon soir, Madame,*" he said, lowering his head. "Good evening." His military coat was very correct, despite the suffocating heat— brass buttons all done up in a row. As soon as he'd spoken he turned away and began striding down the path toward the lower ground. There was room in the *grand'case* only for Toussaint himself, so Marie-Noelle had found pallets for his men in the compound below.

Cléo turned toward Claudine, her face a mask. That same face with its long oval shape and its smooth olive tone, which Claudine had once hated so desperately. The years between had left some lighter lines around Cléo's eyes and at the corners of her mouth, but she was still supple, still attractive, though Arnaud no longer went to her bed. In her frustration, Claudine stretched out her hands to her.

"What was it I shouted in my sleep last night?" she said.

Cléo's face became a degree more closed.

"*M pa konnen,*" she said. *I don't know.*

Claudine felt a stronger pulse of the old jealous rage. The one face before her became all the faces closed against her, yellow or black, withholding the secrets so vital to her life. In those old days she could not visit her anger directly upon Cléo (Arnaud had protected the housekeeper from that) so she had worked it out on others in her vicinity. She took a step forward with her hands still outstretched.

"*Di mwen,*" she said. *Tell me.*

Cléo's expression broke into an awful sadness.

"*Fok w blié sa,*" she said, but tenderly. *You must forget it.* She took Claudine's two hands in hers and pressed them. Claudine felt her anger fade, her frustration melt into a simpler pain, more pure. It was too hot for an embrace, but she lowered her hot forehead to touch Cléo's cooler one, then let the colored woman go and walked down the steps.

In the compound below, Claudine drifted toward her schoolhouse, no more than a frame of sticks roofed over with palm leaves, which the children would replace as needed. There were some solidly made peg benches, and a rough lectern Arnaud had ordered built as a gift to her. This afternoon, four of the benches had been shoved together to make room for two mats on the dirt floor. Guiaou lay on one of these, breathing heavily in sleep, and Riau on the other, his uniform coat neatly folded on the bench beside him. His eyes were lidded but Claudine did not think he was really asleep; she thought he was aware of her presence, though he did not show it. She could see her own spare reflection warped in the curve of the silver helmet he'd set underneath the bench.

Pursued by Etienne, Dieufait ran by outside, rolling a wooden hoop with a stick. The two children disappeared among the clay-walled *cases*. Grazing her fingertips over the lectern, Claudine left the shade of the school roof and walked toward the chapel. En route she passed the little *case* inhabited by Moustique and Marie-Noelle. The cloth that closed the doorway was gathered with a string, and glancing past its edges, Claudine saw Moustique's ivory feet hanging off the edge of the mat where he lay. Marie-Noelle was on her side, turned toward him, and between them their new baby lay curled and quietly sleeping.

Envy pricked at Claudine again as she went into the chapel. There was no door, properly speaking, but close-hung bead strings in place of one whole wall, which could be pulled back to open a view of the altar to the compound outside. The interior space was very small, built on the same plan as a dog shed that had once stood there. The walls were whitewashed, and eight pegged benches like those in the school were arranged in a double row. Claudine sat down on the farthest bench from the altar—no more than an ordinary wooden table. Above it hung a crucifix carved in mahogany from the fevered imagination of one of the Africans of the plantation—or maybe it was drawn from life, for certainly there had been horrors enough, in the last ten years of war, to inspire such a grotesquerie as he had made.

Claudine sat still, her back rigorously straight, hands folded in her lap. The bead curtain hung motionless behind her, and on the roof the heat bore down. She could not pray or think or breathe. That drumbeat she almost thought she heard was only the pulse in the back of her neck, a headache rising; it would not move the spirit through her.

After a long time, the bead curtains rustled and Toussaint Louverture walked into the chapel. Claudine registered his presence without quite turning her head. Reciprocally, Toussaint displayed no consciousness of her. He walked slowly between the two rows of benches, stopped before the altar, and stood looking up at Christ's carved wounds. After some time he crossed himself and sat down on the first bench, to the left of the cross. Reaching both hands to the back of his head, he undid the knot of his yellow madras, which he spent some time folding into a small triangular packet. Claudine had not seen him completely uncovered before. The dome of his head was high and long, the black skin gleaming on the crown. He gave his folded headcloth a couple of firm pats with his right palm, as if he meant to secure it to the bench, then joined his hands and bowed his head to pray.

As time passed, the light seemed to grow dimmer. Claudine did not know if the clouds were thickening outside or if it were only an effect of her own fatigue. She watched Toussaint, whose right hand slowly clicked through the beads of a curiously carved wooden rosary. A movement of the damp air stirred the strings of the curtain behind her, and she felt a current lifting toward the roof, where the eaves had been left open for ventilation.

Finally Toussaint had concluded his prayer. He stood up, gathering his folded headcloth in the hand that held the rosary. When he turned toward Claudine he enacted a startle of surprise.

"O," he said. "Madame Arnaud."

"*Monsieur le général.*" She made a slight movement as if she would rise. A gesture of Toussaint's palm restored her to her seat. She watched him walking slowly toward her. His head was outsized for the wiry jockey's body—the great orb of his skull counterbalanced by the long, jutting lower jaw. The body, whose meagerness was accentuated by the tight riding breeches he wore, carried its burden of head with a concentrated grace that rid Toussaint's whole aspect of any comical quality. He took a seat across the dirt-floored aisle from her, swinging a leg across the bench to straddle it like a saddle.

"It is good to see our Catholic religion so well observed here," he said, "when so often it is neglected elsewhere, among the plantations."

Claudine inclined her head without speaking.

"I have catechized some of the children walking the grounds this afternoon," he told her. "I find them to be well instructed. The boy Dieufait, for example, recites the entire Apostolic Creed with perfect confidence."

"As well might be expected of the son of a priest." Claudine attempted an ambiguous smile, in case Toussaint was moved to find irony in what she had said.

"They say that you give them other instruction too," Toussaint said. "That you teach them their letters as well as their catechism.

This afternoon I passed by your school—of which one hears talk as far away as Le Cap, if not farther."

"Is it so?"

"Why, yes," Toussaint said. "You are notorious."

Claudine felt a bump of her heart. Behind her the strings of the curtain shivered; outside a wind was rising. She was notorious for a great deal more than her little school, and Toussaint must know something of that, though she wasn't sure how much.

"You rather alarm me," she said.

"There is no need, Madame," Toussaint said. "Of course not every comment is favorable, as there are always some who believe that the children of Guinée must be held in the ignorance of oxen and mules."

Claudine lowered her head above her lap. One of her feet had risen to the ball, and the whole leg was shaking; she couldn't seem to make it stop.

"Yes," Toussaint said. "My *parrain,* Jean-Baptiste, taught me my letters when I was a child on the lands of the Comte de Noé."

Claudine raised her head to look at him. He was telling her the true version of the story, she thought, which was unusual. Of late he had been circulating a tale that he had been taught to read and write just before the first rebellion, when he was already past his fiftieth year.

"If not for that," Toussaint said, "I should have remained in slavery."

"And many others also," Claudine said.

"It is so." Toussaint squeezed the bench with his thighs, as if it really were a horse he meant to urge on. "But your husband, Madame. What view does he take of your teaching?"

"He indulges it." Claudine lowered her head.

"Does he not find himself well placed today, Monsieur Arnaud?" Toussaint seemed to be asking the question of a larger audience than was actually present; his voice had become a little louder. "With the restoration of his goods, the men back working in the fields. Why, a field hand may learn to read a book and be no less faithful to his hoe. Does he not find it to be true?"

"I hope so," Claudine said. "I believe so . . . yes, I mostly do."

"You may not be aware that your husband conspired long ago in a royalist plot against the Revolutionary government here," Toussaint said. "Or then again, perhaps you know it. Those men engaged to start a false rising of the slaves in ninety-one—thinking to frighten the Jacobins with a spectacle of the likely outcome of their own beliefs. They thought they could control a slave rising, those conspirators, but as you see they were quite wrong. He was one of them, Michel Arnaud, with the Sieur de Maltrot, and Bayon de Libertat, my former master, and Governor Blanchelande himself, who later lost his head for it, to the guillotine in France."

"As did so many others," Claudine murmured. As she spoke, her eye fell on the rosary, which Toussaint held in one hand against the yellow headcloth, and she saw for the first time that each of the small wooden beads was an intricately rendered human skull.

"What an extraordinary article," she said. It seemed to her that each carved skull was just a little different from all the others.

"It came to me as a spoil of war," Toussaint said, and put the rosary into his pocket, without telling her what other thing it might have come to mean to him now.

Outside she heard voices, the clucking of chickens as they scuttled for shelter. The wind rose further, as the air grew chill with the coming rain.

"Ah well," said Toussaint. "We have our dead."

All at once Claudine's leg stopped trembling and her raised foot relaxed against the floor. How intimately she had her dead! She wondered if Toussaint was similarly placed, sometimes, or always. It was certain that he'd caused the deaths of many more than the considerable number he'd ushered out of the world with his own hands.

"Yes," she burst out. "My husband killed many before the risings, he killed the children of Guinée with no more regard than for ants or for flies, and with torture sometimes, as bad as that—" She flung out her arm toward the crucifix. "Yes, this morning you rode your horse through the place where there once stood a pole, and to that pole my husband used to nail his victims, to die slowly as they hung—like that—" Her rigid fingers thrust toward the cross again. "And there was worse, still worse than that. No doubt you know it—he was famous for it all." Her whole arm dropped, and she felt her face twisting, that alien sensation as she moved a step farther away from her body. The blood beat heavy in her temples, and she heard the other voice beginning to come out from behind her head. *"Four hundred years of abominations—four hundred years for all to endure, and his no larger than a grain among them—"*

She stopped the voice, and came back to herself—she wanted now to remain herself. Toussaint had leaned back a little way from her and regarded her with his chin cupped in one hand.

"During the risings my husband suffered very much," Claudine said. "For a time he was made clean by suffering, as fire will burn corruption from the bone. Oh, he has still cruelty in his nature, and avarice, and too much pride, with contempt for others, white or black, but now he fights against it. I see him fight it every day."

Her voice cracked from hoarseness; her throat felt very dry.

"And yourself, Madame?"

She took it for an answer to the prayer she could not voice. With a lurch she dropped to her knees on the space of packed dirt between them, embraced his legs, and pushed her face into his lap.

"Hear my confession," she said, but her voice was too muffled to be understood. Toussaint was pushing her back by the shoulders.

"Madame, Madame," he said. "Control your feeling."

"No," Claudine said. "No—I want to touch you not in the flesh but in the spirit." But she had grasped his wrists now, to hold his hands firm against her collarbone.

"Hear my confession," she said, clearly now.

"I am no priest," Toussaint informed her. He twisted his hands free and drew them back. "You have your own priest here, who must confess you."

Claudine's arms dropped slack to her sides. To her surprise, he reached for her again, wrapping both hands around her head, balancing it on the point where his fingertips joined in the deepest hollow at the back of her neck.

"It is not easy to enter into the spiritual life," he said. By the soft and absent tone of his voice he might have been talking to himself. But he was looking into her head as if it were transparent to him.

"So you have been walking to the drum, my child," he said. "Sometimes there is a spirit who dances in your head."

The release of his hands let go a flash of light behind her eyes. The wind had blown the bead strings apart and was stirring the dust under the benches around them.

Toussaint cocked his head. "*Lapli k'ap vini,*" he said. *The rain is coming.*

"Yes, you are right," Claudine murmured. "We must go up before we are caught here."

Outside, the sky bulged purple over them, and above the mountains a wire of silent lightning glowed and vanished. Toussaint turned his head to the wind, letting his yellow madras flag out from his hand, then caught it up and bound it over his forehead and temples and knotted it carefully at the back before he followed

100

Claudine, hastening to the *grand'case,* reaching the shelter of the porch's overhang in the seconds before the deluge came down.

Because Toussaint had stated, over dinner, his need for an early departure, the mass commenced exactly at first light. The hour was painfully early for some, and fewer of the plantation's inhabitants turned out for it than might have otherwise, but still there was a respectable crowd for Moustique to part when, with a slow and solemn step, he carried the wooden processional cross into the little chapel. Behind him the children of Claudine's school marched, singing, *Wi, wi, wi, nou se Legliz, Legliz se nou.* . . . Claudine took her seat in the front row, next to the yawning Arnaud, irritable with his too-early rising. *Yes, yes, yes, the church is us, we are the church.* . . . Toussaint, the guest of honor, sat at Arnaud's right hand, while Riau and Guiaou shared the opposite bench with Cléo and Marie-Noelle. The other benches were filled with *commandeurs* and skilled men from the cane mill or distillery and other persons of a similar importance. The bead curtain had been tied up above the eaves, so the whole wall was open to the larger congregation outside, whose members sat cross-legged on the ground as soon as the signal was given.

Claudine paid small attention to the words of Moustique's sermon; her mind was utterly fixed on the cross. *Ah well,* she thought, *we have our dead.* . . . As she stared, she perceived that it was the vertical bar of the cross which pierced the membrane between the world of the living and the world of the dead, and allowed the spirits to rise.

Now Moustique was chanting the Sanctus in Latin, his voice high and whining. Above the altar, the dark crucifix ran and blurred before Claudine's weary eyes, till it became another image. She saw the body of her *bossale* maid Mouche, who'd been lashed quite near to that very same spot in the days when a dog shed stood on the chapel's site, and saw again the flash of the razor in her own hand as it slashed out the child Arnaud had planted in Mouche's womb and let the fetus spill on the dirt of the floor, then cut so viciously at the black girl's throat that it uncorked her blood like a fountain. And now, as Moustique presented the host, the children sang, *"Se Jezi Kri ki limyè ki klere kè nou tout. Li disparèt fènwa pou'l mete klète. . . ."*

The chapel was opened to the east, so that when the rising sun cleared the mountains it struck the whole interior with such force

101

that everything before Claudine's eyes was obliterated in the blaze. But the bread had been torn, the wine consecrated. She groped her way forward and knelt to receive.

It is Jesus Christ who is the light that illuminates all our hearts. He drives out the darkness to put light in its place. . . .

A fringe of cloud drifted over the sun, dimming the interior enough for Claudine to see more plainly. Toussaint, hands clasped before him, opened his mouth for the descending Host as meekly as a baby bird. Claudine's turn followed. Moustique served Arnaud, Riau, and Guiaou and the other two women, then began his second circuit with the chalice made from a carefully trained and hollowed gourd. Claudine held the body of Christ on her tongue. She had confessed her crime many times and to more than one priest, but still the chalice, when raised to her lips, returned to her the salt taste of blood.

Four Poems
Michael Palmer

VAMOS VIVER . . .

Of the paradise that was not,
no one can speak.

Of the place that was,
no one can speak.

Of the owl and the moth,
of the breeze up north.

Of the scorpion and the millipede,
of the windrows of straw,

flecked iris of the eye.
Of the rodents who rule

in the Name of the Lord.
Of the after all and the overall,

the was and because.
The shadow, the wheel of absence,

the past of each space.
So let's drop it all

and head up north
where at least there's a breeze.

UNTITLED (DECEMBER 2002)

And so this book of all the words
and their doubles. We welcome the words
for zero and for one,

for sleep and for space
and their doubles. Of the others
we're not so sure.

We welcome silence and the arcs,
the half-light, the cavalcade,
sorrows of the moon and the sun,

none of the above.
Magpies by the Tam—remember?
Said the one:

I'm burning now, I'm burning up
and still the river runs.
Said the double:

O little book,
enormous, empty book,
the woman and the bird and the man

were never one.
It was a mistake, maybe of the eye.
And this allée of pepper trees

is not endless.
And the book.
The winter day is endless.

UNTITLED (FEBRUARY 2003)

It's true that I've sometimes used the word raisin in place of reason,
true that I'm surprised each time

by the sudden progress of the seasons
and that often when all is said

all comes undone. Look at how the worms
turned into gods

before our filmy eyes
and how the lyric

war machine sings
in the grayness of the morning.

And the name of its song?
But here we are

among the dogs large and small
of the afterdawn.

Is it possible to make love in such light
or read from the first pages of Silence?

The bright, early butterflies
at Pura's place, under the volcano.

Campesinos blockading the roads.
Es bueno.

Michael Palmer

THE TURN (MAY 2003)

What is that turn you took in Beltà, in Beauty?
A blind man is staring out at the sea,

the waves, their foaming crests—
Abed those songs—

and what of the fog that forgives
or only pretends?

That turn, the slight angle of the head,
the wild berries, those to be eaten,

these not. Could you, could anyone
have known it would come to this—

the fragments and chants,
that ringing

that in Beltà, in Beauty
tethers and unties,

embraces and shoves aside?
And the fumblings, the bright, unraveling threads,

the taste that lingers in the mouth,
that turn at last toward *far*.

Too many hours in the poem.
Last one left awake once again.

Four Essays
Eliot Weinberger

ANECDOTAL EVIDENCE

1.

THE *HUAI NAN TZU*, a Taoist book from the 2nd Century B.C.E., tells the story of a man from ancient times, Kung Yu-ai, who for seven days was turned into a tiger. Fur grew over his body; his hands turned into claws; his teeth were those of a wild animal. His brother went to take a look; the tiger leapt and mauled him to death.

The tiger never knew he had once been a man. The man never knew he would someday be a tiger. The tiger was happy being a tiger, following his tiger nature. The man was happy being a man, following his human nature. Both enjoyed the happiness of being themselves, and neither suspected that they were equally happy as something entirely different.

2.

In the Midwest, a student told me how she lay awake at night, planning what she would wear the next day, including an alternative set of clothes in case there was a sudden change of weather. The most important element in her wardrobe was the socks. When wearing tennis shoes, the socks must match their color. However, when wearing leather shoes, the socks must match the blouse or sweater. The color of the pants or skirt served merely as a transition between socks and top.

These strictures, articulated at some length, went far beyond, or deeper than, fashion sense. In her childhood she had seen the Judy Garland movie *Meet Me in St. Louis* and had been impressed, not by the clang clang clang of the trolley, but by—she used the phrase—the *mise en scène.* All of the details of the furnishings and the clothes were historically accurate, and yet they had been color-coded to create a seamless, however unreal, world. The student felt that by similarly color-coding herself, she was transforming her own world and somehow entering into the perfection of that Technicolor Vincente Minnelli St. Louis. An outsider would have been unable to perceive the difference with any other student in a baggy white sweater, blue jeans, white cotton socks, and black leather shoes, but those socks—that is, the whiteness of those socks—were the key to her happiness or a solace in her unhappiness.

3.

The *Lieh Tzu*, a Taoist book from the 3rd Century C.E., tells the story of a man who couldn't find his axe, and suspected the boy next door of stealing it. For days he studied the boy, and from the boy's demeanor, his overly friendly way of saying good morning, his averted glance, and even his way of walking, it was obvious that the boy was the thief.

A few days later the man found his axe in the garden. The next time he saw the boy, there seemed to be nothing suspicious about him at all.

4.

On a cold, rainy February night in New York, I remembered the story André Malraux used to tell—and which, at some remove, was told to me—about Mallarmé's cat, whose name, almost needless to say, was Blanche.

On a cold, rainy February night in Paris, a thin and bedraggled alley cat, wandering the streets, looks in the window of Mallarmé's house and sees a white, fat, and fluffy cat dozing in an overstuffed chair by a blazing fire. He taps on the window:

"Comrade cat, how can you live in luxury and sleep so peacefully when your brothers are out here in the streets starving?"

"Have no fear, comrade," Blanche replied, "I'm only pretending to be Mallarmé's cat."

Eliot Weinberger

THE TREE OF THE WORLD

In *The Sacred and the Profane* (1957), Mircea Eliade writes of a nomadic Australian aboriginal tribe, the Achilpa, whose god Numbakula created the first men and established the tribe's rituals and institutions. Then he made a sacred pole from the trunk of a gum tree, anointed it with blood, climbed it, and disappeared into the sky. "This pole," Eliade says, "represents a cosmic axis, for it is around the sacred pole that territory becomes habitable, hence is transformed into a world." Ever since, the Achilpa have always carried a sacred pole with them; the way it bends each night determines the direction they will go the next morning. But one day the pole was accidentally broken, and the tribe wandered aimlessly and lost, until they finally lay down and waited to die, for they could no longer communicate with the sky and the end of the world had come. Repeating the story in a later book, Eliade wrote that "seldom do we find a more pathetic avowal that man cannot live without a sacred center."

Eliade had taken the story from an ancestor narrative collected by the Australian anthropologists Baldwin Spencer and Francis James Gillen; they published a version in 1899, and expanded it in 1927, based, they said, on new information from an Achilpa [now known as Tjilpa] headman. In 1987, Jonathan Z. Smith reexamined the three texts.

Smith discovered that Eliade, surprisingly, had confused cosmic and secular time. The incident of the broken pole had occurred among the ancestors in the Dreamtime, not among the contemporary or historical Achilpa.

Moreover, the god Numbakula, who appeared in a prologue to Spencer and Gillen's second version (and not at all in the first) as the "supreme ancestor, overshadowing all others," is otherwise unknown in Australian mythology. His name is actually a generic title, referring in the plural to totemic ancestors.

It was equally unusual for an aboriginal ancestor to climb up to the sky, as the ancestors normally return to the earth that gave them birth. And, in the Spencer and Gillen retelling, Numbakula is given an epithet in the Arandan language that the recently arrived missionaries had used for Jesus. It was therefore likely that the story of Numbakula was a syncretic version of the death of Christ.

Moreover, aboriginal ancestor narratives are long and dull accounts of the origins of geographical features: the ancestors in the

109

Dreamtime did this at this place, which is why it is still called this. The Spencer and Gillen narrative has ninety-four incidents. Number 78 tells how the ancestors broke the pole, and how a tall stone still stands to mark the spot. In Number 79—a separate incident that is not a chronological successor—they travel for a long time until they meet the Honeysuckle-Totem People, and are so exhausted by their journey that they lie down and die; now there is a hill covered with large stones that mark the spot.

That is, there is no God Numbakula; there is no connection between the broken pole and the death of the ancestors; there is nothing in the original that suggests either that the pole pointed the direction for their wanderings or that they were lost without it; there is no evidence of an aboriginal axis mundi, linking earth and sky, for the ancestor gods did not climb to the sky and the perpetually nomadic Achilpa never built anything, never stayed in the same place, and had no concept of a sacred center in a landscape where every rock has a meaning that comes from the Dreamtime.

Nevertheless, there is an aboriginal tribe, the Achilpa, whose god Numbakula created the first men, then made a sacred pole, anointed it with blood, and climbed it into the sky. The Achilpa have carried a sacred pole with them ever since, and the way it bends is the way they will go the next day. Once, the pole broke and the tribe wandered aimlessly until they all lay down and died, for they could no longer communicate with the sky and the end of the world had come.

LACANDONS

In the forest of Chiapas, in thatched huts without walls, in hammocks barely rocking, they sleep.

There it is said:

If you dream of a donkey, there will be a strong wind.

If you dream of tacos, you will see an anteater.

If you dream of an anteater, people are coming.

If you dream of a termite, you will see a jaguar.

If you dream of a jaguar, people are coming.

If the jaguar bites you, they are not people.

If you dream you are waking, you'll be frightened in the forest.

If you dream of a mirror, you will see white stones.

If you dream of your tongue, beware.

All birds mean fever; all fish mean pain in your stomach.

If you dream you're worrying about the cost of things, you'll not have to worry about the cost of things.

If you dream of a party, for a long time you'll be bored.

A gourd is a jaguar's head; the old canoe an alligator.

If you dream of a house, you will see a wild boar.

If you dream of a beard, you will see a wild boar.

If you dream of a broom, you will see a wild boar.

If you dream of a radio, you will see a wild boar.

If you dream of a poet, someone will cry.

A shotgun is the tooth of an animal.

Beans are maggots and maggots are beans.

If you dream you are writing, you'll be bitten by a snake.

If you dream of a lake, it is nothing.

If you dream of a frog, it is nothing.

If you dream of a flower, it is nothing.

If you dream of heaven, it is nothing.

If you dream of leaves, it is nothing, but if the leaves are shaking in the wind, grasshoppers will eat the corn.

If you dream of fog, people are coming who are sad and ill.

If you dream you know something, you do not know it.

If you dream of a halo around the moon, the end of the world is coming.

That which is thin in a dream will be thick.

That which is certain in a dream won't happen.

LOUIS-AUGUSTE BLANQUI AS COPIED OUT BY WALTER BENJAMIN

The entire universe is composed of astral systems. To create them, nature has only a hundred *simple bodies* at its disposal. Despite the great advantage it derives from these resources, and the innumerable combinations that these resources afford its fecundity, the result is necessarily a *finite* number, like that of the elements themselves; and in order to fill its expanse, nature must repeat to infinity each of its *original* combinations or *types*.

So each heavenly body, whatever it might be, exists in infinite number in time and space, not only in *one* of its aspects but as it is at each second of its existence, from birth to death. All the beings distributed across its surface, whether large or small, living or inanimate, share the privilege of this perpetuity.

The earth is one of these heavenly bodies. Every human being is thus eternal at every second of his or her existence. What I write at this moment in a cell of the Fort du Taureau I have written and shall write throughout all eternity—at a table, with a pen, clothed as I am now, in circumstances like these. And thus it is for everyone.

All worlds are engulfed, one after another, in the revivifying flames, to be reborn from them and consumed by them once more— monotonous flow of an hourglass that eternally empties and turns itself over. The new is always old, and the old is always new.

Yet won't those who are interested in extraterrestrial life smile at a mathematical deduction which accords them not only immortality but eternity? The number of our doubles is infinite in time and space. One cannot in good conscience demand anything more. These doubles exist in flesh and bone—indeed in trousers and jacket, in crinoline and chignon. They are by no means phantoms; they are the present eternalized.

Here, nonetheless, lies a great drawback: there is no progress, alas, but merely vulgar revisions and reprints. Such are the exemplars, the ostensible "original editions" of all the worlds past and worlds to come. Only the chapter on bifurcations is still open to hope. Let us not forget: *all that one might have been in this world, one is in another.*

In this world, progress is for our descendants alone. They will have more of a chance than we did. All the beautiful things ever seen in our world have, of course, already been seen—are being seen at this instant and will always be seen—by our descendants, and by their doubles who have preceded and will follow them. Scions of a finer humanity, they have already mocked and reviled our existence on dead worlds, while overtaking and succeeding us. They continue to scorn us on the living worlds from which we have disappeared, and their contempt for us will have no end on the worlds to come.

They and we, and all the inhabitants of our planet, are reborn prisoners of the moment and of the place to which destiny has assigned us in the series of Earth's avatars. Our continued life depends on that of the planet. We are merely phenomena that are ancillary to its resurrections. Men of the 19th Century, the hour of our apparitions is fixed forever, and always brings us back the very same ones, or at most with a prospect of felicitous variants. There is nothing here that will much gratify the yearning for improvement. What to do? I have sought not at all my pleasure, but only the truth. Here there is neither revelation nor prophecy, but rather a simple deduction on the basis of spectral analysis and Laplacian cosmogony. These two discoveries make us eternal. Is it a windfall? Let us profit from it. Is it a mystification? Let us resign ourselves to it.

[*Omitted paragraph on "the 'consolation' afforded by the idea that the doubles of loved ones departed from Earth are at this very hour keeping our own doubles company on another planet."*]

At bottom, this eternity of the human being among the stars is a melancholy thing, and this sequestering of kindred worlds by the inexorable barrier of space is even more sad. So many identical populations pass away without suspecting one another's existence! But no—this has finally been discovered, in the 19th Century. Yet who is inclined to believe it? Until now, the past has, for us, meant barbarism, whereas the future has signified progress, science, happiness, illusion! This past, on all our counterpart worlds, has seen the most brilliant civilizations disappear without leaving a trace, and they will continue to disappear without leaving a trace. The future will witness yet again, on billions of worlds, the ignorance, folly, and cruelty of our bygone eras!

At the present time, the entire life of our planet, from birth to death, with all its crimes and miseries, is being lived partly here and partly there, day by day, on myriad kindred planets. What we call "progress" is confined to each particular world, and vanishes with it. Always and everywhere in the terrestrial arena, the same drama, the same setting, on the same narrow stage—a noisy humanity infatuated with its own grandeur, believing itself to be the universe and living in its prison as though in some immense realm, only to founder at an early date along with its globe, which has borne with deepest disdain the burden of human arrogance. The same monotony, the same immobility, on other heavenly bodies. The universe repeats itself endlessly and paws the ground in place. In infinity, eternity performs—imperturbably—the same routines.

De Kooning
William Corbett

I. *Sunday Drive*

Parkway, Thruway, Turnpike
house painter's brushes
wide as dustpans
let the bristle show
splinters in their speed
what wipes the eye in swaths
leaves a fringe,
curves, shoulder, the lawning
straightway, blur of embankments
Toulouse, Havana, Bolton Landing prow,
Parc Rosenberg in Paris
to one who hasn't been there
blur of autumn dirt, spring
crazy about mulberry flowering trees,
skies blue like his pants
mixed mayonnaise in his paint
that juicy touch, greased light
highway landscape a fat knife
spreads color across the eye
wait, the go of the moment
in a convertible hydromatic
flying low, thrust, swerve and pull
ragged blocks of glare stopped
at the plank door to Manhattan's
river light, gray and gold hum
of it, baby pinks flare
into morning openness dew
bright flesh, skies of ocean white
you ride dawn's elevator
what you feel inside
as daybreak divides over Louse Point.

II. *At Black Mountain*

By train to Asheville
summer at Black Mountain
salad of bananas and hot dogs.
"The trouble with that place,"
jokes de Kooning, "is that you go there,
they try to give it to you."
"Asheville" crook of arm, small dome,
sudden slate of green, line
curves, sails, rips a black jag
into gold, all over the place.
Living on Carmine Street
enough room to turn around,
first one-man show,
Egan Gallery, black-and-white paintings
inspired by the cover of *Light in August*
seen in someone's loft, spidery
white outlines of black forms
two fingers raised, a homburg,
something taken apart in pieces
and the pieces scrambled
doesn't know until he sees it
then he isn't sure. Back and forth,
brush stroke and regard
at a dueler's pace.

III. *Woman I*

Doesn't know what he's doing
this then that then another
violent stroke, fierce, decisive
snaggle-tooth, black olive-lamped woman,
locked, unlocked, arrived at
one with her own skin until abandoned,
rolled up, parked in the hallway
outside his studio. Meyer Shapiro
asks to see it, convinces de Kooning
the painting is finished, can have a name,

115

a signature. Easy for Shapiro,
he only had to look at it.

IV. *De Kooning*

Came here on the *Shelley*
certified artist and craftsman
lone English word *yes*
befriended tall Gorky,
Davis and Graham, the smart ones,
painted neighbors Denby
and Burckhardt, troubled
by shoulders. Drew
an imaginary brother,
who worked on the side
while he painted. Saw
André Breton fight off
a butterfly on an uptown
street corner, saw the Wannamaker
Block in flames, paused over
designs in the street: bottle caps,
tinfoil, butts, gum, pennies.
Calmed his nerves with shots
of whiskey, became the King
downtown, wealthy uptown,
moved to Long Island,
drew with his eyes closed,
and, older than Titian,
swiped paint on canvas
with a trowel, whisk, whisk
beautiful dry music like ice
skating down Dutch canals.

Three Poems
Reetika Vazirani

TO COMPARE YOURSELF TO OTHERS

in the beginning of unhappiness
fourteen years
fourteen years
two cycles of exile
       to be Callas or Iman
       a swan she felled my gaze   Seeta's emerald
       I made Radha's notice-me necklace

quest to be fed by the priest
is the first run
ease   grow your wheat
fourteen years in exile
       like a monk I punished myself
       Joan of Arc I took on the wish to be

stopping short of the lit candle
moves you to your level
ingratitude five below the sea's exile
       Regan and Goneril the hard wall grays

breath hallowed lantern husk of a
ring bells pour oils sleep
down panic you are a temple
form the whole note
you turn forty-two cycles of exile
done you're a lean
homegirl Radha roundabout
the next dory anchored to port

THEY LOVED RUIN

wonderful to have lost you
domicile   the life   gigantic
hotel   when I speak to you
I speak of myself   apple in a worm's day
star   parched   this hole-in-one feeling
less plenitude than patience and I
lost your face to another
decade   woman   small coup
d'état to feel age now it is
always a marvel to romp in the body
of this nude world ink I have
loved the moon your candle
on the helmet of Ajanta   cavelit walks
a search for more good
byes   wonderful when they come
at this angle of winter into Krishna
a phone call to say yes
better off on my own because of the
recriminations   and I just
got used to myself keyless
morning in a room-long bed

WORLD

Praise songs   this passage is
my blessing   child's night wisdom
sleep on the hood of the pillow   my worries
and regrets bloom their quiet Allahs
I fly bright-eyed
receipts and dishes in the luggage I shed tatters
    my old woman décolletage harboring love
the snaggle-toothed wintry side of daybreak
comes like ginger in steam and I am
with you child   man fingers curled
around the bent spoke of your umbrella
in the no-rain no-hazard minute we have

Two Faces

Clarence Major

Faces of sorrow
and contentment!—one upright,
another one up side down.
And in that village, under a busy sky,
it was too hot for anybody
to walk about in
the narrow cobbled passageways:
just a village street. And when he was younger
his face reflected in the street
car window, just as he stepped up
onto the moving vehicle. He looked
this way knowing what he saw, and
with the church steeple behind him,
on a cloudy yet sunny day. What a face
of sorrow and expectation! He is like and unlike his father
they say—his father,
a thoughtful man—hand to chin,
unlike himself—hand to cheek.
And the big dreamy sad eyes
of father. Fact—it's unknown who
photographed him, white gloves
and all. But he was never like that,
white gloves and such. Much of his time
was spent in his studio with a view
of the garden, his big easel near the window,
empty bottles all about. Just another
example of his divided self—the studio
up the hill and the apartment
in town where, after all, no one
wanted him, yet he kept going,
even with the village boys
throwing rocks at him,
he kept going.

To the Shadow
W. S. Merwin

Only as long as there is light
as long as there is something
a cloud or mountain or wing
or body reflecting the light
you are there on
the other side
twin shape formed of
nothing but absence
made of what you are not
and we recognize you
when we wave
a part of the darkness
waves at the same moment
not answering though
nor mocking us
no
no you are not the self we know
from night to night

From Streams of Water
Merle Collins

*I turn to the histories of men and the lives of the
peoples
I examine the shower of sparks, the wealth of the
dreams
I am pleased with the glories and sad with the
sorrows
rich with the riches, poor with the loss.*

—Martin Carter, *Poems of Resistance*

THE SHOWER OF SPARKS

A LITTLE MORE THAN three weeks after he died, Normandy told his
daughter to go to the black trunk in his room and pull out the lower
right-hand drawer.

Black, about five feet tall, body scratched and dull with age, the
trunk stood in a corner of the big bedroom. Its brass fittings were
rusty. Nail heads, a gloomy brass, were evenly spaced around it,
holding the body together. The trunk had stood there as far back as
the memory of the house, a part of the room like the bed or the big
press that kept falling open or the old windows you had to push up
and down, windows that creaked and struggled in the memory long
after they had been replaced by lighter ones you had to push out
instead of up. The trunk was not made larger by memory, and so not
specially noticed.

The daughter stood just inside the door of the room and watched
the trunk, not going too far inside in case she had to run back. She
wasn't a coward, not so you would notice anyway, but it wasn't every
day you got that kind of message from that sort of source. This trunk
was no bigger than the other one of its kind, known as the old trunk,
and kept in a corner of the room where the daughter had slept as a
child, long ago, with her grandmother.

Until now, when she was forced to see the trunk not just as a fixture in the room's existence but as having a secretive character of its
own, the daughter hadn't really thought about the two trunks
together. She knew the old trunk had been her mother's because

121

someday, sometime, someone, most likely her mother, had told her this, but there was no particular sense of ownership attached to it. Not like this one. The other one, the old trunk, was the place where, over the years, old schoolbooks were dropped to rest before being given to cousins, friends, or acquaintances. It was the place where old essentials once belonging to the very young stayed for years before being retrieved by older, memory-hunting versions of the young people who had used and discarded them. It was the acknowl-edged resting place for old clothes, old magazines, and a variety of things that would later be taken out and thrown away or given away. Right now there was something in it, perhaps a new set of old books left by a passing cousin.

This trunk in the big bedroom, on the other hand, always had a more private, reserved character. It kept things to itself, and what was in it belonged to one person and had probably been there for years. Although young children, or even older people, might pass by and touch this trunk or even stumble against it in their haste, it wasn't a trunk you would run to and tug open to drop your discarded stuff. When you stumbled against it, you righted yourself and said a nervous *oops*, glancing at the trunk sideways to see how it was affected by the contact. You wouldn't linger around it to leave some-thing that would later become a memory to pick up again. This trunk was known as *Daddy's trunk* or *your father's trunk* or just *The Trunk*.

"Child, remove your clothes from the top of The Trunk, please. Put them in the small room."

Or,

"I could rest these clothes on top of Daddy's trunk before I put them away?"

Or,

"You'd better move those shoes from in front of your father's trunk before he come and find them there and *dekatche* your tail."

The Trunk was tall and slim, opened into more compartments, had more private spaces than the old trunk in the other room. The old trunk was wide and squat, and opened at the top into one large space, with everything immediately visible. Both were bruised from the years. There were bumps and scratches from being pulled and pushed into boats, from being shoved down onto wharves, from stay-ing too long in open spaces and connecting with the hard edges of other traveling trunks. But in spite of the bumps and bruises, this one had kept its status, or most of it. The years had diminished it somewhat. It still stood huge in the memory of childhood, but in the eyes of the adult, it seemed small, wizened, sad, an awesome parody of its giant memory.

The daughter stood looking at The Trunk, wondering what was inside. She knew what it looked like—four drawers on one side, an open area at the bottom, on the other side, a space for hanging things, but she didn't know what it contained.

There had been the occasional order when she was little, on one of those Sunday mornings when her father decided to go to church.— Go to The Trunk for me, look in the top right-hand drawer, and bring me one of the white handkerchiefs you see there.

Or when she was older, adult already, on a morning of an ex-serviceman's parade,—If you wouldn't mind, open The Trunk for me, please. Look on the left-hand side and take out the black jacket you see there. Look at it and tell me if you think I could wear that.

And there'd been her mother, ever irreverent, commenting without being asked—Jacket? You mean *blou?* Something as ancient as that is not jacket. Have to be what we would call a *blou.* Is not today that existing, you know.

These memories made The Trunk seem approachable, and the daughter moved forward. She touched the two tiny rusted keys hanging from the keyhole. The Trunk wasn't locked. She had known it wouldn't be. She had stood and looked at it briefly before this, on her way through the room to get toilet paper from the bathroom cupboard, or when she came into the room to get towels from the big press with its door that insisted on swinging open. One day, she thought, she should go through his things. She knew her mother must have opened The Trunk at some point since his departure, glanced vaguely inside, and closed it, thinking that the children would go through it one day. Perhaps the boys had taken a tie or handkerchief before they left, a keepsake from their father. But each was hesitant to pull things out and make a general clearing out of his belongings. There seemed no reason to.

You didn't just pick up a person's things and throw them out after they'd been part of you for forty-five years, part of your life and your memories and your becoming, there even before you were there, before you traveled, with two trunks and lots of boxes, to this house. Well, you might throw a person out if that person was alive and able to pick up his things and walk away. Might. But after he was gone, leaving things in your keeping, and leaving with you the pull and tug of the memory of those years, the memory of the bumps and bruises

123

of the times, you had to have some respect for the things that were his. And perhaps each knew from the feel of Normandy's memory that he wouldn't like to have his things pulled out and thrown away. At any event, no one wanted to throw them away. And anyway, it was just not possible to pull things out of The Trunk and throw them away. If the children had ever seen their mother looking inside The Trunk during their father's lifetime, they would have known that something was wrong, that she wasn't supposed to be there, would have figured that she was looking for something their father probably wouldn't want her to see.

Up close to The Trunk now, the daughter could remember her father standing there, just a few months ago—September, perhaps, and this was March, so not six months ago. Standing there on one of those days when his eyes, steadily fading in a face drawn and dull with illness, were shifty with an unfamiliar hunger, an anxiety to understand where he was going to from here. If this was the end for him of every tree that he loved, of the mountain he treasured as if he not only knew there was a secret buried in it but knew what that secret was, if for him this was the end of the sprouting weeds he struggled every day to contain, the streams he alone knew the source of, what was the point? His eyes were weak and sorrowful with wondering, watery with the regret of leaving this place. Once, standing under the cocoa, he had explained that the place was called *Bwa Epi Dlo*—Wood and Water—because there were lots of streams all through the high woods. They're drying up, he said, but still anything can grow here. He didn't want to leave. Was there really a Maker on the other side, waiting to point him one direction or the other? The daughter, moved by the recognition of his fear, wanted to tell him that it was OK, that he would be OK, and suddenly, she urgently wanted to know more about him than she had been able to find out in forty-five years. She recognized that she wanted this, not only to reassure him, but also to make sure that he didn't take with him and lock away forever the part of his story that belonged also to her. So as he stood there by The Trunk with his gaunt face and shifting, dimming, hungry eyes, she'd said to him, "Tell me about the place you lived when you were growing up." The question hurt him. It made his lips tremble and his mouth quiver. His eyes said he knew it was asked because she felt he wouldn't be around much longer, knew that she was anxious to get this from him because soon he wouldn't be there to give it. And his eyes had steadied on the trunk as he replied, "What do you want to know?" The daughter looked from him to the trunk and back at him, regretted the thirst that had made her ask, and said, "It's all right. Another time, perhaps." And the moment that would never be gone crept with its awkwardness and uncertainty into the echoing past.

Now the daughter looked again from the trunk to the place near it where her father had stood that day. She turned away from the trunk and went to lie down on what was now her mother's bed. It was early morning, but Nana had already left the room, not able to get over the habit of getting up early and going out to the kitchen. No husband to prepare breakfast for—you want some fry breadfruit this morning, Normandy?—no children to hurry to school—child, hurry up and eat your breakfast if you know what good for you—no chickens to feed anymore in the early morning, no cocks to crow her awake, but still something pulled her up from the bed and pushed her stumbling sleepily to the kitchen at what would be cockcrow if there were cocks to make it that, sent her out to rattle pans, to open windows and look at the grass growing threateningly in the yard, to sing *Jesus Gentlest Savior, thou art in us now,* to lean against the kitchen sink and yawn out loud every now and then. As the daughter watched the trunk, she strained to hear what sounds were coming from the kitchen.

When you die, the secrets you leave are public property, and trunks and their secrets had a history on the island. Once, a man left a locked trunk when he died. His wife opened it. A cock stepped out, crowed, stalked out of the room, and went into the living room, where it flew to the top of the man's framed photograph and stayed with its head held high, never crowing, shifting around, ignoring everyone who came to look at it. And lots of people came. They came from far, in buses, cars, vans. Some came with picnic baskets. Some went to the shop across the road and bought bread and watery red spot in fat, round bottles. They camped outside for hours, going into the living room every so often to see what the cock was doing.

The woman's living room became public property. So she retired. Left the living room to the man's cock and its visitors, closed the bakery from which she had made a living for some thirty years while her husband made money and achieved success in ways he never explained to her. Now, with his secret exposed, the woman went out to walk the streets of the island. She tried to make her living by selling sweet-smelling flowers. As they tell it, *tongue say*—and it's anybody's guess how tongue would know the details so well—that she would walk into a person's garden, pick a rose, prick her finger with the thorns, let the blood touch the rose, put the rose to her nostrils and smell deep of its scent. Then she would cut a bit of fern and go to the door of the house. The owner would know that the flower with its decorative fern came from her own garden (*her* garden because usually it was the women who came to the door), but she would pay for it anyway—twenty-five cents, fifty cents, a dollar. The woman traveled even at night, looking in those dark hours especially for the gardens that called to her with their sweet smell of the flowers called *lady of the night.* Those she picked and went away with, taking them to the house with the man's cock and arranging them in little bunches on the step, sitting and sleeping out there, but never again entering her living room. Everybody bought the flowers when she offered them, but nobody took her in because none knew if the cock would follow her to another living space. And nobody wanted to take chances with a dead man's cock.

The talk went around that after a while the woman started to live in the bakery, that she slept and ate there, that she cooked there in a little pan over an ancient coal pot. Then *tongue say,* and tongue always knows, that the cock started to go into the bakery sometimes, that it perched on a bag that used to belong to the man, that more and more the woman was driven from the bakery to walk and make the streets her home.

Then one early morning, about two years later, the saying goes, and at about five o'clock, *tongue say,* the woman was found dead in the street. After that, after the woman was put into a hole in the ground and they closed the door behind her, no one heard of the cock again. The couple's children, who lived either in England or America and inherited the house, came to claim it. *Tongue say* they had to use prayers to cleanse that house, but that whatever was there wouldn't affect the children anyway. They had been gone too long, and, in any case, the cock had business with their mother, not with them. Eventually the house was pulled down. But still, after that, a fowl farm in the area went out of business. Or rather, the owner closed it because he no longer felt comfortable rearing cocks, or so *tongue say,* and hens alone would not be a profitable business.

So when a dead person specifically sends you to open a trunk after they're gone, you have to think twice. The daughter stretched out on the bed, hands behind her head, and watched the trunk. You know this story, she said to her father, you know the story and you're giving me a message to go and open the trunk. What is it with you all and trunks? But the truth was that the story didn't really worry her. She had enough faith in her father not to expect something physical to come out of the trunk and follow her around. Still, she pushed herself off the bed, glanced at the trunk hesitantly, and walked away from it to the door of the room. She walked through the dining room into the kitchen and stood watching her mother, now leaning against the kitchen sink, yellow mango juice streaming down her hands and inserting itself between her fingers.

"You open your father's trunk yet?"

"Not yet. Tell me, you remember the story about the cock and the trunk?"

Nana giggled and the mango seed, covered with yellow flesh, fell from her hand into the kitchen sink. "Girl, you make me lose my mango. You afraid of what your father leave in there?"

"You want to open it for me?"

"Not a chance. Not me. You're the one he give message. You don't see he didn't tell me anything about that? He always visiting but he never tell me a thing about trunk. The message is for you." Nana let the water run over her hands into the sink. "Go and open the trunk. That man with the cock didn't *send* his wife to open the trunk, you know. She took it upon herself to do that. *I* might have to worry if this one gave me a message, but not you. You know your father wouldn't send you into any nonsense. Girl, go and open the trunk." As the daughter walked away from the kitchen, she thought she heard her mother say, "Afterward, I will tell you a story." She stopped in the dining room and looked back toward the entranceway to the kitchen, but Nana was reaching up to pull open a cupboard.

The daughter held the trunk at the top and pulled it open. A faded, striped papering. Her father had said specifically the bottom drawer. She stooped, pulled out the bottom drawer on the right, and there it was, just as he had shown it to her—a box with a drawing of a sailing ship on the cover. The daughter touched it with reverence, picked it up. Several ships, in fact, petrified in a yellow sunset, sails billowing, one looming large in the foreground, four of significant size scattered in the murky waters around, others, smaller, less distinct shapes on a sunset yellow water. The daughter stood with the box, put it on the top of the open trunk, and lifted the cover.

At the top, a brown-edged photograph of Normandy in military uniform and two identical black-and-white passport pictures. A clean-faced young man, hair cut low, long face, small nose, wide,

127

gentle smile. His shirt was open at the collar so that it formed a V front. On the back of one passport photograph, there were the numbers 5/5/51. He would have been twenty-five. The daughter looked for signs of herself, her brothers, the other, younger girls she had seen and been told were her sisters. Yes, perhaps you could see something there in the spacing of the eyes, the shape of the nose, the mouth. Perhaps, because when you were looking for resemblance, you were almost sure to find it.

There were more passport pictures—three more. Either the V neck was a style or the shirt open at the neck made it one. On the back of one picture, a faded blue 195—something—the last number smudged. In another, there was the same clean-faced, smiling young man. On the back was written *Certified* and a signature the daughter couldn't decipher, something with M-looking strokes, and whoever it was had signed as J. P. The date was 5/8/55. Why had he needed a justice of the peace? Was this for a passport application? At the time this was taken, Normandy must have been approaching thirty, and looking twenty. He was what anybody would call a good-looking young man. The shy smile that touched the corners of the lips said that he knew this. At the bottom of the other photo was part of the curve of a blue stamp and *Aug 196*, with only part of the curve of the last number visible. Nineteen sixty-six, perhaps. He had turned forty a few months before, and didn't look it. Face a bit fuller, though, smile a little more confident, eyes more direct. There were laughter lines around his mouth. In that picture, the daughter thought, he was four years older than his younger son was now.

What else was there in the box? There was a photograph of Nana sitting in a chair and looking straight into the camera. Her hair was long, black, full, held back in a hairnet. She was wearing a white long-sleeved shirt. Not shirt, you would call it, perhaps they would have called it a bodice in those days. It was a very feminine-looking bodice. Nana held her shoulders straight. She was a pretty woman. In her arms she held a baby boy. So this must have been about 1951, with Carl. Standing near Nana and the baby, eyes wide, a ribbon tied in short, thick plaits, one hand holding tight to Nana's skirt, was a little girl of about two. In her hand she held a purse, some sort of bag. You did not so much see her face as see the frown that covered it. Her lips were a determined pout. The set of the child's shoulders said Leave me alone. The daughter had seen this photo of her small self sometime long ago. There were others, one of a chubby-faced boy about six years old—a young Colin—and some color photographs, one a fairly recent picture of a grown Carl holding a baby girl in his arms, and one of Normandy, Nana, and the daughter standing on the steps of the house at *Bwa Epi Dlo*. Normandy had one hand up on gray board shingles. There were receipts for payments made on the family land and right at the bottom of the box, an old book with a soft brown cover. On it was the title *Royal Reader Book Five*. Inside the book was a picture of a gaunt woman with prominent cheek-bones, wearing a print dress and a straw hat. Her shoulders were hunched, her mouth stretched in a pout; a frown bunched together the space between her eyes. Both hands behind her back, she looked with surly suspicion into the eye of the camera.

Inside the book was also a paper wrapped in white plastic. The document inside the plastic, brown with age, was folded so that when opened, the lines divided it into eight squares. There were tiny holes along the center, at the corners of the square. At the top of the document were the words "Military Certificate" and the words "Regimental Number," with the number 876503 in faded ink. And there was some information about the person to whom the certificate belonged.

Surname: **La Porte**
Christian Name: **Normandy**
Enlisted at: **Grenada**
Enlisted on: **12 June 1945**
Corps for which enlisted: **S.C.E.**
Rank: **PTE**

Private Normandy La Porte was listed as five feet seven and a half inches tall. He was born, said the document, on 25 July 1926. Not true, as far as the daughter knew. Complexion, the document noted, dark, eyes black, hair black, and no distinguishing marks or scars. Well, this was probably so at the time the document knew him. The cutlass hadn't yet marked his little finger and pulled it down to point at the palm of his hand. According to the document, Normandy La Porte was discharged from the Volunteer Corps because *Services no longer required on Reduction of Establishment*. Private Normandy La Porte's military conduct was described as *Good*.

The daughter sat on the floor and spread the documents around her. Volunteer Corps, passport pictures, photographs of herself and her brothers in their childhood, her brother and Cara, his baby girl, Nana, Royal Reader, land paper. Was there a pattern? She looked at

The Trunk. Faded brass, dull black, chips, bounces, bruises it had picked up on its travels. What clue was she missing? Had she found what her father sent her to get? She remembered how he used to stand, sometimes, in front of the open trunk, muttering to himself as he took out a pair of pants for an ex-serviceman's day parade, as he folded and refolded a land paper, how he bent and deposited something in the bottom drawer, how he pulled the trunk closed and stood thinking. Sometimes she would watch him from the living room as he stood with one hand on the trunk, turned slightly sideways, his head back, looking in the direction of the mountain, as if, through the walls, he could see the squat cocoa, the tall gliricidia giving the cocoa trees the shade they needed, the breadnut trees, the bananas, the thickness of trees all the way up, the bush pushing through in and between, and behind them all the green *Bwa Epi Dlo* mountain with the constant sound of invisible streams, spreading a mysterious, protective darkness. Most people put their heads down when they were in deep thought, or so the daughter believed. Her father always pushed his head back and twisted his lips.

The daughter took a deep breath, slow, shallow, noisy, in through her nostrils and pushing up her shoulders. She paused, waited to see if anything would present itself as an explanation for the directive to take the box out of The Trunk and open it. She decided to put things back where she had found them. She would take them out again and go through them again later. She gathered and put carefully back into the box the Royal Reader with the picture of Da, her father's mother, the military certificate, photographs. She tried to pack them in the order in which she had found them. She pulled out the drawer. A bird started chattering on the window. The daughter stood up quickly.

Nana had pulled the curtain to the left side. The bird had come through the bottom of the two parts of the new push-out window, and it now hopped on the sill. A small blackbird, it chattered, turned around, moved to peck at the curtain, flew off, and perched on a branch over the callaloo bushes, returned to the window and kept up its chattering. Still holding the box, the daughter watched the bird. In the weeks immediately following a spirit's loss of its body, small animals and insects gained a new importance. You never knew where the spirit might be wandering as it tried to acclimatize itself to new surroundings. As she watched the bird, the daughter heard her mother's dragging footsteps coming through the dining room. Nana came to stand at the door of the room. Still holding the box in her hand, the daughter moved her eyes from the bird and turned to watch her mother.

Though Nana stooped a little, pulled down by the knees, her body looked strong, not fat but definitely not gaunt, not at all like the withering frame of the father in his last days, or in fact, in his last years. The daughter was surprised by the thought, by the fleeting resentment that came with it. The land had always kept the father trim but in the last days the body caved in on itself and then withered quickly. Nana walked forward. She moved with an effort, her heavy body struggling against the bonds that tried to pull it down. When she moved, you could see that the years were attacking the body from the outside, tying knots at her knees, securing her so that eventually she wouldn't be able to resist the tug toward the dust. But her eyes looked forward with determination, nothing like the shifty sadness of the father's expression in his last days. These things presented themselves to the daughter's thoughts during that pause at the door, while Nana measured the four or five steps into the room. Life had attacked the father quietly, secretively, gnawing away at the pit of his stomach while he walked lean and upright. With Nana, it practiced no such dissimulation. Perhaps it wasn't quite ready for her yet. You could see it pulling her down and you could see her refusing to lie down without a struggle. With the mother, everything was obvious. You didn't have to negotiate corners. And so far life was letting her have her way.

"You find what your father send you to look for now?" she asked. And again the daughter noticed what she hadn't really registered in the same way in the kitchen encounter. The mother's voice was like everyone said the father's had been right to the end, far from feeble in spite of the body's degeneration.

"I think so," the daughter said. "The box was right where he told me to look."

"Good. I hope he leave a solid bankbook there so we could see what he do with his life."

The daughter's thumb moved protectively over the box. She looked at the mother as she sank down onto the bed. She saw the picture in the box—the long hair held back in a hairnet, the young, pretty, oval face, the wide eyes staring directly at her, the little girl, tight-faced and fuming, at the woman's side, the baby looking bewildered.

The bird was still chattering on the window. Nana looked at it with distaste and waved her hands at it.

"Get away! What's wrong with you? Let people hear themselves think! Ay!"

"I thought these little creatures supposed to be people's spirit sometimes," the daughter observed.

"Ah chut! A bird is a bird. *Ki spirit sa?* In any case, green crickets are the ones that come as visitors. Not birds so much, as far as I know. If you see a green cricket, your aunt would tell you to make sure and leave it alone."

"And you agree with that?"

"Well, let's just say I wouldn't kill a green cricket, especially not now."

The daughter's eyes traced the lines on the mother's forehead. If you really want to disguise yourself, she thought, I guess you could come as a bird and not a cricket, since everybody expecting a cricket. The bird was moving nervously on the windowsill. In her mother's expression, as she flapped her hands again dismissively at the bird, the daughter recognized some indefinable thing she saw sometimes when she looked into her own mirror—an impatience, an unwillingness to wait and listen. And in that same moment, as she watched the mother's impatience with the visitor, the daughter felt on her face the distaste she was sure she had seen on her father's at times when Nana made some small comment or went close to him in the weeks before his death. It was as if the father hadn't been able to come to terms with the way the mother was so matter-of-fact about dying, as if something about her *being* offended his sensibilities. After all, even if she had always been known to feel more comfortable than he did with the idea of death, this was his death coming, not hers. *She* didn't mind going, but she was staying, in the house surrounded by cocoa and nutmeg trees, the house *he* loved, in the shade of the grapefruit, the gliricidia, the mango, in the protective shadow of the mountain *he* loved and she was so impatient about.

In those days, when death's shadow crouched behind the mountain, when the father's time walked toward him with the slow certainty of an ex-serviceman's parade that was just around the corner, you could see in his eyes a feeling that the body had betrayed him, that he couldn't reconcile himself to the unfairness of it. The daughter remembers the wasting body lying on the living-room couch, hears him say, "But I don't understand it. I wish I could eat, but my body refusing to take a thing." And his bewildered eyes had wandered aimlessly, trying to fix on something to understand that battle with the body that he could only lose because the body had become anxious to return to dust. It was like watching somebody try to hold

back the tears because the house he had lived in and loved passion-
ately since birth was being demolished around him; he was being
forced to move to someplace he knew nothing about, and he could
do nothing about it.

The bird flew away over the callaloo bush and came back. It picked
at the windowsill again. The daughter bent down to push in the
drawer of the trunk, and noticed a silver-blue edge under the brown-
paper lining at the bottom of the drawer. She pulled at the paper,
uncovered a faded blue exercise book. It was heavy, with something
taped to the pages inside. On the cover were the words Presentation
College, and, written in ink, in a confident, watermarked scrawl, the
name Carl La Porte. The daughter flicked open the book and saw,
on the inside cover, the words, like descending steps, Carl La Porte,
Presentation College, St. George's, Grenada, West Indies, The Universe. On the opposite page was the father's handwriting. It was
scrawled across the entire page. She turned the pages carefully. The
father's handwriting was a shaky scrawl on a few other pages of the
book, too. And there was an envelope with more photos. One of
Colin, four or five years old, in the yard with the dog, Bingo, pulling
at the round white O of Bingo's black tail. There was a photo of Carl
at fourteen or fifteen, sitting with other schoolboys on the steps of
Presentation College. The bewildered look he had worn as a baby in
his mother's arms had either disappeared or gone to hide under the
hat pulled down over his eyes.

A few pages on, three or four cassette tapes—four—had been fixed
into the book with a white—whitish—tape. It looked like the tape
that was used to secure banana wrapping when bananas were to be
shipped. The daughter turned back to the first page. She read, *I am
starting to write this and hope that I'll finish.* Had her father written a diary? That seemed very unlikely. He was so nervous about his
writing that she couldn't see him doing that. The daughter bent
down again and pulled at the brown-paper lining at the bottom of the
trunk. Was there anything else? She pulled out the paper, shook it,
turned it over to see if there was anything written on it, put it back.
He hadn't told her about this; he'd mentioned only the box. The
daughter stood up and pushed the trunk closed. She felt like an
agent. She thought of names like CIA, KGB, FBI, and the British one,
whatever it was. And she was suddenly aware of how breathing
happened. Or how it could happen. You pulled the air in through
your mouth, deep. You held it in a bit. You kept your mouth open
and let the breath come out, slow, slow, silent. Then you waited.

Nana, sitting on the bed with her back to the trunk, her body angled toward the bathroom door, looked up from her prayer book. She turned with difficulty, shifting her bottom on the bed and then smoothing out the sheet with her hand. "He leave money?"

"No. He didn't leave money. He left some papers. Photographs and things. I have to look through them." The daughter paused, waited. Then she said, "I took them out of the trunk and I have them here. You want to look at them?"

"No. You handle it." The mother made a dismissive gesture with her left hand. The daughter watched the wedding ring, a thick band, simple, not sparkling, but definitely not as dull as the nails on the trunk. Nana said, "I have enough old papers of my own. I don't want any more."

The daughter looked toward the window. The bird was gone. Nana put both hands on the bed and pushed herself up, said, "Let me go and see what I have to do." She pushed at the bathroom door. One foot went forward, pulled her body into line, and the other followed, carrying her one back-bending step down into the bathroom. "Woy!" she said. "My body not mine."

As the mother moved out of the room, the daughter thought, *his* body not his anymore; yours is yours still.

The daughter turned with the box and walked through the other doorway, out of the big bedroom. She stopped in the living room and went to sit on the chair that had been her father's favorite spot in the latter days of his life. Or perhaps it was just a spot where he felt reasonably comfortable, because in those days it seemed no spot was a favorite, none a place that he enjoyed for itself. In those days, he would lie there, stretched out, looking up at the bright brown of the high rafters and twisting his lips.

In these early hours of the morning, in the house in the cool of the mountain, everything is quiet, or at least, it's only noisy if you've just come back from living somewhere else, and can hear the sound of everyday things like crickets and frogs and birds. You think things like, *Hear* those insects! You'd grown up with them, lived with them shouting at you and singing to you and complaining around you and crying and making every little sound, and yet you'd never even heard these shouting voices until you went far away from them. And then some movement of life or death brings you back one day, and you listen for every little sound, crickets and everything else, and you are excited and surprised to hear so much movement.

The crickets are crying. There is a croaky call from the frogs. The birds are singing an insistent, *green peas sweet, green peas sweet,* starting out in an even tone and lifting their voices each time at the end of the song. It doesn't seem to matter that it is April and green peas season is over. Or perhaps that is the only bird song you know, so the birds are singing it just for you. You lean back to listen and the fridge starts up, mockingly, buzzing and shaking, drowning out the insects. Through the window, you see leaves answering the breeze, moving to and fro, but perhaps their answer is a whisper, because although you can see them moving and then settling back and starting again, so that you know they're saying something, you can't hear them, even though the window is open.

It was only six-thirty by the clock on the living-room wall. The father used to get up early when he was alive. Not early by the mother's standards, but early. Except on weekends, when he would sleep late. He would fret when he didn't want to go to church on a Sunday morning and the mother not only wanted to go but also expected him to drive her there. Usually, on a weekday, in his stronger days, he would be heading outside into the land at about this time. Heading outside to come back in later and have the breakfast that Nana had made for him, and to get ready for the rest of his day.

It was Monday. Washing day for Nana since King Hatchet was a little, little hammer. Long time ago, she would be outside in the yard with a *jooking* board. Now, having moved from the bathroom out into the kitchen, you could hear from her voice that she is moving— limping, or dragging one foot a bit—between the kitchen and the small washroom at the back, praising the Lord, as she did every Monday morning, because although she still had to be careful with water, now she would usually have enough for washing. Not because the pipes carried that much more, but because, she said, she was more sensible now, because her sense—the proper kind, not the common kind—had increased as the children got bigger and money became more available, because now she had a pump and a tank and could even turn off the scarce government water sometimes, because she better appreciated the two seasons Papa God had seen fit to give the island, because she had a reason to thank the Lord on the days that the rain poured, because she could understand the turning and the twisting of life when the grass grew more than she could handle, but still she gave praises that there was a lot of water to do the things that helped to keep life going. The electric pump wasn't getting the water into the machine properly today, so Nana was filling a bucket and transferring the water into the machine so it could do its work.

Small potatoes, she said about this inconvenience, small potatoes when you consider the problems of the past. Young people these days, she would often mutter, they don't know how easy they have it.

The daughter got up and walked through the dining room toward her room. She heard muttering as she passed and glanced toward the kitchen. Had she been in a mood for mother stories, she knew she would have heard how this washing was no trouble at all, how, long time ago, long time in *my* experience, anyway, although we must never forget that some people still experiencing that, on a Monday, especially when I wasn't living with my mother, it would be no school for me because the clothes have to be washed; if you don't have a pipe outside with running water, you know that means help up your bundle and make it down to the river. But the daughter only heard the story from the store of such stories she kept in her head; she felt sure the mother was poised to tell her, but today she clutched the father's box and bent her head to ships sailing in a petrified sunset.

From up the hill, there was a sudden crowing of a cock. As the daughter opened the door to her room, she heard the mother pause in her muttering to say, "It's a long time I don't hear cocks around. I understand Mr. Jones up on the hill have a son that starting to rear fowls."

RICH WITH THE RICHES

They come back often to check on things. That's not surprising, is what Nana La Porte says about it. When you leave a place you like, you would drop in every so often, just to see what it looks like. And if you have family still living there, of course you look in when you could. Some of them are good, she said, and some bad, because that is the way life is. Death, she says, is part of life. There's nothing surprising in that.

Sometimes, when they visit, they stumble against us, or we stumble against them, and we don't even know it, but every so often one of them decides to make it obvious, just to be sure we know they're around. So they might come and walk a little ahead of you as you're going up the hill, and you only realize it when you try to catch up, and however fast you walk, although the person ahead never seems to walk faster, you can't catch up. You run, and the person is still walking, but keeping the same distance ahead. Then you realize what's happening, and you want to panic, because you were always sure that if this ever happened to you, you would die on the spot, but you reach for the panic and there's none inside you, or perhaps this is just what panic is, and unless you make up your mind to die right there on the spot, you have to find some way to go on, so you do it and you just keep walking, until somewhere along the way, you realize that there's somebody you know coming down the hill and there's nobody in front of you going up the hill anymore and you feel too foolish to say anything about it, because people might look at you and say that they used to think you were a sensible person.

Once, a woman came back to visit in such a way that she had the whole island talking, and perhaps that was just to shake people up and make them realize that they only think they're big and they're wonderful, but there are so many things on earth and in the sky and below the ground and in the sea and everywhere that they're really only very, very small potatoes in the ground.

What happened was this. A man from Old Westerhall was coming from Fantazia one night, you know, that club on the beach in Grand Anse, he was partying all night, and even laughing up at the moon and the stars hanging down over the beach, so he was a little bit sweet and he asked his friend to drive for him. So the two of them were in front and two other fellows asked him for a lift and those two with the girlfriend of one were sitting in the back. One of them got off after you go past the roundabout, down the road by White Gun, the other guy and his girlfriend stopped by LaBorie gap and when the friend left him up the road by St. Paul's Police Station, the man was still feeling sweet, but he figured he could make it home now, because he only had to go down the hill and through the Morne Delice road to Old Westerhall, and although traffic is brisk there during the day, it's not really a popular road, and he wouldn't expect to meet much traffic there at night.

So with the little rum in his head, he was going down the hill, and just before the bend by the river, right near to the hog plum tree, a woman stepped out from the little bridge by the side of the road and flagged down the car. Now, in the day, he might have ignored her, but at night, he couldn't even say if he didn't have a few drinks in his head he might have ignored her, because you don't really see a woman in the road there at one o'clock in the morning, looking as if she going home from a party and didn't get a ride, slim and trim-looking, with long, skinny white skirt and yellow top and to tell the truth, somehow he didn't really see the hat, was only when she got into the car and sat down that he realized she was wearing a pretty white hat with yellow flowers on the side. That strike him as a bit strange, but not strange enough to call it alarming, although perhaps that was because the white rum—which is a dangerous thing—was having its effect. He tried to look into her face to see if he would recognize her, but she was bending down to fix something by her foot, perhaps the mat got caught up in her shoe little bit, so he start the car and go on, and he comment, *You late from party, man,* and she answer, *Yes, I couldn't get a ride,* and he going along there, concentrating on blinking his eyes to see the road properly, until, as he was turning the corner by Morne Delice gap, he asked her, *How far you going,* and she say, *Not too far, I will tell you,* and then he say, *Well, I just going around the corner, you know,* so when he reach his gap by the garage there to turn in, he say, *I not going down any further, sorry,* and she say, *Is all right, thanks, I going just round the corner,* and he wondering *where* around the corner, because he knows everybody living there, and she get out of the car and as she was walking in front of the car, he realize she walking sideways so he couldn't see her face and as she walking away from him toward the road down to the old sugar mill, he feel the hair standing up on his arms, and he watching her walking and then she disappear right in front of his eyes, disappear, I tell you, disappear without going forward or back or to the right or to the left, just disappear, and afterward he couldn't tell whether it was that that caused him to wet the car seat or whether the rum was stronger in his head than he realized.

And when the story went around later, Auntie Eva said that a lot of people with rum in their head see things, but another fellow say he passed a woman right there near to the hog plum tree the night before, but that fellow used to live in New York, and regardless of how much rum he drink, no way the night and the road would make him so sympathetic to man, woman, or child that he would stop and give them a lift. Not because he afraid of people from the other side, but because, in New York, people from *this* side make him realize that you don't take that kind of chance with your life.

So really, when you think about all of that, and when you consider how easy it is to take you unawares, you have to feel good about those who want to say something after they're gone, and they come fair and square and say to you, Look, I leave a box I want you to look at; it's in the trunk, go and get it.

The daughter, having removed the box from where she was sent to retrieve it, is anxious to see what her father has to say. The date at the top of the first page of Carl's Presentation College exercise book is 13th February 1963. That date had been crossed out, perhaps by the father, and 10th August, 1993, written directly under it. Carl would have been twelve when he wrote that first date, thirty-three years ago now. The father would have been on the way to his thirty-seventh birthday. That would mean that at the time he was younger than Carl is now, younger than any of his children today.

The daughter tries to remember her father at thirty-six. She would have been thirteen. And now she is aware that the father was twenty-three when he fathered her. She feels a new respect for him. At twenty-three, he actually wanted to start a family. Somehow that wasn't the kind of decision she would have expected of him. The daughter wonders what happened to him, where that joy in family went by the time she was growing up, what he was thinking, how he would tell the story if he could tell it. Thirty-six, thirty-seven, she thinks now, was no huge age, but it was huge then, at the time when Carl was twelve and she was thirteen. Now Time has cut it down to size. And Time stands there looking at her as if it is waiting to see what she will do about this revelation—well, it stands there in the way Time has of standing still; that is, walking on, but looking back at you so steadily that you figure that really it is standing still. It stands there and looks at her, waiting for her reaction. The daughter tries to remember the young man who was her father all those years ago, but her thirteen-year-old self, or what she imagines that self to have been, and her mother's voice get in the way; the father's face is not there, not at that age anyway. So Time smiles and moves on.

As for the young man in the photos taken from the trunk, although the contours of his face are clearly those of the father she knew, he is a stranger to her. She looks at him, that man in the photo, and is amused with Time's amusement, because it is strange, not just to think of her father as someone younger than her younger brother is now, but to look at a photo that suggests a face that could be attached to him. From the period of her life that was her thirteen-year-old youth, the daughter remembers, not so much the face of her mother, who would have been forty-two, heading for forty-three then, but mother movements, gestures, a finger pointing assertively, threateningly in the direction of a chore to be performed, a face frowning and intent as it tries to convey to the daughter the importance of knowing what men are all about, of understanding what her father is all about, of realizing the way the father thought about everyone else but the family he left at home while he roamed the

139

fields, returning home to demand service. As the memory touches her, Time stops again, looks back, and asks, *Is that how it was?*

And then, at last, the daughter sees the father. Or at least, she hears him. She hears a clearing of the throat as he approaches. He is coming in from the fields. She peeks through the window and from the distance, from what she could see of him as he pauses up there near to the golden apple tree, as he stands with his hands crossed behind his back, holding the cutlass in his usual way, she imagines, as he turns slightly to the left so that he is looking up at the mountain, his face is relaxed and warm with the memory of the woods and the water of *Bwa Epi Dlo,* then he is washing his hands at the pipe outside; she pulls further back into the kitchen as he lifts his head and frowns toward the kitchen window; he is walking to the door with lips tight and an expression that says to the mother even though he doesn't see the mother yet, *I know you were talking about me, you and your daughter.* Then he sees the daughter standing there and he is swerving to point toward leaves scattered about under the grapefruit tree and to ask, *Why are those leaves still under the tree, Norma? You waiting for somebody to clean up the place for you?* She watches him and tries to focus on the face of the man speaking, but that face disappears and the daughter, sitting in her room with the box of ships sailing in a petrified sunset, sees the lined, worried, gentle face of the father in his sixties.

And now he is smiling and talking about how he was the best batsman ever in the country and only poor selectors made him miss hitting the big time. He is chuckling about how men went to field on the boundary the moment he touched the bat, then suddenly he is touching his stomach, saying, *I really don't know what this hurt is all about, but it feel like there's something inside of me, right here.* And Time stops again to watch her and Time's face is without expression.

The daughter looks down at the photograph and wonders, Who was he, that man who was thirty-six when Carl was writing with the certainty of life and the assurance of youth in his high-school exercise book? She looks at the cover again and reads: *Carl La Porte, Presentation College, St. George's, Grenada, West Indies, The Universe.*

Inside the exercise book, under the date 10th August, 1993, her father's writing is a careful, disordered scrawl. She looks at it and can remember a younger writing, a time when the father was very proud of his penmanship. Now the daughter sees the teetering of the "l," the drunkenness of the "t," the fumbling uncertainty of the "f" and "h," the shakiness of "g" and "p," the uncertain wavering of "I." In his more robust days, he would make flourishes over the paper with his pen, preparing himself for a decisive stab at the written word. It must have been painful to him to write this much, to bring the pen down and not achieve the decisiveness he always strove for. Or perhaps by this stage he had stopped planning for anything decisive, perhaps there were less flourishes, perhaps he was grateful just to have achieved the shape of the word, and was less concerned about perfection. The daughter read,

> I'm starting to write this and hope that I'll finish. I shouldn't invite bad luck by saying that, because in fact I feel really good now, so I'm keeping my fingers crossed. It's about two months since I came back from the operation in Trinidad. That was 16th June, 1993. Only a week before my 66th birthday. I don't know if your aunt Eva noticed, because she didn't say anything, and you know how she is with numbers. Those two sixes nearly do for me, but I'm here still. I'm feeling good now, and it made me want to write things down. I don't know how long I will continue because this

And that was where the first page ended. The next page, with a shaky "2" written at the top, started:

> is slow going.

The daughter looks back at the first neatly written page, unblotched, even though the letters were wavery, and, remembering the slow deliberateness with which he wrote even when he was healthy, she knows that this was a huge undertaking. And Aunt Eva had of course noticed the sixes. "June," she had said one day, "his life revolve around June. June hit him hard for the two sixes. Although it is as if the two sixes save him, because when he fall apart was the time before that. And you know"—and the daughter remembers her aunt Eva's diminutive figure, the head lifted, gray plaits framing the round face, one finger wagging portentously—"it not surprising this is what he get. He is a June born"—and bringing the hand back to partly cover her mouth, she whispered from inside and around it—"the *Cancer* planet." On the second page of his story, Normandy continues:

141

> I can't write too fast now. To tell you the truth, it's partly
> because of you, Norma, that I'm making the effort. You're
> always talking about how important it is to know what went
> before. And I guess the whole thing just have me feeling so
> frightened that I have to sit down and think about things. I
> can't imagine—I don't even like to write the word, to tell you
> the truth, but, make the sign of the cross—death—that is a
> thing I can't imagine at all. Your mother says you're supposed
> to get rid of that kind of fear once your children get big. That
> was it for her, I guess. Not for me. I'm afraid. Plain as that, so
> I might as well say it.

And now he is at the end of that page. The daughter is sure the
father had stopped often while writing these last two lines. He had
probably stopped just after "Not for me," right before "I'm afraid."
Or perhaps he had stopped after writing "I'm afraid." Or perhaps it
was after "I might as well say it." Or after the next "Afraid."
Somewhere in the midst of all of that "afraid," he would have
stopped to twist his lips, perhaps to run his hand over his head—she
almost thought of it as *through his hair*, but by that time there was
little of hair to run his hand through, even though he went to the barber to cut the gray remainder almost every week. He would have run
his hand over his head and looked up to stare through the walls of
the house at the *Bwa Epi Dlo* mountain. Or, if he was sitting on the
veranda, he would have looked across at the dying palmiste tree. At
the tree standing guard, in splendid leaflessness, over the stone that
served as a marker, *tongue say*, for the grave of some man who had
owned *Bwa Epi Dlo* in the long-ago days when it was a cocoa estate.
The father would probably have looked across there and twisted his
lips at the old palmiste tree, whispering "afraid," inside his head, and
trying not to let the word occupy every bit of space inside him.

And after that, he wrote three more pages, perhaps leaving the
writing and coming back to it, finally admitting that the task was
more than him. He wrote,

> Norma, if you're showing this to anybody after—well, if any-
> thing happens and you want to show it to somebody, I ask
> you please to make the corrections in proper English. I know
> in your job with these school magazines and so, you have a
> style that is in favor of writing our dialect, but that is your
> generation, not mine. People my age think that proper
> English is the best, so I would ask you please to go along with
> my wishes and correct whatever I write to proper English, if
> you are going to show it about in public or anything like that.

I mean, I'm not planning to die or anything, so when I'm finished, if you want to show

And here he came to the end of a page. On the next page he continued:

it to anybody and for some reason I don't tell you, remember that I'm writing it here. I don't even know if I want you to show it around, but in any case, perhaps it doesn't matter. We'll see, and if I'm not around to tell you what I want, just don't put in anything that you know I wouldn't say, please. Just leave what I wrote, and make whatever corrections are necessary. I never forget a time when you used bad words in writing something that you had to talk about in public, out in the raw like that. Your mother and your

He had written less here, turning the page again to write,

godmother were very upset. I was upset, too, to tell you the truth, but I know you younger ones have a strange way of doing things, so that is it. But I hope you will respect my wishes and not put in anything you know I won't agree with. Just put what I say, correct the grammar, and let it be so. If you're putting in anything, let it be clear that it's you doing it, but please don't put bad words. Make corrections to the spelling and the grammar, and leave it at that.

And with the effort of this huge request, he stopped. The next two pages of the exercise book have nothing written on them, nothing, that is, except, on the second one, a couple of small triangles in the top right-hand corner, where Carl must have attempted to make some sort of use of the book. At the top of the next page, there is an equation, in Carl's handwriting: $2x + 4x = 6x$. The page following that contains several strips of banana tape, the long, narrow, whitish yellow tape that the father used, long ago, to tape the covering on bunches of bananas for shipping. Here he had used the banana tape to secure four cassettes, in clear cassette cases. The daughter knows that at least one of the cassettes must be one she had given him. She remembers him asking. He may have taken others. Or asked somebody to take them for him, since he wouldn't normally walk into her room. She keeps a stock of such things in her parents' house in case she needs them when she visits. He may have asked her for more, though she couldn't remember this, or he may have asked her mother, which he tended to count as almost the same thing. The banana tape winds right to the top of the page and down the next side, up again across the page, firmly securing the cassette tapes in place. Now the daughter looks for an end and starts removing the tape, carefully, wincing each time there is the sound of a tear, although there seems nothing written on these pages, so she isn't sure why she fears tearing them. Still, you never know. There might be something to read where you least expect it.

The cassette tapes released, she looks for some writing on the cases or on the cassettes themselves. There is none. The daughter gets up, goes to one of the shelves running along a wall of her room, and reaches up for a cassette player she keeps there for use when her wanderings bring her to *Bwa Epi Dlo*. she hasn't used it in a while, but she knows her father has, and there are batteries in it. It works.

The cassette she picks up first seems to have been stopped somewhere in the middle. The daughter slips it into the player, turns the machine on, puts it on rewind, and presses *Play* again. She sits down slowly and jumps as she hears her father's voice. She turns the volume down quickly, looks around guiltily, hopes her mother hasn't heard. She doesn't know what he said. She was too startled by the voice. The daughter keeps her eyes on the door, nervous that the mother will come to find out what is going on. No sound from outside. She presses *Rewind* briefly. She lets it go and hits *Play* again. Turns the volume down some more. Leans toward the tape. Her father's voice says

> . . . the way my stomach feeling. A few days now, I have this feeling as if I can't eat properly. It's as if there's something in my throat. And the pain. My stomach hurting again.

That was it. The tape is running but the voice is no longer there. The daughter presses *Stop,* then *Rewind.* She presses *Play* again and listens. There is nothing. She fiddles with the tape, going fast forward and rewinding, until she hears again ". . . the way my stomach feeling." What came immediately before that must have been erased because the story the voice tells has no beginning, and its ending is abrupt.

The daughter remembers that some time ago, the father had come into the dining room where she sat; she was on the point of rising from his chair, from the chair that occupied the place he had sat in, when in that room, every day as far back as she could remember.

144

Usually, other people sat in various places around the table, switching chairs all the time, not leaving their mark or their personality written on any one chair. But that one, where she sat, was his. The spot was, anyway. But as she started to get up, a thing she would have resisted in her youth but now did without being required to, he'd said, *No, no, I'm not coming to sit down. I just wanted to ask you, I see you have a tape recorder you use sometimes. Can you lend it to me and show me how to use it?*

She remembers that he'd muttered something about having some work to do for the Ex-Servicemen's Association. And she had gone through everything with him—how to record, how to play back, how to rewind, how to move fast forward. On occasion afterward he came to her and asked if she could put it on *Record* for him, so that he could use it right away. Then he had returned some time later, handing the tape player to her and asking her to turn it off. He had then taken it back and removed the tape. That Christmas she had left the player with him, realizing that he seemed to be working with it a lot. Then just before she left that year, he seemed to have started doing the on and off bit himself. She can't remember if he asked after that.

Now the daughter rewinds the tape and removes it. She doesn't try the other side, but inserts the one that was on top of the others and that she imagines was the first. She starts it from the beginning. She fiddles with the volume, keeps it low, leans forward. His voice confidential, he tells her:

> A few months ago, I started to try to write something, but I couldn't keep up. So since you're here this holiday, I decide to ask you to show me how to use this.

So that was it, the first time she had set the tape for him. This must have been the Christmas holidays, December 1993.

> I admitted to your brother Colin the other day—that—well, sometimes when you're—young—you think the whole world is yours. You do a lot of—well, foolish things. Then, as the years go by and so, you come to realize. And then when you start to think of your—last days, you know—it all come to you. I know what your mother will say to that. She tell me some hurtful things already, you know, but that is all right. Anyway, I—I know she won't believe I really mean that. Well, but—one thing I could say for sure, I never mean any harm. I like my little enjoyment, especially when I was young, and I know I do plenty—well, plenty—that—upset people. But it's

145

just through not thinking, you know, and then, well, it's true that—that—as a man, I suppose—you have more—leeway, I guess you would call it. So, well, that—that is there.

The daughter realizes it was as hard as ever for him to talk. She leans forward, watching the tape machine, wanting to get through to the heart of it, to rub out the pauses and hurry the words along.

It is obvious that—well, you children seem to feel—that what you have as a pattern of how to live—well, I guess that—your mother show you—how to live. You—well, you act like you feel—that way. I never really talk to you about me—sometimes when you ask, I tell you a little bit about—my past and about—what I wanted out of life and—that kind of thing. I was never good at that—I know I was never good at that—you know, talking about how I feel and that kind of thing. Your mother—well, I guess she sort of—had more practice with that kind of thing. She—well, I suppose in a way she—had that to her advantage, and to tell you the truth I guess I didn't really realize that it was important.

The machine is silent. The daughter is just about to press *Stop,* thinking her father had stopped there or for some reason hadn't recorded it properly, when the voice continues:

It wasn't until after you children grow up and I could see— how much you hold to your mother's opinion and never— well, usually, don't really see my side at all—especially you, Norma, but then I guess you are the girl and—well, it wasn't until that time, when you grow up, that I really think about how—well, I wished it wasn't that way. I wished it wasn't that way. The boys—well, the boys—I guess they are more willing—well, to listen, you know—but—I guess, too, you are the girl so you—keep more to your mother's position. I mean, I must admit, though, that lately—you're a bit different, but I feel—well, you don't think about me as you think about your mother. And a few days ago, your mother said some words that hurt me. She said to me—she said it in confusion, is true. I mean, we were quarreling about something, but sometimes that is when you know what people really think, so—she said to me, you live all your life and never achieve a thing.

The daughter leans away from the machine, leans forward and turns it off. So she had said it to him as well! She lies back on the

146

bed, watches the varnished brown of the ceiling. She sits up, leans forward, puts on the tape:

> Imagine that! Not a thing, is what she say. And, well (laughter, short, sharp, straggly) I can't really tell you how much that upset me. Well, I know I'm not leaving—money in the bank when I go, and I never had enough money to pay for anything. But in spite of everything, you know—I believe I achieved *some*thing.

The tape is still running but there are no more words. The daughter waits, then stops the tape and hits *Fast Forward*. She tries to find the father's voice. Nothing. She goes forward again and stops. Hears,

> set your mother off.

Was that all? He must have stopped it and tried to start it himself. Perhaps he had erased something. Perhaps he had been talking and nothing was recorded. The daughter hits *Fast Forward*, stops, and hears a sound. She hits *Rewind* and searches until she finds a place where the voice begins again.

> You should ask your mother to show you exactly where I used to live with my mother and your aunts when I was a little boy. She will show you. Up, near where my mother used to live up there, near to the bridge, up under the cocoa. Well— it used to be cocoa. Now, I believe you will find just houses there. You must ask her to show you. All the way from there, I come to be who I am today.

Silence again. There seems to be nothing more on that side of the tape. The daughter wonders if Side B had been recorded on one of those days when he'd brought the tape to her, and asked her to put it on *Record* for him. She turns the tape over and waits. She searches for the father's voice, but there is nothing but silence. If he had tried to record on that side, he hadn't succeeded. Or perhaps he had been too uncertain of the process to try, had decided to trust that he had recorded something on one side, and had feared that one side would be lost if he tried to engage with the other. The daughter goes forward and back, listens and waits, but there is nothing more here.

How had he fared with the other tapes? Had he recorded anything? He had come more than once to ask her to turn on the tape, and then it seemed he had also tried to communicate without help. She put on Side A of the second tape, starting it from the beginning. When the voice comes, it says:

> . . . so I think we beat that thing.

He had probably begun talking before the machine started recording. He continued,

> In fact, I feeling so good that I went up into the land spraying a few days ago, and, well—that set your mother off. She said all kinds of things. She said that after you children—foolishly—foolishly spend so much money trying to get me well—your mother is something—after that, I put this old can on my back again and going up spraying cancer into the land and—into my lungs. But, you know, I don't think that is true. I put the—the—cloth barrier—you know, the cloth I usually use when I'm spraying—I put it over the lower part of my face and—and that—I think that works—and in any case, if I don't spray the land, how am I going to keep back the bush? Your mother—well, of course she wants things from the land, but she doesn't think about how to maintain it, that is the problem. We—in this business, you have to fight the bush and the only way to do that is to spray it. The government and the agricultural department, and everybody—everybody who know about such things, recommend the spraying. So—what else is there to do? I can't afford to pay people every two weeks to go through the land and cutlass it and I can't do it for myself. When you spray, you keep down the bush for a reasonable amount of time. I don't know how else to fight the bush?

His voice is a question. Then there is silence. The tape is running. The daughter can hear what sounds like small taps. His fingers. She imagines him, agitated, lifting his head and looking toward the mountain—although that depends where he was doing this taping—probably in the dining room in the afternoon when the daughter is outside and the mother is gardening. He would sit at the dining table where he would be sure to hear anyone coming in, and stare through the wall toward the mountain. The small taps must be his fingers tapping on the dining table. The voice comes again.

> Your mother feel—well, she keep saying—that the same way the spray kills the bush, it's the same way it kills people, so

148

that is why she's so annoyed with me and—well—you know
when she gets annoyed, she could say some hurtful things—
so—and—she's implying that—it wasn't worth trying to save
my life because I have no interest in myself.

The daughter hears her mother's shuffling footsteps, coming in
from the kitchen through the dining room, hears her say, "Oh,
Lord, Nana, your body tie up like potato vine, girl." The daughter
hits the *Pause* button on the tape recorder. She hears, "Norma, you
in there?" She turns off the tape recorder and pushes it under
her pillow. She stands up quickly and walks toward the bookshelf, stands looking searchingly at it. "Come," she calls out to her
mother.

Nana asks, "So what your father have to say for himself?" But the
daughter has no intention of sharing the tape with her mother right
now.

She says, "I'm sifting through things still, but he left some old
photos and things. That is the box."

She points toward her bed, to the box with ships on the cover.
What a good thing she had removed the exercise book. It is there,
near the box, but her mother wouldn't realize it belonged to the
package, although she would probably recognize the old Presentation
College exercise book, and wonder about it. The daughter leans over,
picks the box up, and hands it to her mother. Nana eases herself
down on to the bed and opens it. The daughter sits, pulls on the sheet
so that it is bundled up around the exercise book. Nana laughs as she
lifts the top photos.

"Oh yes," she says, "I know he had these old things in there."
Then, looking at the photo of her younger self and two children, she
observes, "Look at Nana in her day. Time could really do things." Of
the passport photos she says only, "Normandy."

The daughter leans over and pulls out the military certificate.
"This is a certificate they gave him when they discharged him from
the army. It says his military conduct was good."

Nana smiles. "Trust him to come and show you where to find
things from his army days, boasting how his conduct good."

"Did you know those things were in the trunk?" the daughter asks.

Nana hadn't known, but she'd known those old photos were
around somewhere. Still picking things out of the box, peering at
them, putting them back down, she says, "And I expect he would
have things from his army days in the trunk somewhere. It's a good

thing he come and point them out to you, so you could get them if
you want them, because when I ready to clean out, all of that going
in the garbage. He realize he can't come and ask me to sort out any
old papers."

The sound of an engine invades the room. It seems the man who
bought Normandy's rover is coming to visit. Nana lifts her hand and
turns her head, listening. The daughter gets up, takes the exercise
book, puts it on her bookshelf. She walks out of the room and on to
the veranda, ready to welcome the unexpected visitor. The engine
falters in the way it did with Normandy just before he changed gears
to make the sharp turn up the hill and into the yard. The daughter
sits on the veranda wall, watching the hill up which the rover will
emerge. Her mother's shuffle follows her out to the veranda. When
Nana reaches the spot where the daughter stands, they watch the
concreted walkway together. "Usually I don't hear so good," Nana
says, "but that sound came to me as clear as ever."

They watch. They wait. Nana turns away before the daughter
does. Inside, as she moves toward the kitchen, she says, "Dead is not
a special condition. All of us going there, so he'd better stop hanging
around waiting, and get used to it. We'll come, like it or not, but why
he trying to hurry me along?"

The daughter says, "He's just letting us know he's around, and
there's nothing wrong with that."

She doesn't try to listen to more of the tape in her room that day.
It is nearly midday, high noon, and Nana likes people to be there on
the double when she says food is ready. There is no waiting until you
are ready, not if you want to avoid irritating the mother, so the
daughter decides she will wait until after lunch and go outside, probably up the hill, to continue listening.

Every day, the sun comes up over the mountain and then aims for
the top of the palmiste tree, moving toward it with hot desperation.
Sometimes, clouds ride up to tone down the fire of the sun a bit;
some days, like today, the sun comes right up and stands glaring over
the palmiste tree just before midday. It would be there for a while
and then, by the time they are finished lunch, it would start walking
across the sky again in that white-gold yellow, wrap itself up in fire
all day, except around January, when the rain would routinely come
out to douse it. Today, at each step it shakes itself and lets fall some
the shimmering yellow, walks down to the sea one today with the
sure promise of another one tomorrow, and then, in the end, satisfied for the day, it will wrap itself in purple and disappear over the

150

horizon for the night, leaving a sheepish, contented glow on the face of the sea.

In the late afternoon, the daughter walks up the hill into the land. The crocus bag over her shoulder is not to pick up stray nutmegs. It contains what she will be listening to on the hillside. The mother doesn't walk up into the *Bwa Epi Dlo* hills these days. Until a couple years ago, she would still do that sometimes, but each day now her knees are weaker, and each time she ventures beyond her new limits, the ground pulls her down to remind her of her destiny. So the daughter can expect to be alone on the hillside, unless some intruder decides to come looking for provisions, and the sound of her father's voice in the land would certainly be protection.

The daughter sits on the ground, under the spread of a nutmeg tree, and puts on the tape. The voice takes up where it had left off.

> In fact, you know, she actually said that. She said that. As if I—deliberately—do things to take advantage because I know, as she says, it's not my money spending for the cure. Imagine that. That is what she implied. Sometimes I think your mother took lessons in how to—how to say hurtful things to people. Anyway, so that is it. I guess it's because of all of that I'm talking all these things here now. I just had to—well, in a way, I suppose I had to—get some things off my chest, and— try and figure out what is what.

The tape stops. The daughter watches it run. "Come on, Daddy," she says. "There's nobody around. You could talk as much as you want to." But there is nothing more on that side. She turns the cassette over.

At the beginning of the next side, there is nothing. The daughter lets it run for a bit and suddenly he says:

> You all to your mother.

Then there is silence. There is nothing else on the tape. What else had he said? The daughter turns the tape recorder on and off. Fast forward, rewind, play, she searches minutely for the sound of a voice, but there is nothing more than "You all to your mother." Imagine having her come all the way up here and still not saying anything. He probably hadn't realized he wasn't recording. The daughter wonders how long he had talked, communicating nothing. She watches the tape as if she could force it to give up its meaning. Her eyes wander beyond the nutmeg to the cocoa trees. She sees the little suckers, weak, pale green, pushing themselves out from the sides of the tree. When they start to come out like that, he had told her once, you have to cut them away, or they will suck the old tree dry. The daughter looks around her. Up the hill behind her, all around, there are old cocoa trees with young suckers poised to suck them dry. For some, it seems the suckers had already been left too long, had already taken over the tree, perhaps to produce for a while, and then to die sooner than the tree would have if it were tended properly. She believes this is what the father told her. That it wasn't right to leave the tree untended so that suckers could take over, because suckers wouldn't be able to do properly the job of the parent tree. Young ones had to wait their time.

There was one more tape, but this was probably the one she had listened to when she started. She searches for a voice and eventually hears what she heard before:

> . . . the way my stomach feeling. A few days now, I have this feeling as if I can't eat properly. It's as if there's something in my throat. And the pain. My stomach hurting again.

There is nothing more, on this side or the other. The voice is gone. No amount of moving fast forward, rewinding, listening, turning the tape over, brings it back.

The Nomadic Text: Exile and Translation
An Interview with Norman Manea

Sean Cotter

—Translated from Romanian by Sean Cotter

SINCE HE LEFT ROMANIA in 1986, during the last decade of Ceauşescu's oppressive rule, Norman Manea has become an important literary voice in the United States. He has published five books, including the collection of essays *On Clowns: The Dictator and the Artist* and the recent memoir *The Hooligan's Return*. Because he writes in the language of the country he left behind, translation has become a lifeline for his literary presence in America. From one perspective, we could say that each of his works must remake the author's transatlantic journey as it moves from Romanian to English. But his new host country exerts its own pressures on the process of creation. From another perspective we could wonder whether, after years of residence abroad, his mother language comes to him somewhat altered, already partially translated, when he uses Romanian words to refer to American events and emotions. By necessity, Manea has found himself preoccupied with translation in both the literal and figurative sense.

In English, Manea has contributed to many journals, including *Conjunctions*, the *New York Review of Books*, *Partisan Review*, *Salmagundi*, and the *New Yorker*. The following books have been translated into English: *October, Eight O'Clock* (1992), *On Clowns: The Dictator and the Artist* (1992), *Compulsory Happiness* (1993), *The Black Envelope* (1995), and *The Hooligan's Return* (2003). His as yet untranslated Romanian books are: *Noaptea pe latura lungă* (1969), *Captivi* (1970), *Atrium* (1974), *Primele porţi* (1975), *Cartea fiului* (1976), *Zilele şi jocul* (1977), *Anii de ucenicie ai lui August Prostul* (1979), *Pe Contur* (1984), and *Casa melcului* (1999).

Norman Manea

SEAN COTTER: As a Romanian writer living in the United States, how important is translation to your life?

NORMAN MANEA: For a writer in exile, the dependence on translation is an even more profound dilemma than regaining a certain social status. The first sentence of my 1984 collection of essays, published in Romania as, not at all accidentally, *On the Outline,* goes like this: "The unity of a people is, above all else, one of language." At that time, I truly believed that language was the matrix, the fundamental, formative factor of communication between the individual and community. I was convinced, by the same token, that writers should be categorized by the language in which they write, not by their ethnicity, religion, gender, political beliefs, or sexual orientation. During that period, I was attacked in the socialist press as "extraterritorial." That is, foreign, cosmopolitan, antinationalist, antiparty. Wasn't my position based, somehow, on the presumption of and the aspiration toward inclusion, not exclusion? Of course. Between "in" and "ex," my choice was clear.

In the end, however, I could not avoid becoming a true extraterritorial, expatriate, exile. Am I still, today, "inseparably" part of the people-language in which I was raised? Were they ever, in fact, "inseparable"? As we now see, I was separable and am now separated. Yet I have brought the language, the homeland, with me, to new shores, to foreign territory, so drastically different from what I had known. I take refuge today in its sinuous shell, like a snail. My relationship with my native country, already damaged in my childhood due to the Holocaust, still causes me tension and bitterness from time to time, but it is now, inevitably, diluted.

For someone who survived the Holocaust and a communist dictatorship, literary survival might seem trivial. What importance could a partial literary survival through translation have? Writing is a bizarre occupation, infantile in its seriousness, ravenous in its consumption of energy, illusions, obsessions, doubts. For a writer, literary survival, even through translation, is not at all negligible. Pompous as it may sound, translation, in my new social and linguistic residence, has become essential.

I have not profited from the opportunity of my dramatic plunge into exile to make an equally dramatic break with writing. Common sense, or the not quite tender age in which my exile occurred, should have been cause enough to disabuse myself of the chimera of writing. Still, I have continued the adventure begun in the difficult political conditions of my own country and language.

An author's exile has proven, more than once, to be his suicide. The simulacrum offered by translation, although just a substitute, a surrogate, a double, can provide some unexpected relief. The liberty given by exile is rather like a hotel room—functional, impersonal, and protective. Translation may be a similar refuge. I have often wished I had a personalized refuge, appropriate to myself and recognizable as such. The lack of a translator gifted enough to be the intermediary feeds my tension. Unable to usurp the new language, as Brodsky tried to do, I hope, at the least, to escape the standardization imposed by that impersonal language, the standard tongue of global translation. Not even Kundera was able to avoid this trap, nor I, nor many others, at the beginning of their exiles. Since then, Kundera has chosen to usurp, I do not know how successfully, the French language. If I had stayed in France or Germany, I too would have been tempted to take this risk. In English, I have the advantage of not being able to try.

COTTER: You have been translated into several languages. How much are you involved? How does the experience of being translated into English compare with that of being translated into other languages?

MANEA: I involve myself with my translations as much as I can. I check fidelity to content; I try to help, sometimes, finding more adequate, more expressive equivalents. I cannot do much more than that or even as much as one should. If I could, I would translate my texts myself. Here is the source of a deep and persistent frustration. Translation, as you well know, is not just an approximate linguistic transportation, but the rebirth, in another mental universe and another social context, of a specific literary reality. That is, of a specific author. As Wittgenstein says, "The boundaries of my language are the boundaries of my world." Romanian, with its Latin structure, is different from its sisters or cousins (French, Italian, Spanish, Portuguese), as much in its unmodernized old Latin roots as in its Slavic, Turkish, and Greek importations. The translation from and into these Latin languages, especially French, still seems easier. But to discourage any naive optimism, it would be useful to quote the opinion of one well versed in the subject. I am thinking of Cioran, the Romanian writer who not only "standardized" himself in the French language but also became one of its best-known stylists. Responding in 1957, from Paris, to the famous letter from his friend Constantin

Noica, still in Romania (the letter which would cost Noica years in a communist prison), Cioran speaks of his successful migration to Latin territory, from Romanian to French:

> It would be the narrative of a nightmare, were I to give you a detailed account of the history of my relations with this borrowed idiom, with all these words so often weighted, worked over, refined, subtle to the point of nonexistence, bowed beneath the exactions of nuance, inexpressive from having expressed everything, alarming in their precision, burdened with fatigue and modesty, discreet even in vulgarity. How should a Scythe come to terms with such terms, grasp their true meaning and wield them with scruple, with probity? There is not one among them whose exhausted elegance fails to dizzy me: no longer a trace of earth, of blood, of soul in such words. A syntax of severe, of cadaverous dignity encompasses them and assigns them a place from which God Himself could not dislodge them. What consumption of coffee, of cigarettes, and of dictionaries merely to write one halfway decent sentence in this unapproachable language, too novel and too distinguished for my taste! (Translated by Richard Howard.)

I quote this long and disturbing passage, not because I would follow his excessive nihilism, or his exaggerated sarcasm, or his typical and always shocking paradoxes, but precisely because these exaggerations convey the terrible trauma of a writer skinned and unsouled, forced to replace the internal organs of his linguistic being.

Should we call into play the "impossible return" of which Cioran writes? "I realized as much, unfortunately, only after the fact, when it was too late to change my course," he writes to his faraway friend, "otherwise I should never have abandoned our own country, whose odor of growth and corruption I occasionally regret, that mixture of sun and dung with all its nostalgic ugliness, in splendid squalor." Even if the nostalgia of the elements did not possess me (no, I am not drawn to dung and ugliness; I imagine they are available in any slang), I have had and do have many moments of hysterical helplessness in my new linguistic residence, where, in contrast to Cioran, I have not been able to reincarnate myself as a writer.

Are there any signs of hope? Yes, but also of paradox. Take, for example, a letter written to me from a Romanian writer who moved to Paris and "standardized" herself in French long ago, with many books in the borrowed language published in France. "It is not my country. . . . I have lost twenty years trying to breathe a bit of it through rhythm, through my frustration, fighting a musty, pompous vocabulary of politeness. You do not know what you avoided by keeping your Romanian. For me, it is a paradise I have lost, my young, vigorous language." Any writer forced into this kind of mutilation would understand her frustration. I think the same thing would happen to someone from China or England if he or she learned Romanian. The suffering is there, and it is not insignificant.

COTTER: I am interested in the collection of novellas *Compulsory Happiness*, which came into English through a French version. Which transformation do you think was more dramatic: the first, out of the original language, or the second, from the Latin culture into the American?

MANEA: *Compulsory Happiness* is, you are right, a translation of a translation. You would have to scrutinize the faithfulness of the translation from Romanian into French, and then the fidelity of the translation from French into English, and then, going back to the original Romanian text, to judge the losses imposed by the two literary transmutations. The solution we chose, far from perfect, seemed the only one available at the time. The result is not inferior, I think, to other books of mine, themselves far from perfectly translated. We were not able to completely avoid some quandaries, especially in some passages from the novella "Composite Biography," a text dense with details of socialist (we could better call it national communist) life in Ceaușescu's sinister last decade. The group of bureaucrats at the Bucharest bank in that novella becomes a miniature of Bakhtin's "laughing chorus of the masses." Their babbling back talk, a daily dialogue both jumbled and distinct, uses an ambiguous, sui generis slang. Their exchanges—which function as communication as well as provocation and entertainment—allow us to rediscover the turbulence and charm of the Romanian language, its fluidity, range of colors, sensuality, all the surprises of a flexible, playful, inventive orality. A kind of freedom—humor and conviviality in defiance of a dark and dangerous authority. Humor is never easy to translate, and an awkward translation can give rise at every step to involuntary ridiculousness.

COTTER: What is it that makes translating into English more difficult than other languages?

MANEA: In English, one encounters another way of thinking. It is difficult to find English equivalents for vaguenesses, metaphors, wordplay, lacunae, equivocal allusions, ironies, intertextual blur-rings, as they are practiced in Romanian literature. To embrace the American idiom, the text has to be retailored, incompatibilities eliminated, all that is too obscure or too specific. Naturally, a great translator, with the necessary time and dedication, can find brilliant equivalents for anything. Intermediaries of genius, unfortunately, are not found on every corner.

COTTER: I would like to ask you about your novel *The Black En-velope* and its long, complicated road toward translation. It is in-teresting that even though you rewrote the Romanian version especially for its translation into English, certain passages were still not translated into English. Why were those pages left out?

MANEA: The story of writing this novel, and its eventual publica-tion in Romania in 1986, is told in the essay "Censor's Report," in *On Clowns: The Dictator and the Artist.* There you can find many grotesque examples of censorship, including the text of a report signed by a former censor, willing to conspire with the publishing house to save my book from the pyre. The report instructs the author how to touch the book up so it could be published. But the censor still writes like a censor, suggesting that things could be arranged more easily if the author were willing to mask his intentions better. She is suggesting, in fact, that the categorical rejection with which censorship honored the manuscript had been, perhaps, rushed, and a deal is still possible. In the end, any bureaucrat, even a censor, is looking for "cover." This is what the censor's report implies. This ambiguity is precisely what makes the report interesting. It is very difficult, however, for a Western reader to see it as such, since the wooden, bureaucratic language of the censor (even smoothed out a bit) comes as a shock. She's not at all stupid or uncultivated. She uses the official code only to assure her credibility. With good intentions toward the press and the author, the censor tried to supply everyone involved with flexible alibis for compromise. Preparing the book for its translation and publication here, I put back some of the sections that had been cut, but I had to keep in mind the excessive codifica-tion the novel had undergone in the hysterical conditions of that era's censorship, and self-censorship. I tried, therefore, to simplify the text, to decode certain situations. Western readers still find the book too esoteric. Too cryptic. Without these simplifications, the book would certainly have been even more demanding, if not impenetrable. The Western reader does not have the "code" of conspiracy which the Eastern author and his public shared. This code worked even for deaf-mutes. The Deaf-Mute Association of the Socialist Republic of Romania plays a more than symbolic role in the novel. It is the key to the *Allegory of Prudence* (Titian's painting) that dominates the texture of the book and the mystifications imposed by the Single Party of a society reduced to autism. By the way, exile has not diminished my interest in deaf-mutes. At least in the beginning, the exile, now himself autistic, was impatient to understand the allegory in which he lived. If America's history had been different, and if John J. Flournoy, a farmer who mistook himself for a politician, had been able to found, in 1855, a state comprised solely of deaf-mutes, to be called Gallaudet, after Thomas Hopkins Gallaudet, the creator of a language of "signs" (American Sign Language), then, who knows, maybe I would have settled in that state. How amusing it is that I happen to hold a chair at Bard College, endowed by a man named Francis Flournoy. You are correct, certain paragraphs were taken out of the revised Romanian edition of *The Black Envelope*. This was due to the difficulties in transmitting the semantic, cultural, and social baggage of certain passages. These lines, for example, did not make the English version:

> —Ah, the letter! The Bachelor's letter . . . yes, the illustrious personage. The gun with a delayed effect . . .
> —Enough, Tolea, stop monkeying around. You didn't come here just to act out the national comedy.
> —Just that. You know, the slightest move, and bang. I draw the lost letter and bang.

The "national comedy" alluded to here is the brilliant and untranslatable *A Lost Letter*, by the classic Romanian author I. L. Caragiale. The parodic language of this passage—intelligible to the Romanian reader, for whom Caragiale's immortal text is fundamental to understanding the Romanian mentality of yesterday and today—has no relevance for the foreign reader. For the same reason, other, small portions of the text were omitted. I wonder how you as a translator would transmit to the American reader the resonance of certain expressions which for the Romanian reader are a part of his spiritual foundation. For example, *"Venerabile domn, în interesul onoarii naționale, te vom așa și pe dincolo. Făclia de pași, răzbunarea Domnului contra celor care l-au răstignit."* ("Venerable sir, in the interests of national honor, you are going to get a such and such. The

159

Easter torch, the Lord's revenge on those who crucified him.") Would an American reader know that the novella *An Easter Torch*, also by Caragiale, is one of the most powerfully anti-anti-Semitic works of Eastern Europe? Or these:

> *—Mizerabilul!*
> *—Nu râde, stimabile, nu râde. Eu merg mai departe şi zic: trădare să fie, dacă o cer interesele amorului, dar să n-o ştim! Baremi, să n-o ştim noi . . . vrei să vorbesc curat şi desluşit?*

> —Miserable cur!
> —Don't laugh, my good man, don't laugh. I will go even further and say: let it be treason, if called for in the interest of love, just do not inform us. Just don't tell us about it . . . do you want me to speak distinctly and plain?

> *Judecă-mă, Bombonel, judecă-mă . . . aşa e, am fost copilă şi copil am fost, şi am făcut nerozii. Dar dacă mă iubeşti, dacă ai ţinut tu la mine măcar un moment în viăţa, scapă-mă. . . de ruşine scapă-mă şi de vise, Bombonel!*

> Judge me, my Bon-bon, judge me . . . it's true, I was a little girl, a child I was, I acted the ninny. But if you love me, if you even cared for me but one moment in your life, save me . . . from shame, save me from dreams as well, my Bon-bon!

The language has not been "purified," as you can see, in the revised version of the book; rather, it has taken the risk of keeping its untranslatable inventions.

I would add that *The Hooligan's Return*, which was published in August, also has an allusion to Caragiale. In the last pages, the hooligan—that is, the author—shortly before he is to return from Bucharest to New York, begins a letter to the two dogs he has just seen passing in front of the hotel, at the other end of a leash from a high school classmate. The two mastiffs are named Lache and Mache, names which would remind a Romanian reader of two emblematic characters from Caragiale's sketches. The fact that an American or Western reader is foreign to this code is, still, in this case, not that important. Less important, probably, than the scene in which the returned exile suddenly encounters, in his hotel room, the ghost of E. M. Cioran, kneeling to ask God to forgive him for having been born Romanian. The nihilist addresses the All-Powerful, naturally, in a somewhat unconventional way: "*Pătlăgică*," he murmurs disconsolately, "forgive me, *Pătlăgică!*" It is difficult for me to believe that "pickled tomato" communicates, really, the entire flavor of the Romanian term *pătlăgică.*

COTTER: How "translated" does the second Romanian version of *The Black Envelope* seem to you?

MANEA: It is, without a doubt, "translated" from Romanian to Romanian, from the heavily amputated version published in 1986 to the version partially reconstructed for its publication in 1995, in the United States, in another language and social-political context. The 1986 version of *The Black Envelope* was supposed to be part of a trilogy that never came into being. The novel that was eventually published in 1995 in the United States was a rewritten, abridged version of the previous one. The book had a complicated fate, like that of its author, for that matter. These things happen in the life of a writer, strange things. Revising is an intense, all-consuming, but also somewhat more detached process, since rewriting, unlike writing, is no longer innocent. It is self-aware, forewarned.

The book is now less ample and layered, and it has stayed true, I'd like to believe, to its initial intentions. I have tried not to betray my project. Rewriting revealed some of the charades hidden in the 1986 pages, making them accessible, intelligible, as much as this was possible. The language of encrypted meaning was no longer necessary, nor were the excessive psychological and descriptive details I used with the intention of overwhelming and misleading the censors, the Romanian reading police. This does not mean that I eluded all traps of translation, bringing the fluid, swampy, lyrical, whirling, slippery language of my Romanian novel into something much more sober, purified, precise, and logical.

COTTER: What can a Romanian reader see in your work that translation obscures for the American? By the same token, what does translation reveal to the American that the Romanian reader cannot see?

MANEA: The Romanian reader gets more of the style, I suppose, than what remains after the simplifications, the inevitable, restrictive rationalizations of English translation. To take two minor examples at random from the revised edition of *The Black Envelope*: when Mila Ianuli is called "*Curvoiul, măreața Circe, putoarea, leoaica, tigresa și scroafa cutreierând, imperială, orașul, ronțăind mereu alte fragede oscioare de cavaleri imprudenți*" (the grandiose

Circe, the scumbag Superwhore, the lioness, the tigress, and sow roaming imperially through the city, crunching the dainty little bones of her careless knights), or when the maid at the Hotel Transit is called, as a joke, *"Vasilică,"* the masculine diminutive of *"Vasile,"* instead of the feminine diminutive, *"Vasilica,"* by the socialist mafioso who wants to humiliate and intimidate her, the Romanian reader understands, I would say, more than the foreigner. When my stories take place in Romania, the Romanian reader is more familiar with the setting. Even when the pieces have a somewhat vague geographic location, Romanian readers may recognize themselves in them more easily. American readers, I imagine, see more of the exoticism of the situation, its bizarreness, which might be exactly what interests them. They encounter another kind of reality, very different from Western societies. I would still hope they find a recognizable sensibility, shared concerns, beyond the different cultural contexts and conflicts. In fact, they may see more clearly and acutely, because of their distance and detachment from the context, the essence of these conflicts.

COTTER: You have lived away from Romania for sixteen years, exiled to a country in which you are dependent upon translation for your literary survival. How is exile like the process of translation? Is translation a kind of textual migration?

MANEA: There are, without a doubt, many similarities. Translation is also a process of migrating from a place (a language) of *departure* to a place (a language) of *destination.* In the same way, it is a process of rebirth and adaptation of the text, the nomadic text, to a new context. Assimilation entails the translation of the ego into another language and culture, where it tries to find its place and its expression. To find, that is, a new identity. The exile, in the end, is a hybrid, a compromise between what he brought with him and what he acquires later. Only the second or third generation can speak, truly, of having been formed by the new country.

Translation provides a new linguistic form for the old content. We find, in the process of linguistic relocation, many of the modulations which the exile experiences himself. The text is a living body, a being. The final product must belong entirely to the new language, to the target language, as they say, not to the old language. The transformation takes a defined period of time, and the result is already beached on the new shore, in the new linguistic territory, the new textual residence. In contrast, the exile often swings, for a long time, if not forever, between the past and the present. Between formation—deformation—reformation, between different possible egos until, gradually, *the double* appears to represent him on the new social stage. This split or even multiple personality needs a long time to coalesce and present itself intelligibly within the new social framework.

Translation operates in the same way, and when it does work, it confers on the foreign, exiled text a legitimacy, residence, "citizenship" in the new language. A cultural and social status. It has partaken, that is, of the flexibility demanded of author, as an exile, so that he can articulate himself in the new world, the world in which he finds himself shipwrecked.

COTTER: Is there an osmosis, through which the new country absorbs the exile?

MANEA: Without a doubt. Osmosis, as you say, is exactly it: loss and gain, wound and revitalization, the fracture of the old and the nutrition of the new, an intense exchange of energies.

Exile is an extraordinary process of education and reeducation, especially for those who come to the new country as adults. Confronted with a different history and social context, a different language, different conventions, the newcomer is reschooled by these various, versatile, new challenges. This self-critical process of reevaluation does not keep him from finding the eternally human in the new conditions, beyond all apparent differences. At some point the circle almost closes on this accidental route, relevant to and revelatory of the human experience, but one does not return to the starting point. Where one begins and where one ends are poles of a privileged existential adventure, with intense suffering and exaltation.

This great school of pointlessness, of dispossession, and in the end, of death, the ultimate dispossession (exile contains, I believe, a profound initiation in, a preparation for the end) does not exclude scenes of extraordinary jubilation. Feelings of rebirth are gifts of inestimable worth to us in our ephemerality.

COTTER: How has your literary language changed since you left Romania?

MANEA: It may, in part, have dried out. It has become essentialized, more laconic now, and I imagine more precise. I am not at all sure that this is a good thing, artistically speaking. Nor perhaps the fact that it has had to become more epic, more factual, more descriptive. My analytical predisposition no longer allows me to spoil myself, as I had often done, with extended, excessive speculations. I face, continually, the danger of domesticating my language. I try to resist, as much as possible, the pressures of translation.

Stylistically speaking, my language has more limitations, probably. It is less risky, with fewer lexical adventures, fewer daring inventions. I am facing a new linguistic universe here but I am also entering another age. Finding a fraternal translator would have stimulated me, possibly, to try extravagant experiments, sure that he would find a seductive linguistic equivalent for even my most exuberant flights of fancy.

Beyond the daily facts of existence, the linguistic shock of exile was, for my sensibility, a kind of second "holocaust." Schooled early on in the traumas of dislocation and dispossession, of foreseeable and unforeseeable danger, I was susceptible, I admit, to this kind of cataclysm. Yet, I can no longer stand the old role of victimhood. It sickens me. I try as much as I can to avoid becoming a specialist in lamentation.

COTTER: What compelled you to keep writing?

MANEA: As Theodor Adorno put it, "For a man who no longer has a homeland, writing becomes a place to live." I would rather say that even for a writer who has a homeland, writing is his real place, his real homeland. This was certainly my case. I could not have survived in Romania without writing; I could not have survived in America without continuing to write, although this time in a drastically different environment.

To go on living, I've always needed some kind of support system. The best choice turned out to be an illusory support. Writing. I didn't have the power to indulge in absolute solitude, absolute depression, absolute muteness. As an old survivor I needed to believe I had a chance at literary survival here, however fantastic or idiotic it may seem. A chance to find my balance through writing. Even a chance to reach some readers? The immersion in writing and the act of communication, though hypothetical, between myself and a virtual reader-interlocutor (I am resigned to having a small audience; even in Romania my readers were not filling stadiums) offered me the necessary illusion. I tried, as best I could, to keep my integrity under Romania's socialist dictatorship as I have tried here too in a free capitalist society with its often carnivalesque literary market.

Compromises are a part of life. Even literary compromises. Some even say that compromise has helped my writing, given it clarity and force. Who knows? The human condition is by definition flawed. Victories and failures and compromises are all imperfect, and we take them as they come. Exile too is not just a negation, but a metamorphosis; sometimes it's regenerative, not just destructive. As with everything human and everything extreme, the extremely human condition of exile contains both loss and gain, hopelessness and hope. The trauma of translation has also had positive effects. It has happened more than once that in checking an imperfect translation, I have discovered certain word choices I like better than in the original. I have then changed the original Romanian to a word translated from English. Translation may sometimes be, as the Romantics said, the best literary criticism. You are forced to see where the text is clumsy.

COTTER: I once heard you quote Hannah Arendt saying, "What remains? The mother tongue remains." What are your thoughts about this?

MANEA: I am a tenant, not an owner of the English language. I have the ordinary linguistic skills necessary for a social life in this second language, but I still write in Romanian. At home with my wife I speak Romanian. Daily events are expressed between us in Romanian.

I was born in Romania, in Romanian. Beyond the complications of my "foreignness" as a Jew, the Romanian language remains at the center of my existence. The machinery that rules my thought is Romanian. Ideas come in Romanian, likewise my dreams and nightmares. The work of a writer, including the work you do while looking at the river or the sky, takes place in the mind, which for me is Romanian. I would love to repeat Joyce's words from *Finnegans Wake:* "The word is my Wife, to exponse and expound, to vend and to velnerate, and may the curlews crown our nuptias! Till Breath us depart!" A eulogy to every language, to the marriage and the incest of language and writer. When I am faced with an American interlocutor, a dialogue takes place, immediately and naturally, in English, the rented language serving social communication. There is an "outsidedness" when you use the new language for personal feelings of love, hate, irony. It appears artificial. You can use broad expressions without dealing with their emotional implications, you simply recite them. They have not won their inner linguistic purchase. The same thing happens, I suppose, during the act of sex, when you whisper in the adopted language interjections demanded by the moment, just as you have heard them in movies or read in books. You borrow clichés for real experiences. These interferences, "osmosis," if you like, appear and grow with time. Some English expressions depict certain situations better, just as some Romanian expressions, without English equivalents, do for others. Paradoxically, you discover in exile not only the language of the country into which you have been translated, but you often rediscover your own language. A forgotten saying suddenly surprises you with its extraordinary flexibility, its uncanny, inspired inventiveness. It is suddenly irresistible. In the midst of your daily routine in the old country, you might take no note of it since it is hidden as it were beneath "normal" language. But now, suddenly, here, so far from home, you suddenly feel its amazing phosphorescence and sonority.

COTTER: Is it possible that a book written in exile would be better, more in its "linguistic skin," once it has been translated?

MANEA: What could "better" mean here? Whether the translated language would be more fitting than the original, than the language of the author? Or whether an excellent translation can make a book better than it was in the original? Such aberrations are probably possible. There is a lot of subjectivity involved in judging a case like this. Some of my Polish friends tell me *Hamlet* sounds better in Polish than in the language of Shakespeare! Pnin, the hero of Nabokov's novel of the same name, argues something similar for the Russian *Hamlet*. We find, for the sake of balance, the following in a recent essay by Stanley Kaufman:

> I, meekly monolingual though I am, will never forget my discomfort at hearing Jean-Louis Barrault's Hamlet say, "Être ou non être," which made me realize, haughtily, that no Frenchman will ever hear the six gigantically simple monosyllables of the original line. I felt that Shakespeare was not being translated but was being drowned in French. (On the other hand, it was depressing because it emphasized that I will never know—really know—Molière.)

I won't exclude the possibility that certain phrasings may be more successful in a language other than the original. If it happens, so much the better. We don't have to be scandalized by such surprises, however absurd they seem. We should take advantage of such miracles. Lord knows, we have too many unpleasant and ominous surprises to cope with every day to ignore the benefits of unexpected opportunities. In any case, we should not forget that without the original text, the translation—good or bad—would not exist. It is interesting for an author to note that the same book, translated into different languages, can enjoy very different receptions—great success in one place, utter silence in another. I have sometimes wondered if the lesser success of my books in France, setting aside some trivial reasons for this that are obvious to me, is not due to that which is non-Latin about me, my expressionist side, my Nordic, Bucovinan airs, but this would not explain the success my books have enjoyed in Italy.

COTTER: You have written that one of the problems facing a writer under communism was the risk that his work would remain readable only to those who have lived under the same rule. Twelve years after the fall of communism, do you still feel the same?

MANEA: In the summer of 1989, while Eastern Europe was caught up in the excitement of freedom, Richard Lourie, who translated from Russian to English, and Alekesei Mikhalev, who translated from English to Russian, co-authored an interesting article in the *New York Times Book Review*. "Why You'll Never Have Fun in Russian" lists some of the incompatibilities of the two languages and cultures. Words such as *kommunalka, vozhd, gosudarstve, normalno* have no English equivalents, and "privacy," "to have fun," "efficiency," and "take care," cannot be understood, entirely, by a Russian reader. The difference between a communist society and global capitalism is reflected in everyday language. But beyond these circumstantial disjunctions, the authors mention that Nabokov devoted roughly ten percent of his book on Gogol to the translation of the word *poshlost*—an abstract noun meaning the consequences of moral "viscosity," false self-regard and false beauty, mediocrity proud of itself. Let me quote just one short passage of the two translators:

> English no longer has "thou," no pronoun for the intimacies of love and contempt, and Russian has no verb "to be" in the present tense, so that the simplest affirmation—I am— becomes an uncommon construction. In English we are always "getting"—getting married, getting promoted—but the Russian verb for getting, *dostat*, reflects a society of scarcity and implies chancy expeditions or fabulous strokes

of luck. Russian has a single word for "happiness" and "luck," suggesting that happiness is more a matter of good fortune than an inalienable right.

These differences will not disappear in the course of the planetary convergence of modernity and capitalism. Seamus Heaney's essay "The Impact of Translation" analyzes the poem "Incantation," written by Czeslaw Milosz and translated by the author and Robert Pinsky. Heaney notes that "unabashed abstract nouns and conceptually aerated adjectives (glorious, beautiful, universal, despair, and so on) should have been altogether out of the question." He means a poem which "aspire[s] to deliver what we had once long ago been assured it was not any poem's business to deliver: a message." That is, truths, which "we assumed to be previous to poetry, so richly established outside its formal citadel that they could never be admitted undisguised or untransmuted through the eye of the lyric needle." He is describing another age of poetry, connected to different ages of civilization in the two countries of the poem and its translation. Although he allows that the poem's force consists, in the end, in "the intense loss we recognize behind its proclamation of trust," Heaney admits that the emotional connection the poem creates between its author and its Western reader "is effected in great part by our awareness of the context from which Czeslaw Milosz's text emerges." Translations from East European "dissident" poetry have created a conception of a new literary tradition, as well as "a modern martyrology, a record of courage and sacrifice which elicits our unstinted admiration."

When we speak of the isolation of East European literature under communism, we do not mean, obviously, official literature, good or bad, but literature which is directly or indirectly anticommunist, often encrypted, connected to a dramatic situation and specific to a place, at times excessively so. We also mean a literary tradition which communism, as a result of its attempted rapes, forced to return to its old obligations: inspiration and message. Referring to poets "tested by dangerous times," the future Nobel laureate distinguishes those who write in the *indicative* and thereby become a shadowy challenge for those who have remained in the *conditional*, the undetermined which "has grown characteristic of so much poetry one has grown used to reading in journals and new books, particularly in the United States." I admit that I, in Romania, often wrote in the conditional, optative, presumptive, and so forth. We may well wonder how precise or approximate this generalization may be, but it is certain that today, more than a decade later, the world of the East, and therefore its literature, is moving closer, however slowly and protractedly, toward the West. Thematically there will be more and more similarities, even while the dissimilarities, not just in terms of style, will remain, for some time, marked, just as the individual will remain, always, the true subject of literature. The exotic, extreme situations of the past have slowly become clichés, more digestible for the masses, but, maybe, more perishable at the same time. Of the enormous volume of literature written under and about communism, not many books will last. The reader will find in them sufficient cause for reflection, not just on the past but also the present, on some of the bizarre and maybe marginal similarities of communist dictatorship to democratic society, in fact on human nature itself.

COTTER: What is the context of the exile?

MANEA: "Context" refers to the relations between the individual and the collective, between the citizen and the state, as well as among the numerous individuals who live inside each one of us. Comparing the exile with people who stay at home in the place of their birth reveals some distinguishing features, naturally. Aggressive "distortions" (to recall, again, dispossession and dependence) bring with them the incentive of uncertainty. Conscious or unconscious mimeticism often marks the childishness inherent in the spectacle of assimilation. The exile has new, particular themes for reflection. He spends most of his time analyzing the changes in himself and in those around him, but always under the monopolizing pressure of survival within a situation whose code he does not yet grasp. His only relaxation is the happiness of expressing himself, completely, in his native tongue, exiled together with him. The acute sensation of uncertainty—of having been hurled, unexpectedly, into the void, forced to accept the absolute ineffability of fate, robbed of his familiar expressions, both true and false—this is exile. The terror of negation, of annulment, can either drastically undermine one's mental stability, or it can fuel its creativity. It does not allow that much time, however, for the analytical exercise it deserves. For a writer, the danger of ending up as a character is not negligible.

COTTER: What does it mean for an Eastern European author to be translated today, as opposed to before the fall of communism in 1989?

MANEA: Translations from Eastern Europe no longer benefit from the more strictly political interests in the area. The situation today has become more or less normalized—cultural foundations, professional connections, frequent visits. None of which means that there is a great interest in that part of the world. The East has lost some of its extravagance and provocation. Even "exile" has lost its former vogue, "multiculturalism" having moved in other directions. In the end, the pulse of global cultural life today is dominated by economic-commercial factors. Translations have to contend with the small interest in literature in general. The pressures of television, of the Internet, of all that is vulgar, politics included, remain the most obvious causes. Still, this situation is not that unnatural.

COTTER: You have called translation "a terrible trauma." Are there authors better suited for translation?

MANEA: Balzac, of course, seems easier to translate than Proust. Modern literature is more complicated, generally speaking. It revolves around rupture, with a certain Baroque style. Art comes in all shapes and sizes. The fact that an author is hard to translate has nothing to do with his value, nor does the fact that he is not translated at all, if that's the case. In recent years, several articles have been written on new translations of Thomas Mann and Dostoevsky, which are supposed (finally!) to show their true worth. After how many decades and editions and millions of readers? As a young man, all the authors who fascinated me I read in translation. Russians, French, English, Americans, Germans, Latin Americans, Italians, Scandinavians. During the years of Stalinism, the great literature of Russia, as well as French and English realism, and German romanticism. Then, as much as liberalization allowed, contemporary Western literature. Who can tell now whether I had the best possible translations? In Romania after 1960 several excellent translations exerted a strong influence on the culture: the Kafka moment and the Proust moment and the Joyce moment, the Faulkner moment, the Latin American moment, as well as the Orwell, Koestler, and Solzhenitsyn moments, acquired and read in secret, in languages other than Romanian. The cultural and educational role of translations cannot be underestimated. In today's world of conglomerates,

English, corrupted through intense use around the globe, has become the planetary language.

COTTER: What and who should be translated from Romanian?

MANEA: Hard to say. I have tried, from time to time, to convince various American presses to publish a range of different Romanians, some already translated into other languages. Lucian Raicu, George Bălăiţă, Gabriela Adameşteanu, M. Blecher, Marta Petreu, Virgil Duda, Mihail Sebastian, Mircea Cărtărescu, Florin Mugur, Mariana Marin, Ion Vartic, and others. No success. I have other proposals in mind as well, plenty of names, new and old. There are many talented Romanian authors who deserve attention. They are not easy to promote, I can assure you. Again, this does not seem unnatural to me. It happens in all cultures and especially so in dominant cultures. History, including the history of literature, has shown that it is not easy to love your neighbors as yourself.

COTTER: Can we imagine a particular way in which Romanian literature would have an impact on American culture?

MANEA: I could not even define a literature precisely, be it American, Romanian, or Iraqi. Writers are very different, one from the other, and we prize them precisely for their originality, their distinctiveness. A mosaic impossible to synthesize, each literature having some of all possible currents of creativity and the most wanton individual experiments.

In 1989, Seamus Heaney spoke of "the note sounded by translated poetry from that world beyond—pitched intently and in spite of occupation, holocaust, concentration camps, and whole apparatus of totalitarianism" defining it as "credible, desolating, and resuscitative." Poetry in English of the century did not follow these kinds of creative directions, and the Irish poet explains why:

> We have not lived the tragic scenario which such imaginations presented to us as the life appropriate to our times, our capacity to make a complete act of faith in our vernacular poetic possessions has been undermined. Consequently, we are all the more susceptible to translations which arrive like messages from those holding their own much, much further down the road not taken by us—because, happily, it was a road not open to us.

Impressed, yes, even susceptible to outside influences, but without

171

great consequence for the landscape of English and American poetry. Individually, influences can be, possibly, probably, detected. Writers are first of all readers. They form themselves through their often chaotic readings, which create the catharsis of miraculous encounters, unleashing kinetic energies. Readings can be and actually are, most often, not only domestic, but also foreign: French, Russian, Nigerian, Japanese, Indian, Australian. Novels and poems and children's books or travel books or even cookbooks (Flaubert once called a famous contemporary chef the greatest prose writer of his time).

Formative influences are sometimes widely felt, of course, especially at a literature's beginning (the influence of France on Romanian literature, for example, or that of England on American literature). Once the culture has matured, however, these influences remain, at the most, individual.

I was completely shocked to hear, a few months ago, of a young American intellectual, who upon hearing my name mentioned at a party of Bard College professors, declared that my collection of essays *On Clowns* had changed his "life," awakening a great interest in Eastern Europe and the issues discussed in the book. I should balance out this unexpected event by telling what an American writer around my age said to me about ten years ago. She had decided never to read East and Central European literature again. It was supposedly too "claustrophobic." I don't know if she had read Hasek, but I'm sure she didn't know of Caragiale, Tudor Arghezi, Mihail Sadoveanu, Panait Istrati, or other writers from a pool of remarkable creative diversity. Whatever they may be—Romanian, Czech, Russian, Baltic, or Greek—they are not claustrophobic. So there you are: the impact you speak of has, sometimes, a wide range of effects, often contradictory. But only for individuals, as is natural. We should remind ourselves that Proust only found himself through Ruskin's translations. In translation, in writing as translation, he found a model and voice. "I have two more Ruskins to finish," he wrote to Barrés in 1904, "and after that I will try to translate my poor heart, if I haven't died by then." We can never emphasize the importance of translations enough, for the expansion of knowledge, for dialogue among nations. Especially, though, for the individual discovery of unforeseen, great friends. More important friends than those we meet in the morning for a coffee.

From The Gravedigger's Daughter
Joyce Carol Oates

I.

SCHWART! THAT'S A JEW-NAME, yes? Or do I mean—He-brew?

No. A German name. He and his family were German Protestants. Their Christian faith derived from a Protestant sect founded by a contemporary of Martin Luther in the sixteenth century.

A very small sect with very few followers in America.

II.

In America. Surrounded by crosses.

He'd brought his family across the Atlantic Ocean to this: a grave-yard of stone crosses.

"What a joke! Joke-on-Jay-cob."

He laughed, there was genuine merriment in his laughter. His fingers scratching his underarms, his belly, his crotch, for God is a joker. Weak with laughter sometimes, snorting with merriment, leaning on his shovel until tears streamed down his whiskery cheeks and dribbled the shovel with rust.

"Jay-cob rubs his eyes, this is a dream! I have shat in my pants, this is my dream! *Am-er-i-ka.* Every morning the identical dream, eh? Jay-cob a ghost wandering this place tending the Christian dead."

Talk to yourself, there's no one else. Could not talk to Anna. Could not talk to his children. Saw in their eyes how they feared him. Saw in the eyes of *those others* how they pitied him.

But there was the *little one.* He had not wanted to love her for he had expected her to die. Yet she had not died of the bronchial infection, she had not died of the measles.

"Rebecca."

He was coming to speak that name, slowly. For a long time he had not dared.

One day, Rebecca was old enough to walk unassisted! Old enough to play Not-See with her father. First inside the house, and then outside in the cemetery.

Oh! oh! where is the little one hiding!

Behind that grave marker, is she? He would Not-See her.

She would giggle, and squeal in excitement, peeking out. And still Pa would Not-See.

Eyes squinted and pinched for he'd lost his damn glasses some-where. Taken from him and snapped in two.

The owl of Minerva soars only at dusk.

That was Hegel: the very priest of philosophy admitting the failure of human reason.

Oh! Pa's eyes scraped over the *little one* without seeing her!

It was a wild tickle of a game. So funny!

Not a large man but in his cunning he'd become strong. He was a short stocky man with the hands and feet, shameful to him, of a woman. Yet he wore the previous caretaker's boots, cleverly fitted out with rags.

174

To the Milburn officials he had presented himself with such courtesy, for a common laborer, they had had to be impressed, yes?

"Gentlemen, I am suited. For such labor. I am not a large man but
I am strong, I promise. And I am—" (what were the words? he knew
the words!) "—a faithful one. I do not *cease.*"

In the game of Not-See the *little one* would slip from the house
and follow him into the cemetery. This was so delicious! Hiding
from him she was invisible, peeking out to see him she was invisible, ducking back behind a grave marker quivering like a little animal, and his eyes scraping over her as if she was no more than one of
those tiny white butterflies hovering in the grass. . . .

"Nobody. There is nobody there. Is there? A little ghostie, I see?
No!—nobody."

At this early hour, Pa would not be drinking. He would not be
impatient with her. He would wink at her, and make the smack-
smack noise with his lips, even as (oh, she could see this, it was like
light fading) he was forgetting her.

His work trousers were tucked into his rubber boots, his flannel
shirt loosely tucked into the beltless waist of his trousers. Shirt
sleeves rolled up, the wiry hairs on his forearms glinting like metal.
He wore the gray cloth cap. His shirt was open at the collar. His jaws
moved, he smiled and grimaced as he swung the scythe, turning
from her.

"Little ghostie, go back to the house, eh? Go, now."

The wonderful game of Not-See was over—was it? How could you
tell when the game was over? For suddenly Pa would not-see her, as
if his eyes had gone blind. Like the bulb-eyes of the stone angels in
the cemetery, that made her feel so strange when she approached
them. For if Pa didn't see her, she was not his *little one;* she was not
Rebecca; she had no name.

Like the narrow grave markers, some of them laid down flat in
the grass like tablets so weathered and worn you could not see the
names any longer. Graves of babies and small children, these were.

"Pa . . . !"

She didn't want to be invisible anymore. Behind a squat little grave
marker tilting above a hillock of grass she stood, trembling.

Could she ride in the wheelbarrow? Would he push her? She would
not kick or squeal or act silly she promised! If there was mown
grass in the wheelbarrow, not briars or grave-dirt, he would push
her. The funny old wheelbarrow lurching and bumping like a
drunken horse.

175

Her plaintive voice lifted thinly. "Pa . . . ?"

He seemed not to hear her. He was absorbed in his work. He was lost to her now. Her child-heart contracted in hurt, and in shame.

She was jealous of her brothers. Herschel and August helped Pa in the cemetery because they were boys. Herschel was growing tall like his father but Gus was still a little boy, spindly-limbed, his hair shaved close to his bumpy skull so that his head was small and silly as a doll's bald head.

Gus had been sent home from school with lice. Crying 'cause he'd been called Cootie! Cootie! and some of the kids had thrown stones at him. It was Ma who shaved his head, for Pa would not come near.

Who was she: Rebecca? "Reb-ek-ah." Ma said it was a beautiful name for it was the name of her great-grandmother she would never see in this lifetime. But Rebecca wasn't so sure she liked her name. Most of all she did not like who-she-was: *a girl*.

For Ma was always brushing her hair, plaiting her hair to make her scalp hurt. And scolding her if she protested. And if she got dirty, or ripped her clothes. Or shouted loud like her brothers.

Rebecca, you are a *girl*, you are *not a boy* like Herschel and August.

"Pa."

She was whining, half-sobbing. Oh she knew this was wrong, this was a mistake, yet she could not help herself. Trailing after Pa when it was clear he didn't want her, asking could she help? Could she help him?

What Rebecca could do in the cemetery: pull some of the smaller weeds, carry broken tree branches and storm debris to the wheelbarrow. She would not scratch herself on the briars or stumble on the hill and hurt herself. (Her legs were covered in bruises. Her elbows were scabbed.) She was overcome by a need to help her father, to make him see her again; and a wink and make the smack-smack noise that was a noise only just for *her*.

That light in Pa's eyes, she yearned to see that light in Pa's eyes, a flash of love for her, even if it was annoyed love, even if it so quickly faded.

She ran, and she stumbled.

"Damn! I *said*."

He was impatient with her. He was not smiling. His face was shut up tight as a fist.

He was pushing the wheelbarrow through the dense grass like he hoped to break it. His back was to her, his flannel shirt sweated through. In a sudden terror of childish helplessness she watched him move away from her as if oblivious of her. This was Not-Seeing, now. This was death.

Pa shouted to her brothers who were working some distance away. His words were scarcely more than grunts with an edge of annoyance, no affection in them and yet: she yearned for him to speak to her in that way, as his helper, not a mere girl to be sent back to the house.

Back to Ma, in the house that smelled of kerosene and cooking odors.

Deeply wounded she was. So many times. Till at last she would tell herself that she hated him. Long before his death and the terrible circumstances of his death she would come to hate him. Long she would have forgotten how once she'd adored him, when she was a little girl and he had seemed to love her, sometimes.

The game of Not-See.

III.

Herschel growled, Promise you won't tell 'em?

Oh, she promised!

'Cause if she did, Herschel warned, what he'd do is shove the poker up her little be-hind—"Red hot, too."

Rebecca giggled, and shivered. Her big brother Herschel was always scaring her like this. Oh no oh *no.* She would *never tell.*

It was Herschel who told her how she'd been born.

Been born like this was something Rebecca had done for herself but could not remember, it was so long ago.

Never would Rebecca's parents have told her. Never-never!

No more speaking of such a secret thing than they would have disrobed and displayed their naked bodies before their staring children.

So it was Herschel. Saying how she, just a tiny wriggly thing, had gotten born on the boat from Europe, she'd been born in *New York Harbor.*

On the boat, see? On the water.

The only one of the damn family, Herschel said, born this side of the 'Lantic Ozean that never needed any damn vissas or papers.

Rebecca was astonished, and listened eagerly. No one would tell her such things as her big brother Herschel would tell her, in all the world.

But it was scary, what Herschel might say. Words flew out of Herschel's mouth like bats. For in the Milburn cemetery amid the crosses, funerals, mourners, and graves festooned with flowerpots, in the village of Milburn where boys called after him *Gravedigger! Kraut!* Herschel was growing into a rough mean-mouth boy himself. He hadn't been a child for very long. His eyes were small and lashless and gave an unnerving impression of being on opposing sides of his face like a fish's eyes. And his face was angular, with a bony forehead and a predator's wide jaws. His skin was coarse, mottled, with a scattering of moles and pimples that flared into rashes when he was upset or angry, which was often. Like their father, he had fleshy, wormy lips whose natural expression was disdainful. His teeth were big and chunky and discolored. By the age of twelve, Herschel stood as tall as Jacob Schwart, who was a man of moderate height, five feet eight or nine, though with rounded shoulders and a stooped head that made him appear shorter. From working with his father in the cemetery, Herschel was acquiring a bull-neck and a back and

178

shoulders dense with muscle; by degrees he was coming more and more to resemble Jacob Schwart, but a Jacob Schwart smudged, distorted, coarsened: a dwarf grown man-sized. Herschel had bitterly disappointed his father by doing poorly in school, "kept behind" not once but twice.

As soon as they'd arrived in Milburn, Jacob Schwart had forbidden the speaking of German by his family, for this was an era of German hatred in America and a suspicion of German spies everywhere. Also, his native language had become loathsome to Jacob Schwart— "A language of beasts." And so Herschel, who'd learned German as a child, was forbidden to speak it now; yet scarcely knew the "new" language, either. Often he spoke with an explosive stammer. Often it sounded as if he was trying not to laugh. Talkin, it was some kind of joke? Was it? You had to know the right sounds to talk, how to move your mouth, God damn they had to be the sounds other people knew, but how'd these people *know?* The connection between a sound coming out of a mouth (where your damn tongue got in the way) and what it was supposed to mean drove him wild. And printed words! Books! Fuckin school! That some stranger, an adult, would talk to *him*, he was expected to sit his ass in a desk where his damn legs didn't fit, because it was New York State fuckin law, an look in their damn face? With them little kids, half his size? That stared at him scared like he was some kind of freak? And some old bitch titless female teacher? Why the hell? At the Milburn school where Herschel Schwart was ostensibly in seventh grade, by far the biggest boy in his class, he took "special education" courses and under state law would be allowed to quit at age sixteen. What a relief, to his teachers and classmates! As he could not speak any language coherently he could not read at all. His father's effort to teach him simple arithmetic came to nothing. Printed materials aroused him to scorn and, beyond scorn, if they weren't quickly removed from his glaring eyes, fury. His brother Gus's textbooks and even his sister's primers had been discovered torn and mutilated, tossed on the floor. In the Port Oriskany newspaper which Jacob Schwart occasionally brought home, only the comic strips engaged Herschel's interest and some of these—"Terry and the Pirates," "Dick Tracy"—gave him difficulty. Herschel had always been fond of his baby sister, the *little one*, as she was called in the household, and yet he often teased her, a wicked light came into his yellowish eyes and she could not trust him not to make her cry. Herschel would tug at her braids that had been so neatly plaited by their mother; he would grin and tickle her

179

roughly beneath the arms, on her belly, between her legs to make her squeal and kick. Here he comes! Herschel would warn her. The *boa 'stricter!* This was a giant snake that wrapped itself around you but also had the power to tickle.

Even with Ma in the room staring at Herschel he would so behave. Even with Ma rushing at him crying, *Schwein! Flegel!*, slapping and punching him about the head, he would so behave. Physical blows from their mother made him laugh, even blows from their father. Rebecca feared her hulking big brother yet was fascinated by him, those lips expelling the most astonishing words like spittle.

That day, when Herschel told Rebecca the story of how she'd been born.

Been born! She was such a little girl, her brain had yet to comprehend that she hadn't always *been.*

Yah, she was a squirmy red-face monkey-thing, Herschel said fondly. Ugliest little thing you ever saw like somethin skinned. No hair, neither.

'Cause why it took so long, eleven damn hours, and everybody else dis-em-barkin the fuckin ship except them, her baby-head come out backward and her arm got twisted up. So it took time. Why there was so much blood.

So she *got born.* All slimy and red, out of their Ma. What's it called—'gina. Ma's hole, like. A hairy hole it is, Herschel had never seen anything like it. Nasty! Like a big open bloody mouth. Later he'd seen it, the hairs, between Ma's legs and up on Ma's belly like a man's whiskers, in the bedroom by accident pushing open the damn door and there's Ma tryin to hide, changin her nightgown or tryin to wash. You ever seen it? Thick hairs like a squirrel.

Hey, Herschel said, snapping his fingers in Rebecca's blank face.

Hey you think I'm fuckin lyin or somethin? Lookin at me like that?

Rebecca tried to smile. There was a roaring like thousands of mosquitoes in her ears.

You askin for the *boa 'stricter*, honey, are you?

Not the *boa 'stricter*, oh! Please not him.

Herschel liked to see Rebecca scared, it quieted him some. Saying she maybe thought he was makin' all this up, but he wa'nt. How'd you think you got born, eh? You somebody special? How'd you think anything gets born? Out of their Ma's hole. Not her asshole, nah not like a shit, that's somethin else, there's this other hole it starts out small then gets bigger, girls and wimmen got em, you got one too, want me ta show ya?

Rebecca shook her head no. No no!

You're just a li'l gal so you got one but it'd be real small like pea-size but for sure it's there inside your legs where you go pee-pee and where you're gonna get pinched, see? You don't b'lieve your brother Hershl.

Quickly Rebecca said yes she believed him! She did.

Herschel scratched his chest, frowning. Trying to recall. The shit-hole cabin they was stayin in, on the ship. Size of a doghouse. No windows. "Bunk beds." Damn mess of rags, squashed roaches an stale puke from Gus being sick, and everywhere stinkin of shit. Then, Ma's blood. Stuff comin out of her layin in the bunk bed. At last they was in New York Harbor and everybody crazy to leave the stinkin boat except them, they had to stay behind, 'cause of *her* wantin to be born. Pa said you wa'nt spost to be born for another month, like he could argue with it. We was all starvin, Christ sake. Ma got so 'lirious, it was like she wudna h'self but some wild animal-like. Screamin, some muscle or somethin in her throat broke, why she don't talk right now. An you know she ain't right in the head neither.

Some old lady was gonna help Ma get you born, but there we wuz "em-barkin" so she had to leave the boat, see. So it was just Pa. Poor Pa out of his head. All along, Pa was goin nuts with worry he said. Sayin what if they wudna let us land? in the Yoo Ess? what if they send us back to fuckin Nazizz they're gonna kill us like hogs. See, these Nazizz was comin after Pa at where he worked, he hadta leave. We hadta leave, where we was livin. We didn't always live like ani-mals, see, we wa'nt like this. . . . Shit, I don't remember too well, I was just a little kid scared all the time. They was tellin us there's Nazizz submarines—"torpedoes"—tryin to sink us, why we was zigzaggin an took so long to cross. Poor Pa, all the time he's lookin through this "money-belt" thing he got around his middle checkin the papers, the vissas. God damn you got to have them vissas with all kinds-a stamps an things, you ain't a Yoo Ess cit'zen, see the fuckers won't let you in if they can. Fuckers sure didn't want us lookin at us like we stunk! Like we was worse'n hogs 'cause we cudna speak right. All Pa could worry about on the boat was this papers gonna be stolen. Everybody stealin what they could, see. That's where I learned, snatchin things. You run, old people ain't gonna run after you. You're little enough, you can hide like a rat. A rat is littler than I am, I learned from em. Pa goes around sayin his guts was eat out by rats on that crossin. It's some joke of Pa's you got to 'preciate the old man's sense-humor. My guts was eat out by rats on the 'Lantic Ozean I heard him sayin to some old lady in the cemetery here she's puttin flowers on some grave an Pa gets to talkin to her, like he says for us never to do, talkin to *those others* you can't trust, but he's talkin an laughin that dog-bark laugh of his so she's lookin at him like she's scared of him. So I was thinkin Pa is drunk, he ain't got his right judgment.

On the boat, we had to eat what they give us. Spoiled food with weevils in it, roaches. You pick em out, squash em under your foot and keep on eatin, you're hungry enough. It's that or starve. All our guts was eat out by the time we landed and everybody shittin bloody stuff like pus but Pa was the worst 'cause of ulcers he said the fuckin Nazizz give Pa ulcers way back years before. Pa's guts ain't normal, see. Look at Pa, he wa'nt always like he is now.

Rebecca wanted to know how Pa used to be.

A vague look came over Herschel like a thought the wrong size for his skull. He scratched at his crotch.

Oh shit, I dunno. He wa'nt so excitable I guess. He was more happy I guess. Before the trouble started. Before I got too big, he'd carry me around, see? Like he does with you. Used to call me *Leeeb*—somethin like that. Used to kiss me! Yeah, he did. And this music him an Ma liked, loud singin on the radio—"oper-a." In the house they'd be singin. Pa would sing some, and Ma she'd be in some other room and she'd sing back, an they'd laugh, like.

Rebecca tried, but could not imagine her parents singing.

She could not imagine her father kissing Herschel!

They was diffr'nt then, see. They was younger. Leavin where we lived wore em out, see. They was scared, like somebody was followin em. Like the police maybe. "Nazizz." There was trains we rode on, real noisy. Real crowded. And the damn boat, you'd think the 'Lantic Ozean would be nice to look at, but it ain't, all-the-time the wind's blowin and it's damn cold an people pushin you an coughin in your damn face. I was little then, not like now, see nobody gave a damn about a kid if they stepped on me the bastids! The crossing, that wore em out. Havin' you 'bout killed Ma, an him, too. Nah it wa'nt your fault, honey, don't feel bad. It's the Nazizz. "Storm trooperz." Ma had nice soft hair and was pretty. Talkin diffr'nt langidge, see. Christ I was talkin this diffr'nt langidge "German" it was, bettern I can talk what-the-fuck's-this-now—"English." God damn why they got to be so diffr'nt I don't know! Makin more trouble. I mostly forget that other now but I don't know fuckin Eng-lish worth shit, either. Pa was like that, too. He knew to talk real well. He was a schoolteacher they said. Now, Christ they'd laugh! 'Magine Pa teachin in school!

Herschel guffawed. Rebecca giggled. It was funny: seeing Pa in front of a classroom, in his old work clothes and cloth cap, a stick of chalk in his hands, blinking and squinting.

No. You could not. You could not 'magine.

Herschel had been nine years old at the time of the 'Lantic crossing and would not forget through his fuckin life except he could not remember, either. Not clearly. Some kind of mist came down over his brain that ain't lifted since. For when Rebecca asked how long did it take to cross the ocean, how many days Herschel began to count on his fingers slowly then gave up saying it was a long fuckin time an there was lots of people died an dumped over the side of the boat like garbage for the sharks to eat, you was always scared you would die, this "dyzen-tery" sickness in the guts—that's all he knew. A long time.

Ten days? Rebecca asked. Twenty?

Nah it wa'nt days it was fuckin weeks, Herschel snorted.

Rebecca was just a little girl but already she needed to know: numbers, facts. What was *real* and what was only *made-up.*

Ask Pa, Herschel said, flaring up suddenly. Herschel would get mad if you asked him any question he couldn't answer like he'd gotten mad at his teacher at school once, she'd run out of the classroom for help. That cobweb look in Herschel's eyes and baring his yellow teeth like a dog. Saying, Ask Pa you're so hot to know all this old crap.

Looming over her, and his hand shot out, the edge of his hand, *whack!* on the side of her face so, next thing Rebecca knew, she was fallen over sideways like a rag doll, too surprised to cry, and Herschel was stomping out of the room.

Ask Pa. But Rebecca knew not to ask their father anything, none of them dared approach Pa in any way likely to *set him off.*

Letters to Peter
Fanny Howe

1955

Dear Peter:

When we met on the beach in Killiney, I was running away from my mother. She was driving me insane. I hope you didn't think I was crazy when I threw my teacup into the sea. Then, when it smashed on the rock, and you came up to me with a pair of false teeth, it was all really funny. I was just nervous. That's why I backed away laughing. I wasn't really scared of the teeth. You were nice, but I am back in America now and I doubt if we will ever meet again. I am fourteen. If you feel like it, write to me about your life.

1955

Dear Peter:

Well, now I am back in America. Everything seems really speedy and bright, but I can't stop remembering Ireland anyway. Even that gooseberry fool with Devonshire cream that we ate, and the smell of boxwood. Our walk around Sandymount and Ballsbridge. You are so tall, I feel like June Allyson or something. My uncle John did not approve of me seeing you. He knew your family but that wasn't why. He is so romantic with his motorcycle and his good looks and girlfriends, I don't know why he would be so suspicious and judging. But I can never really tell what he feels about anything, even me. He just doesn't trust me because I am American, or something. As if I would do anything!

He didn't need to worry since I hardly ever saw you all summer.
I don't blame you. You have your normal life and friends and I am a
stranger. At least we had a couple of good days together, and they
say that the way two people are together, when they first meet, is
the way they are always deep down.

Write to me, if you feel like it, though I doubt that you will.

1956

Dear Peter:

Thank you for your letter. Today it is snowing here. My parents are
out at a dinner party and I am babysitting my sister who is five.
Yes. I have a boyfriend now. You won't believe it but he is from
Ireland, named Liam Clancy. I am fifteen. He is seventeen. His
brother Tom lived in our basement for ages and my older sister
used to have a crush on his older brother Paddy. He's not at all
snobby like you. There is always a lot of theater stuff going on
around our house. Liam is writing beautiful songs for the Countess
Cathleen. He plays Aleel. He sings to me and plays the guitar. I bet
you have a girlfriend or two. I still think of that day we walked
over the stones to Sweet Pea Lane, and stood in the tunnel
together. You probably don't remember but you recited "The Song
of Wandering Aengus." You made a few promises you didn't keep.
But don't worry, I am used to that. My mother is sort of like you.
But she keeps promises, she just doesn't tell the truth. I am really
glad anyway to know you are at home from school for the
Christmas holidays.

1956

Dear Peter:

For some reason I bet you are lying. It just doesn't sound right. You
are having an affair with an actress twenty years older than you????
Well, maybe it is true. Liam is going to New York a lot to sing, and

an older woman wants to sleep with him and help his career, but
he won't. He always tells the truth. I still get furious at my mother
when she exaggerates, but I like coming home from school to see
her when she is still fine and funny. When she is working at the
Poets Theater she is fine too. I go there after school almost every
day and watch rehearsals or help out. Once I was in a play where
I said, one line, "Virtue's been struck a blow, a dreadful blow,"
and I stammered. I ruined it. Before that I was in a play and the
reviewer said, "She played the part of a child and acted like one."
In another play I said three words at the end: "Goodnight, Mr.
Ashbery."

It's fun being around the theater but I HATE being in plays. The
costume room next to the theater is a riot. Mr. Pankhurst lives
there and on freezing nights people dressed like fairies and pirates
run up Palmer Street to the theater from his place. Tell me more
about your life. I doubt if we will ever see each other again.

1956

Dear Peter:

Thank you for writing. I was amazed when the letter came. I wish
you could see where I live. To answer your question: I'm really
lucky. My father is a professor. McCarthy called him "pink."
Sometimes FBI men would come to the door at night. Alger Hiss
was his friend. Do you know any of these people? America is scary.
Our house is on the top of a hill with lots of trees around and my
mother has made a beautiful garden in back. We have a big screen
porch and a dog. We also have a piano for you to play if you ever
come here, which you won't.

I don't think my father likes Irish people much and he is married
to one. They seem wild to him, or something. He kicked one out
of the house (Desmond O'Grady, a poet) for being drunk. My
mother is not like other mothers in Cambridge. She acts
outrageous and lots of people don't get her jokes. She can be
a bitch. New Englanders get nervous easily. She makes them
nervous. They are so prissy. I hate grown-ups. Sometimes I hate

my mother. When she gulps down vodka in orange juice and gets all sloppy and vicious. My father hides in his study. They aren't happily married but like the same jokes. This is boring. Tell me about your family.

1958

Dear Peter:

My mother thinks she knows your mother and your family, and we might be related. Anyway, your life sounds exciting with all the music, riding your bike to conduct concerts, your brother and sisters, etc. Wow! I am boring. But guess what I did? I jumped over the wall like a nun. I escaped from a school outside Sèvres, where I was sent to improve my French. I hated it and got the gardener to help me escape. Then I went into Paris on a train, with no money, and called Mr. Beckett for help. He was my mother's friend in Ireland. We went to his play in London years ago and I sat beside him and dropped my candy bar down the seat in front of us and it stuck to a fat man's back and melted all through the play. The play was called "Waiting For Godot." That was just before I met you, I think, that summer.

Mr. Beckett has helped me survive for two weeks before my mother comes over. He is kind but not gooey. I feel he is telling me important things that I can't quite understand. I think he's an existentialist.

Well, I didn't get in to any colleges because I am such a bad student, so I am being sent into exile. To college in California where they still want people from the east coast. Even idiots. I was always bad in school, unlike you. I HATE it. It is JAIL! It's embarrassing because my older sister is superior to me. She is really beautiful, she reads all the time, she is a good student, and she looks like Orson Welles when she tips down her head and looks up from under. My mother worships her, and wants her to be an actress. They both read everything. I stupidly read the same things over and over again. I am better than my sister at languages, but that's not saying too much. Luckily I write poetry and she doesn't, so this gives me a thing that is completely my own. I love French poetry, even in French.

Is your older brother mean to you? Is he a musician too? Do you feel inferior to him? Liam went to New York with his brothers and all these older women who seduced him. He actually acted like he still liked me, but it is too hard for us to stay close. He is getting famous and far away. Sometimes I visit him in Greenwich Village but it doesn't make us happy the way it used to when we "both sat down together like sister and brother and listened to the nightingale sing." That was our song. Oh well, tell me about your life if you have time. It's raining today but the magnolias are in bloom and I have e. e. cummings to cheer me up with his spring poems. See you in three months, maybe, I hope.

1958

Dear Peter:

It was so great that you came all the way to Paris to see me! But my mother can be unbelievable. Sorry. She was spying on us, just as you thought, when we went into the hotel room alone and meanwhile she was flirting madly with Mr. Beckett. And we didn't do anything wrong. The best part was walking in the Tuileries with you while Mr. B peed in that pissoir by the tree. He wasn't even embarrassed. Did you like what he said about Descartes writing in the fireplace? I did. Supposedly Mr. Beckett's a good writer. Once someone came over and asked for his autograph while we were in a café. He was irritated and embarrassed. Then we went to see a great movie called "The Cranes Are Flying." His wife came with us. She didn't say anything. You weren't there yet and I never thought you would come because you don't know me. I want to be a writer, really a poet. Why, I don't know. I love poetry. I have a book with pictures of all the poets. The handsome men ones— Wilbur and Merwin—look so poetic, it seems that they were made to be what they were. But I guess I like Baudelaire better even if he looks stern and not handsome. Do you like his poems? I love Rilke and Anna Akhmatova. (I am a failure at school, by the way.)

You are obviously really smart and good at school. Why did you disappear? You don't keep your word very well. That's horrible. I waited at the Louvre. That night at the hotel I kept listening to the elevator coming and going and thinking maybe you would show up, but you didn't. I'm glad I never kissed you! Be brave. Tell me where you went and why. Will you be a composer and come to America someday? Mr. Beckett was very impressed. He said you had a very good mind and therefore you would find a way to ruin it!

1960

Dear Peter:

It has actually been two years since we saw each other. You never answered my last letter. So I don't know why I am writing to you. I am now at college in California. All my best friends went to college in Boston and New York, so I am very homesick. My parents put me on a plane and sent me here. They have never been to California, so I just got off the plane and found my way to a bus and the dorm alone. I am not feeling sorry for myself because it is so beautiful here. You would be too European to like it, but for some reason I love the palm trees and the flowers everywhere. Eucalyptus smells like boxwood.

I am still writing poetry and taking some great classes. One teacher in the Western Civilization class we have to take started on the first day by announcing, "Jesus was the first communist." All these students almost fainted with shock, but I knew what he meant. I was really glad to hear that about Jesus. The girls here are all blonde and perfect, except for my friends. I hate the ones we call "dollies" which is what they are. Weirdly, they are smart too. Everyone seems rich.

I love San Francisco!!!! It is the most beautiful city I ever saw. We take the train there on weekends and go to jazz concerts and poetry readings. I love the Beatniks. Some of them came from Cambridge. I love Kenneth Patchen and the Modern Jazz Quartet. You wouldn't know anything about these people, I bet. I wish I could show you around out here, but honestly I think you are probably way too

Fanny Howe

Irish to like California. And you would hate what a communist
I am.

So anyway I wonder what you look like now, and what you do.
Maybe we are really long-lost cousins. Maybe you don't even
remember me or the way we felt about each other inside the tunnel
in Sweet Pea Lane. I bet I will never see you again since we have
nothing in common. Apparently.

Love, Fanny

Night Music
Rebecca Seiferle

1.

"voice" is not only a manner of utterance
    there is so much light in the dark water
but a *mater* of being,
    the water bird seems to be fishing for nothing
so that form, even the apparent absence of
    but light, its beak, a thin needle of light
form
    threading the waters
is the attempt to create
    all the dark at its back, luminous,
another order
    like that river which was believed to circle
of time,
    the ancient world where we are still
that river which is full of prehistories and intoxicating
    watching for the winged messengers
drinks offered to lips of water
    so that we always begin with the simplest of faiths
naked or the color of blueberries
    full of the dust of ourselves

2.

that word, like many words,
    I kept confusing
has a *person*
    the vessel of the supposed
buried within it,
    hero with the monster he went to kill
so the mask is fashioned
    its eyes as many as mercy, its mouths as many as death,
until we forget ourselves

trying to stay alive as a happy animal,
though at moments in another's eyes
for what is a love but that
we still glimpse the face of the beautiful daughter
night music
peering out beneath that white skull,
of the human heart
a strange and terrible prize

3.

there was this ancient rule
full of a pain
that words could not be
as I am now
uttered
my own horned toad
as a thumb jammed into the mouth
weeping tears of blood
would choke off crying,
out in the garden,
piercing the ear of that most distant angel
the fear of love, the fear of death, the fear of not
who falls to the ground like a dead wren
that idle cat brought home

4.

he said that everything would change
I was listening to the radio
if the word "radio" were used in a poem
dancing not in body but in mind
because what is a poet
when suddenly I am, oh, somewhere else
but a night music
in another realm of being,
so full of pain and sounding so much like you,
and in that world, too, I love you and love you
for what are "you" finally
and I'm holding out my hand to you,
but the very body of night,

192

your hand resting lightly on my palm
a folded wing,
    our fingertips just touching
a tree full of birds
    as we begin to move . . .
A music
    So close and reserved
It will not show itself
    except by a dark light

5.

where am I
    I've gone miles past the turn back
when I'm absent-
    to my life, to the errands of the hungry
minded?
    cats and dogs, which I do easily, mindlessly
my mind, humming,
    loaded down
with bags and papers,
    walking into the house
my skin still strange and full of that night music
    into the bright and busy rooms

Spirit Birds
Stanley Plumly

The spirit world the negative of this one,
soft outlines of soft whites against soft darks,
someone crossing Broadway at Cathedral, walking
toward the god taking the picture, but now,
inside the camera, suddenly still. Or the spirit
world the detail through the window, manifest
if stared at long enough, the shapes of this
or that, the lights left on, the lights turned off,
the spirits under arcs of sycamores the gray-gold
mists of migratory birds and spotted leaves recognize.

Autumnal evening chill, knife-edges of the avenues,
wind kicking up newspaper off the street,
those ghost peripheral moments you catch yourself
beside yourself going down a stair or through
a door—the spirit world surprising: those birds,
for instance, bursting from the trees and turning
into shadow, then nothing, like spirit birds
called back to life from memory or a book,
those shadows in my hands I held, surprised.
I found them interspersed among the posthumous pages

of a friend, some hundreds of saved poems: dun
sparrows and a few lyrical wrens in photocopied
profile perched in air, focused on an abstract
abrupt edge. Blurred, their natural color bled,
they'd passed from one world to another: the poems,
too, sung in the twilit middle of the night, loved,
half-typed, half-written-over, flawed, images
of images. He'd kept them to forget them.
And every twenty pages, in xerox ash-and-frost,
Gray Eastern, Gold Western, ranging across borders.

Guests of Space (II)
Anselm Hollo

When in a mood of fair-
Ground music mortality   Drift
Down Feral Boulevard
Wearing your sentimental formal
To the bar called "The Far"
Sit down to a think
I won't be back
You won't be back
He She It won't
Nor will We You They
In the Twenty-First's air
And none of them
Will ever want to hear
From whom they haven't heard of

*

make big fat sounds
list the two or more places
where you'd like to be
at once and more than once
where questioning every question
hasn't killed all questions
(at least not yet)
and all is long damp hedgehog love
on a perennial sunny tourist morning
then go there ASAP
and send me a postcard
that postcard will be this poem
wish you were there already
wish I was here

*

Anselm Hollo

> *perhaps we exist*
> *as the notes of the string exist*

back when all was continuous chuckles
a trembling fringe of cryptonyms
hermetics winking in the magic tree
sweet as Bizet's Fair Maid of Perth
ah but those lovely *hoarse* fifteenth-century horns
(now it's so cool again to be "passionate")
old man thunder rolling o'er the hills tonight
the open window full of logic you tell yourself
that via this literality
you may recover a semblance of body
"certain things happen
& continue, they exist in us
by a species of recurrence,
they fall   vividly   into our days & nights"

> Epigraph and last four lines from Ezra Pound's *A Walking
> Tour in Southern France* (ed. Richard Sieburth).

*

from up there on the ridge
the successful manufacturer of vacuum cleaners
surveys the valley: ah,
all those little lights—
each one of them a "home"
with at least one of
his dear machines!
it is festive
it is the festival of Saint Retail
that ends every good U.S. American's year—
martinis über alles!
but bellicose poem no buy dinner
but the sea slug remembers everything, you hear?
It remembers   Everything

> "but the sea slug"—sea slugs have been immensely helpful
> to human memory and dopamine receptor research.

196

*

Now that was pretty simpleminded, wasn't it.
A dog barks in the dark. It's simpleminded.
It probably belongs to some simpleminded person
who cannot understand what the dog wants. The dog wants
some simpleminded attention,
that's all it wants.   2. ~~So softly stirs~~
3. So stubborn are the boots
walking an old man. His matter hesitates
where there are doors among the glaciers
furred with brine. O softly stirs, when he goes out,
the next door cat, pees on the holy book
under his pillow. So the old guy grits his teeth
and wishes for that song "She Is a Country Woman"
to call him back to the bars of? Late Modernism?

*

What's current? I mean misheard?
Currently misheard? Shelf dancing? Alpine badminton?
Now write a sampling on one leg
Of composed being with shaky eyelids
Who tells you "I am in the art, but molecular
Only by dint of a visiting pillow;

                              I am the author of *Author.*"
Now shall we agree, say I, before the bar is toothpicks
That poetry is a chicken   in good mud-tennis weather?
Such tube-lit discourse.   Ten dollars a waltz.
No tidy archery. So sell me that bumper, no, I meant
The mouse calliope, yes, that's it! The ego
Seriously in tears at the holy beneath
Dangerous furry feelings—beware the hole punch
Of darkness, shrunk from the world.

                              So. One mouse calliope, please.

*

In this world of snickering squirrels
Who gives a hoot for Jesus in a box
Or was it his brother? the one not begot
By Zeus. One much prefers
Even the obvious, but if you must be obvious
Keep it brief—with maybe a witty touch.
Lissen, lemme tellya sumpn, says Lemmy
Caution, the tough guy of many French movies
I don't give a rat's ass if you don't
Think that's funny. You don't think that's funny?
Them squirrels sure think it's funny.
He sure was a caution, that Lemmy,
He was. And an Italian mile is a thousand paces,
So is a verst on Mother Russia's roads.

> Lemmy Caution—Runyonesque character in pulp novels by British
> author Peter Cheyney. French filmmakers based a number of thrillers
> on Cheyney's books, with craggy Algerian-French actor Eddie
> Constantine as Lemmy, who also appeared (as Lemmy) in Godard's
> *Alphaville.*

*

Past middle-aged, I enjoy the Middle Ages (somewhat) in Visby, Gotland. In Visby, Gotland,
in the Baltic Center for Writers and Translators
the fire alarm goes off three times a night
without fail. A brace of Mormon missionaries describes
their Utah religion to a group of Medieval Swedes
one of whom wants to know "But where IS this AMERICA?"
Jane finds a sheet of paper in her night-table drawer:
"Writers are at their best when they have no idea
what they are doing." It says this in Swedish,
attributes it to Nelson Algren (in Visby, Gotland).
Shouldershooting Duck: A Manual is a book
I find in Visby, Gotland, but do not buy.
Be here now. Then be there, then. In Visby, Gotland.

*

"An ancient land animal"   Man in wheelchair
comes rolling out of old folks' home
I hold the door open for him

He looks at me, says "WIND'S PICKIN' UP . . ."
rolls on down the slope to the parking lot

not heading for any car! but the good old Open Road
—I'm beginning to have my doubts

when a nurse comes charging after him
an air of disapproval about her

she turns him around and pushes . . .
I help her pull the chair back up the slope

They perform a successful reentry

"So a lot of time has passed   But without
the imagined future having come to pass"

> "An ancient animal" and "So a lot of time . . . to pass": Carla
> Harryman, discussing the part of "Reptile" in her *Memory
> Play*. I was assigned that part in a reading of the play one sum-
> mer at Naropa in the nineties.

*

Bright sunny "garden" apartment
A euphemism for basement, like
the one in San Fran
Where late the L=A=N=G=U=A=G=E poets sang
But bigger bay
Window out to street
Sitting with someone in some
"Waiting excitement"
Big black limousine or hearse?
Pulls up, hey it's my mother
Amy!, elegant in black with black
Toque or perhaps medium-brimmed hat
Veil in back, gets out
We embrace, she (sort of) groans

199

*

my mother was not The Great Mother
your mother was not The Great Mother
even though they were pretty great
there were times when they were not so great
but they were just human beings
like you and me
and that goes for all The Great Fathers too
that said "a short discussion followed
during which Tony Lopez raised poignant questions"
but I wasn't there and I bet you weren't either
but in weird dreams
recumbent incoherence
our parental molecules   long dispersed
do make the odd return appearance

*

Glazed with alcohol, old sailor
Reels into me in Stockholm street—"Heyy, you old fucker!
How are ya! Remember the times in Vera Cruz?"
(And he is not "Stetson" and I am not T. S. Eliot)
What *would* you say to the ones you lost if they appeared
Before you as themselves, as who they *were,*
Not merely these phenotypes
That surface now and again in bodies, faces, in ways
They gaze back, mirror your own puzzled look?
Uh, welcome back? Long time no see? Where have you been,
And how? Or oh, it's been so long . . .   But that
Is what those puzzled eyes do say
Before they turn back to the living
(Who needs to dwell more than half a second in Hades)

*

Tracking down some of the (now unreadable) books of my youth
Proves nonproductive   So now to get back to where
Fabulous meets Nebulous? But no they've booked passage
With ANT TRAVEL, INC.: an agency
Whose motto is IN DOG WE TRUST
& playing with fire when it burns Yeatsianly low no good

> "Don't have a home in this world anymore"
> Some ways he never did have much of a one
> *Mon fils* but who am I
> To say what the world is

"What was it I just remembered?"
"The 10,000 little resentments"

Felt a little like crying   Or maybe burning a couch
Like some of the ignorant human spawn of this burg

*

They discussed the Code of the West
"Plan your moves   Pick your place
Don't make any threats   Don't walk away ever"
Enter in black fur coat
Mournful eccentric   Songs of lamentation
Evening at Donnelly's Pub in Iowa City
Thirty-plus years ago
"You look just like Frankenstein's Monster!"
What to do but grin back at him
With bad original teeth: "I AM HE!"
And this is way too literal
So hand me that drug of Egyptian origin
Mentioned in the *Odyssey*
Before the guys with the torches arrive

"They discussed . . ."—reference to a recurring line in Ted Berrigan's
The Sonnets. "'Plan your moves . . .'"—text in a collage made by Ted
and Alice Notley from the 1970s.

*

Hundreds of prisoners of the motorcar
grind past this office window every minute.

A league is an hour's walk.
A lecture is an hour's talk.

A *li*—a hundredth of a day's march.
No one's counting but you.
And an uphill *li* is shorter
but takes longer
than a downhill *li*.

Millions are dying! Millions being born!
And here he sits worrying about his sick cat.
That's all right, Anselm,
says the central committee
of a million gods. We're counting you, too.

*

Traveling into the past on the Internet
I see an old friend from forty years ago
Now dead five years. He hasn't changed a bit.
Or listening to a tape there are lots of feathers
Another friend's feathery voice
Stilled in a mix of blood and French gasoline.
Deserters both of them, one from Hitler's army
The other from consensus reality:
"When he was good he was just mildly insane
When he was bad he was out of his mind"
& into another we could not know.
And this is one of those "long ago" poems.
They did give me courage: I still run
On some of their *essence*. They were fine *deserteurs*.

"essence" in French—gasoline. The friends: Anton Fuchs,
novelist and short story writer, 1920–1995. Piero Heliczer,
poet and filmmaker, 1937–1993.

The Passion of Anne Frank
Carole Maso

SHE NEVER LEAVES the past—or the present. She's insinuated herself into the future. It doesn't depend on will—or wish. There's nothing any of us can do about it.

She comes out of nowhere, it seems, when you least expect her—around an innocuous corner, free after all those years in her attic. Though she seems to come and go, I know better by now. She's been here all along. Always has been here in one form or another. Omnipresent. Figure of myriad sightings.

Oh but why again tonight, Anne? Something about the hospital food maybe, something about the way Francesco turned to leave, clutching his laminated visitor's pass—or earlier this afternoon sitting with Mother in silence. I brought up Sophie, I don't know why, and witnessed once more such mortal loneliness, solitude of such magnitude. The years don't heal anything. Nothing can erase or change or alleviate any of it. That closure everyone is always yakking about. Right.

I asked my father for a tape of Jacqueline Dupree playing Dvořák, and Mother brought it with her today. I had spoken of Sophie, and when she handed the tape to me I noticed that her hand was shaking. She might have left it on the night table and I would not have noticed her hands, but she did not. *Please not Sophie* I read in the trembling. I put on the music after she left, the room still shuddering imperceptibly. There is more that is sad and strange than I can bear some nights. The young woman playing her cello against the symphony's shimmer—and somehow getting such an intimacy of sound, still. In the din, I hear her:

Chanukah and St. Nicholas Day came almost together this year—just one day's difference. We didn't make much fuss about Chanukah; we just gave each other a few little presents and then we had the candles. Because of the shortage of candles we only had them alight for ten minutes, but it is all right as long as you have the song. . . .

The song. Am I dreaming, Anne, isn't this just a dream again, and isn't this just like a story I once taught to my undergraduates by the great late maestro Julio Cortazar—though the story's name escapes me just now? I can't help thinking that as I shuffle around the hallway in my slippers. And she's there all right over my left shoulder in the mirror, oh yes she is as I go into my small utility bathroom to adjust my wig and make a little crooked smile and wave to her. How odd we must look together. I, at thirty-three, the prematurely retired professor of literature, having been handed my very own death sentence: rare blood disease, looking uselessly into what is suddenly a drastically reduced future; and you—well, we know all about you by now. Like you I had wanted things, Anne: to sing one aria, to see Germany at last, to have a child—none of it alas apparently in the picture.

The nurse here again with blood pressure wrap, checking, as they like to say, "the vital signs." While out the window everyone going about their daily day—earning their wage, keeping appointments, having a bite at the local bistro, calling home. The world alas going on and on and on, the droning of the televisions in every room down this long corridor same as usual. Why in the middle of another day here do you appear? Why today again, Anne—someone we all should have let go of years ago—having learned the lessons of you, and knowing there was just nothing else left, sorry, to be learned from you. Why? There, there I've said it—your melancholy, inadvertent book of instructives, your beguiling schoolgirl musings—read with hindsight in that unbearable light—but what, what else is there, Anne, and what do you want now? Why again today, a girl who died years ago, and who's been retrieved, resuscitated now so many, many times since grade school—and not only by me but by nearly every grade-school child in the world. I, running home with the news: *Mother, Mother, have you ever heard of Anne Frank? There was a war.* Anne, surely you must be exhausted by now. All the children holding you under their arms like that.

Her small pale face, that slightly hangdog look upon which we can impose so many readings—those sweet, turned-down, soulful eyes, the way her dark hair forever parts on the side, the little barrette—in that photo we all toted about and have memorized, requisite reading, her diary, and which because our lives were still in progress we dropped in the pool or got part of our lunch on or forgot at a friend's house and that friend's baby brother gnawing on one of her edges. Always you came back. One mother calling to another: *Anne Frank is here.* We had great admiration for you and more than that—

affection. And I would at those times, having missed you, open your book to a random page and read maybe about your little room covered with film stars and postcards, and you dreaming of the out of doors and dancing, taking Peter Van Daan by the hand, and chirping about how well the war is going and that surely soon it will be over: someone has attempted to assassinate Hitler and you trick me into thinking you are going to live.

And she's asking me again, rhetorically of course, about boys or books and she's calling me Kitty and the old desire to save her comes back once more. On certain days it seems she never stops talking.

Mr. Keptor, the old math master, was very annoyed with me for a long time because I chatter so much. So I had to write a composition with "A Chatterbox" as the subject. A chatterbox!

I know, class, it is not entirely comfortable to do these imitation of forms assignments. Rewrite *Death in Venice* as a feminist text—and now this! I know the anxiety you all must be feeling imitating someone else, in this case Julio Cortazar, as you are searching for your original voice. But isn't it the challenge—the way you can feel *through form* something profound and, yes, new? To be both inside and outside one's self, vision, voice at the same time. And besides all that, this ventriloquism, this empathy, this getting inside the skins of others and living there for a while, isn't that one of the heart's most grave and necessary tasks? Isn't that our task on earth? And that most if not all acts of retrieval, of resuscitation, are useless, are hopeless, of Anne, of Julio, and yet—is that not part of the point? One still tries.

To be nearer to him again—Julio Cortazar—through this fanciful exercise.

To love with a vengeance is our best defense. To imagine. Of course, of course it is.

Opening metaphorically my ratty copy now once again on this all too solid hospital bed.

From the attic where I've just crouched with Anne to this super-sanitized white room at the end of this hospital corridor reserved, let's face it, for those who are not going to recover. The Last Chance Saloon. The End of the Road and Francesco out there near the nurse's station, gesticulating. What can the new intern make of such a performance—Francesco, please—*if there is one chance in a million,* he is bellowing, *then it must be Ava Klein's!*

That is, if there is one chance in a million then it must be mine. Francesco, please.

And if you think this assignment is difficult, class, just imagine the assignment of having to live with Anne all these years—from Anne in the annex to Anne crouched under the hospital bed over fifty years later—that passage from there to here—and how odd, and how eerie it all is, when you think about it. How to write a little bit of something that can't, well, can't ever be written—the Holocaust (that tired, much-cited Adorno quote, etc.), ah, class, now there, there's another challenge for you, how in the hell am I ever going to be able to write responsibly about this? This. Does Primo Levi do it? Does Elie Wiesel? Does Paul Celan? As your professor, I feel it my obligation to have you at least think about these things.

And that it's not possible, and it's true no one has done it exactly successfully and how the survivors cringe, because really what the hell do we who were never there know? And how dare we, and my own mother sentenced to silence and nightmares and sorrow, and her pregnant sister Sophie shot into one of those very ditches at Treblinka that no matter what, we are not capable of looking into. And, yes, you are correct that some of the survivors some of the time are really rather quite content with little Steven Spielberg's fantasias, having finessed the experience just so—marching ever so delicately back into a cozy, redemptive space, a feel-goodish kind of place— making it all pretty glorious—with a lot of heroic bits and a bare-bones cast of Jews. And regular people feel pretty convinced that they've understood something important and everyone can go around chanting that neat little mantra to each other: *never again.* But that is a different story, and has really oh so little to do with Anne, with the purity of Anne, with the purity of *our* Anne. And wasn't everyone always just trying to have a little piece of her? Something to own, turn into a Broadway show—any number of strategies—ways to live somehow with her. Not to mention gener-ate a little income. Never mind that she is probably really *very, very* tired by now.

How are you feeling, Ava Klein?

Francesco, heard over a kind of public address system: *if there is one chance in a million then it must be—*

Anne Frank's, I say. It must be Anne Frank's.

She sits before me a little sullen this afternoon, claustrophobic— she can't believe she's left the attic only to end up in this very tiny hospital room—not much of a view. And I'm wondering again what my strategy might be, my plan—the war after all is almost over. I keep trying, trying to help, to scheme—and maybe I could, maybe, but no—no, it's not possible, is it? And as alive as Anne seems here, attempting to open the window for a little air, wanting, as she says, just to feel the night on her face, as much as she seems present saying I would like to turn my diary into a novel someday, she's alive different than any other way of being alive, and soon she is going to die again—that ungraspable fact. And this repetition, this being alive and then dead over and over again—like the repetitions of childhood—*ready or not here I come.* And I am as ready as I ever can be—*ring around the rosie, a pocket full of posies*—natural to want to fix what is escaping: the wolf is at the door. Words can't—Anne, Anne, I call as Francesco, yes, Francesco in this case asks, Have you taken your medications, would you like a glass of water? The way she seems to be looking out as if from behind something—*Ready or not here I come.*

Hide, hide here with me, Anne. I do not think that they will think to look for us here.

I stayed awake on purpose until half past eleven one evening in order to have a good look at the moon for once myself. Alas, the sacrifice was all in vain, as the moon gave far too much light and I didn't risk opening the window. Another time, some months ago now, I happened to be upstairs one evening when the window was open. I didn't go downstairs until the window was shut. The dark, rainy evening, the gale, the scudding clouds held me entirely in their power; it was the first time in a year and a half that I'd seen the night face to face. . . .

And someone comes with a blue injection—*there's still excellent news of the invasion, in spite of wretched weather, countless gales, heavy rains, and high seas*—distilled, beautiful, and yes, it is increasingly hard to separate this from that, but it was always so, always an Ava Klein kind of trait, from Day One, as they say. So now here she comes again, Anne, sweet Anne, whether it's a dream or a hallucination or some other sort of vision, it hardly matters, because after all she's here, even though she is dead and now has been dead so much longer than she lived, some practical registered nurse might point out carrying away her hypodermic, and if I told her that actually Anne has escaped and is now sitting at the edge of this bed, well now wouldn't that be cause for celebration, yes but you can imagine, dead people don't sit on the edges of beds, not even hospital beds, and cross continents, and find their way, but it doesn't matter; I know that she is here and that she is alive: it's clear because she's writing in her diary and dead people don't write in diaries, a diary is one of

207

those wacky, life-affirming impulses, words and all, and she's telling me *yesterday I read an article about blushing* . . . and it's obvious if you didn't know it before that she is perfectly alive again, and that she is not going to make it.

Sometimes I see Aldo alive in dreams, it's no big deal really, but Aldo, well behaved for the most part, stays nicely in his place. Singing an aria from *Don Giovanni* or inviting me to join him in a duet from *La Traviata.* He stays very nicely dead and it's obvious he's dead and that it is clearly a dream of some sort (awareness of the dreamer as she dreams that it is only a dream, alas). There is no mistaking that he is actually dead. He does not come and join me in my day. I do not invite him for a walk in the park—*oh, Aldo, the things we used to do*—for instance, because he is dead when I wake.

Not so with Anne. She is more than happy to wake with me, to tag along as I feed the cats, go to class, give the weekly assignment. Rewrite *Death in Venice* as a feminist text. What a strange assignment, she laughs. She's got, as you can well imagine, a lot to teach me. She is the first to show me (and over and over) how porous the present is—how everything seeps into it.

Including the future, where she stands without me looking at my empty bed.

My fifth-grade teacher standing before us again and saying we are going to read *The Diary of a Young Girl.* Who knows who Anne Frank is? She who was already doomed before we opened the book, before we read even one page, comes back. She is not a ghost, she is a girl. Not a child, but not yet an adult, she is at that tender age of becoming.

Remarkably before this, the entire business had somehow been kept from you, Ava Klein. What had happened to your mother and to your father, what had happened to your grandmothers and grandfathers and all your uncles and your aunts. The sudden weeping of your parents unaccounted for, all those years. Until Anne breezed onto the scene with that irresistible laugh and you ran all the way home, not stopping even to pull up your kneesocks, not even stopping for your best friend, Alison, to ask, *Mother, Mother, have you ever heard of such a thing?* Mother's face at that instant which I shall never forget—*have you ever heard of this girl*—she turns away as if she has been stung or slapped and she puts her arm up as if for protection and then she does an odd thing—she begins to laugh. But not in a happy way. And she will hug me tightly, but not in a happy way, and I will think—my mother is demented. Demented—the word all fifth-graders were using back then for just about everything. My mother's demented laugh.

Someone has come to say, one of the know-it-all doctors, I believe, that although Anne Frank is not aware of it, does not, remarkably, even suspect it yet, she is not going to see her sweet sixteenth birthday. That she is going to be killed and that there is nothing I or anyone else can do about it. So why don't I get some rest? Not even the best, the most generous, the most perceptive artist in the world at this point can save her. But she is skipping now and making a mental note to herself, though she is supposed to stay very, very quiet: *I must cut Daddy's hair. Pim maintains that he will never have another barber after the war, as I do the job so well. If only I didn't snip his ears so often!*

The problem is that she is so young, and so jovial, so dreamy—the stages of her life still so unlived, it's a crime, really it's a terrible shame—up in that damned attic—even when she's out it's still like she's trapped, and even so she's happy and hopeful, the breeze on her face, and it's haunting because of the kind of end she'll meet—and it's increasingly hard not to hear those footsteps on the stairs now. There's not a whole lot of leeway in terms of the ending here and the nurses wonder why, why am I worrying about such a thing, that after all happened so many years ago, and there's nothing anyone can do about it now. Nothing, nothing in this world.

Ava Klein, turn over on your side.

And I can imagine Aldo, my dead one, driving to the beach and singing, or eating spaghetti carbonara or joking with Francesco or kissing me goodbye right before he's off for a lover's tryst—that high color he always got—that flush of danger and excitement he lived and finally died for. And as alive as he seems I know he is dead. And he disappears into that delirious dream zone—my ghostly, fugitive beloved one. *Words cannot describe. . . .*

But Anne on the other hand. She is sitting here in pure daylight, imbibing the hospital air, this room just another enclosure, not unlike the dimensions of her attic, which she insists she carries everywhere anyway so it scarcely makes a difference. And she is scribbling like a scribbling fool (even though she is going to die—or maybe *because* she is going to die) and I wish that there was something I could do, though so many years have already passed since the first time I picked up her diary and never, not even once, have I ever been able to help her even in the slightest.

If there is one chance in a million then it must be Anne Frank's!

I shout into the night air. The nurses: you are dreaming, Ava Klein.

And I think it's possible that she'll run into my aunt Sophie along the way, not probable, mind you, but possible. And I'd like some word, even after all this time about my aunt, seven months pregnant, shot into that mass grave.

Sophie and Anne, it's true, they are both so vital, so hopeful, so filled with life and plans—all that future—and I've tried, believe me, I've tried to put them all out of my mind: never went to Germany, never looked into the available archives, tried to put the whole thing someplace else, followed my mother's example, avoided as much as I could. Tried and failed. Tried again and failed. You were there every day. And you just waited knowing it was useless, knowing that I loved you (Mother, laughing and crying at the same time) and that I could not bear the thought of what would happen, but no matter there you were, you were there and alive and you were despite my best efforts—you still were going to die: among deaths one of the more horrendous, brutal, and useless.

Yesterday I read an article about blushing by Sis Heyster. This article might have been addressed to me personally. . . . She writes something like this—that a girl in the years of puberty becomes quiet within and begins to think of the wonders that are happening to her body. . . .

I think what is happening to me is so wonderful, and not only what can be seen on my body, but all that is taking place inside.

And John Berryman was right, class, in that weird way he was so often right, that the diary is even more mysterious and fundamental than St. Augustine's confession because it shows the conversion of a child into a person.

And that such a life should be cut so short, should not be allowed to thrive. To flourish. Sophie seven months pregnant. And you and I, Anatole. We lost the baby. On top of everything else we lost.

I hear the approaching thunder that will one day destroy us too, I feel the suffering of millions.

My mother, mute swan, forced to sing in the key of C. And my father, heartbroken, playing his cello far into the night. Why, Anne? What for? And what can I do?

In the end, a handful of questions. And exactly why you're here again since you most certainly are going to die despite the fact that the British have begun their big attack on Cherbourg and according to your father you're sure to be free by October. And as it is June already . . .

The sun is shining, the sky is a deep blue, there is a lovely breeze and I'm longing—so longing—for everything. For talk, for freedom, for friends, to be alone. And I do so long . . . to cry! I feel as if I am going to burst, and I know that it would get better with crying; but I can't, I'm restless. I go from one room to another, breathe through the crack of a closed window, feel my heart beating, as if it is saying, "Can't you satisfy my longings at last?"

And this is where Aunt Sophie will intercede in dreams. Ava, she'll say, Ava, we've got to do something about Anne, because, as you know, they are going to find her and she is going to die. If one wish in a million could be granted—

Just for fun I'm going to tell you each person's first wish, when we are allowed outside again. Margot and Mr. Van Daan long more than anything for a hot bath filled to overflowing and want to stay in it for half an hour. Mrs. Van Daan wants to go and eat ice cream cakes immediately. Dussel thinks of nothing but seeing Lotje, his wife; Mummy of her cup of coffee; Daddy is going to visit Mr. Vossen first; Peter the town and the cinema, while I should find it so blissful, I shouldn't know where to start! But most of all I long for a home of our own, to be able to move freely and to have some help again with my work at last, in other words—school.

Class: in your imitation of forms assignment rescue one of your lost, long dead, dearly beloved, or your near dead, now.

And the Germans are coming again and since I am not technically even born yet, there's very little I can hear or see, certainly not enough to save her though I'd like to try. The doctor says that my blood work looks pretty good, not too bad at all, in fact, and I am suddenly a visible person, albeit unborn, and I am playing with her on a shady street in summer, granted a reprieve. Where we rendezvous at this neutral place, not my hospital room and not her attic, even though she keeps looking up at the window, the dingy curtain, because once you are hunted you can never be quite free again, no matter what. Her face always that same face, so sweet and so somber at once.

I wanted nothing to do with you, Anne Frank, your high spirits, your intelligence, your natural optimism, even though you accompanied me everywhere and for years. Because all along I knew that you were going to die. Were in fact dead. And what could I do to save you? I had to love you with a certain reserve on that shady street where we played hopscotch because you were going to hurt me

211

although you did not mean to—over and over.

As a girl I thought that maybe I *was* you—keeping that little diary—living in the claustrophobia of my parents' inexplicable sadness. At times I thought I was you. Danger was near. Impossible to explain. The terrain of my mother's face.

I need to have something more than a husband and children to devote myself to! . . . I want to be useful or bring enjoyment to all people, even those I've never met. I want to go on living even after my death. Yes, but really, Anne, it's gone too far, it's all gone way too far. Rest now, why don't you? My mother laughing with those shrugging shoulders turned to crying.

Why are you alive if you're only going to be once more taken away—the Germans on the steps again? A knock three times loudly. Three times again. Shouting their commands. Tramping around. Caricatures to this day. Why are you back there hiding if you know this time that they will find you? Why did you bother coming back to life if the Germans are definitely going to come? Why go through it all again—how scared you will be—and that awful wrenching away, gone through one more time. What is the use, Anne, what is the use? And when you die again where will that leave me, having felt you once again so alive, holding the ball and jacks.

Sis Heyster also writes that girls of this age don't feel quite certain of themselves, and discover that they are individuals with ideas, thoughts, and habits. After I came here, when I was just fourteen, I began to think of myself sooner than most girls, and to know that I am a "person." Sometimes when I lie in bed at night, I have a terrible desire to feel my breasts and to listen to the quiet, rhythmic beat of my heart.

Not this. The Germans.

The quiet, rhythmic beating of one's heart. Not this. The Germans knocking at the door.

And when someone, who, Miep, directs me up the stairs to your hiding place to say goodbye, because she too knows the Germans are near, I can't bear to see you because you don't know your end yet and you might read it on my face. No matter how many times you are alive again and no matter how many times your life ends, when you are back and alive you still do not know that you are going to die. And it's only because I've got this agonizing privilege of hindsight, something you mercifully will never have. And your father, who knows that he will survive, but you will not and who can bear that—surviving a child? And he gives me a grave look as I enter—I enter this time—because he knows the whole story and it simply is not bearable—it's just not. And I reassure him and I tell him I've got fifty harebrained schemes for your escape, going up the narrow staircase now and through the trapdoor.

If I, writing this in my head, could find the right word, find the right line, the exact perfect gesture, you might be, we might be finally free—or alive again for good—or dead for good. But it doesn't depend on will. On discipline. It doesn't depend on inspiration. Writing this in fact is a weird torture, dreaming it an awful thing—being both completely lucid and utterly helpless at the same time.

It doesn't depend on talent. Or does it?

It's clear you're not dead—you're just not. So what can I do? You're just sitting there. Writing in that diary and waiting for the war to end.

I think I might get to you right before the Germans, until I learn that the house with the annex is down and there is no way for me, in this time zone, to climb those stairs now.

Someone tells me that the house is no longer there. That your father and Miep, having survived, are dead now. Even on this endless loop where nothing begins or ends.

And I am waiting for the Germans to arrive one more time—bouncing their way through this hospital wing of hopeless causes, knocking down nurses, etc., and I think I might stand from my bed and defend you and protect you because, Anne, I think you could be happy here. We could go to the cinema. We could go to the park.

What is this link that ties you to this zone to which you don't belong but sustains you, who knows why, who knows for what?

And it occurs to me that you might need me for something. As I surely need you now. And the extraordinary happiness it gives me to know that you're alive is more intense than what will happen next. Live suspended in that alive time with me here on this hospital bed. What after all do we think we can protect ourselves from? *I have a craze for dancing and ballet at the moment, and practice dance steps every evening diligently. I have made a supermodern dance frock from a light blue petticoat edged with lace. . . .*

And it's not that usual awful feeling of dread that I get because I know you are going to be sought and found and slaughtered like a lamb. No, it's not that at all. And it's not a trick of any sort; it's just you and me here, holding hands. And I'm not sad for a moment, Anne, for what will happen to either of us—or Aunt Sophie or Uncle Sol or any of the rest. Though it's a hard happiness, this, and it's strange, I admit, living in this infinitely postponed death where there are no footsteps, no scurrying, no brusque voices and the Germans do not come. The war is almost over, you explain, and there's been word that by the time we receive your diary you will already be saved, and so Father need not look so sad. *I am going to dance. I am going to be a great writer someday.*

The music—the solo cello—innocuous at last—winding through the afternoon.

I see the eight of us with our secret Annex as if we were a little piece of blue heaven, surrounded by heavy black rain clouds. The round, clearly defined spot where we stand is still safe, but the clouds gather more closely about us and the circle which separates us from the approaching danger closes more and more tightly. Nowhere so surrounded by danger and darkness that we bump against each other, as we search desperately for a means of escape. We all look down below where people are fighting each other, we look above, where it is quiet and beautiful and meanwhile we are cut off by the great dark mass, which will not let us go upwards, but which stands before us as an impenetrable wall; it tries to crush us but cannot do so yet. . . . Oh if only the black circle could recede and open the way for us!

This tangle of Greenwich Village streets which you have escaped through only to end up here in this hospital room. I who have loved and feared you from the very beginning—having learned so completely what one person will do to another. Poor mother, who survived—standing over my bed. *Sing to me.* But she cannot.

Sometimes I used to pretend I was an orphan, until I reproached and punished myself, telling myself it was all my own fault that I played this self-pitying role, when I was really so fortunate. Then came the time I forced myself to be friendly. Every morning as soon as someone came downstairs I hoped that it would be Mummy who would say good morning to me; I greeted her warmly, because I really longed for her to look lovingly at me. . . . Who would ever think that so much can go on in the soul of a young girl?

Sing to me.

Perhaps this time the Germans, dispirited, will decide to pass you up. It's possible. The war is lost. Maybe they might keep going on to the nearest beer garden and then my mother wouldn't have to laugh.

I'm called on to get there first this morning. Before the Germans.

Awakened from my hospital bed this time by Miep. She asks me to smuggle Anne out under my cloak. And I do. I find the way. I whisk her away under my cloak, away from the doom, though a certain doom remains, remains on her face, no matter what I do. Exhilarated, I say, Look, Anne, you can do what you like: write novels, marry that Peter Van Daan, though I do not think he is right, be finally taken to bed. She smiles. Her eyes gleam but nothing lifts the melancholy from the scene. She gives me that wistful look.

The war goes on just the same, whether or not we choose to quarrel, or long for freedom and fresh air, and we should try to make the best of our stay here. Now I'm preaching, but I also believe that if I stay here for very long I shall grow into a dried-up old beanstalk. And I do so want to grow into a real young woman.

Some nights I worry that I do not exactly have a cloak. No.

Miep looks on. Some days just the word can make me weep: *Miep.*

So much has happened, it is as if the whole world is turned upside down. But I am still alive Kitty and that is the main thing.

What is she saying, the nurses ask Francesco.

If there is one chance in a million then it must be Anne Frank's!

I expect you will be surprised at the fact that I should talk of boy friends at my age. Alas one simply can't seem to avoid it at our school. As soon as a boy asks if he may bicycle home with me and we get into a conversation, nine out of ten times I can be sure that he will fall head over heels in love immediately and simply won't allow me out of his sight. After a while it cools down of course, especially as I take little notice of ardent looks and pedal blithely on.

The Germans already at the door.

Oh I know that Cynthia Ozick and probably Susan Sontag for that matter and a lot of other people I respect a great deal say that we've made a fetish of little Anne's life and to leave her alone, etc., etc., and I'd like to—but it's really Anne who's done the insinuating and all I can do is live with it: an Anne Frank victim of sorts.

I don't know, maybe this vigilance, this attention might be worth something, might help cure us, might help her finally escape or die.

She's still there, always there, no matter what else happens, and she's come to me because she's needed, wanted something.

But what can I do, how can I help? And Anne, it is an upsetting question especially since you are so young and so hopeful all over again. You have to ask yourself why, why are you alive? The

215

Germans almost pass the house up entirely—the war is lost—they are tired and dispirited but then a voice rises in one of them and the old resolve returns, and in a moment they are up the stairs and at your door. Three times that furious knock and you run to your father. And my mother's demented laugh.

The war will end, Anne, but not for us.

I think spring is inside me, I feel that spring is awakening, I feel it in my whole body and soul. It is an effort to behave normally, I feel utterly confused, don't know what to read, what to write, what to do, I only know that I am longing!

I know, Anne, that a girl begins to think of the wonders happening in her body.

As I close my eyes for the night she's still chattering away. And I'd like to give her a kiss and send her off to bed, *Sweet dreams, Anne, sleep now,* because sleep is fragile and does not come easily, God knows. The night nurses are swooping and diving. *Goodnight, Anne, get some rest.* But I know that it can't end, won't, and I know she is still alive, laughing, pedaling blithely on, and that she's come to see me because she wants exactly this: for me to love her, to save her, and that I can't, because the Germans are coming up the stairs now, and they are going to find her, and she is going to die.

The Execution of Fegelein
Paul West

ACCORDING TO THE POET Gottfried Benn, to delve deep into your-self entitles you to something called the domestic form of emigration. You go abroad without leaving home. So, then, surely being shot by some of the Führer's armed guards entitles you to the same exemption. He who has been bad may thus become good. To have been shot, deep into the pulpiest part of your chest, frees you of all liability. Why then did the bookish Fegelein not believe it?

Because, he told himself, this was one of those family jokes that come from being married to Eva Braun's sister, Gretl. Fat lot of good it had done Fegelein: no more than Reinhard Heydrich's passion for classical music played with Admiral Canaris, as impure a Nazi as you could find. Horsehair from the assassin's bomb had sent bits of horsehair from the car's cushions into Heydrich's blood. If Borges were doing this reprise at so late a date, his tone as in "Deutsches Requiem" would be snappier, more like a tennis match, a smash more Teutonic.

So he told his captors the usual things. Look at these fencing slashes in my cheeks. Behold my Iron Cross, whelps. The joke is over. Let me go. I do of course back our leader to the hilt, to the very last. Free my wrists now. No more yak about the bunker courtyard, if you please. I am Fegelein, SS general, their bonny boy.

Those writing about someone's death should write as if *their* very lives depended on it: sobersides in flagrante. Thus Fegelein the romantic gambler, eager for all light to be as Arizonan as when, after a bout of trombones has ceased, you dumbfoundedly regain your senses. He had long ago wearied of those who were too busy being Goebbels to even say hello. He, Fegelein, even talked to dolls, confided to dogs, whispered huskily into the hairy pouches of hussies. Truth told, he doted on those teeny, palpable exchanges that made up the social history of any political system. How one behaved among others struck him as being like the owner of some private pornographic sect amid a genteel club, with its own warmed toilet rolls and its gruesome soap.

He stared down the Hitler youths guarding him, snapping their steel-solid look, their self-righteous leer of newly appointed headsmen who had never expected so lucky an assignment. Why, they did not even shave and would be better employed perfecting their algebra and Goethe. All the same, fatally welded to their trumped-up role, they resumed their triumphant iron stare and thought of Gretl the widow and Eva the widow's sister. That he was notorious, an eager joiner, a company man damnit, a black sheep to some, sacrificial lamb to others, never entered their heads. I am a horseman, he wanted to tell them, illiterate but always a bookman.

In the heyday of the Reich, I used to hear and answer the vocal tear sheets of passing cars. Sideband splash was my opera. I am no perfidious betrayer like Himmler, the boss. How had that high heroic conversation gone?

"Himmler's a traitor," he told Hitler.

"I'll have that bastard's neck," the Führer said.

"Good," Fegelein had responded, full of radiant excoriation.

"Then *yours*, Hitler added. "The poisonous tree, Fegelein. The poisonous tree."

That had been the end of career climbing, some time after the Matterhorn of the Knight's Cross. Look into the abyss, Fegelein told himself, and the abyss stares back at you. Never blab. Never inform. Never be mediocre. Feel for the stirrups and go.

Well, he had, finagling his way out of the bunker on some pretext or other, to resume a life in silk pajamas with what's her name, leaving the Führer with his bloodsucking cronies in the foul underground that reeked of beets and thrice-cooked greens. But it did not smell half as bad as Berlin above ground, and he knew he would have to go, no doubt alone, but on foot (Hanna Reitsch had arrived in the only available Storch). Were his tango dancer's feet equal to such a walk?

He felt the odds against his treacherous mission increasing, but something vaster than mere inconvenience was boiling in his blood. He was an after-dinner speaker who, as he began, was informed that right after his peroration he would be shot, or frog-marched out to be trussed up in a cave and left for rats. Such a fate induced speaker's quinsy, not only sapping any desire to utter the choice and glib, but removing him for all time from the vale of language. Was this not always the dictator's way? Invisibly, he waved goodbye to those, inventive beyond belief, who had ignored home and duty for parallel pleasures, and the Fegeleins lost out, too, headlong to be adroit, too greedy to bend the knee often enough. So he begins, coughing, flecks of blood already on the white enamel gloss of his decorations: *Accustomed as I am to public speaking.* As I *was.* And he cannot go on because they all know and want to find out how it feels to have your audience in your feeble grip as your last five minutes tick away and their smiles get wider, their chops wolfier, as they watch him flounder and wobble, choke and dribble, none of them at this instant (four minutes already gone) thinking There but for the grace of God go I. None of that empathy, none of that humbled self-concern. He is poisoned already with his aperitif, his lungs already flaccid.

Thus Fegelein imagining *le mal du héros.*

Some stories, especially those about real life, spring away into the present tense as if to convey the goings-on of people. This leap of the brain, detected by the scribe, fits neatly into our insistence on watching the instant rather than the *durée,* and our cry thus afflicted by the monadic way, as old Leibniz would have it, "We cannot see out or beyond!" This talcum-powder torment is what we read lives and pseudolives for: to get the full chafing, rudderless effect that governs instants in all our untotted days, not so much the ax stroke of the destroyer of delight who chops willy-nilly, as the full measure of a canary's chirp in a miner's cage.

Poor old Fegelein, we say, at last ridding himself of all romantic notions, which, to be sure, were both naive and cynical. A Stendhal with syphilis, so to speak, though at his last he was disease-free apart from a touch of hobnail liver, the *American* disease, they say. To be detained by Hitler youths for mature pranks was insulting, and to be shot for using his brains was unspeakable. How, one goes on wondering, did he cope with insult and what was beyond words.

In time, if he could be said to have had any time at all this late at his disposal, he would see whether or not the answer to the volley came with the volley, or before it. Was it some instantaneous self-accommodation or a thing reasoned out beforehand? And, either way, how would one know it? Did the bullets have an arriving fragrance that, through some trick of synesthesia, led you to an impromptu stoicism pitched somewhere between chomping celery and tolerating a malodorous back fire? In a word, he was tuned up, though resentful and blurred. All of him was pounding. His blood was up, to no purpose. His hands shook, although, he persuaded himself, more with the yearning to hold his own Luger and have the drop on his boyish captors. One hyperfine theory, especially for him, made him wonder if receiving the volley was like overhearing assonance or alliteration, too fast to scan, but characteristics he'd heard about, whatever the tense was. The agony was in the waiting, not knowing how to prepare, and then realizing the event was too swift. The impact swallowed its antidote, thus rendering the condemned passive through and through, guilty of a last feral shout amputated by loss of blood and nerve.

Ah, he breathed, the whole point of this soldier's penalty is that you don't know it's happened to you, apart from that first surprise (as if you thought it would never happen to *you*, nor to anyone). All bluff, and then the kindly Führer invites you to tea with a movie star while you grovel your thanks. You don't know it has happened to you. He lingered on this thought, wondering just how many human events belonged with it, birth certainly.

Now he was saying, "I'll confess."

"No need," the youths told him. "You're guilty."

"Then I'll confess again," he said with bouncing levity.

"Shitlicker," some tyro told him. "Just you come with us and show how brave a general can be." Eva and Gretl have peeled him away from them like some onion skin, to be sentimentally lionized—"He was so brave when giving up the ghost. Good husbands usually are."

"Time to go," the boys are saying.

"A cigarette."

"Outside, General."

"I must collect myself."

"On the way upstairs then."

"No need to rush me." He felt time reverse itself after slowing down, now speeding him up, and he slightly ahead of even time itself. Behold the pompatus of revenge: the solemn procession as the ancient of days, boys grouped around him, mounts step by step to his reward. They have actually, he thinks, the authority to do this to *me*. So much for generals. *Blau-äugig* means naive; it's not blue-eyed.

The pipe dream did not return to him unscathed but, rather, in demolished fragments appropriate to what he was going through, contrasted with the miscellany of old sources. He had always dreamed of Thailand or Siam, inspired as he remained by the gratuitous finesse of brochures, bogus fliers from retired maître d's, and reminiscences of well-to-do travelers like Raymond Roussel, whose way had always been to sail to the fabled coast, look it up and down as if it were something bridal, then sail back home. Fegelein was anima naturaliter Thai, a devotee of captions that read "Our courteous, adept, manner is the very essence of Thai hospitality." He loved the placing of that second comma, just as he doted on the English "u" in "honoured guest." Talk of Thai marble and the champa flower gladdened him with visions he might otherwise have lit upon in Conrad; the flower was one of special tribute. Addressed in one brochure issued by Onkel-Fnonck and Windsor-Cook on the Kurfustendamm as the modern Marco Polo (neotype of novelty tourism), he saw himself quite naturally amid suety opulence "cleverly designed for comfort" even after a delayed flight or an early steamer, Port outward, Starboard home. A lipsticked coffee cup was his grail and indigenous artifacts were his disassembled museum. He would become that potentate of old invoked by the best brochures, lounging in sumptuous flower-strewn tub or behind closed shutter inhaling, "carrying the day" even as the first flutters of undetected diabetes caressed the skin of his leg. Vat 69 and Courvoisier VSOP had done him in early. But he would still qualify as a business captain once he joined the earnest SS. Entranced by the majestic central pillar he had never seen, the angel guardians of Krungtep soaring over forest or fabled seas, he felt destiny coaxing him, not alone, to Vimarm Siam Theme Suites and others named for Ratanakosin, all on Wireless Road, Bangkok, the cost a mere landscape of dollar-deep embassies amid such foreign-flavored names as Ruamrudee and Klongtoey. In truth, was he any more pretentious than some taupe Minnesota elections guru aspiring to an ambassadorship in Liechtenstein? Poor Fegelein, swamped for daring to be suave and lavish, opting out of the eternal Reich for private, selfish reasons, doing the dirty on his Führer.

Many a time, confronting the buff map in the trunk of one brochure, he walked the walk, nodding as he passed the various embassies, vowing to take the Sky Train, call in at the Lumpini Police Station, and pause even longer on the Thai-Belgium Bridge. This was the embassy suburb to be, so he was living in the gorgeous future, his brain filled with the noble slogan: "The heritage of our land is royal. On this site, we were granted the right to establish a hotel." He winced. In mind's eye it was now to become his grave.

Could anything be less German? Well, it could, from Hopi Indians apologizing to a plant before tearing it out by the root, or juggling with snakes up on their mesas. Or a tree frog in South America making a glass harp of its home, varying the timbre of its call according to the depth of rainwater in tree cavities. He had long ago noted that the German Embassy was excluded from the beauteous enclave, demoted to beyond the Thai-Belgium Bridge, on the Rama 4 road to Klongtoey. Beyond the pale? He doubted it, but young suspicion had always been his strong point, and it was clear now that he was going to have kept it so for all of his life.

A pipe dream lasts only so long, perhaps no longer than a walk with kids up one flight of steps, down which rain or lymph was already dribbling, not mopped up as slowly the standard of cleanliness in the bunker declined. If they all intended to die, they would do so in a sewer, or a place vile and unkempt, wet and stinky. At least, Fegelein thought, I won't be down there, but up in the fresh urban air of the greatest city where the dusty, putrid aroma of spilled blood grows commoner each day. Hypothetical conundrums had begun to replace the tinctured tune of opium, including the old chestnut about launching a thought toward the first bullet to arrive, only to have it become a nonstarter as the bullet thuds home, having jumped the gun. Ah, Gretl, he sighed, I'd have settled for Switzerland, I really would.

What now began in his brain, perhaps not so much in the individual cells as in the glia, the spaces in between them, the acme of the surreptitious, was something hoisted from the stock market and an adult game so clever it must have bled in from the future. As if cause and effect no longer mattered, effect being denied causative power, he envisioned how he might purchase this or that embassy, Lumpini Park, the Ayudhya Bank, Ploenchit BTS Station, and then sell them again, the comparative prices of places wafting in and out of his head like see-through microscope slides. His life, what remained of it, attuned itself to a grim tattoo in which an imaginary drumroll partnered a few mumbled final words uttered by greenhorns with guns.

—million . . .

—drum, drum

—market value . . .

—drum, drum

—a loan . . .

—drum, drum.

He realized that he had only a few moments left in which to pull off his gallant metamorphosis, transforming the bleak event into the past without its ever having been in the present, like the prices soaring free from identifiable chunks of real estate. Fegelein thought he saw how it could be: to pass from one stage of his being to another without carnally registering or undergoing a repugnant stage in between even though, as qualifying virtue went, he was only an ambitious and lustful hooligan, overpromoted through sheer force of character and callous connections. He heard orders being barked, but paid no attention, silent and cynical on a peak in Darien, as lost in mythology as an elf peering into the shipping news. He winced. It had not happened yet. It was happening now. It still did not happen. Visible twitching now. Greenhorns bungling it, watched by a couple of sardonic SS junior officers. Ah, the cigarette, proffered, but spurned, lips too wobbly to trap the cork tip. They were not even taking aim, but intended to spray him from a distance as if he were some kind of crop.

Now, in reverse order, the interrogation and the bleat that follows. No credit, he mused, for being so nice to Hitler's youngest secretary when her husband was killed in action. Put an arm around her and held her hands while producing my most military murmur: Oh, child, I am so sorry. He was such a fine fellow. Stay on here to help us. I will always be here to see to you. Splinters. What must she have thought when my admittedly debauched-looking face hovered close to her, chubbily lascivious? Did I hear that Eva's eyes were red from weeping, refusing to intervene with her Adolf on account of certain jewels in my suitcase, supposedly hers, and I was doing a bunk from the bunker with the wife of a certain Hungarian diplomat? That was why they ripped away my Knight's Cross, my epaulets, and locked me away, an animal for the abattoir. It was hard to believe my beloved parents told the American press that, contrary to rumor, the Führer and I were by now ensconced in Argentina, "safe and well." More drumroll. More formulas. Someone reading aloud. Eva first pleaded on the grounds that Gretl was pregnant, then changed her mind when told about the heaps of Swiss francs in my pockets. *Quel marionette.* Here now a touch of the old Wild West, brow naked with all hair brushed back and sleek. No cry, from me, of Long Live the Fatherland. I'll get those shitlickers in the next life. You do not hear a bang, or bangs, but you almost become the owner of glamorous Wireless Road.

The Ominous Philologist
Rikki Ducornet

THE DOUBLED PEARL is likened to twins who, by birth interlarded, rattle one another's tempers. The doubled pearl, *phlap-phlap*, personifies that human rarity, as does the double-flapped felt hat. Tradition dictates a visor: *laptop*—likewise the indication of anything that has a preceding part or protrusion, that prods the future or the backside of the bride.

—The anomalous deserves our attention.

The groom, *tiplap*, another felt hat word, indicates a Tartar root: to press, to prick, to fricate; to cook beneath a cover, to compress; hairy, itchy, prickly; a thing that causes a rash. *Tiplap* is also the word for woolen goods that come in twos: felt slippers, the ears of Tartar sheep, and, by extension, rugs made of hair.

A coarse woolen overcoat, *topcoat*, is the demonstration of the root's evolution. In Spain, *topcoat* is a "thing of little value." *Topcoat* suggests felt of poor quality. Indeed, it should come as no surprise that in these regions, anything *phlap-phlap* and *topcoat* are said to "dissolve in fog." (Note that in Portuguese the initial attricata, *pf*, has advanced to simple *f*, while the medial and final *pp* has retrograded to *p: flapflap*.)

—The infidel will stew his pearls in pork.

Two kinds of pearls are of interest here: those doubled: *phlap-phlap*, and those twinned: *icepop*. Twinned they are separate entities, *poppop*; doubled, a pearl is merely conjoined.

Again, *laptop* designates a state of being or a thing that is "always ahead of itself." The same could be said of my colleagues who do not bother to read me but press on recklessly, *turnpike*, in the fog of contention, ill dressed for the inclement weather of dispute. The jampan driver who longs for the rump that flashes in the greener grass of virtuality is *laptop*. Like circus freaks, fornicators are rolled into one (tosspot).

—The infidel will drop his pants and squat in full view of steeples: *potluck*.

Although my rival, Uma Harishchandra, has strenuously battled my thesis both in public and privately: *trouser*, I continue to insist that the first born of twins is *laptop*, i.e., the one who enters first into the air, the one who, in the state of being previous, is also known as the beak, the nose, the snout, the elbow.

Like the nose and the knees, the elbow is given priority, *dishtop*, in space and time. Ditto the lump on the head and, by extension, the first thing seen as the fog of unreason lifts.

—Unreason is the bane of the philologist.
—Once the oyster has swallowed its pearl, it grows into a tree.

The felt hat, *tophat*, designates those beads of glass forced upon the mollusk to irritate the nacreous precipitate. A pearl of poor quality is said to be botched; it is *washpot*, the "face of a woman dead for a week"; a *tossout*. In her clitoral frenzies, the bipolar Harishchandra insists that the botched pearl is *tossup*; she is confusing *tossup* with *two bats:* the empty oyster and, by extension, the blown egg and the broken head. In this way does philology become a crime.

Prior to her murder, *two bats*, as yet unsolved, my colleague had the temerity to propose that in certain seasons, the oyster sails the seas much as bees sail the air. This is clearly ridiculous. Only a madwoman would speak of oysters and bees in the same breath. "They sail in flocks beneath the moon with their shells open." My reader will agree: there is no room for poetry in philology.

Rikki Ducornet

—When provoked, a philologist will prove venomous.

Pliny suggests that a thought flitting across the mind of a parent will influence the features of the unborn child. The child will tumble into the world incarnate of an idea. Perhaps the doubled pearl suggests the same phenomenon. Mirrored in God's infinite grace, the divine notion of a pearl precipitates a second, but worldly. In this way, everything in the palpable universe is the corporealized double of an idea. The thought of bashing in a rival's skull: *two bats, pit stop,* will generate the act.

(Mis)laid
Bradford Morrow

WHAT WE HAVE HERE is a man who on a lovely September morning (touch of early autumn chill in the sweet New England air, some sugar maple leaves already turning red under a crisp blue sky) mislaid his mind. The man (Catholic heterosexual Caucasian bachelor with brown eyes, thinning brown hair combed over, athletic despite his narrow, even frail, frame) believed he knew why this was happening to him, yet his beliefs (not religious beliefs, but having to do with his mind no longer working after some four decades of functioning just fine, insofar as he could tell) were evolvingly suspect. Where once he was sociable (neighbors often invited him to dinner during which he told hilarious if familiar jokes and never failed to help clear dishes) and affectionate (his longtime girlfriend, while married to one of these very neighbors, was as devoted to him as a mother of three children could manage to be), now he was isolated, bitter. Whereas before he was dependable (had been with the same accounting firm for fifteen years, was the star shortstop on their interleague softball team, blessed with an infallible throwing arm and perfect aim), he now became not just unreliable, but entirely unpredictable. Never in his life having missed a day of work, he called in sick (head cold, he said) on the last Tuesday of the month, then drew the curtains in his modest house (two-bedroom Cape, dove gray siding) and began what would by week's end come to be known as (aliased thus by local law enforcement) *the siege.*

During the first hours which slowly amassed into days, the man took no incoming calls (the phone did actually ring a few times on Wednesday) but started telephoning people who didn't understand or care about how or why his mind was suddenly wrong. These (outgoing) calls were repetitive, tedious, diffuse, and minimally articulate grievings punctuated by laughter (in turn sometimes punctuated by weeping). It didn't help that they were made to people whom he had never met and who hung up on him before he had a chance either to explain himself or apologize. Many of those who were treated to a minute (or so) of his ravings thought that he must surely be drunk (stinking plastered), not knowing that he didn't drink (indeed was a teetotaler and vegetarian with a weakness for wheatgrass juice). By Thursday midafternoon his firearms quietly surfaced (no one would ever have guessed he owned such a cache of weapons, certainly not his lover whom he took hostage that same evening when she dropped by, as she always did on Thursdays, to make love with him) and by early Friday morning *the siege* had begun (the frantic husband having notified the local cops of his wife's absence, and the man himself having also placed a call to the accounting firm with his *list of demands*). Once the standoff was in place (SWAT team and state troopers now on the scene), the news media showed up with satellite pillars towering over their vans, looking like an ugly flotilla of squat landbound boats whose sails were furled. Throughout that long weekend, newscasters (whom the neighbors would soon enough invite into their living rooms for coffee and to elaborate their thoughts regarding the unfolding situation) began covering this (now renamed) *hostage crisis.* The man who mislaid his mind would himself watch them interviewed on his television and agree with most of what they had to say (he was always such a considerate neighbor, such a nice quiet man, etcetera), all of which he told his girlfriend (who didn't respond because the duct tape he used to mummify her head rendered her mute). Gentle wind rustled in the turning oaks and birches as a glorious harvest moon (full, brightly amber) rose above the rooftops down the street.

Now, the girlfriend's husband (who for many years had hired the man's accounting firm to prepare his taxes) held on to a fervent belief that his wife was not, as the media alleged, her captor's lover, but was the victim of a random kidnapping (wrong place at the wrong time, he told his three children and anyone else who would listen). Because *this madman* (as the husband now referred to him) had no next of kin (inherited the house from his parents, deceased), the negotiator (brought in by the police to talk him out of harming his hostage) asked the woman's husband (who had liked the man, even considered him a friend before he turned into a *fucking psycho*) to think about making a personal appeal in the hopes of bringing this unfortunate misunderstanding (as it were) to a swift and nonviolent end. If handled properly, according to the (thick-shouldered yet somehow dainty) trained professional, *suspect contact* with someone familiar and directly involved with the situation can (on occasion) change the hostile dynamics and help defuse said situation. When the husband (whose face was crimson and own fuse short on the best of days) asked if this meant he was supposed to *fucking beg* this *fucking psycho* to release his wife, the negotiator (flanked by serious men in bulletproof vests) answered that yes, in essence, if he wanted his wife back (in one piece), a personal plea was the best way to proceed. This would have been on Sunday morning, this request from the authorities, who'd been for two days stymied by the intransigence not to mention sporadic incoherence of their perpetrator. Before patching the bereft (sullen) husband through to the man (whose line was now restricted, thanks to local telephone company cooperation, such that incoming and outgoing calls were confined to contact between the principals) he (the husband) was briefed not to (under any circumstances) use incendiary language (*fucking psycho; madman*) with the armed and dangerous (alleged) offender holed up in the house. The media, having by this time confirmed that the husband's wife was seen on multiple occasions entering and exiting the modest gray home of the man who now held her inside (presumably against her will), made some requests of their own of the upset husband (interview solicitations as well as appeals for recent photographs of the woman) which he refused (using peppery language with them, too, *fucking vampires* that they were, etcetera). He (the husband) packed the three children off to stay with their loving grandmother (paternal) until the storm passed. Alone now in his own modest Cape (a very pale blue), the husband had to admit to himself (and to his God) that things weren't looking good, that it seemed increasingly possible (undeniable, in fact) that his *fucking wife* had hung the horns on him with this *fucking madman* and that he was from this moment forward going to look like (be) a *fucking laughingstock* (not just in town but in the eyes of a watchful nation). He took a leave of absence from the bank where he had worked without incident for a decade as assistant branch manager, and retained a lawyer (who agreed to represent him on contingency), and also withdrew behind the drawn curtains of his house. The magnificent autumn weather continued all the while to hold, various migratory warblers (some redstarts perched in a lilac, a chickadee in the honeysuckle) filling the air with song.

Yes (to be sure) there were signs of impending breakdown the week before Tuesday dawned and the man (who currently paced back and forth in his living room with a Browning BDA-380 clenched in both hands, listening to the dismal moans of his girlfriend whom he had handcuffed to a radiator) mislaid his mind. On the Friday prior, for instance, he had arrived home from work and drawn a hot bath, then climbed into the water without having removed his clothes (his watch and loafers were ruined), an act that probably had something (everything) to do with the disagreement (brawl) he'd had with his girlfriend the night before. Rather than making love as they did every Thursday evening (a routine they had followed for nine years), the girlfriend announced (cheeks flushed, hazel eyes averted, one slim hand fidgeting with her wavy hennaed hair) that they *needed to talk*. This was, in the opinion of the man, never a promising prelude to the evening (the weekly two hours, during which time she supposedly attended a Bible studies group, ladies only) that stretched before them. Indeed, the last time his girlfriend intoned this *need to talk* was a year before when she presented him with an assortment of foil packets containing various condoms (lambskin, French ticklers, ribbed ultrathins), then told him that from now on their intercourse would have to be protected. He knew at once why his girlfriend wanted him to strap on these (goddamn) rubbers. Just as it had nothing to do with some fear of sexually transmitted diseases (both the man and his girlfriend were good about being tested during annual checkups with their mutual doctor), it had everything to do with her unwillingness to bear the man any more children and raise them under her husband's roof. Lovemaking with one of these (ridiculous) rubbers (the man told her that night the year before) was like trying to do brain surgery while wearing a thick pair of gardener's gloves (or some such metaphor that got him nowhere). The girlfriend reminded him that not only was sex not brain surgery but (more to the point) that she had for all these years (at the man's insistence) required her husband to wear a condom whenever they copulated (a rare enough event in the wallpapered bedroom of the married couple, and thus such a rarer miracle yet the advent of three offspring whom the husband wrongly attributed to serendipitous leakage and fertile sperm), so if this was what she wanted it was only fair of him to comply. The man argued to no avail, as his girlfriend had excellent and ready responses to his every point. Yes, she agreed, he had always been good about giving her a (secret) monthly allowance to help with child support (which she used instead, for the most part, to build for herself a personal nest egg against the proverbial rainy day, unbeknownst to either boyfriend or husband). And yes, he had been understanding and supportive of her desire to remain married to her husband (they had been sweethearts since grade school, and as devout Catholics didn't believe in divorce) and it was true he had not (very often, at least) expressed jealousy toward her husband or resentment about the children's ignorance of their true paternity or (even any real marked) rancor with regard to their (singular) circumstances. But at the end of the day none of this mattered because (at the end of the day), she said, she wanted *no more kids.* He acquiesced (having no viable option) and their Thursday evening rendezvous continued through winter and spring much as they always had, the man not wanting to upset what seemed to him (sanely or not) a basically good situation and his girlfriend thinking (more or less) along similar lines. Given all this, then, why did she suddenly *need to talk* last Thursday?

Because she was pregnant. Three months along according to the doctor who (himself an old-school Catholic) embraced the Pope's call (this would be Pius II) for Catholics to conceive, thus to propagate large families so that the universal flock be increased according to the (ironic, if not plausibly hypocritical) wishes of the Virgin Mary. Being an accountant (a good one, it should be acknowledged), the man (whose chalky face blanched as his mouth went dry) made some quick calculations and comprehended immediately the deeper meaning of his girlfriend's unexpected revelation. This was not *his* child, he breathed (lower lip quivering in a way she had never seen before, as if he'd been touched by an invisible taser mildly electrocuting him there) and waited for her to respond, suspecting she was going to tell him (as in fact she did) that she wasn't sure. He (however) was. As the man marched from the kitchen to the bedroom to the living room and back into the kitchen (where she sat, trying her best to *remain calm*), he recounted (at the top of his lungs and with awful precision) both his own itineraries, locations, and agendas for the month of June, and then hers. She had missed (as she did by joint agreement and without fuss each year) being available to him the first three Thursdays of that month (because her family made their annual trip to the Midwest to visit her parents), and in a (rare) disruption to their arrangement he himself managed to miss the last Thursday that June because one of his interleague softball games ran into extra innings (they lost). The woman sat listening to this (quite accurate) appraisal of things, feigning a certain interest in the logic of the man's assessment, nodding her head sometimes and other times shaking it (all the while warily observing that grotesque shuddering of his lower lip), knowing he wasn't wrong in concluding that (for once) the baby was not his. It was when the man fell silent, strode smoothly over to the kitchen table, and quite unexpectedly slapped her (not hard, but it came as a shock), that she told him (through a

veil of warm tears) that he was right about everything. She'd felt
sorry for her needy husband one night at her parents' (couldn't he
understand such a simple thing) and, having left the condoms at
home, figured nothing would come of it (so to speak). Granted,
they'd only (discreetly and perfectly silent in the guest bedroom of
her mother and father's old clapboard house) *done it* once, but, as the
adage goes, In for a penny, in for a pound (she didn't say as much that
evening, though it occurred to her as she walked back home under a
pretty waxing moon, wondering what she was going to do about *this
total mess* she found herself in, drying her eyes on her jacket sleeve
while elegant bats dropped in and out of the streetlamp light). They
had agreed before she left (embracing tentatively after exchanging a
few choice words about the unacceptable slap) to give it a week to
cool off and meet Thursday next to pursue a reconciliation.

Over the course of that protracted and galling weekend, the man
found himself thinking (if thinking it was, given he was by then well
into the process of mislaying his mind) at cross-purposes. Now he
was calm (it doesn't matter), now hurt (how could she), now enraged
(the time had come inevitably that everyone had to be taken off the
ledger, zero summed). He wished she would telephone him and (on
a whim, for instance) propose that (perhaps, barring he had other
plans) he might drop over for dinner with her husband and kids
(vegetable lasagna night), so that he could accept her invitation or
else slam down the phone in disgust (she didn't call). But no, he was
banished now and there was no making up with her next Thursday
(she should have at least called to see how he was faring, given he
had done *nothing* wrong and she had done *everything* wrong), and
this was why he filled his (father's old Waterman) fountain pen with
black ink and took a sheet of paper and began to draw up his *list
of demands* not having (initially) a definite concept (clue) what his
demands should be, but writing in the confident knowledge that
(because of her *ruthless betrayal*) what had been private would soon
become (very) public (indeed). She'd *get hers* (he thought). That
Monday at work he found himself studying the (seven) faces (three
female, four male) of his (soon to be former) colleagues, wondering
whether they fathomed the darkness that haunted their coworker's
heart. They didn't (it seemed to the man), and this only angered him
all the more, even though he had spent years (and a great deal of
effort) keeping secret from them the source (his girlfriend and three
bastard children) of what now infuriated him. He tidied his (already
meticulous) desk the next day, knowing it would be his last, then

walked straight home, pausing (briefly) to throw a rock (small but with cruelly perfect aim) at a mockingbird perched in an elm tree.

When the telephone rang (fast forward to late Sunday night on *day three of the hostage crisis*), the man (startled from his quiet reverie about how his life was falling to pieces faster than autumn leaves) inadvertently squeezed the trigger of his Browning BDA-380 causing his (hitherto inert) girlfriend to scream, however muffled she was by the duct tape (which she'd managed to chew through in order to breathe better), while also causing the sharpshooters and other peace officers outside the house (illuminated by klieg lights) to move into *maximum alert mode.* The man himself screamed before picking up the phone (after a good dozen rings) and asking, What do you want? as the acrid bouquet of discharged primer smoke settled in the living room and the fresh (impressively huge) hole in his hardwood floor gaped at his feet. He recognized the voice as that of his girlfriend's husband. What I want is to know what you want, answered the husband (reasonably enough), containing his fury with great effort. Brief silence, then more from the husband. What (he said) I don't want to do is cause trouble here (words prescripted by the negotiator), I just want to know if my wife is all right. A (lengthy and sinister) silence ensued before the man assured his neighbor, this *totally retarded* former friend, client, and husband of his gagged and handcuffed pregnant (by now very ex-) girlfriend, that she was doing *really great.* What was that gunfire all about? pressed the husband (again reading the scribbled prompt written in the negotiator's notepad). As if snapping out of a daydream, the man told the husband to pass the (goddamn) phone to somebody who had some (goddamn) authority here. What was being done (for instance) about his *list of demands?* The cuckold (just before the negotiator snatched the phone out of his hand and two troopers gently if firmly escorted him away from the *staging area*) told the man (dramatically, very audibly) that he didn't give a *rat's ass* whether he killed his *fucking wife* or not, and that he hoped (sincerely) that he put a bullet through his own *fucking brain* (if he had one) while he was at it. Screw you, thought the man who was now confronted with a very different voice (the negotiator said hello to him, winningly), making the man think (wisely) that here (most definitely) was someone (he asked for authority and got it) more frightening (or else appalling) than even the (goddamn) husband, because he was (or *it*, since it was a voice) smooth (as honeyed yogurt), and cool (as a wasp's dart) and sober (unafraid of the darkness, anyone's darkness), all of which suddenly shocked (as the expression goes) the man back to (as it were, fleeting) reality.

This negotiator (knowing what was of primary interest to his perp) asked first how the man was doing, did he have enough to eat, did the woman (never *hostage*) have enough to eat, or have other (uh) needs (prescription medicines). The woman, the man said (curiously sheepish given the imbalance of power at play here, the world being in *his* hands), was *doing better than ever* (disdain intended), though he realized for the first time since he took his girlfriend hostage that neither he nor she had slept or eaten (much, old tofu salvaged from the fridge before the electricity was cut off, washed down with tap rather than customary bottled water, which he'd shared with his captive, duct tape temporarily removed, who accepted his largesse with reluctance) and (thus) his (already mislaid) mind was not as (razor) sharp as it (undoubtedly) ought to be under the (developing) circumstances.

That (*doing better than ever*) sounded (not so) encouraging to the negotiator who (in his most concerned voice) wanted to address the man's demands. There seemed to be five of them, all of which would be taken with (utmost) seriousness (to be sure). It was just that the message (you see) that he had left earlier on the phone machine at the accountants' office was a little garbled (utterly unintelligible) and so in order to accommodate his needs (in the most immediate and efficient manner) it would be useful for the man to (now) repeat these ultimatums. The man cleared his throat and (wanting to cooperate fully, given things were going his way, it decidedly seemed) articulated his *list of demands.*

First off was a private jet (fully fueled) with an experienced (unarmed) pilot prepared to fly the man and his girlfriend to the destination of his choice (the man made this first demand despite the fact he had never been on a plane in his life, was in fact terrified of flying, and had concocted the idea from having seen numerous action films that featured *hostage situations*). Further, he demanded that the sum of one million dollars (unmarked bills, twenties and fifties, once more inspired by those selfsame movies) be delivered to him (leather attaché) in exchange for his (written) guarantee to release the girlfriend once his destination (Cuba, he was thinking, certain—not quite—he wouldn't be extradited if, as he'd additionally mused, he donated most of the ransom money to Cuban baseball for the purchase of new gloves, uniforms, etcetera) had been reached. And furthermore, he demanded (lest he not summon the courage to board the jet and fly to Cuba) that he be granted legal immunity for his (unsavory to some, but surely not felonious to him) actions, since (logically) none of this was *his goddamn fault* but rather the fault of his (treacherous goddamn) girlfriend, not to mention her (goddamn Lothario of a) husband (plus also that he had, solely *because of them*, mislaid his mind). And moreover, what he demanded was an apology (in front of television cameras, preferably in prime time) from all his fellow employees at the accounting firm, for each and every thing they ever did to make him unhappy (not fathoming, for instance, *the darkness that haunted their coworker's heart* on Tuesday last, damn them all to hell). Finally, the man demanded (noticing as he spoke that the negotiator had been very quiet, which he mistakenly attributed to attentiveness and even conscientiousness, perhaps to the fact that the negotiator must surely be taking notes, if not scrambling his qualified staff of sublieutenants, or whomever, even as they lived and breathed, to make arrangements for the flight and ransom money) that his children be made aware of the fact that their father was not their father but that their *real father* (and here, more instantaneous than the crack of a bat against a ball, or a slap in the face, the bullet from the husband's handgun broke the living-room window glass, tore neatly through the drawn curtains, and entered the man's cranium, dropping him in a stunned heap on the hardwood floor, killing him immediately and without recourse)—.

At this juncture the husband's wife screamed again, this time unremittingly until the peace officers (having placed the husband under arrest, quite incensed and not a little chagrined that, while focusing on raiding the house through the kitchen door in back, they had failed to notice the husband who had walked home after the officers removed him from the *staging area*, and there had a few *nice stiff ones* while he loaded his own handgun, no Browning BDA-380 but sufficient to the task, and marched back, keeping himself more or less hidden in neighborhood shrubbery, and aimed at the living room window not caring one way or another whether he happened to hit the *fucking psycho* or his *fucking wife*, just hoping he succeeded in murdering one of the *fucking motherfuckers*) entered the house (firearms unnecessarily drawn) to discover the (dead) man on the floor (still clutching one of his dozen or so guns, the others having been neatly laid out on the plaid sofa and matching wingback chair) and the woman by the radiator (who stopped screaming once they uncuffed her and removed the duct tape), and (after searching the rest of the modest house) radioed the negotiator and commanding officer (both smoking unfiltered cigarettes in the *staging area*) that the crime scene was secured. The woman's husband gave himself up without a struggle and was led off (himself now in handcuffs) to be driven downtown for booking (he called his lawyer and so forth). That he expressed (in front of several witnesses at the precinct house before his aforementioned attorney arrived) delight (not to mention astonishment) upon hearing he had somehow managed (sheer luck) to slay the *fucking psycho* would not help his case in the months to come (found guilty of first-degree murder by a thoughtful *jury of his peers*). The man's corpse was (after being photographed from many angles) removed (body bag), and the media vans (pros in them) thereafter left (this particular crisis being *a wrap*), as did the SWAT contingent and many officers (two detectives and a forensic expert remained behind *collecting evidence* such as it was), and soon the neighborhood settled back to (some semblance of) normalcy while a harsh early frost (this would be toward the end of the month) hastened the (magnificent) autumn foliage even as it killed chrysanthemums in flower beds up and down the street, while geese flew in (loud and traditional) formation across the (cobalt) sky overhead. As for the ex-wife of the (imprisoned) husband (and girlfriend of the deceased), she sold both (the dove gray and very pale blue) Capes (having inherited the former from her ex-boyfriend, who had thoughtfully included their offspring in his will, and the latter in her divorce settlement) and moved (with all four of her children) into a larger house (different neighborhood, as might be presumed). During her (understandably quite lengthy) period of mourning and recovery (from the many traumas she was forced to endure) she relied on the (combined) comforts afforded her by her doctor (who determined which pharmaceuticals would help her through her difficult days and nights) and priest (whose dulcet voice, not unlike that of the doctor, was so soothing to her in the shadowy solace of the confessional), each of whom (generous to *a fault*) took her (as it were) under their mortal wings.

Five Poems

James Tate

THE REENACTORS

    I was just standing on the corner watching the people
go by. Occasionally, an acquaintance would stop to make small
talk. "I'm just back from a year in China." "Oh, I didn't
realize you were gone." "My dog just gave birth to a litter
of eight puppies. Would you like one?" "Thanks, I'd like all
eight, but not today." "Hey, Blake, I saw you in the papers.
That was really a weird article. It's not true, is it?" "I'm
hardly the one to ask. I mean, it's my life, but who can say
what's really going on?" I must admit, I don't even know the
names of any of these people. But I know who they are. He's
the one who talks out loud to himself in bookstores. And that
one's unemployed. And that one's a scam artist. And that one
won a million dollars in a personal injury lawsuit. Then, a
motorcycle convoy roared through town, old men with a lot of
pride in their machines, on a Saturday outing. No one pays them
any attention, and soon they're gone. I saw my friend, Blaine,
crossing the street toward me. "You're just the man I wanted
to see," he said. "You won't believe what's going on. Some
out-of-town investors are planning to take over this whole town
and turn us into a theme park." "It could be fun," I said. "What's
the theme?" "I think they want to call it The Last Small Town
in America, or something like that, and everything is going to
be a replica, a fake hardware store, with a professional actor
reenacting the role of an old-timer hardware store owner, etc. . . .
The whole town reenacting small-town America as it once ostensibly
was, according to the billionaire investors who have never even
seen an honest-to-God small town. We've got to stop them, Blake.
This is where we live. It isn't perfect, but at least it's real,"
he said. I had never seen Blaine quite so agitated. Normally,
he was a real cool customer. "Where did you hear about this?"
I said. "They're trying to buy up every business on Main Street.

They're offering the owners prices they can't refuse. It's going
to happen before you know it," he said. "Well, I'm not moving,"
I said, "and I can't change. I'll still be standing right here."
"But people will be taking pictures of you, and talking about you
right to your face, as though you weren't an actual human being,"
he said. "Sounds like a mighty poor theme park, if you ask me.
Are you telling me that people are going to travel halfway around
the world and pay money to see me standing on a street corner?"
I said. He paused and looked me over. "Listen, I have to run now.
I just thought you should be the first to know, Blake. I know
you love this town as much as I do. Hey, I'll call you when I
know more," he said, and took off running down the street. Nothing
ever changes in this town. One restaurant closes, and another
opens up, and they're pretty much the same. Fears come in all
colors, as they always have, and dreams, too. You stand on the
corner long enough, and it all goes by. But I don't need to see
it all, just a glimpse of Blaine on the run. Tomorrow he won't
remember a thing. We'll reenact our lives as if they were the
real thing.

THE FORMAL INVITATION

I was invited to a formal dinner party given by Marguerite Farnish
Burridge and her husband, Knelm Oswald Lancelot Burridge. I
had never met either of them, and had no idea why I was invited.
When the butler announced me, Mrs. Burridge came up and greeted me
quite graciously. "I'm so happy you could join us," she said.
"I know Knelm is looking forward to talking to you later." "I
can't wait," I said, "I mean, the pleasure's all mine." Nothing
came out right. I wanted to escape right then, but Mrs. Burridge
dragged me and introduced me to some of her friends. "This is
Nicholas and Sondra Pepperdene. Nicholas is a spy," she said.
"I am not," he said. "Yes, you are, darling. Everyone knows it,"
she said. "And Sondra does something with swans, I'm not
sure what. She probably mates them, knowing Sondra." "Really!
I'm saving them from extinction," Mrs. Pepperdene said. "And this
is Mordecai Rhinelander, and, as you might guess from his name,
he's a Nazi. And his wife, Dagmar, is a Nazi too. Still, lovely
people," she said. "Marguerite, you're giving our new friend

a very bad impression," Mr. Rhinelander said. "Oh, it's my party
and I can say what I want," Mrs. Burridge said. A servant was
passing with cocktails and she grabbed two off the tray and handed
me one. "I hope you like martinis," she said, and left me standing
there. "My name is Theodore Fullerton," I said, "and I'm a depraved
jazz musician. I prey on young women, take drugs whenever possible,
but most of the time I just sleep all day and am out of work."
They looked at one another, and then broke out laughing. I smiled
like an idiot and sipped my drink. I thought it was going to be
an awful party, but I just told the truth whenever I was spoken
to, and people thought I was hilariously funny. At dinner, I was
seated between Carmen Milanca and Godina Barnafi. The first course was
fresh crabmeat on a slice of kiwi. Mine managed to slip off the
plate and landed in the lap of Carmen Milanca. She had on a
very tight, short black dress. She smiled at me, waiting to see
what I would do. I reached over and plucked it from its nest.
"Nice shot," she said. "It was something of a bull's-eye, wasn't
it?" I said. Godina Barnafi asked me if I found wealthy women
to be sexy. "Oh yes, of course," I said, "but I generally prefer
poor, homeless waifs, you know, runaways, mentally addled,
unwashed, sickly, starving women." "Fascinating," she said. A leg of lamb
was served. Knelm Burridge proposed a toast. "To my good friends
gathered here tonight, and to your great achievements in the further-
ance of peace on earth." I still had no idea what I was doing
there. I mentioned this to Carmen since we'd almost been intimate.
"You're probably the sacrificial lamb," she said. "The what?" I
said. "The human sacrifice, you know, to the gods, for peace,"
she said. "I figure it's got to be you, because I recognize all
the rest of them, and they're friends." "You've got to be kidding
me," I said. "No, we all work for peace in our various ways, and
then once a year we get together and have this dinner." "But why
me?" I said. "That's Marguerite's job. She does the research all
year, and she tries to pick someone who won't be missed, someone
who's not giving in a positive way to society, someone who
is essentially selfish. Her choices are very carefully considered
and fair, I think, though I am sorry it's you this time. I think
I could get to like you," she said. I picked at my food. "Well,
I guess I was a rather good choice, except that some people really
like my music. They even say it heals them," I said. "I'm sure
it does," Carmen said, "but Marguerite takes everything into
consideration. She's very thorough."

James Tate

THE GREAT HORNED OWL HAS FLOWN

I bought a stuffed owl at a tag sale and immediately
regretted it. The man had said it was a great horned owl,
and his grandfather had shot it in the woods around here
maybe fifty or sixty years ago. He let me have it for three
dollars. I thought it was a bargain until I saw what it looked
like in the backseat. Even that dead, I thought it was going
to tear my head off. I waved goodbye and tore out of there
mindlessly, the fierce yellow and black eyes staring at me
in the mirror with an undisguised hatred. I waited for it
to spread its wings any moment, to flap and fill the car with
terror. I was driving erratically, too slow, then too fast,
not staying on my side of the road. Finally, I pulled over
and hid the owl under a blanket. When I got home, Sally said,
"Where's the milk?" "The milk," I said, "I forgot the milk."
"How could you forget the milk?" "I bought an owl instead,"
I said. I took the blanket off the owl and just stood there
trying to smile. She walked around examining it. After a while,
she announced, "He's very attractive. Let's put him on the
mantel. Now go get that milk." I placed the thing gently on
the mantel. It looked stern and imposing, as though it un-
questionably ruled this world. I couldn't believe Sally didn't
notice that. I went out and got the milk, cursing the tag sale
as I passed. When I got home, it wasn't there. Sally was in
the kitchen and as I handed her the milk, I said, "Where'd you
move the owl?" "I didn't move the owl," she said. "It's
right where you left it, on the mantel." She walked into the
living room and said, "See." The owl was staring right at
me. Sally looked at me as though I was slightly addled. "Oh,"
I said, and she went back into the kitchen. Already it was
playing tricks on me. Then it sits there like Mr. Innocent stuffed
bird. His powerful beak and claws were just a small part of
the problem. It was his mind that really alarmed me. He was
smarter than I was. One look at him would tell you that. He
was capable of operating on several levels of reality at once,
while I was barely holding onto one. I was definitely at a
disadvantage here. Sally called to me to come help her with
something in the kitchen. I looked at him and said, "You bastard."
I changed a lightbulb, and then grated some cheese. One thing
led to another, and soon I had forgotten all about the owl.

We had a pleasant dinner, during which we discussed the possibility
of remodeling the bathroom and getting a dog. Then we went
into the living room, and the owl had moved. "Why did you move
it?" Sally said. "I didn't," I said. "It moved on its own."
"That's cute, Jay, that's real cute," she said. "It can do
anything it wants," I said. "It's not really dead. I mean, I
know it was shot and supposedly killed fifty or sixty years ago,
and it was stuffed and mounted, so you'd think it would be dead.
Maybe it's just us, but I saw its ears twitch and its eyes move."
"Jay, I can't believe you're talking like this. Are you sure
you feel all right?" she said. "It's had a long rest, and now
it's waking up," I said. I couldn't believe I was talking like
this either. Even so, I blamed it on the owl. "But I like it,"
she said. "Maybe it's the wisdom thing." "I'm going to release
it tomorrow," I said. "Release it? It's dead," she said. In
the morning, it was gone. No opened windows and doors, but
somehow it was gone. I said to Sally, "Did you see that, it's
gone, the owl's flown out on its own." "Yeah, it's flown into
the trash and on its way to the dump," she said. "The poor thing
was making you far too upset, no fault of its own."

THE THEORY OF MOWING

Rather than dwell on my son's upcoming marriage to a
minor starlet of questionable repute, I went out to the
garage and cranked up the lawnmower. I start along the
property line, and always try to gain an inch or two from
my neighbor. He'll take it back when he mows his next week,
but still I like to irritate him. When I stop to pick up
small stones or fallen branches, I always toss them into his
yard. Back and forth they go all summer. I try to make the
rows as perfectly straight as I can. But when the mind drifts,
so goes the machine, and there's no telling where you can end up.
Once I start thinking about my ex-wife, it is possible for me
to mow my neighbor's entire yard. And I hate it when he comes
out and thanks me. I say, "Herb, you're my friend. It was the least I
could do for you," and am immediately overcome with
self-loathing. Libby, my ex-wife, doesn't even speak to me.
She's married some handsome, wealthy younger man, who, I'm almost

certain, is a criminal. Maybe she's protecting me, that's the
only thing I can think of. But I miss her, I mean, my God, we
were together for twenty-five years. By now I'm mowing in
crazy-eights, and have wiped out half the flower garden. Herb,
my neighbor, is watching me from his window, and laughing up
a storm. I push the machine back to the beginning of the last
straight row and start again. I try to concentrate on nothing
but the grass in front of me. I push and sweat and think, straight
line, a straight line is your way to heaven, row after row after
row without end, well, that's an exaggeration to pump me up.
And my daughter, Tamara, living in Thailand, supposedly doing
volunteer work for the Red Cross, she writes to me in what feels
like code: ". . . lonely nights on the beach under the bright moonlight, I feel like a dying rose." What is that supposed to mean?
Am I supposed to have a code book for this kind of writing?
By now my lawn looks like I am trying to send a message to aliens.
It says, SAFE TO LAND HERE, FRIENDLY EARTHLING. The whole idea
was to relax and concentrate on mowing. So I start again, neat,
precise, and straight, no wavering, no slip-sliding around, trim
around what's left of the garden, circle the maple tree, then
straight to the back property line, quick turn, and so on.
I am aware that Herb is still watching me, but I act for all the
world as if there was a plan and a purpose to all my previous
diversions. I accomplish this through an air of high confidence, as
though no mere mortal could fathom the supreme, final design of
my creation.

SPECIAL OPERATIONS

There were some bald men in a field pushing a huge ball,
but the ball wasn't moving. They appeared to be straining
with all their might, but the ball wouldn't move. Then they
sat down and cried for a few minutes. But soon they jumped
up and charged the ball with war cries, and the ball moved a
few inches. They shouted with joy, and jumped up and down,
hugging one another. A woman walked by and stopped beside me.
"What are those men doing down there?" she said. "It's a
warrior thing," I said. "They're working out some technical
problems. They're protecting us from evil, but the plan is

242

still in the early stages of development." "Does that big ball
represent evil?" she said. "It's either evil or good. They're
still trying to work that one out," I said. "Some men live on
such an exalted plane, it's a wonder anything ever gets done,"
she said. "I meant that as a compliment, of course," she said.
"Only a few are chosen," I added. The men were butting their
heads against the ball and kicking it. "I've always been amazed
that we don't just fall off the planet and float around like so
much space debris. I have a goldfish in my purse swimming around
in a little plastic bag. Would you like to see it?" she said.
I didn't have much choice in the matter. "Sure," I said, "let's
see the little devil." She opened her purse and looked around.
"It's not here," she said, looking terribly distraught. "It
got away, or somebody stole it from me when I was on the bus."
"Maybe one of the bald men conscripted it for the war against
evil," I said. "A fish like that could be used in special
operations." "But it was for my son. He's sick, and I thought
it could comfort him," she said. "Things are different now," I
said. "You'll see, it's all for the better." "I'm feeling a little
weak. I know we've just met, but would it be too much if I asked
you to walk me home? I don't live far from here," she said.
What was I supposed to say? "That would be no problem at all.
By the way, my name is Rudy Byers," I said. "And mine is Paula
Kozen," she said. "How old is your boy?" I said, for the sake of
conversation. "He's nine," she said. A flock of pigeons took
flight from the roof of the hardware store. They flew in a wide
arc, then landed back on the roof in the same spot, all but one,
who landed on the sidewalk to savor a piece of bread someone had
dropped. "What's his name?" I said. "Colin," she said. "What's
wrong with him? You said he was sick," I said. "I don't know,"
she said, "he won't talk. And he won't get out of bed." I was
sorry I had asked. I was trying to take her mind off the goldfish.
"How long has he been like that?" I asked, against my better judgment. "For as long as I can remember," she said. "You could get
another goldfish," I said. "They're cheap." "Do you honestly
think one of those bald men stole it?" she asked. "They couldn't
even move that ball," I said. It was quite a spectacle. "Well,
this is where I live. Thank you for your help. I'll be all right
now," she said. "Are you sure?" I said. "Oh yes, I have my Colin
to look after. I have to be strong for him," she said. "Right,"
I said. "Well, nice to meet you." I walked back to the center of

town and sat on a bench in the park. The flag was snapping on its long pole. Lovers walked by holding hands. A fire engine returned to the station. A dog was waiting for the light to change. Then, it changed.

Untitled
Renee Gladman

"CHOOSE THIS WALK," I hear through the headphones as I read along in the accompanying book. "When you finish you will discard the weight." I assume the travel writer means the bags we've brought with us. But why would we get rid of them, particularly this far from home? We're standing in line, waiting to get in to eat. I turn the page: a photo of a champagne-colored car with Texas plates, no occupants. The caption reads, "They stepped away." The voice continues, "Now take this car, for example. It belongs to a rental company. Two people borrowed it for the weekend. When Sunday came, it was agreed they would return it. However, some time before Sunday the car was abandoned. . . ."

The hostess walks out of the door of the restaurant with a clipboard in her hand. "Gladman, party of two," she calls. But she doesn't mean us. I can't explain how I know. My name is Gladman and there are two of us and we've been here nearly an hour, but that call, it's for a different sort of folk. Indeed, a couple walks out of line and approaches the door. Clearly Gladmans of a different sort. A. looks at me, not quite agreeing. "The book says," I add urgently, though out of sync with the voice in my ears, "the occupants never think of the car again," and show her a photo of two women in a parking lot, their backs to the camera.

Then a young man stands in front of us. He has bright eyes that suggest intelligence: he's probably asking about the wait. I can't hear him of course. The headphones are on my ears. He mouths: open, spread, open, close, and his teeth show every so often. I look at A., relying on her to be our ears. I want her to smile and be normal. She opens her mouth, like his, but instead of open, spread, open, close, with teeth periodically, she closes, opens, spreads, opens, with no teeth. I want to pull the phones off to beg her to cooperate, but the guide is saying, "Travel light in New Mexico," and I'm responsible for this information.

Being in a place "Colorado" that doesn't quite look like "Colorado," and headed to a place "New Mexico" makes you begin to wonder about maps and orientation. I look up. There is nothing in the sky indicating which way is north. And that's what I mean. Why is mathematics here? When I'm done gazing at what I believe to be up, I say to A., though I can't hear myself, "You've got to be nicer to people. We couldn't be more alone than we are here." And she nods and gives a face that reads, "I know. I'm trying." We're cooperating because we're underrepresented in this town, where she's starving and I'm absorbing this book. I remove my headphones and ask the woman in front of us where we are. She smiles and answers, "pueblo," which I presume is a joke.

The hostess opens the door and says, "Brown, party of two." A. turns to me, "That's us." I shake my head. "No," she says, "I went in while you were reading and wrote my name in place of yours, thinking surely they would call *my* Brown before they called *your* Gladman." She looks at me reasonably, challenging my need-to-be-blurted, "They already called *my* Gladman."

"The best direction to enter New Mexico is from the north," I read without listening to the guide's voice. More of this relying on signals for comfort. "From the north one is able to see the dramatic change in terrain from forest to desert without having to negotiate boundaries. If time allows, take the family to Cimarron Canyon, where you can get a great close-up."

"Hey, they are ready to seat us. Are you coming?" she asks as if she might go in without me. For unity, I acquiesce to eat as a Brown, though I am most certifiably a Gladman. "What are you so afraid of?" she wants to know. I ignore the question. "The book says," I try to explain the women's disappearance a different way, "officials found traces of cigar tobacco on the floor of the backseat and that's the extent of their evidence: the women may have been taken away."

246

*

A. towers above me as we walk to the ladies' room. The restaurant is working out fine, but the conversation we need to have can't take place at the table where we're sitting. So we agree to continue it in the bathroom. A. worries that her beer will be taken while we're gone and I'm worried about my wallet, which I left in the middle of the table, under a pile of napkins surrounded by hot-sauce bottles. The bathroom is unoccupied. Once inside, I pull her tank top over her head and seize her left nipple with my mouth. I have to stand on the toilet to do this. Well, I have to kneel on the toilet. I tug on the nipple, and wrap my arms around her waist. She does next what all day I've been hoping she would do, and afterward screams, "Renee!"

Time to go back to our table.

I recognize the Gladmans sitting in a corner of the smoking section. But I don't want to talk about them. So I turn back to the book and replace the headphones. A.'s been nearly serene since our return from the ladies' room, dipping her spoon in a yellowish pudding. I must say, there are other Gladmans here as well—besides me and the smoking couple. Everybody's white. I'm trying to rewind the book back to that photo of the fleeing couple. "Some time before Sunday the car was abandoned," I read. "Shut it," A. signs to me. She mouths something like, "You're talking too loud." And I lose my temper, yelling, "Yeah, well whack it." And I know what to expect. The waiter rushes over and I have to clear my ears. "Is there a problem?" he asks. I'm just going to eat this shrimp, I tell myself. But aloud I say nothing. "Ladies, could you come with me?"

What makes those smoking Gladmans want to get involved? The man of the pair shuffles toward our table. A. and I have not risen to the waiter's request. But with her eyes she's trying to ask me what I want. Mr. Gladman and the waiter stand to our right, obscuring us from the remaining diners. "Young man," Mr. Gladman begins, "why are you harassing these girls?" His chivalry embarrasses me; I look down. Below my hand, which rests on the book, I make out, ". . . evidence that the women spent some time in a hostel outside

247

Taos. Sight reportings have been the fuel for this case; there are no other records. No credit cards used." I'm dying to replace the headphones. What do you think happened to them, I ask A. She shrugs, closes her eyes. "Give me some time to sit with the information." Then she takes her last spoonful of pudding and leans back against her chair. Meanwhile, words between the waiter and old Mr. Gladman are destabilizing. The waiter is tapping Mr. G. on the shoulder saying, "Sir, you have no idea what you're doing." And Mr. G. is flailing his arms.

When I realize A. is speaking I'm surprised. The four of us have been talking at intervals, each pair at a time (the waiter and Mr. G., then A. and I), but something has caused A. to overlap with the waiter. Now he is saying, "These women have been negracious since they entered" against A.'s "What's peculiar about this case is how quickly it became folklore. And nobody was murdered. And no obvious sins were committed. The book doesn't even suggest they were lovers." All true, I respond, then grimace because I'm speaking alongside Mr. G.

Suddenly we four fall silent.

Then just as suddenly we begin again. Now A. and I cannot harmonize our conversation. But at least we're trying to say the same thing. She wants us to pay the bill and go, and that is also what I want. How awkward our timing. I say, "Get the check so we can split," and she says, "Get the check so we can go," only perhaps a second faster. Old Mr. Gladman startles us when he snatches something out of the waiter's hand and shouts, "Here you go, girls." I reach for my wallet, assuming it's the check, but soon realize it's a napkin.

Outside nothing has changed. The car is still in the parking lot; the sun is still out. I want to go somewhere and vacuum the seats, but A. says not yet. We're pulling away from the restaurant and I'm thinking about Mr. Gladman, comparing him to my father. "What happened back there?" I ask her. And, against her "Nothing," replace the headphones.

The Reincarnate
Michael Bergstein

IF I UNDERSTAND the karmic principle, after one's death, one is reborn into another, subsequent life to fulfill unfinished earthly tasks
and paradise can never be achieved until all the cycles are complete,
one after another, birth following death. My lives, though, the three
of which I can speak, took place more or less concurrently. That is,
upon each death I returned to another lifetime overlapping the one
before it, so all three of my lives were lived to a large extent at the
same time. This strikes me as awry, and has led to a perplexing
conundrum: what indeed is the true nature of time and rebirth? My
existences did not adhere to calendar years and clocks. Nor have I
been entirely unaware of my various selves during the long course of
me.

In my first life, if I may call it the first, I was Michael Patrick
O'Malley, born the son of Anne and James Robert O'Malley, in South
Boston, 17 April 1903, and there died of cirrhosis in May 1952. My
existence might have ended there had I not been reborn, so to say, as
Henry Stone, also of Boston, in 1911. Obviously these selves lived for
many years in the same city at the same time, unaware of each other,
which is to say unaware of me, but that changed early in October
1937 during my second life. Henry Stone, as it were, was twenty-six
years old, unmarried, and working as a line cook at a downtown
hotel. On this particular morning my chance reading of the *Herald*
revealed a photograph taken the day before in front of a school on the
corner of Dartmouth and Newbury streets, in Back Bay. The building was undergoing renovation, and the photographer took a picture
of a few workmen posing around an open pit, leaning rakishly on
their shovels. On the left, a slight man in his midthirties with large
eyes and greasy dark hair pulled behind his ears had his head turned
slightly and looked to one side, as if noticing something or someone
just beyond the frame. I don't know what triggered the memory—if
memory it was—but even though the newspaper did not identify the
workers, in a flash of cognition I knew this man was Michael Patrick
O'Malley, then thirty-four years of age, day laborer, alcoholic, and

living in a third-floor bed-sitter in the Fens. I knew this because he was me. Or perhaps I was him. It is difficult to now describe just how this knowledge took shape in my consciousness, though the effect was both aural and hallucinatory. I knew the sound of his voice—a low, rough Boston burr—and what his childhood home looked like. I saw his father's face and remembered the taste of his mother's Irish stew. I knew Michael Patrick had been working at the school site for only a week. I knew he kept a bottle of inexpensive whiskey under his bed, and I knew the ceiling in his bathroom needed painting.

Evidence of my reincarnation was generally like this—never clear as a whole, but detailed enough to convince me. I knew I had lived before. Or, rather, lived again, and the notion both confused and frightened me. I had no doubt that I "was" Michael Patrick, or "had been" him, from the moment I saw the photograph. There was much sadness in his life, with more troubles and worries to come, and in a way I felt sorry for him—for me—for having to endure so many woes. For myself, Henry Stone, my life by comparison was grand. I enjoyed my job, had fine health, and was engaged to my kind and plain-faced girlfriend, Louise, currently finishing her course work at Tufts. We planned marriage, children, a home, all the typical middle-class dreams of the late Depression, so this sudden discovery that I was a reincarnated soul who had lived "before" forced me to reconsider my identity and motives. Why had Michael Patrick "come back" as me? Which endeavors in the great universe had I failed to complete?

With my dharma thus broken, several days of torpor and melancholy followed, which even Louise noticed, though I never mentioned its true source. I carried an interior darkness along the sun-brightened autumn streets of Boston, and could not escape feeling split between my former and current life. This duality changed everything. Each thought I had, each action, these all now took place in relation to Michael Patrick O'Malley, if it is true that the second life owes back debts to the first, that is. The newspaper photograph haunted me and I vowed to see me in person, though it took a few days more before I screwed up the courage. On my day off I walked over to the intersection of Dartmouth and Newbury and mingled with the passersby. It was lunchtime, and most of the workmen sat on the ground eating, but I did not see me. I walked the length of the block and back again, then noticed a couple of workers standing beside a frankfurter stand at the edge of Copley Square. When I approached I saw that one of them was me, Michael Patrick. I looked sickly, almost tubercular, and though I refused to get closer than a hundred feet I saw how shabby I was, a man more defeated by life than nourished by it. I sadly watched me sadly eat my hot dog and took pity on myself, this former, older me. After only a minute I was sorry I had done it and walked away. In the reincarnation business, past lives are perhaps best left on their own. But now that I had seen me, witnessed proof of personal rebirth, I had to alter the whole way I looked at Henry Stone and the expectations of my life. I knew what would happen to Michael Patrick O'Malley in the end, and wondered whether I was now supposed to make up for all that his life lacked. Was my happiness and satisfaction meant to ease the pain of my former life and take me to a higher place? Or were my pleasures disrespectful of my suffering? I did not want to repeat mistakes of "the past," for then I would be doomed to another life on this earthly floor.

Baffled and distracted, I kept Louise mollified and hid my feelings from her. Indeed, I often hid them from myself. I never dared to go looking for Michael Patrick again, and as 1937 crept up on 1938 I promised myself that by the year's end I would decide on a rightful path for this life and stop beleaguering myself about it. At Christmastime we visited Louise's parents on Buzzards Bay and I was glad to be away from the city. The change of atmosphere gave me perspective, and their big house on the water was always a warm and welcoming haven. After dinner Louise's mother took her sherry glass and narrated a tour along the walls of family pictures, at my request. Photographs of faces in this century and painted ones of those in the previous smiled or scowled back at us from their dusty time traps, and when I noticed a resemblance to people still living I knew that that was another kind of reincarnation. By sequential birth and blood, perhaps, but in a way little different from the kind I experienced. The saga and connection were still evident.

Louise and I walked on the beach in the dark, and held each other and smooched, as the saying went, under the cold stammer of starlight. We pledged our love and promised to wed as soon as she graduated, and as we talked I realized that our plans were right and true after all. Having seen Michael Patrick made me more aware of my own good fortune, that of Henry Stone, and then and there I decided to make the most of it to counterbalance the misery and disease of my first life. Louise and I married, as discussed, on 12 June 1939, and by then the influence of Michael Patrick O'Malley had receded. As a reincarnated soul I accepted the inevitable (life, after all, is a wheel), so while I never forgot me or my other existence just across town, in a way Michael Patrick was already dead. I would stay true to my former self, but there was nothing I could do for me now.

Life in Boston settled into a normal state, though every now and then I wondered how many of the people around me—at work, in the streets, on the trolley—were also reincarnated. Surely there must be many, and which of these had experienced what I had: running across a previous life in the midst of the current one? If they did they never showed it. Nor did I, of course. I had no intention of letting people think I was mad, and haven't spoken of this to anyone until now. Louise and I intended to reproduce ourselves in a less karmic way, and by the time I had worked myself up to kitchen manager at the Lennox Hotel we prepared to have our first child. Before she had a chance to get pregnant, however, the Japanese destroyed our fleet on Hawaii, and out of duty I immediately enlisted. It meant abandoning my young wife for the time being, but I would have been eventually drafted anyway, the way things turned out, and also I felt I somehow owed this to Michael Patrick. Fight the fight on his behalf. Can you understand?

Uncle Sam sent me to the Pacific, attached to a Liberator crew. At age thirty-three I easily made captain, and was sitting copilot the afternoon of 29 September 1944 when, flying over a small atoll we assumed was unmanned, antiaircraft fire came up from nowhere and took out both starboard engines, followed instantly by a huge cabin explosion. Our plunge was fiery and thankfully brief, and the image of this wreckage splintering into the ocean began as a series of short nightmares in my third life, at the age of five or six, incidentally well before the era of aviation. On and off, usually for several nights in a row, I would awaken crying in my Beacon Hill bedroom, disturbed by visions of a flying machine coming apart in flames and hitting the sea. I had no idea, of course, that I was "remembering" the death of Henry Stone, a person who was me, or would be me, this being about 1892, nearly twenty years before Henry's "birth." Yes, my third life, the one from which I now speak, as Dr. Charles Saltonstall, semi-retired, ironically came into being earlier than those of my two predecessors. My reincarnations did not follow any chronology, as I said from the outset, and this poignancy grew as I did. My nightmares eventually stopped, and it wasn't until I was much older, as a student at Harvard Medical, that the life of Henry Stone and, by association, that of Michael Patrick O'Malley entered my consciousness in a significant way. I came by this in part through a colleague from India, also studying ocular surgery, who often spoke of the tenets of Hinduism, and I believe this may have induced my sensitivity to the presence of my previous lives. It was soon after meeting him, at any rate, that I began to "see" or "relive" my first two incarnations.

Details of these, as you see, are few yet specific, and I cannot recall everything. Each life overlaps but remains distinct, and it is not possible to fully experience previous selves. You exist and you know you and the rest is kismet. By 1922 I had read some Indian poetry and tried my hand at meditation, and this, too, helped open my consciousness. For short periods, if I wanted to, I could usually conjure what Michael Patrick and Henry were doing at any particular moment during the run of time when all three of us were still alive in Boston, but beyond that I could not know their worlds. For example, though I realized that Henry Stone died falling from the sky in the far future of 1944, I remembered nothing of the surrounding circumstances. Further yet, regarding the demise of Michael Patrick O'Malley in 1952, I only recalled the chromium instruments in my white room and a dull pain deep in my abdomen, but nothing else. It wasn't until much later that I researched Henry's war record, or attended my own funeral in Southie three days after Michael Patrick passed away, rest my soul.

Like my immediate forebear, I couldn't help visiting myself, even at death. Otherwise, three of me lived on, in sequence and yet out of it, and frankly my studies and internship left little time to contemplate the finer points of life in the cosmos. Flashes of my other lives came to me intermittently, usually during moments of pathos or enjoyment (for instance, I was quite distinctly three intoxicated people at Thanksgiving 1928, and paid dearly for it the next morning in triplicate), but in the main I was busy enough just being Chuck Saltonstall. After joining the eye surgery unit at St. Jerome's in 1930, I married and had two daughters, and by mid-decade had settled into my practice. I accepted the conditions of reincarnation and hoped that my acts on earth were worthy of a promotion. After three turns on the ground I was getting tired and wouldn't have minded skipping any more lives. Three seemed like enough and still does. My old selves were not through with me, however, and as October 1937 approached I began to "remember" that on the twelfth of that month Henry Stone made his private observation of Michael Patrick O'Malley in Copley Square. As the date neared (coincidentally, my fiftieth birthday), I had a mind to go and see them both. I was curious to actually lay eyes on me, as if a part of me did not quite believe it all. I remembered the exact time of the encounter—12:15 P.M.—so when the day and appointed hour came I ignored any misgivings and took a stroll from the hospital toward the square.

I would be fibbing if I said my heart didn't race as I approached the spot near the frankfurter stand, which stood exactly as it had in my recollections. Michael Patrick was there next to it, in the flesh and pallid, munching on a roll, and when I looked down the street I saw Henry Stone watching, recognizing myself from my own service photo: six-foot-two, lanky build, sandy hair. I looked cautious and furtive, motionless next to a lamppost and gazing at the me eating a frankfurter. Dr. Saltonstall's presence seemed at once an interruption to this amazing and, to Henry, devastatingly emotional scene. My own take on reincarnation was not as passionate anymore—perhaps I had lost interest during the very course of multiple lives—but as I watched my two previous selves engage in a bizarre, one-way intro-duction terrible questions suddenly arose: what if all these people filling the square were actually me in my future lives; what if Charles Saltonstall was merely the third in hundreds or thousands of lives yet to come, but all lived at the same time? Was I every-body, and was everybody me? Did each of these people, if me, always come to Copley Square on this day and at this hour to observe the amassing of our collected selves? Had it become a reunion of one, assuming each self reborn is aware of the other lives that came before (or during) it?

I, too, did not stay long and left when Henry Stone did, walking in the opposite direction. The encounter left me breathless though satisfied. I had proof I existed twice, but from here on I planned to leave my other selves alone. Like Henry, I did not want to meddle too much with the past. I never saw them again, except, as I said, when I attended Michael Patrick's funeral, but even here I did not enter the chapel until after my casket was completely closed.

The years carried forward, as years will, and though they were usu-ally far from my mind I occasionally relived moments in the days of Michael Patrick O'Malley and Henry Stone, and still do, if only to compare my present life with my past ones, keeping an eye on my karmic progression. There must be reasons for my lives, just as I think there are reasons why I am aware of them. I pay homage to my star-crossed precursors for all they have taught me, but I do want this life to be my last and hope my lifelong dedication to healing quali-fies me for a final place in Nirvana. By the time I reached seventy, in 1957, my wife was dead and our daughters had grown and married, thus I retired from St. Jerome's and came out here to India. The clinic in Agra was new then, as was the concept of eye banks, so I settled here and volunteered my services. If I was to halt the cycle of reincarnation and escape my earthly bonds, what better place to finish up than here in the cradle of ancient teaching?

That was eight years ago, and since then I have learned much. Enough, in fact, to become a legal convert to Hinduism. As to performing surgery, it has only been a couple of weeks since I have had to give that up, and only because of the pain. It is not so bad now and requires only small doses of morphine to keep it tolerable. I am bedridden, and expect the end to come any day now. I could have had an operation of my own to forestall growth of the tumor, but at my age I am ready to go. And, as I stress, go permanently. I have no desire for a fourth chukker and pray frequently for a different outcome. In the meantime my stenographer, Mr. Djinn Chatterjee, who has kindly taken down this dictation in flawless shorthand and will presently type it into readable manuscript form, has proven a capable and trustworthy secretary as I settle the affairs of a dying man.

Here, Dr. Saltonstall drew a long breath and exhaled, coughed, and lay still. I put down my pad and pencil and looked at me. The burra sahib was dead. My familiar bulk looked suddenly small on the bed, and my face had gone white as my thick mane of hair. I knew this moment would arrive, but only since a month ago, when sheer coincidence (was it?) led me to be employed as a real pukka steno, temporarily, as it turns out, by my own previous self, whom I instantly remembered upon sight, I must say. Despite my fatal condition, I certainly did not want me to die, but interaction with myself disturbed me and created all sorts of dharmic repercussions in my life. That is, in my fourth. I got up from my chair and thought: here I go again. Somewhere in the hospital a radio broadcast the BBC and I heard Harry James playing "It Seems to Me I've Heard That Song Before" on his trumpet, and with that I went to the dresser, opened Dr. Saltonstall's wallet, and removed all the rupees, of which there was a considerable amount.

Whereupon Mr. Djinn Chatterjee stepped outside under the hot Indian moonlight and hailed a tonga to the nearest bordello.

The Messenger
David Antin

     i was on the way to binghamton and took along something to read
because it was a long trip from san diego   even with a stop in pittsburgh
     the book was marquez's one hundred years of solitude   its a long
book id started several times before and always found interesting and
always put down because the print was so small   i figured this might be
the time
     because it takes a long time to get from san diego to binghamton but
i took a notebook along just in case   as i always do
     i climbed over a gray haired man in a business suit to slide into my
seat beside the window and i opened up my copy of the new york times
while my neighbor was going over some kind of statistical documents in a
sort of portfolio   because i didnt want to start on any serious reading till
after breakfast   id only had time for orange juice before blaise drove me
to the airport
                so i opened my copy of the times to see that the italian
government was about ready to collapse over the achille lauro affair
     chrysler was going on strike   a rare documents dealer had been
blown out of his sportcar near the mormon temple in salt lake city
     st louis and kansas city had just clinched the playoffs   a new jersey
company was being charged with manslaughter for shipping paint soaked
sawdust to a dump site in akron
     and they were starting repairs on the st lawrence seaway
     it took a while for me to process all this but when i looked up my
neighbor was still going through his charts with a pencil and i looked at
him a bit more closely   he was a graying haired man with a big pleasant
face but a pale complexion   a little rumpled in his bluish business suit
     a small bulge of gut folded over his belt   a salesman engineer i
figured   middle aged   a little gone to seed   probably my age i figured
     when the stewardess   a handsome honey blonde with the impeccable
paint job and meticulous hair style that keeps every strand in place which
used to be the mark of the profession came by to take our breakfast orders
and noticed the marquez lying on the seat between us
                           are you reading

that she asked
     intelligent blue eyes looked out at me from under her rococo mask
     i nodded   its a wonderful book she said   those brazilians are so
powerful   so mystical and realistic at the same time   she shook her
head in amazement and smiled at me a sweet brilliant smile filled with
shared and secret knowledge   to which i responded with a kind of lame
agreement and watched her disappear
     my neighbor turned out to be a computer person   a mathematician
working as a sales rep for a seattle outfit that marketed a master program
to power companies to increase their efficiency and reduce their costs
     not a cheap program he said   it costs about fifty million   but it
saves the companies so much money they can make it all back in a year or
two   i was fascinated by the idea of a system that could pare twenty five
million dollars a year off these fat giants and i pressed him with questions
     its really based on a simple algorithm as elementary as kerckhoffs
laws   but it monitors every generator and transformer in every central
power plant and substation and plots the instantaneous output against
maximum capacity and the anticipated load   at any given moment it can
tell you how much load you can carry   how much youll have to import
or sell to other power companies   once youve put in all the statistical
data for seasonal and daily load for the region   it even lets you make
optimal judgments on parts replacement on marketing and hiring and
firing. . . .
     so   i suggested   it ought to prevent those great blackouts and
brownouts like the ones that hit new york in the sixties
     it ought to help anticipate them   he said   even if you cant
eliminate them   sometimes in a business boom   during a heat wave
     the demand is great all over   and the system simply doesnt have any
more power to give   and your neighboring systems dont have any surplus
to lend
     but all other things being equal   which they usually arent   he
smiled
     it gives you the best idea of where you are in your network at any
moment and how youre doing with all your power sources   whether
theyre nuclear or fossil fuels or hydro   it tells you at any second where
you are and where youre going to be
     this sounded marvelous and i was starting to get into the spirit of this
rational magic act   i suppose   i said   it counts in all the new energy
sources   the wind farms and solar and geothermal fields that have started
up in the last few years
     now there   he said   is a bit of a problem   wind and solar are

pretty unpredictable   and the systems are still pretty much just one level
above do it yourself kits   so theyre not standardized   and though by law
   the power companies have to buy up all the power these sources have to
sell and pay for it at a standard rate   to the power companies theyre
more trouble than theyre worth   theres just no algorithm for them   and
between you and i   the power companies would just as soon theyd go
away
        but how about hydro i said   i mean based on rainfall and snow   the
meteorologists havent had too much luck   what kind of algorithm have
you got for that
        sure he said   but weve got more experience with water   hey weve
been working with it longer and we have some pretty good statistics
        though mother natures always unpredictable   he grinned   but then
so are people   and you have the politics of the gulf countries affecting oil
supplies   and now youve got environmental pressures against certain
kinds of coals
                    strictly speaking he said   nuclear would be the cleanest
and the easiest to predict   but with all the publicity around that near
disaster at three mile island   public opinion being what it is   theres not
much chance for it to fly   at least for now   and with the delays in
licensing and all sorts of new safeguards and standards   thats going to
raise the costs of financing unpredictably   but as they say nothing is sure
but death and taxes anyway   still within that frame   all other things
   being equal   the program saves everyone lots of money and lots of grief
as well
        our lunch came by and while we were unwrapping our chicken
à l'orange from its foil cover and our green salad from its plastic covering
we got into a discussion of the computer revolution
        its a whole new world he said   i thought i was going to be a pure
mathematician maybe teaching at some college   and now im in
computers im on my way to make a sales presentation in binghamton and
i havent done any mathematics in years
        we started talking about how everything from tuning your car to
sending out junk mail or working out your sex problems could all be done
with computers now   and i remarked how even in the art department
where i was teaching we were opening up a computer wing   and he said
he wasnt at all surprised   even if he didnt know much about it   art was
something he never had much to do with but he knew that music was
starting to make use of computer aids to simulate all kinds of instruments
and even help in composition   so he supposed that artists could make use
   of all the graphic aids macintosh was putting out and there was more

complicated stuff some of which you could even see on television   but i
explained that wasnt really what my department was interested in as much
as the kind of conceptualizing power the computer made available   that
we expected the artists we were interested in educating would want to
write their own programs even develop their own hardware
    beats me he said   i would never have expected that   but if the
whole world is changing why not art
    and we drank to that with the wine we were using to wash down the
glazed chicken wed been eating   and my neighbor reflected on how
strange it was for almost everyone unconnected with the reality of
computers to concentrate on the problems they created instead of the
problems they solved   like the unemployment they created through the
jobs they eliminated in industries like chemicals or steel   and forget
about the new jobs they created in new technologies and services they
required and made possible
    and just at that moment the blonde stewardess reappeared beside our
seat and at the first break in our conversation smiled politely at my
companion and handed me a magazine
    theres a wonderful article there on brazil i thought you might be
interested in she said smiling once more at us before returning to the front
of the plane   and we went on talking   but after that our conversation
couldnt quite pick up again   the stewardess had handed me the magazine
face down and i was curious to see what it was   but out of politeness for
my neighbor i hadnt turned it over   id simply accepted it as it was offered
nodded thanks and gone on with our conversation   but i was anxious to
see what id been given   and i followed my neighbors conversation a bit
abstractedly   he seemed to sense this and discovered when hed finished
dessert that he had to review his portfolio again while i turned over the
magazine
    it was a copy of rolling stone   and there sandwiched between an
article on billy crystal   "billy and his wife janice have been married
fifteen years   their first date was on casey stengels birthday   johnny
carson will just have to wait"   record reviews   ads for videocassettes
memorabilia peewee herman fans   there was a photo essay on the
brazilian city of cubatao   a refinery city on an oily inlet two or three
miles from the port of santos   its the center of brazils economic miracle
    the smoking center of petrobras' cracking plants and the fiery
foundries of cosipas' iron works
    the sky above it turns red when its iron dust turns black when its coal
    and the twenty three other chemical and fertilizer plants that spew
carbon monoxide ammonia sulfur dioxide benzene pentachlorophenol and

coal dust into the air and into the muck that runs in slimy streams
under the stilt supported shacks where the people have come to participate
in the prosperity of brazils economic miracle   and they participate in it
    because theres work in cubatao and a man can earn two hundred
dollars a month working instead of starving in the back country or dying of
malnutrition like the indians while the states bulldozers are chopping out
roads through their homelands to exploit the bauxite iron ore and oil
    necessary for development and progress   but at a price the article made
clear in lurid photographs of lesions and lumps the size of golf balls on the
bodies of the workers   and of infants born dead or brainless   so many
they have to bury them in numbered boxes like packages in some infernal
post office   and of accidents like the rupture of a benzene pipe that
incinerated a whole section of a worker suburb or leaks of ammonia gas
from the fertilizer plant   and of regular trips to the hospital for oxygen
or adrenaline shots while the trees and shrubs along the hillsides near the
factories blacken and die and the rains carry the soil back to the grassy
river that runs out to the atlantic
    the story wasnt new   the underside of development and progress
for the people who dont have the computers and never will have them   it
was terrible and i knew that   but it was like a message given to me at the
moment of my technological intoxication   but what of the messenger
    the beautiful blonde stewardess with her gold polished fingernails in
her neat little continental airlines costume   what kind of message did she
intend   had she been listening to my computer conversation and seen me
getting caught up in a social fantasy triggered by an excess of
neighborliness and a momentary delight at being in someone elses skin
    was she trying to tell me something about the price of this kind of
progress thats never counted by the people who benefit from that progress
    or about the price of all progress paid for by the planet   or did she
simply think that because i was reading marquez i would be interested in
all things latin american and there was a nice article on brazil shed noticed
in rolling stone that i might have wanted to read   i wanted to ask her
what did she mean by giving me this copy of the magazine   and i got up
to look for her at the end of the aisle   but i couldnt find her   so i just
slipped my copy of rolling stone back into the magazine rack and made up
my mind to speak to her as we were getting off the plane   and i looked
for her as we debarked in pittsburgh   but she was nowhere to be seen

Duality
Hayden Carruth

Two roads converged in the woods, and I
Turned around and came back.

Arrow

Elizabeth Robinson

If the arrow
hits its mark,
it breaks flesh.

Then the body
divides in two,
and the arrow
as well.

This is how
the world divides,

and the result of pain
is its secrecy. The two
bodies it creates:

a mouth around
a barb, and essential

that word
choked back.

The I adopts a verb
and becomes its lover.

Then arrows become
indicators

pointing at them
in their duress.

If there are now
two arrows

coming late to their
target, they see

the breaking of split
selves that ought

to have happened.

Where the body arcs

it waits and expects

to meet them.

One verb
in many tenses

traces the feather
on the arrow's tail

in all the bodies' motion.

Arrow
not divisible

from the sender
as the point of
its final contact.

To revise the body
by any means

from its solitary
habit,

Elizabeth Robinson

this taking aim
and releasing.

Late and later
the air

compressing on motion

to deter

the arrow
from this recognition—

bouquet splaying
in air,

all possible motions

caught in the net
of the verb

swathing the body.
What word

can rise and incline

as target.
To injury

as it divides

give grasp.

The Pink Dress
Honor Moore

I AM WRITING THIS because you asked me to.

Every afternoon, I lay on the roof. It was the summer before I took my first woman lover, and I had left a man in Paris where I'd bought a dress of thin Indian cotton whose color was what they call rose, with a tinge of purple.

I thought of the sun as a god, opened my legs to him, and became wet in the clear heat.

There's your heat.

The Indian dress was short and I took it off. Slats of wood under me. Wind in the high branches of the maples. Cars passing on the road, like whips.

The man who had prized apart my legs was in Paris, so I would lie on the flat part of the roof, opening my own legs, watching the sun hit what it made wet.

The dress I took off is the only dress I remember wearing that summer.

I would lay my palms on the outsides of my thighs, and, pressing in, move them down and then up the outside lengths of my thighs as I opened them, as the sun picked up a wet shine of cunt, of labia.

Waves of heat, you said.

But you haven't told me what you like. Whether you like the word *cunt*, the word *labia*, or if in this circumstance you prefer the word *lips*, which if you translate *labia* into English is what you get.

Honor Moore

After a while I go into the house, where a sharp darkness makes white grainy, gives color edge. I have abandoned the master bedroom for a room at the side where I feel free to do what I like to myself. To my cunt.

If that's the word you like. Tonight it's raining hard. If the telephone rings, it's you. I open my legs. You've said that to me at least once. Open your legs. I like it when you say that. Just the definitive baritone of your voice brings—unspeakable.

I don't put my hand between my legs into my cunt when I lie outside, but when I go into the bright shade I meet my own hands and the white sheets that bring relief from the hard wood and give refuge from the sun.

I'm wet now, again, or if you'd like, My cunt is wet. I open my legs now to remember what I did then. Place one hand inside each thigh and push them apart against my own feigned resistance, my ass—

Is that the word you like?

Ass rising, fingers breaching—

Later I will hear of women who bend and tongue their own cunts. It seemed a terrible injustice I couldn't do that, and that what my fingers could do to my own cunt was not what his cock had done. What your cock might do.

What about *that* word? Will you allow it?

Cock. I like how it almost rhymes with fuck, and how when I say it, I feel the back of my throat open, something that doesn't happen with other words I might offer: *penis*, for instance, or *dick*.

I couldn't bend far enough to see it, so I got up and lifted a mirror from the wall. I wanted to see my cunt as hot and wet as it is now. I took the mirror down, lay on my back, and positioned the edges of the frame between my legs, just above the knees.

Naked on her back, a framed mirror between her bent, pale legs: I'm curious what you make of the spectacle.

266

Her bent pale legs holding it in place—oval, twenty-four by thirty-six inches—and then I reach for a lamp, remove the shade, switch it on, and move it close enough to light my cunt, which I have never seen, its slick creases the color of my thin dress, pink with a tinge of violet, twisting like glass in a kaleidoscope.

My hand is there now.

Exhilarating to be so free, holding the lamp as close as I want to, feeling its heat, the hard edges of the frame imprinting the insides of my thighs, cunt rising as I lift my pelvis, clench hard then open as if I am ready, as if you had pulled up the Indian dress with a rapid gesture, as if I were in your dream.

Again.

Because you ask me to.

Every afternoon, she lay on the roof. It was the summer of motorcycles on the road, the summer before she took her first woman lover, just two months after she'd left the hard-bodied man in Paris where, on rue St. André des Arts, she bought a cheap dress of thin Indian cotton whose color was what they call rose, with a tinge of purple.

She thought of the sun as a god, opened her legs to him, and became wet in the clear heat.

There's your heat.

The Indian dress was short in the style of the time, and she took it off. Rough slats of wood under the naked verso of her body. Wind in the high branches of the maples. Cars passing on the road, like whips. It was Sunday.

The man who had coaxed apart her legs, who had fucked and licked her, was in Paris or somewhere, so she would lie there on the flat part of the roof opening her own legs, watching the sun hit her black pubic hair, heat her cunt.

The only dress she remembers wearing that summer, a drawstring at the waist.

Her palms on the outsides of her thighs, pressing in, move down and then up the outsides of her legs.

Waves of heat, you said, but you haven't told me whether you like the word *cunt*, the word *labia*, the word *pussy*, some other. You would not, I think, tolerate the word *lips*. In that usage, it becomes a euphemism, don't you agree?

After a while she will go into the house, where sharp summer shadow turns white grainy, gives color edge. She has left behind the master bedroom. In the small room at the side of the house she feels free to do what she likes to herself.

To her cunt.

I'm beginning to find that word descriptive.

Tonight it's raining hard. If the telephone rings, it's you. I open my legs. I've heard you say that, Open your legs. I like the commands you issue in that definitive baritone. Open your legs, I want to see your cunt. And then you watch for a while, an animal intent on quarry.

On the roof outside, she doesn't put her hand between her legs, fingers into her cunt, but when she goes inside, into that bright shade, her own hands and the white sheets serve to bring relief from the hard wood, to offer refuge from the sun.

She's wet now, again, or if you'd prefer, her cunt is wet. And I? My legs are open now, an *aide memoir*.

One hand inside each thigh pushes outward against her feigned and symmetrical resistance. She lifts her ass.

I know you like that word. You've used it with me: Turn around. I want to kiss your ass. I liked that. I liked it because what is colloquially an insult—kiss my ass—became a devotion.

She lifts her buttocks and her cunt opens. She holds herself there,
the exertion a form of sex.

Later she will hear of a woman who can bend and tongue her
own cunt. She will meet that woman once, before learning of her
extraordinary flexibility. What an injustice she herself cannot reach
her cunt with her mouth, with her own tongue! What an inequity
her fingers cannot do to her cunt what her mouth might do, her
tongue.

Or what your cock might do.

Suddenly I like that word, how it almost rhymes with fuck,
and how when I say it, *cock,* I feel the back of my throat open,
something that doesn't happen with other words like that, *penis,*
for instance, or *dick.*

She could not bend far enough even to see it, so she lifted a mirror
from the wall. She wanted to see what her cunt looked like when it
burned like mine does now. She carried the mirror to her bed, lay
on her back, and positioned the edges of the mirror frame between
her legs, just above the knees.

Her bent pale legs holding it in place—a Victorian oval, twenty-four
by thirty-six inches—she reaches for a lamp, removes its shade,
switches the light on, and moves the hot bright bulb close enough
to illuminate her cunt, which she has never seen. For a while she
watches as its slick creases twist and reconfigure like strands of
shattered glass in a kaleidoscope.

Do you like the word *slick?*

Slippery.

To be so free, hold the lamp as close as she wants, the hard edges
of the frame marking her thighs, cunt rising and opening as if she
were being fucked, as if you had pulled at the Indian rose dress
with a rapid gesture.

Write it, you said.

It was the last summer before the years of women lovers. I had
left him in Paris, where I had bought an Indian cotton dress
whose color was the color they call rose, but with a tinge of purple.
I lay on the roof in the sun. For the first time I was living alone
here, maples overhead, the sky saturated blue, sun on my naked
skin. Sometimes I thought of the sun as a god and I opened my
legs to him and became wet from his clear heat. Waves of heat,
you said.

I took off the Indian cotton dress, the narrow slats of wood pressing
into my naked back, wind in the high branches of the maples. It
was Sunday, the day motorcycles pass in packs on the road, their
roars repeating as if I were being teased, as if the sound of each bike
were a soft whip.

The man who had opened my legs in the dark Paris flat was either
still in Paris or somewhere else, which was why it was necessary
to lie alone on the flat part of the roof, on the narrow rough slats of
wood, opening my own legs, watching the sun hit what it made
wet.

The dress was also pink, the dress I took off, the only dress I
remember wearing that summer. It had a drawstring waist. I kept it
for years.

I was just past thirty. I would open my legs, press the palms of my
hands to the outsides of my thighs, move them down and then up
the outside lengths of my thighs as I opened, as the sun picked
up cuntshine.

Heat is required, you said, but you haven't elaborated or told me
what you like, whether you use the word *cunt* in this circumstance,
or the word *pussy*, or if, suddenly, precision is unnecessary.

After a while I go into the house, which when it is that bright
outdoors has a sharp darkness that gives color edge. I had forsaken
the master bedroom for a room at the side whose ceiling slanted,
where I felt free to do what I liked to my cunt.

If that's the word you like. Tonight it's dark and raining. If the
telephone rings, I will open my legs. You've said that to me at least

once, Open your legs. I like it, just the definitive baritone of your voice.

I didn't dare put my hands between my legs, into my cunt, when I lay outside on the roof.

But when I went inside, into the sharp bright darkness, it was as if I were going to meet my lovers, and though my lovers were my own hands, I waited as if they were strangers.

Wet.

I do it now so I can remember what I did then: Open my legs. Place my hands, one inside each thigh, and pull my legs apart, at the same time pressing them closed. I resist, and so I must become forceful as my ass rises, my fingers breaching, loosening, sliding.

I had never done this.

Later I would hear the story of a woman with long black hair who could bend and reach her own cunt with her own mouth and tongue. It seemed an injustice my fingers could not do in my cunt what his cock had done, what yours could.

Cock: it almost rhymes with fuck, and when I say it I feel the back of my throat open.

I couldn't bend far enough to look at it, so I got up and lifted a mirror from the white wall. I wanted to see what my cunt looked like. I took the mirror down, lay on my back, and positioned the edges of the frame between my legs just above the knees, holding it steady with my thighs.

A woman naked on her back, a framed mirror between her bent, pale legs.

Holding it in place—oval, about twenty-four by thirty-six inches—I reached for a lamp, switched it on, and moved it close so that as I lifted my haunches, it lit my cunt. I saw a reflection of flesh the same color as the Indian cotton dress, creases twisting and untwisting like shiny strands of broken glass in a kaleidoscope.

271

Honor Moore

Still naked on her back.

My cunt opened. It seemed at the time exhilarating to be holding the lamp as close as I wished, the hard edges of the mirror's frame digging into my thighs as I rose and clenched, as if by clenching, I might more than conjure being fucked. At last, carefully, reverently, with my left hand, I put the lamp on the floor beside the low bed, then opened my legs to release the mirror, but this time, as my fingers rush in to pull it open, I know what my cunt looks like.

What it looked like to me.

What did it look like to you?

I am on the roof. I am lying in the heat on the slats of the roof. I am opening my legs as if the sun were your mouth saying open your legs. I do so because you do not hesitate, because you ask me to, because there are no niceties. You do not wheedle and you are not polite.

Again, you said . . .

It was the summer before I took my first woman lover. I had left a man in Paris, but the sun was a god and for him I opened my legs, cars passing on the road like whips. I had bought the dress in Paris, of thin Indian cotton whose color was what they call rose, with a tinge of purple.

Crease. Do you like that word? My hand is there.

The Art of Thinking
Ron Padgett

IT MUST HAVE BEEN in Harold's News that I found *The Art of Thinking*, for in 1956 there was no other bookstore that I frequented at the age of thirteen. Harold's was a deep, narrow shop in downtown Tulsa, its shelves and racks lined with magazines, newspapers, comic books, greeting cards, and books, mostly Bibles, how-to titles, and other volumes likely to sell to a very general public. At the checkout counter you could buy chewing gum and candy, and at the very front of the store you could rotate the several freestanding wire racks and peruse crime novels, cowboy stories, and joke books, alongside a few "contemporary classics" such as Somerset Maugham's *Moon and Sixpence* and some ancient classics such as *Great Dialogues of Plato*. It must have been on one of those racks that I noticed a yellow paperback whose title alone no doubt caused me to take it home on the bus that day, for it offered no other attraction: its cover design was pedestrian and its author was unknown to me. I must have been ready for the idea that there is such a thing as an art of thinking, though I don't recall having had, at that age, any personal experience of it.

Of course I had had ideas and thoughts. In fact, my mind was fairly quick to learn whatever it was presented with. But, until around the time I discovered *The Art of Thinking*, I don't recall ever being aware that I thought, let alone that I could have any control over the process of my thinking. It had never occurred to me that I could, as it were, stand outside myself and watch the flow of my own mentality. In short, although I was at times self-conscious, I was not self-aware. I was Ronnie.

But it had dawned on me that physically I was no longer who I had been. The evidence was unavoidable: before my very eyes my body had started to change. Over the years I had grown larger, of course, but it was always the same me. Now there was a different me, a me whose facial skin had begun to feel oily, a me who, like the Wolf Man, was transformed by the magical appearance of body hair that seemed to grow from some malevolent impulse of its own. I was both the old me and the new me, and these two versions allowed me—or rather forced me—to begin to see myself from another point of view. This was the divided and confused adolescent who reached out and picked up *The Art of Thinking* by Ernest Dimnet and purchased it for thirty-five cents.

The book's effect on me was enormous, as it was on my best friend, Dickie Gallup, who lived across the street and with whom I often had serious discussions. It was a book that not only described an art of thinking but also ennobled it. And since Dickie and I were essentially fleeing from our own bodies, what better place to go than into our minds? Dimnet made us feel that this was a perfectly fine place to spend one's time, and he cited numerous great thinkers and writers from the past to illustrate his theses. Later in my adolescence, whenever I winced at being called an egghead or brain-boy, I took refuge in the notion that thinking is an elevated practice far above the "common herd," though such defensive snobbery was not characteristic of Dimnet.

By the time I went to college, I had passed the book on to someone else. And though Dimnet was never the subject of study in my college years, his book was largely responsible for my being there at all. Because he had instilled in me a respect for thought, I was ready and even eager to see what Saint Bonaventure, Descartes, Locke, Hume, Kant, and company had to say.

The years went by. In fact, about thirty-five of them. During that time I never saw another copy of *The Art of Thinking*. I never saw a single reference to its author. It was as if he was part of a forgotten dream I had once had. Then, two years ago, I remembered the dream, and remembered that it wasn't a dream, and began to wonder: what was that book really like? I could barely remember it. A search of the card catalogs in several libraries turned up no copies of *The Art of Thinking* by Ernest Dimnet. It was nowhere to be seen in the used bookstores I tried. Then someone suggested that I search for it on the Internet. For me, Dimnet's book was so closely associated with the past that I hadn't imagined it could be found on anything so contemporary as the Internet, but when I got around to checking a rare and used book Web site, I was surprised to find not one but forty-two copies available. I was even more surprised to learn that it had originally appeared in 1928, twenty-eight years (approximately two of my young lifetimes) before I had found it, and that it had gone through numerous editions and printings throughout the 1930s, '40s, '50s, and '60s. The copy I ordered was from the eleventh printing (July 1929), at which point the number of copies in print came to a nice round one hundred thousand—in only eight months! By 1949 it had gone through thirty-six printings. I don't know the print runs of all the editions, but, given the book's longevity, they must have formed a substantial total. I cannot account for the fact that, not long after I bought my first copy, the book seems to have vanished from the marketplace, its author quickly forgotten.

Who was he, anyway? The cover of the paperback edition had said that Dimnet was an abbé. He had written books in both French and English (not to mention one in Latin) as far back as 1905. We also learn, in reading the book itself, that he was an intellectual, a non-conformist, and a man who, in his avuncular way, wanted to counsel and encourage his readers. But he was perhaps not an ideal uncle: his glimmer of admiration for Mussolini gives me pause, but we are now hearing that in the late 1920s Mussolini was not yet the posturing disaster that he would become. I'll have to do some research on this. (My refusal to condemn Dimnet automatically on this point is perhaps a result of his emphasis on the importance of examining accepted ideas before repeating them.) In any case, aside from whatever general impression the reader forms of Dimnet's personality and character, this is all we learn about him from the book.

The 1957 edition of the *Encyclopedia Americana* tells us that Ernest Dimnet was born in Trélon, France, on July 9, 1866, and died in Paris on December 8, 1954. He was educated at the Cathedral School in Cambrai, not far from his hometown in northern France. He specialized in English and visited England often, eventually becoming an authority on the Brontës. He taught at Catholic University in Lille until 1902, then at the Collège Stanislas in Paris until 1923. Afterward Dimnet devoted himself to writing and lecturing. For many years (1899–1919) he was the Paris correspondent for the *Pilot* and the London *Saturday Review* and for the *North American Review* (1904–1909). In 1908 he made the first of his many lecture trips to the U.S., including one in 1919 as the Lowell lecturer at Harvard. At some point he became the canon of Cambrai cathedral. Dimnet wrote a number of other books, including two autobiographical volumes, *My Old World* (1935) and *My New World* (1937). My impression is that he was overshadowed by other French Catholic intellectuals, such as Jacques Maritain and Gabriel Marcel. Dimnet was more of a popularizer.

Ron Padgett

A few weeks ago, as I read my newly arrived copy of *The Art of Thinking*, I was struck by several things. First, I wondered how I, as an unsophisticated thirteen-year-old, had managed to get all the way through the book, with its frequent allusions to authors and historical figures then unknown to me—Plutarch, Madame de Staël, Sainte-Beuve, Spinoza, Bossuet, etc. I also wondered how I, whose reading consisted of the most simplistic literature (*The Mickey Mantle Story* by Mickey Mantle, as told to . . .), had been able to puzzle out some of Dimnet's more difficult sentences (written in English, his second language). For example, referring to schoolchildren, he writes:

> At an age when impressions are as deep as they are insidious, uneducating education can produce mental parasites which, in time, are apt to result in inferiority complexes, or—a worse evil—can distort our whole outlook on life.

Or:

> Open Clemenceau's little book on Demosthenes and you will see and positively touch as with your own hand the effect of a constant preference for great patriots and great thinkers in an existence which journalism, politics, duelling and all that empty effervescence of the Forum might otherwise have made shallow.

Or:

> The notion that one is writing for the public, for criticalness and often for misinterpretation, produces ill effects from which the person writing only to help his powers of concentration is free.

Obviously, I had understood what I was able to, and something in the book kept me turning its pages, eager to learn whatever I could about the art of thinking, about those who practiced it, and how I might join their company. It turned out that I never quite did engross myself in pure thought, soon having gravitated into the art of poetry, but I have never outgrown the way Dimnet's book awoke me to the very idea of thought, its role as fundamental to human existence, and its accessibility for anyone who realizes that it is there, always ready for whoever is willing to wade into its rewarding, fascinating, and sometimes baffling flow.

*

If only it were all that easy. That is, what I wrote above was called into question when, going through a box of old papers a few days later, I happened upon a list of all the books I read between the ages of twelve and fourteen, a list I compiled on a chart for Miss Lillie Roberts, my English teacher during those three years, and zealously updated for her inspection. Eager to please her, I even listed books I had not read in their entirety. It chagrins me to say that *The Art of Thinking* is not on that list!

What *is* on it, however, supports some of the points I made earlier. In seventh grade, I read twenty-two books, the great majority of them about cars and auto racing. The eighth grade (twenty-four books) began with the same fare, but around the middle of the school year I shifted into science fiction and astronomy. The ninth grade (twenty-eight books) continued the previous year's interests, but quickly moved into more varied (and usually deeper) material: a volume on reincarnation, *Einstein's Theory of Relativity* by Max Born, *The Wisdom and Ideas of Plato* by Eugene Freeman and David Appel, *The Adventures of Baron Munchausen*, the *Iliad* and *Odyssey*, *Better Bowling* by Joe Wilman, *The Greek Way* by Edith Hamilton, *Ballads* by Rudyard Kipling, *Romeo and Juliet*, *A Tale of Two Cities*, *The World As I See It* by Albert Einstein, and so on. In other words, my intellectual awakening had been gradual, extending over the course of reading seventy-four books, not one.

It is possible that I read *The Art of Thinking* the summer after ninth grade, when I turned fifteen, by which time I would have been less daunted by Dimnet's literary allusions and his occasional citations in French. In fact, a notebook entry I made only a few weeks into tenth grade strongly suggests the influence of Dimnet:

> From various cases illustrated every day in every school it is obvious that there has been a terrible failure of teaching our children to think. . . . I have found a failure in my thinking process which should not occur. I call it "stagnated confusion." The case is as follows: I was sitting at my desk, when the teacher suddenly called upon me to answer a question which I was not prepared for. I looked at my book, and I knew that I had studied it last year, yet the answer did not come. I began to sweat as the class quieted and began staring at me. The only thing I could think of is, "They are waiting I must think must hurry what is the answer they're looking at me as if I'm stupid I must hurry . . . ," etc. My mind was in a

277

psychological rut, and my processes were stagnated. It was a good picture of mental confusion, and all I could think of was confusion. After a small hint, I quickly remembered the answer, and the class continued.

It is highly unlikely that I read Dimnet any later than age fifteen, though given my revisionist memory, there is room for doubt.

So what, if anything, does remain valid in my earlier version of events? Discovering the book at Harold's News seems rock solid, partly because of the visual nature of the memory of doing so and partly because there was virtually no place else I *could* have found it. But did *I* find it? Perhaps not. Maybe my friend Dickie—a much more cerebral person than I, even at that age—found it and lent it to me. Or it's possible that we found it together, on one of our bus jaunts downtown.

The comments on puberty and my emerging self-awareness ring true as well, though the latter probably took place more slowly than I, pegging it to the discovery of this single book, would have had it.

Also true is the sense I had—and which Dimnet reinforced—that henceforth I could live on a different level, one that implicitly linked me to the thinkers of the past and thus to a tradition that was much longer and wider than those I had known until then, those of family, school, city, state, and country.

The question remains: Why did I, in remembering my adolescence, ascribe so much importance to *The Art of Thinking* that I seem to have altered my memories to fit that book? One reason might be that its title was so attractive and inclusive, as if Dimnet's book had encompassed the intellectual structures of all the books I read during that period. Among the seventy-four books on my list, not one serves such a purpose so well. *The Art of Thinking* was not only the epitome of all the books I read during those three years, it was the culmination of them, a turning point, for the pitifully small number of works of serious literature and poetry that I read during that time would, beginning in tenth grade, swell to a flood, as my reading of works of science and philosophy slowed to a trickle. And though the evidence shows that *The Art of Thinking* was not the crucial volume that I had always remembered it as, nor was it a great piece of writing, I still feel an inexplicable loyalty to it, and gratitude to its author, after all these years.

Early in his book, Dimnet writes:

> The flux in our brain carries along images—remembered or modified—feelings, resolves and intellectual, or partly intellectual conclusions, in vague or seething confusion. And this process never stops, not even in our sleep. . . . When we look in we are conscious of [this] perpetual motion.

He then urges us to "do more than merely peep and at once look away." Perhaps my willingness to examine my excessive zeal for "organizing" the past owes something of its origin to the canon of Cambrai.

If you have read this far, you might well be thinking, "OK, enough about you, Padgett. You keep referring to this interesting book, but you don't tell us what it says. You dangle it in front of us like a carrot, but you never allow us to take a bite."

That is because I made the mistake of assuming that you would be more interested in me than in yourself, and unwittingly revealed my stinginess by keeping the book's riches to myself. In this respect I was the opposite of Dimnet, who early on tells us that his primary wish is to be useful to the reader.

But the persona he creates is not that simple. The first sentence of his book is: "What writer would dare to appropriate Voltaire's verse in *Le Pauvre Diable,* and would dare to say of his reader: *Il me choisit pour l'aider à penser?*" The real question here is: What writer would dare to begin his book with a quotation that refers to a poem unknown to the vast majority of his readers, and to conclude with a question in a foreign language incomprehensible to most of them? Either a writer who mistakenly assumed that his audience knew French or one who was willing to lord it over them, no?

But in the very next sentence Dimnet allays the apprehension he has just caused us: "Yet, it is a fact that millions of men and women are anxious to take lessons in the Art of Thinking and that some other men and women have to take the risk of seeming presumptuous in offering those lessons." Thus in only two sentences he presents himself as both a literary highbrow and an unpretentious fellow who is modestly offering advice. From this point on, Dimnet modulates between these two roles—waspish don and unassuming uncle.

The Art of Thinking consists of four major parts: On Thinking: Obstacles to Thought; Helps to Thought; and Creative Thought, each of which has sections and subsections, demarcated and elaborated on in the table of contents and framed by a preface and a conclusion. Dimnet outlined his book before writing it, partly, I think, to give himself the freedom to ramble a bit inside any given paragraph without wandering *too* far off the path.

He is shrewd enough to know that he must hook the reader early on. After describing thinking as a mental stream, he pulls the charming trick of turning to face the reader and abruptly asking, "What are you thinking of?" There follows a conversation between him and "the reader," whom I, and I assume many others, easily identified with, so natural and fitting are the reader's answers—a conversation about what we are experiencing as we read the book at that very moment. This fusing of our here and now (reading) with the author's "back then" (writing) creates an immediate bond that erases space and time, especially time, for we have been transported to a mental realm outside of it.

It would be difficult for Dimnet to sustain this level of literary sleight of hand, and not useful for his ultimate goal: to inspire us to a better intellectual and moral life by advising us how to think. To do so, he must first describe the nature of thought. Here thought as stream gives way to thought as movie, sometimes with two or more films superimposed. He then asks what types of images the reader habitually entertains: Are they material, artistic, moral, religious? Note the ascending scale of the "nobility" of thought. His ultimate subject is human nature, about which he periodically injects an aphorism, such as: "It is one of the humiliating features of human nature that we resent a few little things which happen to irritate us more than we appreciate a great deal for which we ought to be grateful." People can be petty and all sorts of other bad things, but a few can rise above it all. Dimnet accepts "us" into this superior group when he says, "We know that nineteen people in twenty do not think but live like automata." (The word *robot*, in both French and English, had come into use only a few years before Dimnet's book was published.) But Dimnet the high-minded sage is quickly supplanted by Dimnet the regular guy, when he gives, as an example of a thinker, a mechanic!

Soon Dimnet begins to make thought sound quite attractive: "As Léon Daudet says it, à propos of Marcel Proust, we love a conversation 'full of flowers and stars,' the stars being the rare thoughts and the flowers their fascinating expression." And then thought becomes awesome: in pointing out how certain ideas take on a life of their own, independent of their creators, he leads us to

> an exalted idea of the greatness of thought. Measure Descartes, the refugee to Holland, or his disciple Spinoza, the artisan, or that typical provincial professor, Kant, or Karl Marx, by confronting their personalities with their influence. The contrast between these humble lives and the mental effervescence they have left behind them is startling. One flash through a human brain, and, in spite of a total lack of wordly influence, in spite of the recondite character of the doctrines, in spite of the absence of literary talent, the whole intellectual trend of mankind will be changed for several generations.

He concludes with the assurance that we need not be a philosopher or a genius in order to practice the art of thinking. In fact, the art is accessible to everyone.

So why don't we all have great thoughts? The reasons are many, and in Part Two Dimnet discusses the salient ones: obsessions, inferiority complexes, pretence, self-consciousness, imitation of others, excessive gregariousness, bad education, the pressures of daily life, reading inferior books, and wasting time in trivial conversation. Of course most readers will recognize some of their own habits here, but the negativity of the subject is offset from time to time by perceptions such as this:

> Two notions juxtaposed in the mind invariably hinder its working. You do not see a picture as it really is when you have been told it is a copy whereas it really is original. The moment you hear that it is not a copy, the picture returns on you with an energy that it did not possess a few minutes before.

Although Dimnet also encourages us with a passage on the virtues of individuality (original perception) and entertains us with an amusing description of a man reading a newspaper on a train, Part Two makes us wonder if we can surmount all these obstacles to thought.

Part Three (Helps to Thought) comes to the rescue. The early sections of this chapter point out the desirability of solitude (for thinking and for just being oneself), concentration, and time management—all discussed in a general manner, followed by some rather commonplace specific tips. But his flair for aphorism comes to the fore:

> If you try to think, you must expect to be a little apart and not a little above.

> Nobody has ever been able to explain why a Latin education should give that curious superiority to people, but it does.

> An hour in the morning is worth two, and the nothingness that must inevitably come in the silly hours afterward will not submerge you.

He continues in this positive vein by suggesting again the nobility of thinking, in his subhead "Living One's Life on a Higher Plane," but soon afterward he decries the "general inferiority of the images filling the minds of most human beings." He pontificates in the opposite direction as well: "It is impossible to spend an hour in a room with a man approaching greatness without feeling the contagiousness of distinguished thinking." But he quickly wins back our affection when he says that "Plutarch's *Parallel Lives* gave first-rate food to the minds of the *élite* in all nations until it was regarded as a classic instead of an amusing book."

Then he reactivates the device he used in the opening pages of his book: "Stop the stream of your consciousness for an instant, look into your soul, arrest the images forming and dissolving there." Notice that the focus has shifted from the mind to the soul. The cleric in Dimnet shows even more clearly in his declaration that "we can drive out soul visitors we are not proud of." But he comes down from the pulpit and gives us this lucid and agreeable passage:

> Have you ever analyzed what has been going on in your mind when you have been pleased with a lecture or a concert? Sometimes you may have enjoyed following the argument or the music with more than usual clarity; oftener the speech or the motif have [sic] given a chance to some lurking activity deep in you and, during an hour, you have been at your most personal. The Art of Thinking is merely the art of being that, as easily and as frequently as possible.

A lovely vignette of a little girl on a train—apparently Dimnet spent a lot of time on trains—totally absorbed in reading Roman history illustrates his belief that great books make terrific reading, and that only a bad education, which the little girl is too young to have had, makes us think otherwise.

Though Dimnet offers a few specific techniques for improving the way we think, they are not nearly so memorable as his anecdotes, such as: " 'How did you discover the law of gravitation?' somebody once asked Newton. 'By thinking about it all the time,' was the answer." Or this maxim: "The habit of never seeing a thing without visualizing another beside it, or behind it, has in it something vital." By this time, however, the pragmatic (American) reader, sensing that the chapter is drawing to a close, wonders whether it will fulfill the promise of its title. Where is the list of those helps to thought?

Dimnet, ever the clever tactician, concludes the chapter with another dialogue, in which "the reader" expresses disappointment at finding not the quick and easy recipes for thinking that he or she had expected, but an "avalanche" of advice. The author brushes aside these remarks by replying, "Yes, it is a shame that thought-lozenges do not exist. I should buy some too." Then he sweet-talks the reader into going back to the avalanche and trying each bit of counsel one at a time. Yes, it requires patience and work, but he knows that the reader is an "exceptional candidate" because he or she is reading this very book.

In the fourth and final chapter ("Creative Thought"), Dimnet is at his best as a dignified cheerleader for serious thinking. He begins by pointing out that being creative means more than being an artist or a writer. It can also mean being an inspiring person. Besides, we all have inspired moments, in which we experience states of mind that allow our individuality to shine through. And we all have intuitions, including minor ones; all we have to do is capture and follow our intuitive flow:

> These minor intuitions often come in clusters, or in a quick succession, but most often without any apparent connection. When we are dreaming awake, or under the influence of music, their number is so great that no calculation can approximate it. We then squander them freely. Yet, we know their value, for, sometimes, they develop into protracted trains of thought, during which we realize that our brain is doing its best work, yet doing it without taxing our coöperation. This is what we want to reproduce after the spell has been interrupted, this is what we call thinking, and the mention of an Art of Thinking means to us chiefly the possibility of recreating at will a similar state of mind. What we call understanding or comprehension is this superior annexation of some intellectual growth.

The chapter concludes with a final dialogue with the reader, in which Dimnet affirms that literary production (such as writing a good letter) is something that everyone is capable of, so long as we do not think of it as literature while producing it.

This inspiring and democratic passage is followed by a brief conclusion (the same length as the preface) in which Dimnet reiterates that he "cherishes no greater hope than that of being useful," a hope that I think probably is fulfilled in the great majority of readers who complete the book.

After writing this brief overview of *The Art of Thinking*, I realized that it is essentially a book report—overdue by more than four decades—that I wish I could hand in to my teacher, Miss Roberts. Though she was nothing like a French cleric, she did show Dimnet's tendency to oscillate between gentle encouragement and firm injunction. I can still see her at the front of the classroom, standing at her desk, removing her glasses and narrowing her eyes as she begins, "The best grammarians believe . . ." and then, turning to the jungle of sticks she has drawn on the blackboard—it is the diagram of a long complex sentence—and smiling back at us over her shoulder, she continues, "the subordinate clause modifies *this* word." A light goes on in my head *and* my heart. I love this diagram and the old woman who made it. I love *subordinate clause.*

It's too late to show Miss Roberts this essay now—she has been dead for at least thirty years—but in thinking of her and in writing these words, in some sense I become her for a moment, just as I become Dimnet, and though both of them would want me to be no one other than myself, I like to think that they would be secretly pleased by these transformations, however fleeting.

Five Poems
Jackson Mac Low

WE DEPLORE THE ATLANTIC
[Hopkins 11]

We deplore
vein-lancing shrines,
limbs of her,
this snowstorm,
prideful mothers boast of.

Motionable sailors
are motionably straining
motionable shrines.
Quartz fret? Ay.
All, sweetheart.

Heart-springs
and heart-springs' master,
son of his captain,
veins dared and azured,
nobler and guiltier.

Speaking of captains,
a captain, speaking,
wrings at times
mothers of captains,
worse than daring.

Oh, occasions of riches
the Atlantic makes righteous.
Providence warned him
motherhood's an afterdraft,
a snowstorm infinity.

285

Jackson Mac Low

Unrolled,
dared,
the Atlantic dwindled.
Did Providence dwindle
with the Atlantic?

Please pause for one beat between stanzas.
New York: 13 May 2001; 16 May, 13 July 2003;
source poem by G. M. Hopkins

WRINKLES' WISDOM
DESPAIRS
MOST LEADENLY,
BAYS AT AGE,
LONG MAY LONG

[Hopkins 12]

Wrinkles' wisdom despairs:
the winding motion of wisdom
is there, sighs.

Echoes have, strongly
tall, everything that's
to be done.

Yet, fashioned, slept.
Despair. Drooping despair.
Be beginning, Beauty.

Beauty's sign's motion:
known messengers begin,
begin, sparely begin

where morning's never
matched by sunny
places not within,

never too motionable
with soaring, soaring,
hurling care, care

fondly, but told
none to keep
no sheet there.

Air of despair,
airway of death,
no sheeted way

echoes age's evils,
everything swiftly least:
gallantry, looks, hair.

Not least, every
place's sighing maidens
fly away gracefully.

Hair replaces whatever
gallant messengers numbered,
prized, and fastened.

Swiftly walking past
sad places, they
prize the past,

every weary, everlasting
way of us:
fast maidens' eyelashes,

early everything's eyelashes,
everything's beauty's ghost
fastened sweetly, freely.

Keep these deaths
fresh and fast,
fastened freely, sweetly.

Jackson Mac Low

Truth freely keys
flying elsewhere, waving
us off, undone.

Yet some, them,
us, seem sweetly
sighing "no worse."

O somewhere away
from us, not
matched by morning,

come winning ways
following mournful beauty
long singeing you.

Beauty, fearing death,
follows yonder, mournfully
passes all gallantry.

No, none now
wrinkles sheets gracefully,
freely walks carelessly.

What do mournful
wrinkles do yonder,
delivering what ways?

We most leadenly
bay at age,
long may long.

Please pause for one beat between stanzas.
Source text: Gerard Manley Hopkins's poem
"The Leaden Echo and the Golden Echo
(Maidens' song from St. Winefred's Well)."
New York: 16 May 2001; 15–17 April, 13 July 2003

THE LAMP ON THE LEFT
WAS NEVER TO RETURN

[HSC 9]

*In Memoriam Charles Hartshorne (1895–2000), Gertrude Stein (1874–1946),
and Lewis Carroll (Charles Lutwidge Dodgson, 1832–1898)*

The lamp on the *left* was *trimmed.*
It was only a *lamp* and didn't *need* red *wheels.*

If their *banderole* caught *fire*, I wouldn't snatch it *out* for 'em.

That lamp ain't gonna be trimmed no *more.*
She was only a *kitty*, but she was the one and *only* kitty.
If they weren't going to return it *neatly*, they shouldn't have bothered returning it at *all.*

You're returning our *things?*
Thanks for understanding   how necessary they *are* for us.
You can never tell *exactually*   what an upside-down speech like that *means.*
Try breathing quickly through your left *nostril*   to replace the breath you've *lost.*

Sunday made the queen   *frown* among the *trees*,   but she *needn't*'ve frowned and
shouldn't've.
She explained that she herself was learning all *about* frowning.
When the queen caught a trim little *feather*, she trimmed her *hat* with it.
She *trimmed* it with it because of its *whiteness*—and trimmed it—and *trimmed* it—and then
she *stored* it.

Someone said-she-should've trimmed her *feet* with that feather.
Any light *sign* might or might *not* be a sign of *light*.
You *must* buy a *light*.

        And then he was *made* to.

Please, you *mustn't*,   you must *not*,   catch a feather *anyplace*   near that little *well!!*
  The king said he was no longer *clever*, thanks to the *fearfulness* of that *era*.
  It was like explaining and learning what exactually could be stored *again*.
        Frowning can say a *lot*.

So Duncan must have had *difficulty* with that letter   only after he'd been made to *pause*.
  The queen didn't set much *store* on explaining how strong her *outrage* was.
    The fact that she was *frowning told* us that.
      Who are *you*, sir,   the *driver*?

  Speaking *directly* won't necessarily carry-you-in-the-right *direction*.
Explaining his *words* and his *posture*,   he remarked that his joking *bugged* 'em
        like-a-fast *left*.

        I'd like to go more in *that* direction.
        What does that *whiteness* mean?
        I gotta go to the *kitty*, I said.
Harold's-little-*trees* were *banded*   *long* before anyone ventured to snatch 'em *away*.
      All of a sudden a red   *wind*   returned her *letters*.
  The agèd king   stored-his-*words*-away   as well as his *other* necessities.
    You needn't replace your band*on*eon with a strong *engine*.

Wooden remarks like *that*   don't make a hit with *any*-of-us.
Why don't you post that feathery joke on a *website?*
You'd need something very *strong,*   maybe with *wheels,*   to get over *that* wall.
Duncan told Harold he mustn't try to *do* it.

Suddenly, Andrea went and replaced   a *lot* of her white *necessities.*
She *wasn't very clever.*
But one of her *cakes* could make *all* of 'em *stop.*

Her speech among the *trees* was pretty *catchy.*

Should the *moon* be replaced by an *engine?*
Only if you want it   never to *return.*

Eleven strophes in which the numbers of single-sentence lines in consecutive strophes follow the rising and falling Lucas sequence 2, 1, 3, 4, 7, 11, 7, 4, 3, 1, 2. The roots of the lexical words in the poem come from three sources: a group of essays by the philosopher Charles Hartshorne, Gertrude Stein's *Tender Buttons,* and Lewis Carroll's *Through the Looking-glass and What Alice Found There.* The poem was freely composed from the output of a diastic method I'd devised in 1963, which Charles O. Hartman digitized in the early nineties. The source text was a mix of sentences from the sources, and the seed text came from somewhere in that mix. Lexical words in the poem are various forms of the lexical words the method found in the output. Some "helping words" (prepositions, conjunctions, and other structure words; pronouns; and forms of "to be") were found in the output, but others were inserted freely when needed. Spaces within lines signify short pauses. Words connected by hyphens are spoken more rapidly than others. *Please pause between strophes for three andante beats (a thousand and one, a thousand and two, a thousand and three).*
New York: 21 August–17 October 2002; 31 March, 14 May, 3 July 2003

THE PAWNS WERE NONEXISTENT

[HSC 11]

With thanks to Charles Hartshorne, Gertrude Stein, and Lewis Carroll for lexical root morphemes

—*For The Poetry Project at Saint Mark's in-the-Bouwerie*

The pawns were placed quite otherwise than I remembered their having been ever before.

They saw trees in those parts that were said to be subjects of the moon.
We support ourselves by subjugating our own and other matter.

He started to shake whenever he dared to write.
If it were a question of hanging her, he'd've been moved by looking through a hedge at her.
She ended up balancing a roundly generic consciousness of others with hers of herself.

The principles underlying Whitehead's panpsychism are unlikely to be deemed foundational by more than a few now.

Many grew up looking at physics as having at best a subjective validity.
It seemed fairly evident that its applications would come to furnish questions.
They would enable too many—far from the best—to risk inclusive levels of mischief.

Continuing subjugation counts more than observation or experience in the ordering of patterns of events.
We knew from many a subject of the queen that water is a better remedy for dirty teeth than any potato could be.

For nearly every subject, every other subject may be something on a par with a *thing*.
Sam subjected the structure of his back to more than the queen thought necessary.
How could the wise be haunted by a fundamental question if that question itself were questionable?

That relativity causes the same forms as a looking glass is not de facto true.
What she left in the boat there could never be repeated.
After the subject of white experience was nearly over and past, she'd not quite glanced at him.
Each minute meant a lot to her.
Shake it well unless there's only one interpretation of that rhubarb cage.
She picked completely great ones there—sometimes.

Material entities there were apparently wilder than most of their pieces.
The subject of rooms seemed hardly related to ones that were more universal.
He meant that in less than a minute he could pick a harmonious land.
They argued that idealism seldom causes enduring experience.
She only promised an idealistic process.
Which of them claimed that instants of the rivers of God are really power ordeals?
Her proboscis was subjected to Justice's round trip.

A string is still rated a means to pain or an even more inharmonious purpose.
Most choking is an event with a bodily motive.
Is it true that three hundred or so were watching the soup?
Outside, their conditions were piercing, but their plates were mighty pretty.
Knowing the past can soon subject the knower to subjection.
They said that the sand was knitting it.

293

Both of them must often drink from a couple of broken cocups.
One round bottle is worth several embroideries.

Many idealists are willy-nilly interdependent.
Their kitten's poles are never wildly poor though often cried about.
The subjectivity of a subject isn't physically accessible to other subjects.
This morning's simple particularity may not be at hand for me tonight.
I dare say you never picked up on your head's impatient relationship with an idea.
Who says that God's power contemptuously separates the memory of a pleasing wrong from the subject's understanding of it, preventing it though it shouldn't?
Annalisa thought the last reason for looking at a place was that it might be of use.
But hardly anyone one bought that.
Before a certain science showed some people there that nestling was their common right, they considered it nearly as precious as pearls.

There's never enough subjectivity around, the cynical would-be idealist claimed, to make it evident that subjectivity provides the ultimate spectacle.
One of your hands, of course, is not suitable for counting pink things.
You need more of the same.
This question could seldom have been looked into by others.
Before the question was made to include the one place you were looking at, it should have been widened by a subjective collection of generic entities.
A strong situation may evidently have a microscopic meaning.
Is materialism always marked by shaking?
Or is that due to changes cooked up by vapors of astonishment?

Twiddle that little one again.
She is likely politely to bridle at his questions, though the subject is merely a conceivable garment for her stomach.

All we said was that every falling slice might join a greater one.
Meeting a particular may cause confusing talk.
Is it, she asked, that she, like other poor, could never expect a certain objection?
How pityingly she cleared away that other pretty past!
Eagerly she marked the necessary rain.
It was a foolish subject, much like a package of useless curtains.
That evening it seemed their so-called truth-directed theory was brushing off experience.
They presented their feelings as if they were really being governed by prayer.
It's a broad subject, winter—closely connected with values, they say.
Augusta turned and swept the meaning of the day into the back garden.
She was sure the specs for anything there were nonexistent.

Please pause for three andante beats between every two strophes.
Numbers of single-sentence verses in successive strophes are 1 through 11.
New York: 13 September–8 October 2002; 1 January, 31 March 2003

AGNES CRIED IN JULY

[HSC 5]

Agnes cried   when she merely admitted reproachfully that scientists   are philósophers.

That observation was literally   too fully in cháracter.
What was the name of the quéen whose possible rélative she was?

Basically coherent   even at the end   Agnes had a keen   awareness of blúe.
Just as súmmer was coming   she'd dréss herself in blue whenever the wind was stróng.
For her   the woods were getting to be lacking personálity.

Although she was only watching   it's certain she was púrring none the léss.
Because this didn't check her acceptance of ríddles   she could simultaneously báck
    creative mechánics   and loudly voice complete astónishment at them with féar in her
    eyes.

She claimed they were flákes to their fáces.
But they were a míld   áudience.

She knew she wasn't wanted.
They always attributed her ways to too-many-bóoks.
Yet Agnes's crackling violence   would always kind-of-fade-awáy.

296

Was anything happening that somehow could surprise her?
Her thinking up inorganic chóices   was partially realistic.

That must have been why she went to Eúrope to eat in July.

The roots of lexical words in the sixteen single-sentence lines of "Agnes Cried in July" come from essays by the philosopher Charles Hartshorne, Gertrude Stein's *Tender Buttons*, and Lewis Carroll's *Through the Looking-glass and What Alice Found There*. The numbers of single-sentence lines in successive strophes follow the sequence 1, 2, 3, 4, 3, 2, 1. Spaces *within lines* indicate short pauses, often occasioned by readers' fully sounding the consonant groups before the spaces. Each space *between strophes* calls for a pause of three andante beats ("a thousand and one, a thousand and two, a thousand and three"). Neither overemphasize nor slight the pauses.
New York: 14–15 July, 22 October 2002; 22 April, 2 July 2003

Two Poems
Rae Armantrout

THE SUBJECT

It's as if we've just been turned human
in order to learn
that the beetle we've caught
and are now devouring
is our elder brother
and that we
are a young prince.

*

I was just going to click
on "Phoebe is changed
into a mermaid
tomorrow!" when suddenly
it all changed
into the image
of a Citizen watch.

*

If each moment is in love
with its image
in the mirror of
adjacent moments

(as if matter stuttered),

then, of course, we're restless!

"What is a surface?"
we ask,

trying to change the subject.

EMPTY

The present
must be kept empty
so that anything
can happen:

    The Queen of England visits
    Amanda's hot tub

    as a prophylaxis?

a discrepancy
between one's view of things
and what comes to pass.

            *

It's ironic when something
has a meaning to someone

    "Gotta go
    Gotta go
    Gotta go
    right now"

other than that
intended by the speaker.

sings the bladder-control model
from the fidgety TV
above the dying woman's bed.

*

It's ironic when a set
contains no elements.

Of a person, frivolous.
Of a body, shrunken.

'Can't' is 'Night'
Leslie Scalapino

—For June Watanabe in a collaboration for text, dance, and music

(1)   re—separation of character and

night.

'no language' 'with it'—movement or language, here

(2)   the real-time event (occurring) is the only thing there is/ *'was'*
they've destroyed language so we have to destroy it in it not
movement

night exists at day—but is not the same night so

night is not-existing *then then* is open to the senses

she (someone) says our language is to remove boundless character of

night,

that's terror.   when?

their 'lie'—as that one's

is to substitute for night, hers night 'terror'—say how _____. to

reverse *'their'* reverse of the boundless character of night can't be

said

or moved either

even though outside

blues can't exist outside either—as separation of character and

night.

so it's separation of character and night 2

301

Leslie Scalapino

(3)   our prisoner

was found on the ground outside standing before Bagram U.S.

military prison in Afghanistan which we've decimated, lie to, for

something they didn't do—

the U.S. military   take him in

beat him to death, prisoners who interrogated chained hang while

'our' marines beat them to keep them

awake if they fall asleep when hanging there

present—blues can't exist outside—or in character

no night being—as woman who

says '*our*' language is to reverse

night's

being—without edge—any night

terror

he'd committed no crime standing outside might

be

terrorist

her separation of '*our*' language from any real-

time night

order

(4)   Major Elizabeth Rouse, pathologist, checked the homicide box

to say he was murdered by U.S. military—events don't fit

in, at all—aren't in language either—Major Elizabeth Rouse

told the truth

blues can't exist outside now for

Leslie Scalapino

        night is not-existing *then then* is open to the senses to
newspapers say (their corpses) one Iraqi man walks

                       forward holds his AK47
above his head, he defies our huge army somehow to walk to it
what's he thinking? as our soldiers kill him in movement he

                                 can't do

(5)   says

        after the person's attack on one in his
        saying one's motion—is fixed, fixing it—where its

                           intent
          is to have no place its motion is its theory

                              he
      says the motion is one's fixed self, which, if one speaks, one
                 he says *'imagines'* attack of his
                      on one, that *is*
         that (*is* his reverse of one and others)
    he says one is self-centered in seeing it—not one is seeing his
    actions outside in fact—so, there is no event, no real-time
    —at all in that their/his language changes it always—is then
'only'
        not its past action—or occurrence *now*

                separation of thinking and being
the same is occurring outside *'from'* war they make saying to them
                it's liberating them not attacking
before, our language is only coercion, in every conversation reverse

event—any except

themselves in *'our'* language

—in space at all—language is then

(6)   since

an event's—not language—separation of character

                                                        and

night—is outside movement's—separation of character and

                                                        night 2

day. as. bud 'dis-placing' is

           lineage.—both. (both the bud and 'dis-placing') single is 'tree's'

                                                        buds

                                                        there

           day. "we dropped a few civilians, but what do you do?" the sniper
           says "1 Iraqi soldier and 25 women and children, I didn't take the
                                                        shot,

                        but 1 Iraqi soldier standing among 2 or 3 civilians,"

                        sharp-shooter Sergeant Schrumpf remembering the

                        woman going down—"the chick was in the way"

                 events are against movement   can't be in

                 one's movement

           'dis-placing' terror by killing. not movement dis-placing language

                                   the Kurds just move in that space

                        waves on a line across it ('we've') courted to fight and

                        dropped them to be, were, slaughtered again court

                                   to have them attack on the lands

                        where they're slaughtered then wave on lines on one side in

Leslie Scalapino

space 'we'

label them freedom fighters on the line's other side the same

ones 'we' label terror

ists

as words labels space—one—is there difference between the

'basic space of

phenomena'

and

the space of planets

moon

outside

movement?

(7)   "I expected them to surrender I thought they would all capitulate."

in the 3 days that followed,

they did not.—many of the Iraqis, Sergeant Redmond

said, attacked headlong into the cutting fire of tanks

and Bradley fighting vehicles

"I wouldn't call it bravery," he

said. "I'd call it stupidity. we value a
soldier's life so much more than they
do. an AK47 isn't going to do
nothing against a Bradley"
since we're to reverse with 'our' language—boundless

characteristic of night

as   day order

Iraqis are fighting   tanks, aircraft, artillery, prison camps, torture

305

Leslie Scalapino

Sergeant Redmond thinks that's stupid. for him relation

of language to movement: is

none?

the relation of language to movement is: 'none' in order to make

that   relation—*there*

the only chance they have is

at all

night

(8)   the phrase

'the basic space of phenomena' is different from night space?

night's in

event is 'the basic space of phenomena' before occurrence

of the phenomena

'we're' 'our'

language is to reverse the boundless characteristic of night,

she (someone) says,   to reverse night's

night is everywhere fierce fighting in Kut the south where

desperate

Iraqis armed with rifles charged tanks in suicide

raid. 'we'

mowed them down

says Lt. Col. B.P. McCoy—tracer rounds   lit night

sky

there

the battalion arrived after dark and settled

Leslie Scalapino

down for the night

night is in the newspaper page only

(9)   with no

warning shot, fire killing
family of fifteen—or they fight *'our'* tanks with AK47s
from pickup trucks 'ours' say those others are only lied to, not

brave   in 'our' movement

(10)   there is no way ('reason') to live, following the day. I thought.

'our' language is to (she says) reverse—

the 'basic space of phenomena' (phrase) and the space of planets moon's

not outside

(11)   he characterizes 'our' enemy, Iraqis, as murderers,

cowards, thugs—and he praises the U.S. force

for their kindness and goodness.   their Iraqi bodies lay

along the road. living these are all across night, they cross night, are

not

its

character

to reverse trees

marines came and Iraqis left so quickly left cooking fires alight

and their guns they need them

Baghdad plunges into darkness   —can't *be.*

'our' war everywhere—isn't/is—in 'our' language

in movement of

one

(12)   has made living impossible. any way. 'they'

destroy

language. destroy

night

fight with your hands

they exhorted   the Iraqi people

the Kurds just move in that space

waves on a line across it ('we've') courted to fight and

dropped them to be, were, slaughtered again

'we' have nowhere ahead—either—any way.

she says 'our' language is to reverse the bound

less characteristic of night

to

destroy night to—without language—in it—two—outside

(13)   destroy that language

for that

night

there

Leslie Scalapino

(14)   this isn't about suffering we'd be suffering if 'we' *were*

happy

she (someone) says 'our' language is reverse of the bound

less that's terrorist

terror characteristic of night's everything

in my language / is 'ours' only—to enter the boundless

night

night's

without language any

basic space of phenomena's not outside or in—is it *there*

also?

a man (someone) says a (this) syntax is a state of being

insanity—but it's attention only—to itself

I thought attention, and as its subject, cannot be insane? or

may be breaking 'his' reason this   now phenomena

'our' being 'happy' (emotion that's convention) is 'ours'

not

in events outside is insane

the outside and the inside cannot be *there*

in 'our' character? if it is uncompounded

or re—in attention (one cannot be regarding), either—

that

separation of character and

night

night cannot be seen

regarding is separation of one from others   only

here   not-regarding

309

collective now—having driven the Iraqis insane

attention now is insane—is dependent on the separation

of character and night 2, not in movement—either—them

in 'our' thought, language, 'our' movement is before

(language) and later.

'the civilians had to be killed on the road

fleeing Baghdad because the civilians were there as

'we're' (invading)'—they were there before—

—is not 'our' movement in that it has occurred already—

people speaking see   now the breaking of reason

theirs/'our' that's killing   reason

to reverse

'our' language's reverse of nights night-boundless-

ness   terror

or movement

(15)   the breaking of reason not inside movement of

one's

_____   moon and movement—of one's or

at all (and moon)—is the breaking of reason.

one's is 'theirs'

(16)   their despair is one's physical movement (not).

language is

crushed.

Leslie Scalapino

"2   Iraqis sat in despair." after their dead
                            coincide with night after
        (and after night's over). the breaking of reason—a
                                        man seeing.

(17)   as if by favoring war
                                    is meant its reverse
                                        reverse trees
                                        (that are)
                                    night characteristic
        I can't see/comprehend it's (before night) 'the basic
                                    space of phenomena'
        he's been reversed in language—'we're' 'killing as its
                                            reverse'
                'our' character is even in night_____ how?

(18)   the breaking of reason
                    is silent seeing   movement (of one's)
                            language
        since these 're in utter isolation only,   that is
        everyone

                                                    is
        as language   as social/*and* dawn.
        their despair is one's physical movement (not).

311

Leslie Scalapino

(19)   long movement (single)   does not repeat

the outside

'isn't'/ 'is' the same as 'his' night crushing language

of one—night's

space even?

he/someone else intends actual

sky even to reverse its night/as language/one not—

while (one) dawn-waking actually ('at' dawn *yet* one *there*

also)

dawn in the same space

as one   is.

someone/it's not possible for him to do any thing even

without attacking someone else first,   *he can't,*

he's never done so.   defensive

is

be-dualistic

he can't stand (in front of others) without first

attacking someone what is

this space   (in front of others)?

he can't sustain

others because he

will not.   *'then'*

present.

isn't reason—reason is insane

movement of one's

is theirs

their despair

312

Leslie Scalapino

already   it?

that space/social even and not dualistic isn't

                                                    even

            because that would be dualistic,

it   night sky *would.*   'be-dualistic'

                              in   nights not mirror

and: 'our' tyrant makes/'is' the war expanding in

an outside the outside breaking reason

is—

'isn't'/ 'is'—the same as 'his' night crushing language

                                            of one—night's

space even.   long movement (single)

sky even to reverse its night/as language/'one not'—

                    while (one) dawn-waking actually ('at'

            dawn *yet* one *there* dawn also)

(20)   it's 'not repeated'—'to produce'—that is:

                    'be-dualistic'.—at all

                    is   night's space

                    even—   not

(21)   A wave is sucked into sleep then

                the forest is completely separate from the

                people always—   outside and

                                    separate from the war

313

Leslie Scalapino

though

the forest destroyed or growing

is in the war

the forest is balanced on the night and

then balanced on the day

at the same time. after—is the same time later

the forest wave if the trees

are still even on night

is one wave moving on day

that's war whether day

appears still. day is in war. separate from the forest

day still appears. the forest

is black at night black

fire goes away at night though night's still

the dark gangly sleek moose come out and shy

away

vertically

though one moves

across night for long distances wave of

forest

(22)

immense light on the endless lake at

night black

the ducks fly across it

night vertically

the dark gangly sleek moose roam at

314

Leslie Scalapino

will in the forest

wave on the endless still lake

never black

then

the endless lake moves night

black

(23)   the forest rushes to the road

push

steel rumpled thunderous clouds are

at the road at

the forest meeting ahead—at one's side

forest wave rushing horizontally

to

the rumpled steel clouds everywhere ver-

tically

race to the endless lake steel light in it

sky of rain descends everywhere vertically

then

black bear rambles gracefully in the sheets

rain-vertical-grass

in day separating night horizontally

above

Leslie Scalapino

(24)   occurrence in structure unseen
                        words on a sign "owl rafting" the
                        dark mist separates morning from night so the
                                                        forest wave
                                                        begins
                                                        to rush
                                        but the forest moved at night
                                                unseen by one rafting
                        the night rafting the owl, unseen by one, the
                        forest rafting
                                                                the owl
                                        rafting the night forest—one rafting
                        only   and unseen owl-night
                        at   forest-wave
                                                                there

(25)   —woman saying our language is to reverse
                                night—is 'for' that—not producing—
                                night uncontrolled
                                is occurrence in structure unseen
                                                at all
                        not producing at all—one's seeing—
                                        but the forest moved
                                                        at
                                        night rafting

316

How They Took My Body Apart and Made Another Me

Robert Kelly

IN THE CAVE THEY STOPPED, *brought me here, where was here, here was just some other time, three hours later, later or the next day, desert or mountain, I had never been there, it looked familiar, I've known it all my life, it's the Cowboy Movie place. I saw the butte and the arroyo and the buzzards circling and the pitiless sun, the striations of red and ocher and buff and taupe in the sandstone sediments, the dark notch of wall they dragged me, floated me, toward, cave mouth they brought me in, and I was glad at first for the shade. I have always hated the sun.*

They took him to a cave they had used before in their investigations, but this was the first time these researches had involved a human male. They had not expected to find one this particular night, since their mission of the moment, as well as their professional training, was in *tlalorisn*, or geology, as we would call it. So Smarakd and Kavdil had to work with what they could find in their own mind-stock to get to the root of the particular matter who had wandered through apple trees into their hands.

Their tools, though that name is hardly fair for the elegant sinuous exiguous wands and probes and lancets they used so deftly, their tools were all back at the metarsic ship, and the boy was here, heavy in three-space, and they needed to know what beings like them need to know.

This need to know: is that the root of things, the root of hell?

Smarakd had been reading the *Sifer Dovvar,* which always got him excited. Book of Words or Book of Things. Which is it? How can you tell them apart? I can, I can tell them. You can kick a stone, you can't kick the word. But who are you?

Robert Kelly

So they opened me up with some fractured black obsidian they found and then flaked even sharper on a harder stone. My sternum they cracked with a narrow pebble punched down and in with a fistworth of stone. Then they eagled my ribcage out and got to work. There and below. They told me what they were doing, and the telling made the pain less, anyhow it was less than I would have expected. Maybe they had ways of changing my rhythm, Smarakd was breathing in a strange way I unconsciously began to imitate. The way we do. And the pain was there, but I wasn't screaming. It helps to imitate somebody else's breathing. Was it hers? Where was she?

Of course he was screaming. Or had been. When the first cut, shell-shaped, curved down through the skin above the breastbone, then the cartilage, he screamed. So they stuffed a leaf into his mouth that instantly took most of the pain away, and calmed him about the rest of what he felt.

Calmed him, but he began to talk. His two examiners, Smarakd and Kavdil, like all the traveling philosophers of their kind, had long pondered the relationship in humans between language and anxiety, seeing each as a facet of the other. So it was always interesting to them to observe whether and how sedated humans spoke. Thus, rather than taking his words now as mere reactive whimpering, they paid a little attention to him while they were concentrating otherwise on the members of his committee, as they thought of the juicy, messy, mysterious wholenesses that were mere parts of him.

Why are you cutting me? What have I done to you? Why are you doing this? Who are you?

Answering the first question they thought would serve to answer all of them.

We are cutting you open to find and examine your soul.

The language of the catechism rose gracefully to his mouth, and his sedated syntax let him express:

But the soul is immaterial!

So is the body, they said.

No, he said. The soul is immaterial, and lodges like a wary guest in the slovenly guesthouse of the body, always ready to crumble or burn down.

No, they said. The soul is immaterial, and body is immaterial as well. Matter has a touch of material about it, but the only material stuff in the cosmos is words and what they do to your head. We are looking into you to see what language has done to your soul.

But I'm a child, I have only in recent years come to express myself by way of language.

No, they said, you see this wrongly. (Meantime they had removed several ribs, and pulled the spleen out and away, that mystery organ, and stuffed a squat black glass bottle of liqueur in its place, Latvian balsam, he was later to be told.)

You see this wrongly, in that long before you began to express yourself (what a funny expression that is, too) with language, language was busy shaping—is that what you mean by expressing? No, I guess not—language was busy shaping you.

But the soul is deathless, he cried, slightly shifting the ground of the argument.

If it is deathless, what is it doing in the body?

He tried to answer: it isn't in, exactly, the body, not in the body but sort of around it. A poem we read in school said: "The body stands in soul." So get your hands out of my thorax.

They were taking out his organs one by one, cutting them loose with the sharp conchoidal volcanic glass, then licking the cut with their own tongues, finally shoving the rifled vein or stripped tendon back to reconnect with the replacement item they had found to do the work.

They took out his urinary bladder and put in an alarm clock, an old round windup brass clock with two bells and a striker on top. It was

319

ticking as they settled it down snug into his abdomen. Some days he can still hear it ticking. Tick, tick, when he hears the word he thinks: urine, urinate, now. The clock is always telling me to go. When he learns the word *ticking* later, which means the soft striped cotton cloth that binds the straw and hair and strapwork of a mattress and covers it all round, he thinks, pissy mattress, bedwetting, a mattress wrapped in what defiles it, urinary stripes, the stripes of man, old men with stains round the gaping fly in the once-white broadcloth of their underwear, tick, they wake at night to pee. Old men wake at night to pee, little boys pee without waking, Christ, what a life, tick.

And in their busy cave they went on working, lifting out his young pure smokeless lungs. In their place they carefully tucked two gray squirrels, apparently alive and breathing, and nested together like a pair of shoes in a shoe box, tail of one to the head of the other. And when they pulled the liver out slimy with blood, they shoved a live hawk in its place, which fluttered its wings once or twice and then kept quiet, its wild eye looking here and there.

They told me they used a shoe for my heart and they laughed. I said what kind of shoe? They said it was leather, and stuffed my old tennis socks with the orange rings round the shank deep in it to make the shoe keep its shape. Why is that funny, the coat hanger for my clavicle isn't funny, what's so funny about a fucking shoe? They said it goes. A heart goes, get it? I got it but I don't think it's so funny.

He worried the ways boys do that they were thinking about pushing the wooden coat hanger up his anus to see what would happen as it spread him open but they didn't. He was sure he could hear them thinking about it, and it scared him. But other people's thoughts are always frightening. At least to him.

But they had hung the hanger in his chest, and neatly festooned some of the loose vessels, vena, aorta, over the trouser rod to keep them out of harm's way as they worked. Now they were ready for the big exchange. They took away the sternum and one of them, Kavdil, I think, shoved it in his hip pocket like a kind of money. In its place they spread a postcard from Bolzano in northern Italy, with cardboard glued to the back to stiffen it, so you couldn't read the address or message or sender anymore, just the blank cardboard backing the picture of a mountain called *The Rose Garden* glowing from the setting sun.

The aliens seemed fully absorbed by this examination, which they called a Vivi-redaction, of his interior. They talked to one another steadily, in quiet, discovering tones that strangely calmed him. It is not all that bad, being an object of interest.

His pancreas they replaced with a pink rubber tobacco pouch still half-full of Red Rapparee. The left kidney they lifted out and replaced with a big green emerald—where could they have gotten it?—all faceted and glittering. The right kidney they sliced out more neatly, and stuffed a blue forty-watt lightbulb in its place.

I was watching them take things out of me, I couldn't believe it, stuff dripping with blood and lymph and bile and piss, and then shoving things in. Shove with a little twist, a little tap, and each time one of them would do that, the other would say tza! It sounded as if the sound had some work to do in the process. The little Peruvian ocarina they put into my midriff to replace my gall bladder made a soft too-tootling sound as I breathed and as they twisted things out and in. It was dark glazed, with a blue pattern in it, a five-pointed star with blunt rays. I guess it still is making that sound inside me, I never listen to what's going on inside me. Can you hear it?

When they heard it they grew intent, listened carefully. Was it the soul, or just a vagabond breeze wasting time in the reeds on Lake Titicaca, idling till some indio laid hands on it roughly and wrestled it into the goose-shaped clay whistle they call *oca, ocarina,* goose or gosling. From the shape.

And then the shape of the sound.

But when they realized it was just the sound of the gizmo they had themselves inserted into the living body of this momentary Beloved, this boy, this anguished loser blood-eagled out on the table, why, why they said to each other, No, this sound is just us. Just a noise we put inside him, not his sound. We don't want to listen to ourselves. It's not his soul yet. Not the sound of him.

321

Robert Kelly

We can't hear it. Not yet. But we've got to make it speak.

—What did we learn from him so far? (It is a him, isn't it, just a young one of its kind?)

Young. The first thing that came up is this, that when they put on a new pair of those coarse blue trousers they call dungarees, especially in summer, when those trousers are most often worn, after the first day of wear, the skin of the wearer's thighs, his thighs at least, are stained pale with blue. He thinks of this as *indigo.*

—Is he right to call it so?

Hard to say, these beings make a lot of trouble for themselves with words. On the one hand, a word like *indigo* has a clear specific range of referent: a flowering plant called Baptisia tinctoria, as well as the dyestuff made from it, or, later, a synthetic dye resembling it in hue and saturation. On the other hand, the word has a resonance for them, and a bifid

—bifid?

Split in two, divided, forked. The word has a resonance for them, and that resonance seems divided—part worked by the psychological and cultural associations of the word (for example, indigo = sailors who wear these dungarees and thus the sea, which is also usually described as blue, though seldom as indigo, or indigo = Quaker merchants and dry goods shops and cottage gardens and homespun wool dyed blue, and linsey-woolsey and bunting, the field or canton on which the forty-eight pentagrams of the republic glow white, wagon trains and the blue shadows of cloth left on a boy's thighs after he's taken off his new dungarees on an August night, the smell of his inchoate maleness and the color blue—these are just examples). Partly the resonance seems generated by the sound of the word itself—and here too there is a forking path—the sound as echoing or resembling or parodying other distinct but apparently unrelated statements in the language, thus *indigo* may bring to mind in they go, Indy go, in the goo, Wendigo—one of their old gods, by the way.

On the other hand, the sound can take off all by itself in them, the narrow fronted vowel soaring to a nasal, resounding just off the alveolus where the *d* takes flight and thrusts the tense dinky little front vowel like a dart from a blowgun that is then, only then, re-strained by a rough command from the back of the throat, the fauces from which a sonant summons it back, to dissolve it in the awe-filled cavern of the wide-open mouth, the awe trailing off to you, oooo I mean, and the word is done. But the mind of the speaker and the mind of the hearers are brought through this glossodrama by the sound of the word alone. When the silence comes back, speaker and listeners alike stand reverent in the vast caverns of their own mouths, where all the sacred dances come to spell. Mammoth Cavern. Secret Places of the Earth.

—I think they know about us, don't you?

I do. We are after all characters in their glossodrama—the act or action a word performs in the world or in the mind by sound alone. We are who they mean when they think that words mean any-thing. Words mean us. We inhabit their speaking. We ride on their breath.

—But that seems to be a metaphor you're speaking now.

I am allowed—the sons of Mne Seraphim are permitted metonymy.

—I know you are, we are, I know you as I know myself. But when they know about us, they think it's themselves they know, their whims, desires—their breaths. Can we ride so fickle a breeze for long?

—Drives too we can ride.

Yes. So we have to come down in our craft and bite them before they know it's not all inside them, not all inside.

—Even if it is?

It is, but it comes out.

—True, here we are, with a dumb kid in our hands, his constituents all over the table, his replica half done.

323

Robert Kelly

Replicas are always unfinished. The copy always lacks the presence of the original. The cry of presence.

And I was listening all the while they were talking. I had nothing to do but listen to them, and to the cry.

It was me becoming two people.

The solace of a mountain is lost to me. Plains. I was in the flat land so long that even now when I am on a mountain I can take no pleasure in it. I am afraid that it will fall. Or they will come and bring me down again, the way they do.

One went up and one went down, one went to earth, one went to heaven, one went to symmetry, one went to the actual.

I am lost. Lost the way a sound is lost. I hear the honking of the gyaling near my cave, wooden tube with a brass bell, a double reed that shatters the calm inside the air. For a moment it is louder than anything can ever be. And then it dies and is gone. A minute and a half later I can hardly even imagine the sound.

There was a cry.

There was a cry and it was me. Or what was left of me after the dividing. It was a divided cry, I died in the dividing and left me to live on. All the me I can come to be.

I remember the beginning of the cry. It was when they had torn out all the parts of my body and thrown them into a basin in the corner, when they had finished stuffing all that crap into me, clocks and animals and flowers, and sewed me up, quick and harsh, with thick red twine. Then they did things to the basin in the corner, tossed handfuls of things into it, then shoved a shiny metal rod into it, and out of the parts of my body and whatever else was in there, a boy stood up who wasn't there before. He looked just like me.

Will he always look like me? Will he be a man when I am a man, an old man when I retire? Just like me then and just like me now, I bet, though I haven't seen him since.

324

The alien came toward me with a silver rod, while the other alien approached my look-alike, who was standing slack jawed and dumb, a fleshy, dopey kid, just like me, so that's what I look like, red hair and white skin and looking dumb, dumb. The other alien put his rod against the chest of my look-alike and squeezed a switch. My look-alike opened his mouth and squeezed his eyes shut, and a second or so out of sync a scream began to come out of his mouth.

Then I heard it in my chest, and it began coming out of my mouth too, though my alien hadn't touched me, not at all, with his wand. The scream came out of my mouth and I could feel the pain breaking things inside me but the scream was louder than the pain.

The cry went on, and on, and sounded just like I, an I that kept on and on, a warble of a sound, aaaaaaaaaaaeeeeeeeeeee, and I realized as I heard it that I was the smallest word, but it still had two sounds in it, aaaaa and eeee

and we were both screaming, the sound came out of my throat, my mouth, even my chest, and it converged on the tip of my alien's wand and the tip of that began to glow.

The two aliens began backing away from us then, us meaning me and whatever in God's name it was standing over there. Whatever it was, it was made from my guts and looked just like me. The aliens backed away until they were back to back, then each whipped the wand, which had been pointed at us, up and joined them above their heads.

At that moment, the cry broke in half. I was sobbing aaaaaaaaa and he was screaming eeeeeee, and we were born apart, separate, done. The pain stopped then, and the broken cry soon after. The aliens led him away into the trees and left me alone.

Why didn't I escape then? Or try to? I didn't even think about it. I didn't know what had become of me. I didn't know how to go home. How could I go home and say, Mommy, I have two squirrels in my chest and they do my breathing for me?

What happened to you, son? my father would say.

Robert Kelly

And I would have to answer, they took me apart, I heard a cry, the cry said why, then fell apart and I was two. And now this one of me comes home, to you, do you want me?

So I couldn't go anywhere, just stayed there, trembling and crying, this time just ordinary crying, soft and stupid and wet.

I lay on my right side, and saw along the dusty rock floor of the cave, which now seemed not at all like a cave, seemed just an old shed in the woods. I smelled wet earth outside; it still was Pennsylvania. As I watched, the aliens were putting my clothing on the other me, brushing him carefully, sweeping back the forelock over his, my, right eyebrow, just the way my mother always did it, licking spit on their fingers and plastering the lock back. My jeans were snug on him, so must have been snug on me. I looked down at my legs and of course found them naked, I was naked and never knew it. And now I did, and folded my hands over my groin to hide the silky pubic hair that had just started to come out these past few months. I didn't fully understand this hair yet. But I didn't want anybody to see it before I had it figured out.

Two Stories
Brian Evenson

GIRLS IN TENTS

IN THE LATE AFTERNOONS, after school, in the days just after their father had left their mother, the two girls would strip all the blankets off their beds. Gathering them up as best they could, they carried them out of their rooms and down the narrow hall to drop them in a heap in the living room. They tucked blanket edges under couch cushions or put them on furniture with encyclopedias piled on them and then stretched the blankets from couch to chair or chair to window ledge. When done, they had a series of tents, all overlapping, the living room become a field of billows and dips under which they could crouch.

For several months they lived each afternoon under these tents, light coming mottled through the fabric. They felt good there. Sometimes they read or drew or talked there, other times just sat. When their mother came home from work she often knelt down and asked how they were doing, and what. The youngest girl mostly half-shrugged and said *fine*, they were doing *fine*. The oldest girl never answered unless she had to, unless the mother addressed her directly and more than once. It was not that she disliked her mother, only that she thought it was none of the mother's business. The tents had been the oldest girl's idea; she had made them so as to have a substitute house within the larger house, for now that the father was gone the house no longer felt like it was her house. It was only in the tents that she began to feel at home again. In tents it was the two of them, the two girls, alone but together, and nothing changing unless they wanted it to. So when the mother knelt down to ask what they were doing in the tents, the oldest girl didn't feel she should have to answer: the tents were not about the mother.

When the father had left it was as if he had taken part of the house with him. It no longer felt like the oldest girl's house, but neither did it feel like her house at the apartment the father rented across town. Every other week their father showed up looking somewhat disoriented to take them away to his apartment where they stayed for almost two full days, the father trying to keep them entertained until the mother arrived Sunday afternoon to take them to church. At the father's house, in his apartment, the girls slept on the front-room floor in sleeping bags. This practice the father sometimes referred to as *camping,* which made the oldest girl try to imagine she was out in the open, under the stars. But still she never felt at home in the sleeping bag like she did in the tents.

One problem with the father's new house was that there were not enough blankets to make a good tent. The father was what the mother called a *cold sleeper;* he had only one blanket in his apartment and usually slept (so the eldest girl had found sometimes late at night when she couldn't sleep and went in to the father's bedroom to see if the father was asleep himself) on the edge of the bed, half his body uncovered, the blanket splitting him in two. During the day the girls were allowed to take this single blanket from the bed and stretch it from the back of the couch to the bookshelves behind, tucking it in tightly among the books, but one blanket was not enough; it made a tunnel but hardly a tent. They had tried, the two girls, unzipping the sleeping bags to use them as blankets to make tents, but the sleeping-bag fabric was heavy and thick—light didn't come through in the way it did with a good blanket. And in any case, the father didn't have enough furniture to make good tents. All he had was a couch and a chair. Now that he was out of the house, the father didn't have much of anything. In the kitchen, all he had in the way of utensils was three of each: three knives, three forks, three spoons, all taken from the larger collection of wedding flatware that still resided with the mother. If he and the girls ate anything, the father would have to wash utensils before they could eat again.

The father, when he was feeling exuberant, when he was at his best, would claim that they were lucky girls, that most little girls did not have two houses like they did. But the oldest girl felt that no, they did not now have two houses: they were between houses and thus in a way had no house. And it was clear to the eldest girl that their father did not feel at home in his new house, that in a way he had no home of his own either. Unlike the father, the oldest girl at least had the tents to go to, and after school, each day, she and her sister would make the tents and lie beneath in the warm space, watching the mottled light filter through.

*

Near the end of his fourth month out of the house the father began to let them down. He still showed up on Friday to take them to his house, to his apartment, but they never could count on when. Before, he had always been sitting on the porch when they came home from school, but now it was hard to say. Sometimes he was there, waiting, but most days he would not show up until the mother was long home from work and it had begun to grow dark outside. A few times the mother got tired of waiting and called him, and when he showed up ten minutes later he was shamefaced and apologetic.

The oldest girl knew something was going wrong with the father, but could not say what exactly. She knew he was distracted but could not say why. In a way what or why did not matter. The youngest girl, too, felt something going wrong with her father, and the youngest girl was nervous about him. The youngest girl was, so the mother always said, *high-strung,* and thus needed from time to time to be soothed and calmed down. The oldest girl always tried to calm her down. The youngest girl did not always notice things as quickly as the oldest girl did, but when she did notice them she seemed to feel them more, and since the father had left, it somehow had become the oldest girl's job to help calm her down. Because of that, the oldest girl had learned not to show when she knew something or felt it, so that sometimes she felt like she was just watching things happening but nothing really was ever happening to her. The oldest girl thus had learned to cope with everything alone and quickly, so that by the time the youngest girl began to get wind of things she could be there, calm and placid as glass, to comfort her.

So while it was true that the oldest girl knew something was wrong with the father well before the youngest girl, by the time the youngest girl began to notice and feel it, the oldest girl had stopped worrying and already saw this wrongness now instead as a condition of life to be adapted to. The youngest girl worried about what was happening with the father, but the oldest girl, while calming the youngest girl and distracting her and making up games in the tent for her, was not so much worried as only curious about where it would all lead.

The father kept coming to get them, mostly late but occasionally on time. Sometimes he seemed so distracted that he could not even be talked to. They would ride back with him to his apartment in silence. Once there he would sometimes notice them and smile, and sometimes they would even walk a few blocks together for ice cream and then figure out something else to do, but mostly they would just sit around the apartment in their inadequate blanket tunnel while the father lay on the blanketless bed reading a book or just staring up at the ceiling. Sometimes he would come out of the bedroom and sit at one end of the blanket tunnel and give them choices about what they could do. They could order a pizza or they could have pasta. They could go to a movie or they could go to the zoo. Which did they want to do? The oldest girl had developed a system of not putting any demands on the father, figuring that putting demands on him would make him even less dependable than he already was, so mostly she shrugged and said she didn't care. The youngest girl usually followed her lead. But somehow not caring put another sort of demand on the father so that he just shook his head and often went back into the bedroom without deciding on any particular thing, and nothing was done. Something was happening to the father so that he was slowly disengaging himself from them, even when they were actually present and there. The oldest girl could guess where it was going, that they would see the father less and less and one day see him not at all. But all she could do while she comforted the youngest girl and kept her from the truth was steel herself for what would happen next.

On the day the father failed to arrive, the mother had made *other arrangements*. She would not be home after work, had an *engagement*, would not be back until the next day. She had in fact called the father the night before to let him know this, to stress that he must come on time. This, the youngest girl thought later, once night had fallen and she and her sister were alone in the tents, had been a mistake on the mother's part. The mother did not understand how the father worked since she herself, the mother, worked so differently. She did not see that saying such things to the father made him not more dependable but less so.

So, when they left in the morning the mother gave them their lunches and reminded them that she would not be home, that when they got back from school the father would be there waiting for them. She kissed them and drove them to school and left them there like she always did, and they went to their classes and ate lunch and went to their classes again. When school was over, the oldest girl went to the youngest girl's classroom and got her and together they walked home.

At the house, the father wasn't there yet. They took the key from under the doormat and cleaned it off and let themselves in. *Hello,* the youngest girl called out hopefully as they entered the house, but there was no answer.

They put their schoolbooks down on the couch and then went to get their already packed overnight bags out of their rooms and put them next to the front door, up against the wall right beside the door, so that when the father arrived they would be all ready to go. They sat on the couch, waiting. Usually, the oldest girl thought, the mother was there and would have them do something while she herself called the father, but they were alone, the oldest girl thought; that was fine, they would manage. Or at least she would, she thought. The youngest girl, she could see, was beginning to fidget and get anxious. She was sitting on the couch and trying to figure out what was happening, or rather not happening, and soon she was going to start to panic.

"Let's go get a snack," said the oldest girl to her, poker-faced, as if getting a snack and their father's absence weren't actually connected. They went into the kitchen and the oldest girl boosted the youngest girl up onto the counter so that she could stand there and open the cabinet and get the snacks out. Getting up on the counter was a special treat for the youngest girl, the oldest girl knew. The youngest girl got down the sandwich cookies and sat on the edge of the counter while the oldest girl opened the packages and divided out the cookies. The way the girls liked to eat sandwich cookies was to break them open and scrape the cream out with their teeth and then eat the cookie part later, dipped in milk. But even when they were done, cream and cookie halves and milk gone, the father still hadn't arrived.

The sun was getting low in the sky outside, the oldest girl noticed. She wondered how long it would be before the youngest girl noticed. The oldest girl helped her sister off the counter and they went back into the living room and the oldest girl, trying to be casual about it, turned on the light.

"When is he coming?" asked the youngest girl.

"He's on his way," said the oldest girl. And then she said, "Time for tents."

They did it the way they always did. The oldest girl went into her room and pulled her blankets into a pile and carried them out all at once, dumping them on the living-room floor. The youngest girl carried out just one of her blankets and then waited for the oldest girl to come get the other one. Together, they pushed the armchair closer to the couch and brought in the kitchen chairs as well. They got the encyclopedias down from the shelf and then set about spreading the blankets out, tucking them into the couch cushions and anchoring them down with books.

When they were done, the tents overlapped and stretched from couch to fireplace, in some places as high as the sitting girls and in others almost touching the ground. They crawled under an edge and got in and moved into the middle, where, near the armchair, they could sit upright without the tents touching them, the overhead light coming differently through the different blankets around them, shining oddly on their flesh.

"I'm hungry," said the youngest girl.

"We had a snack," said her sister.

"When is he coming?"

"Soon."

"Did you call him?"

The oldest girl did not answer. She did not want to call the father, though she knew that was what the mother would do. She wanted the father to come on his own. Instead, she crawled out and got some bread and a knife and a mostly empty jar of peanut butter and crawled with it back into the tents.

"We're not supposed to eat in the living room," said the youngest girl.

"We're not in the living room," said the oldest girl, "we're in the tents. Besides, Mother isn't here."

When the bread was gone and they had scraped the rest of the peanut butter out of the jar, they sat and waited. The oldest girl watched the youngest girl's pale and anxious face, and wondered how her own face looked. And while she was sitting there, looking at her sister's face and wondering about her own, she saw the face begin to change and her sister begin to cry. The oldest girl reached out across the tent and put her hand on her sister's back and began to move her hand. It was like she was petting an animal—or rather, since she herself, concentrating on staying calm as glass for the sake of her sister, felt distant not only from her sister's back but from her own hand, as if she were watching someone else pet an animal.

The youngest girl, she realized, was asking about the father. Where was he? Wasn't he coming? Where was he? Why wasn't he here? The oldest girl just kept patting her back. And where was the mother, the youngest girl wanted to know. Not only where was the father but where was the mother?

"She's not here," said the oldest girl.

The youngest girl kept crying and asking questions, which made the oldest girl think that she didn't really want an answer, or at least didn't want the real answer. The oldest girl kept patting her sister on the back and waiting for it to be over, waiting for her to calm down. When she finally did, her face was blotched red and her eyes were puffy. She sat in the tents looking drained and not looking at anything at all.

"What do we do?" the youngest girl asked.

"We wait for him to come," said the oldest girl.

"But what if he doesn't come?"

"He'll come," said the oldest girl.

"But what if he doesn't?"

"He will," said the oldest girl firmly.

She crawled out of the tents and got some pillows from their bedrooms. She brought them back into the tents and coaxed her sister into lying down. *We'll just wait,* she told her. *We'll just lie down and relax and wait for him to come.*

Later, the oldest girl was not sure how long they stayed there together, waiting, the oldest girl sitting, the youngest girl lying down. The oldest girl watched the youngest girl's eyes narrow and finally close. Then she kept sitting and watching, the blanket fabric brushing her head lightly. She waited.

When her own head began to nod, she shook it and got up, crawled out of the tents. In the kitchen she checked the clock; it was after eleven, later than she was allowed to stay up. She looked out the window; there was no moon, the night thick and dark. She could see the dim shape of the porch supports, the ghost of the garage a dozen feet past them, but little more. It was as if the world had dissolved.

She locked the back door, left the front door unlocked so the father could get in. She went around the house turning lights on. When she was done, she went back into the living room, and sat just outside the tents.

She could hear her sister inside the tents, breathing softly. Otherwise the house was quiet. Why not telephone the father? she wondered. But that was the sort of thing the mother would do, the sort of thing, the oldest girl thought, that made the father less dependable. The father, she felt, had to come on his own.

She sat there cross-legged, just outside the tents, guarding her sister, waiting for the father to come. Eventually, he would come, she was sure. He would remember them. He would remember her.

And when the father did burst through the door, she thought as her eyes grew heavy, wild-eyed and unshaven, wearing only his pajama bottoms, she would still be there, she was certain, sitting cross-legged just outside the tents. He would look at her and she would look back, and then she would turn and crawl back into the tents and lay her head down next to her sister's on the pillow and sleep. If the father wanted to follow her in, that was fine—there was plenty of room in the tents, and for the mother too if she wanted to come. But they would have to understand that in the tents it was the two girls who made the rules. It would be up to the girls now to be in charge, she thought, yawning. It was up to them, not the parents, which meant it was mostly up to the oldest girl. The father would have to understand that.

But if he didn't come, she finally thought hours later, her legs tingling from being crossed so long, the sky beginning to grow light outside, if he didn't come, she could learn to live with that too.

STOCKWELL

I.

He told again the story of Bates, and then the one about himself—Jansen—and then about Gerhardie. Stack just sat as always with his chin resting on the head of his cane, listening, sometimes grunting a bit. He told like beads of Bates with that leg and the rest of him you could put a knife right into and him not feel a thing. He told of himself, Jansen, who had crept up to slit a disloyal throat mostly out of curiosity, damn the risk. And he told of Gerhardie, goddamn handsome bastard who had done fine, not a flicker of doubt through the whole struggle. The handsome, in Jansen's opinion, tended to be like that. But then two months later the car crash and Gerhardie thrown out, the ground breaking his neck and the asphalt scraping the skin all off an already dead face. *Ayeh,* responded Stack, his head hiccoughing atop the cane, *Ayeh.* And Jansen told of Bates crossing a parking lot alone late at night and being attacked. The numb bastard walked three miles home with a knife stuck deep in his back, not feeling a thing, not even knowing the knife was there until he tried to shuck his clothes at home and found the shirt wouldn't come free. Didn't even call the police, Bates, just laid down on the bed on his stomach and bled to death.

You and me, said Jansen to Stack, *sorry pair, the only ones still drawing breath.* Jansen always claimed he was still alive because he had remained curious, because he took anything at all that life threw at him and worked it back in. Nothing could touch him. Stack just nodded, as he did to everything. *What about you, Stack? What was it kept you alive?* Stack just sat there, his chin on the cane and eyes rheumy, saying nothing at all. Which perhaps was an answer in its own way.

So Jansen told on, told about the fifth and last of them, Stockwell, who was what you would refer to as a *creeper,* had a creeping way about him, and then he had died too, like the others, how was it exactly he had died, Stack?

"Never was a Stockwell," said Stack.

Jansen stared and then said, no, there goddamn was a Stockwell, there were five all told. Jansen, Stack, Gerhardie, Bates, Stockwell. He could recall them all now plain as day.

"No Stockwell," said Stack.

No Stockwell? But he had been telling of Stockwell for years now. Stack had never said *no Stockwell* up to now.

"Never had to," said Stack, finally lifting his chin from his cane. He pushed himself off the chair and slowly stood. "Today's the first time you ever mentioned a Stockwell. Nobody by that name ever was alive."

II.

Lunch and then dinner, a slow round from cafeteria to bedroom and back, and, between, the slow journey out the door and to the grounds, around the paths. Stack there on the bench awaiting him but Jansen passing the traitor by. Stack seemed not to notice. Jansen kept on, right down the garden path. *What about you? What was it kept you alive?* he asked of himself, and knew the reply he always gave, *Curiosity and working it all back in, nothing can touch me,* but it had been more than that: he had Stockwell to thank, he thought, *the creeper.* There was a certain dogged persistence to the man that Jansen had stolen for his own. But here was Stack, who never said anything, now saying no, there was no Stockwell, just the four of them, no one further. It was not to be believed, he thought. But there, too, in the photograph he kept in the dresser beside his bed, only four of them: Jansen, Stack, Gerhardie, Bates. And in Stack's pictures as well, no sign of Stockwell. Yet he was certain there had been a Stockwell, Stockwell had been there. *What about you, Stockwell?* he wondered, *What was it killed you dead?* Was the answer that Stockwell was dead now because he had never been alive in the first place?

The slow sound of the generator dying down, the light above him slowly fading and then flickering as he marked his book by folding the page back. It was the moment he hated most, that slow vanishing of light. Then the light went out altogether and he hated that even more.

If there was a moon, he would turn his chair window-ward and continue reading, stumbling on until he fell asleep in the chair, woke stiff and aching a few hours later, stumbled to his bed. If no moon, as tonight, then he would lie there for hours, the stories springing into his head again, but more vividly this time. He played their lives out again, thrashing against the sheets. Gerhardie: sliding along the asphalt, perhaps hearing the sound of his skull rubbing the pavement. Bates: lying in bed, dying, sheets growing wet with his own blood.

But where was Stockwell? After Bates, every night until this night, had come Stockwell.

And then Stack: not as he had been when they were all loyal together, but as he was now, chin resting on his cane, listening to stories, nearly wordless himself.

And there he was, he himself, Jansen, first seeing the man he planned to kill and then slowly moving forward. Inches from him now, then directly behind. Knife jabbed through the throat, a strange gurgle as the flesh opened warm over his hand and then air hissing out bloodflecked as the man continued to try to breathe, finally going limp. In bed, he saw himself laying the body down, but doing it poorly so that the body rolled faceup and he could not help but see the face.

But tonight there was more. Tonight he saw, above the gash, Stockwell's pale face. Thrashing in bed, he was not certain if the face was there because that was how it had happened—that he had killed some unknown man that he later christened Stockwell so as to work him back in with the alive and loyal—or because there was now merely no other place for Stockwell's face to go.

I will make it to morning, Jansen told himself, staring into the slit throat. Nothing can touch me. I will wake up into light and I will put on clothing. I will go out and make the world over again. I will never sleep again.

Two Poems
Catherine Imbriglio

PSALM

—For Reginald Shepherd

I.

Each now dropped

Lay your hands upon me, you in the black bent grass, the body in motion that stays in motion, so too in your drifting to or from me, in the pictures of the body that provoke the body, *judica me,* you in the blackpoll warbler, *judica me,* you in the black-tailed godwit. It wasn't on purpose, was it, in the way you get it down or keep it down, my texture to your texture, in the body as motion that stays as motion, *judica me,* which one of us, like spit. One of us should try breathing in the mirror, each mirror holding yet another mirror, it *was* something like communication, wasn't it, how many persons to a copper or silver goblet, how many persons from holding out their bowls. So too you in this drifting to or from me, in the pictures of the body that provoke the body, let me not from the circulation of impediments, let me not from accommodation to the pose.

II.

No internally fixed order of stages stop. Under incremental light conditions stop. I look out and see under the lilacs stop. From woodbine to woodbine stop. Day unto day one tree frog two duckboards three goat moths stop. Made you look made you look made you look you stop. Were word of godetia real word stop. If without if without finding stop. What impudicity what who me stop. There is stop no speech no language where the voice from the wilderness stop. When it comes a'courtin' and we all go stop. Yours to then yours to wend watch stop. Day unto day while we take its sweet time stop all rise.

III.

Spiny wings that, suppose that

Break their teeth with your lips, break the teeth of the dumb flowers, open wide the calyx, for when you do what you do, I who you your honor, broke out in teeth, the alleged teeth, for at just that time, admit, for open wide, admit, were you or were you not, *selah,* down beside me among the cow wheats, the bull thistles. Go for the throat. Now we see it, now we, in sun mouth, in ripened seed head, casual, seriatim, party of the first part wreak party of the second. Rattle the big pharmaceuticals. Reign in with limit list. Rattle for rattle, rattle *of* rattle, constrained by, gag ordered, most wanted, grift. So moved. Hoop ash, basket ash, a set of promises, a mimicry. And then, an if then, a nothing to me. I lost my place. Partings of the first part beneath a parting of the second. So moved. Ballast love, when a rain coursing through me. Here. Hearsay. In here you'd say.

RECITATIVE

I.

A photograph is an index that fractures your mobility.
Odd her oddness, like zero as a place marker, a unit of measure in the
    photograph that's set to anchor in a system of counting.
It says it happened.
It collapses from an interior.
Look at the moments when you say you watch carefully.
Weighing bottle. Salt mouth bottle.
This is the part where evil is subsumed by religiosity.
It is not a question of whether to pin the towers down or be evocative, your
    mobility consumed by their immobility, you trying to stop you from not
    having to address what's passed.
To describe the excavation, take a photograph and put circles around its
    archaeology.
The numbers in the circles represent a faux interiority, steel, flesh, ash, air.
When you turn the vessel turns.
The flattened picture of the street fills to her reactive body.
At the same time, cordially, you could say, we have a photographic bypass.
It is all in the timing. She assumes the uncaptioned photograph is a
    retrogressive case shot for military fire.

339

It is not combinatory, as with a formula, but a depth perception, even though
    "the concept of image-as-opinion is difficult for most people to grasp."
In this manner looking is both assault and being assaulted.
We see through that which sees through that.
Some of which I may be imagining.
Its supplies.
Its demands.

II.

In her right eye, the degree of visual definition measured along the vertical
    and horizontal axes is unsatisfactory, because a spiked cataract is growing.
The film of the developing cataract distorts her image transfer, as in a glut of
    information, what things her brain selects, sausage, ricotta, for a hasty
    meal preparation.
In the immunity of a photograph, think: you can go now, you can go back in.
Her right eye is her default eye, i.e., her dominant eye, to whose imagery the
    brain submits, so you won't see the stunned woman stunned totally.
Light teases out a latent action in the lens, hope in proximity, what you now
    do or then did.
She anoints herself with such narratives.
Sunspots in her mind's eye correspond to the mating parts of the external to
    the internal thread, as from a table of oils, pressed radially.
She experiences an indwelling, terms she wants to break into, deep fascia,
    deep femoral artery, deep epigastric artery, for a moment of second sight
    that is once again temporary.
That could be me, breaking the window, the third one from the left.
I begin dinner by pouring olive oil into a pan.
I select fish, bread, greens, carrots, candles, wine.
Outside he may be planting.
The light on the cherry trees elaborates the fallen petals of the cherry trees.
As with a waterway, she takes a sounding.
At the extreme point, the incline of a roof, one half pitch, one whole pitch,
    the ratio of the height to the span, like arms around a stranger.
You can pave a street with the rubble, as with a series of undressed stones.
She plays a tape she keeps of beloved voices, here and not here, as if sound
    were a mending instrument.
The voices rise as from a carpet, ash to petal, in degree, number, rate,
    proportion, kind, the force of a transparency.
The voices rise, as from a carpet, blown.
They relay a periphrastic present, a strain on the values of her photoelasticity.

I Remember Her as a Study in Red
Julie Agoos

Her scattered fractions leaving nothing whole,
no wonder that I cannot bring her close.
Her fingernails the rose on a lacquered box.
Her lips that would later bleed fresh raspberries
in the day's heat just forming an ice of sweat.
The fabric of her coat was Thai silk,
her suit a lightweight wool from the Hebrides,
the scarf of seafoam mixing with the dawn
against which the gold teeth of her spoils shone.
I'd seen her boots in the Musée du Costume,
her hat and gloves a fashionable hoax
perpetrated on the silver screen.
I learned at her knee, not knowing the protocol.
I fingered the wealth of empires like pennies.
I learned the genuine and female art,
150 proof against a barbarous world.
And her ship, a barge of honeyed white and gold
hard at it over the depths, nowhere at home;
not yet exquisite under green glass.

Birthday Call
Mark Rudman

"How are your bones?"

"Ashes."

"Happy birthday."

"Restless."

"What?"

"I'm restless in death.
I want to get back."

"That's a good sign."

"But what's it worth?
What are you doing with your time
other than killing it?"

"Let's see, this week, jury duty."

"That's not what I meant."

"I'm working on . . ."

"That's not what I meant."

"A party. I went to a party."

"What did they serve?
What were the women wearing?"

"Bare midriffs."

(*She guffaws.*)

"And your wife, was she dressed in black?"

"With a purple blouse."

"Well I wish I could go to a party."

"I thought death was a continual party."

"Some joke. You're very funny.
Did anyone ever tell you that?

That's not the way to talk to your mother.

Right?"

(*Bats her eyes flirtatiously.*)

"Did you meet anyone interesting?"

(*He thinks.*)

"The beautiful and animated sister of an actor."

"Well that's very nice.
I'd like to meet someone like that."

"Give her time."

"Very funny."

"Why in LA and New York City is everyone
someone's sister or son or daughter?"

"You know." (*Pause. Scrunches up face. Slurs her words, like a
45 on 33 rpms.*)

"That'saveryinterestingquestion."

(*Recovers voice.*)

"But you don't have that problem, do you?
You're an orphan, aren't you, Mark?
You certainly behaved like one."

(*Pause.*)

"I meant the offspring of a famous so-and-so."

"Was Generatia there?"

"Why do you always ask if she was wherever I've gone?"

"I don't know. She's your friend, isn't she?
I met her at your apartment."

"I only see her on the street."

343

"Oh. That's too bad.

Maybe you should be more careful to keep your friends."

"You're giving me a lump in my throat."

"Well you do want me to be honest, don't you?"

"We've been so busy."

"That's too bad too.

I think you should write a grand adventure.

Something people want to read."

"A book you'd like to read?"

(—*I just have!*)

"Now what would you do if you weren't so busy?
If every minute weren't accounted for?

I don't know how you can be so busy.
You only teach two afternoons a week.
Sounds like a swell job to me.

More like a vacation."

(*His face grows red. Voice grows hoarse.*)

"That's to earn the money to give myself time to write, remember,
Mom?"

"I'm sorry, I forgot. I must be stupid."

(*Hits herself on forehead to emphasize "stupidity."*)

"I need a day to recover.
It leaves a few days to write and live.
And I need time to waste."

"Well you've always wasted plenty of time.
I never saw you do anything except listen to music in your room.
Never saw you pick up a book."

(*Thump of body as it falls to wood floor. Beats fists weakly on
ground. Dry tears.*)

"I wasn't aware that you were spying."

"I used to read a lot, and I read to you too, Mark, when you were little—
that's how come you know so much—
but now I just don't have the energy.
Or the incentive."

(*Pause.*)

"If I did write that book I'd write about you."

"Now that's what I'd call stupid.
My life was just one big mistake."

"Thanks."

"I don't mean you."

"Then why are you so critical? So unsatisfied?"

(*Assumes little girl/little old lady voice.*)

"I don't mean to be dear."

"Maybe it was the longings that counted.

You were so open in your letters.

What a difference between the honest and anguished
you of your letters and the frowning groaner
you were in person.

Maybe there's an epistolary novel in your correspondence."

"I doubt it. Who would care anyway
about the groanings of an insignificant woman?
No one cares about my misery.

What's so special?

Now your life, that would be interesting."

"Doing what I do?"

"Oh no, oh no.

I mean, you live in New York City and you never go
to any fine restaurants or Broadway plays."

"Not never."

"When was the last time you went to a museum?

Mark Rudman

You didn't see *Phantom.*
I just don't get you."

(Shakes her head vehemently.)

"I'd go to Broadway plays. Musicals!"

"*The Producers?*"

"I'll bet that's a howl.

Who the hell can afford the lifestyle?
The stockbrokers have made a killing."

"Had."

"Well, while I was alive.

I told you to study law.
Or medicine.
Then you wouldn't have to run to doctors."

"You did have every disease—except cancer."

"The big C.

(Counts on fingers methodically.)

The psoriasis, the rheumatoid, the varicose veins (remember I had
that operation?); the psoriatic arthritis that made the scabs burn;
then . . . diabetes, emphysema, and arteriosclerosis."

"The latter three could have been avoided."

"That's probably true, if I had given a damn.

Terrible, terrible stress."

(Lowers voice, mumbles: "And the valgus heel.)

(Let's not forget the hysterectomy that was the beginning of my
mood fall, they were hysterectomy crazy in the sixties, those
bastards, they just love to cut; I think they're misogynists.)

And of course I swelled up like a balloon when you had the
appendicitis."

"So I've heard."

"You don't know what you put me through."

346

(Visibly upset, she wrings her hands.)

"And the only thing that helped."

(Pause.)

"The swimming.

I was a beautiful swimmer, don't you think so, Mark?
In Beverly Hills they all said I swam like Esther Williams."

(Displays her "effortless, smooth, slow" stroke.)

"I never saw her swim."

"You don't know who Esther Williams was?"

"The swimming actress."

"She happened to have been an Olympic swimmer!"

"No she wasn't."

"Oh yes she was."

"The team was heading for Tokyo when World War II intervened,
canceling the games and her hopes for gold."

"Now where did you get that misinformation?"

"The Internet.

I looked her up as we spoke."

(She composes herself. Delivers dignified reply.)

"It doesn't take away from that fact that they all said
I swam like Esther Williams."

"Why can't people just be themselves?
Why do they have to look like a prototype?"

"A simulacra."

(Pause.)

"You smile, Mark.

The dead read their Baudrillard."

Three Poems
Elizabeth Arnold

BARRIER ISLAND

—barriered itself now
by another sandbar-turned-to-land

two sandbars east—

was the only thing between him
and the ocean's never-ending

fist-fights-to-the-death

against the river's outbound current,
gouging from the inlet floor

deep-runneled beds,

their underwater banks
thrust up like breaching whales

into the air

then sinking back. He
taught himself to sail there in the twenties

in a heavy wood-keeled gaff-rig boat.

Slumped in his chair at home now
back in town, his circle—

though already letting no one

but my mother, sometimes
(distantly)

a daughter in—

is closing further.
I can almost see the line

as if he'd drawn it

on the rug around his chair,
behind him the room-high windows

and the river

—wider this far south, less rough, sailboats
cutting back and forth across its back,

chimney swifts that dart past dusk.

Wanting to hurry time, it seems,
he gets up for the day

at 2 a.m. He's sure it's later,

fights against my mother's
talking sense into him,

sense not making sense.

As when I found him
in the middle of their bedroom

lost, leaning

toward the sunlight's leaving
—as from some high coastal point, some

sand dune barely held intact

by sea oats' roots,
their tassels blown back

with his still-blond hair, sand

everywhere and flying off.
As can happen

with an island, which may one day

(if anyone is there to call it
"day") become

(who knows?) a whole

continent, or
(more than likely)

cloud the sea with its dispersion.

EXPERIMENTS OF THE HEART

The body of the Earth's core
rolls

—current-driven

just as experiments of the heart
mix their component parts, the force

of one

pulling at the other
checks itself then

dives for cover

•

People of societies that emerged from ice,
they cry like seals.

•

Who's to say what's worse, the powder blue
infinity of sky?

—or the sea inside its metal coat as the beach
assaults it one more time,

the sea clattering up again, as if
it weren't about to break?

•

A light broke out of it, his face
—as fire

out of earth: everything suddenly
there

then disappearing, hope veering.

•

And the bird—so high it, from the desert,
looks like dust

—observes and disregards its shadow.

Elizabeth Arnold

TWO POEMS

1. *Person*

And I can't know itself, how could *I* hope to,
looking from a face, a cover

through which voices sound as through a mask?
The eyes can't turn around to see

the lightless brain behind them, how could others?

2. Altercation

I let his words steer mine, his anger
—*this* is what it is

to run, to

not let what would let one
let oneself wait

—as for some

possibility, an
opening

in a bid. Turn toward the

outer world now,
make a bridge.

Scotch and an Orange
Donald Berger

This is exactly where Whitman
Used to stand and watch the president
Go by in his shabby cart
Or on his calm gray horse,
The man himself ugly as everyone else
Ever said he was, and his clothes
Beautifully threadbare and black
And ill-fitting. They even bowed
To each other, Whitman says,
Which must mean that one of them
Bent at the neck or the top half
Of the upper body, slightly,
And then the other did the same,
Which had to be the case because
One of them, Whitman, was standing
But Lincoln was most often sitting
Unless he means (Whitman) that the bows
Came at the other times, almost daily,
That the two men were in proximity,
I mean the same room
Like in the White House, there,
Which anyone could just walk around in
At any time you wanted as a citizen,
And at the receptions and feasts
I know Whitman stared at him, noting
His dark face and his ugliness that became
Beautiful, his lines in such a way,
His eyes looking out at someone like
Whitman saying there you are, and once
Whitman says the two men caught each other's
Eye, and held the look, while Lincoln
Was heading off on a horse with the cortege,
If you want to call it that,

Donald Berger

Toward the soldier's home near our house
Where he summered. I think Lincoln
Knew what the guy did, I think he even
Legendarily noted that Whitman looked like a man
Somebody says, the one person to stop
And steadily looked when the horses passed
With the sound of the swords and
Whatever else. I think Whitman watched
Him closely every time, when he wasn't
Reading to the amputee, or attending to his
Amputation. Anyhow, the two never met,
Never spoke to each other and probably
Did not even shake hands, the legend goes.
I plan to write a screenplay about this
For a movie that will never be seen.
I plan to come back to Washington
Tomorrow, to stand at the other corner
Of 14th and L where the carriage
A lot of times passed, and where Whitman
Could see and then go up to his third-
Floor room and toast the bread and sleep
Etc., like the actual person it may have
Been forgotten he was, holding a bottle
Of Scotch and I think an orange at
The O'Connors' door one day one floor
Below at Christmas even though that might be
Wrong, his hair and beard much longer
Than Lincoln's (but not by much), and his clothes a little
Dirtier maybe, and sometimes with blood
But not on that day, and that will be in
The screenplay too, and the words they never
Speak will not be in it, the two of them,
After Whitman's brother dies and his other
Becomes a prisoner and his sister a
Prostitute, they will not ever speak,
As they did not. Please follow with me
Here one day while we are still
Living and by then I will have found
The exact spot where the poet
Finally caught his eye.

Trees of the Epistolary Life
Howard Norman

Drawings by Jake Berthot

1. JAKE: "YOU CAN'T JUDGE a person by his lowest moment of despair" (overheard). Possibly. Depends on the person. Still, as Wm Bronk suggests, happiness passes like a shadow, fleetingly, whereas sadness has an adhesive quality in the mind. Today I was thinking about my uncle Saul. He built me a three-room tree house. I can scarcely fathom that project today. I think it took him nearly a year; he worked through the winter! "Don't worry," he said, "this is as much for me as it is for you. I don't have no kids and you don't hardly have a father." He owned a shoe store. "This store's just a front," he liked to say, conspiratorially. "Yeah," his enormous wife, my aunt Haddassah, said, "a front for it seeming like you actually do any work!" Anyway, he collected WWII posters. He kept them in a chest of wide drawers he'd bought from a print shop. He had "Loose Lips Sink Ships," he had "The Devil Has Big Ears." There was a type of poster in which a familiar circumstance, just a tableau of daily life in America, took on a menacing air. A family of blonds stands in front of a church in Middle America. The blond man holds a swastika-headed cane behind his back; the blonde woman wears a swastika necklace barely visible at her neckline; the blonde girl holds a Bible, but a copy of *Mein Kampf* peeks out of her big snap-purse; the snarling German shepherd is stiffly poised behind a fence as innocent families walk home on an average Sunday morning. The virulent concept of ambush. "No Jews ever in these posters," he'd say without fail. "What, we aren't Americans?" Uncle Saul, an opportunistic dramatist, insisted I view the posters only by flashlight, even during the day. The storeroom was windowless. I had a penknife flashlight he had given me expressly for this purpose. The long and short of it was, Saul died while fitting a pair of shoes on a woman's feet, just on an average working Tuesday. "He must've known it was coming," Aunt Haddassah said, back at their house after the funeral. "How do you mean?" I said. "Go climb up into your tree house and take a look, that's what I mean." I walked

directly out of the house, then the four blocks to the huge oak tree. My uncle Saul, architect, carpenter, painter of the tree house, had festooned the walls with WWII posters. What's more, he had fixed a kind of leather holster to a wall, in which was a flashlight and extra batteries. In fact, I do judge my uncle—because he judged his own life by it—by his lowest moment of despair, which must've happened in Poland, or Russo-Poland, in that vicinity, circa 1939, when he was "smuggled out of hell in the false backseat of a motorcar," as he put it. "That incident defined everything from then on."

2. JAKE: I've just been sent a lovely paragraph by a friend in Vancouver. She deals in antiquarian books and is the most dedicated vicarious Arctic traveler I could imagine. She obsessively searches out, reads, rereads Arctic journals, expedition logbooks, nineteenth-century zoological field reports, and so forth. "I go to the Arctic every night," she wrote me. Anyway, the paragraph pertained to a British expedition of 1890; in the naturalist's log, it says, "I have taken a native English seedling with me, about three feet high, so as to attempt to fend off the inevitable ravages of homesickness in the bleak, treeless land toward which we are sailing." (If only he had had one of your tree drawings!) / In "Anecdotes and Incidents of Reincarnation," by Bernard Heuvelmans, one reads of a so-called "moving orchard" in Ceylon. (I think today designated Sri Lanka.) Apparently, the belief was in a kind of portable, hallucinatory orchard, of "rather pinched, almost papery-skinned peaches of some kind." Nonetheless, according to local belief, should you eat one of these peaches, it offered an "aggressively erotic result," thus on the whole it was an aphrodisiacal orchard. The most obvious correspondence was, in Heuvelmans's mind, to the Garden of Eden. Yet in the biblical garden, the temptation was fixed in time and space, specific knowledge obtainable—that was the point; the apple was locatable. Whereas, in the Ceylonese situation, the taste of the peaches was "often perpetually out of reach, so that lovers had to invent alternatives. So the ancient Ceylonese lovers simply turned to each other's bodies in the rain or moonlight. At least that is how the stories were told." / In California, once, I literally got lost in an orange grove, when fog filled the corridors of orange trees. The acoustics, too, were ventriloquial; I heard my then girlfriend's voice say, "Are you there?" from what I thought was my left; in fact, she was down a lane to my right. To be honest about it, given the feel of fog drifted in from the

sea on the skin, the muffled, beckoning voice, "Are you there" as if from the afterlife, the acute sense of possible reunion (like Gina Berriault's splendid title, *The Infinite Passion of Expectation*), was when I felt the most desire. A day later we went separate ways. I took a job picking oranges for three weeks, after which I took myself out to a seaside café and saw my first movie actor, a very frail-looking Peter Lorre.

3. JAKE: In "Anecdotes and Incidents of Reincarnation," Heuvelmans remarks that trees in Ceylon seem to be the "place of most comfort for wandering souls." He apparently was not referring to the condition of purgatory. This was not a Christian country. He was referring to the *choice* of wandering souls to rest the night in an orchard, or in a tree. Last night I dreamt you were in one of "your" trees, I was in another of "your" trees; we each sat in drawn trees. I was conducting an interview. Here are the questions; I jotted them

down when I woke up. Remember, they are from a dream. (You may wish to answer them only in a dream.) 1. Kandinsky said that when people change locales, they often require different music, either in their memory, or they simply put different records on the turntable. Did this apply to you? 2. Did the light of upstate NY "remind you" of Ryder, especially storm light? 3. How many hours a day do you spend locating a tree to draw? Is this done basically by looking out a window? 4. I am assuming you detest the word "figurative" when it comes to drawing trees; am I correct? 5. Was it true, that after sharing a seven-dollar bottle of merlot, the most expensive vintage available in the local general store, you stood up, bowed, said to your guest, "Well, shall we walk out among the trees?" completely unaware of your pompous diction? 6. Did the walk take place? 7. Do you draw trees, or do you draw the "idea" of trees? 8. Why would you ever speak to a person who would ask such a question as number 7? 9. Remember the cramped, musty, cluttered museum in the small town that had dioramas of stuffed mammals, birds, insects; at the far end of a corridor, it had examples of the types of local trees, and amidst them was a piece of rough-hewn wood, a handle, whose label read, "from Noah's adze"—and you said, "A secret religious nut must be curator here!"—? / A double rainbow last evening; dear, old friends standing on the back porch, salmon and risotto cooling on plates; through the lower part of each arc, the trees seemed awash in color. "It's fine, keep looking, the food is just as good cold, actually." Lemon, rosemary, tiny bits of apricot slightly blackened. Later, someone said, "I hear you're building a screened porch. Well, now you can sleep almost among the trees." The big maples in front of the house; sometimes at dawn and dusk, their shadows hinge around, almost at a right angle, shadowing the side porch. How does that work? It could be researched, I suppose. But that might diminish the mystery, if not the happiness based on it.

4. JAKE: Took a walk up our curving dirt road at five A.M., a pair of mourning doves near the neighbor's mailboxes. Remembered that I forgot to give the four mailpersons at our village office holiday gifts last year; "Don't give those nice people books again," my daughter said. "What they read is none of your business. Try something from Chet and Viiu." They're glassblowers. Good idea. I rehearsed, "We meant to give these vases to you in December. Absentminded. Our apologies." More and more of late I'm talking to myself out loud.

The doves were farther down the road on the return walk. In "Anecdotes and Incidents of Reincarnation," Heuvelmans writes a very evocative scenario: "The dilapidated wicker mailboxes along the river are serviced by a ten-year-old girl in an outrigger canoe. She was never paid wages, but the position allowed for great enhancement of possibility for her ambitions as a stamp collector, though few letters arrived from foreign lands. Still, in all the neighboring river villages she was known as worldly. When she drowned, her deliveries continued without abeyance the next day, and on to the next and the next, and none were in noticeable alarm having a ghost girl deliver and collect as they would have protested a halt in the service, and, perhaps especially, the expert way she steamed postage stamps off envelopes or packages, using an oil lantern at night on the river." What more description do you need to get a full sense of village life? / My bid on a defunct ice-cream truck, I was told by telephone, fell short by five hundred dollars. For about two years the truck was situated amongst a stand of Russian birch trees, near the village of Craftsbury Common. It was a squarish truck with a fairly small freezer space, faded decals of Popsicles, Fudgsicles, Creamsicles, and ice cream sandwiches on the side. The cab fit just the driver, the steering wheel was on the right side, like a British car. What did I imagine doing with this truck past owning it? "A writer of my acquaintance," wrote Edward Lear in a letter, "seems always to be looking for a menial profession; instead, he writes about it. Whereas I am content to draw parrots on commission—trees, harbours, birds, alas." I laugh when thinking of Lear's comment: "It's true, Audubon perhaps drew more emotionally at times than I; however, I often chose more emotional birds to draw." Have you seen Lear's landscapes; his trees are magnificent.

5. JAKE: Friendship is provisional; it takes work; nothing can be taken for granted. I am sorry not to have written in so long. Life got complicated; "Physical pain is a drag" (kidney stones); writing letters usually organizes if not simplifies it. I should have written you every day and night. Of late I have imagined you "awake half the night, only because the other half is yet to come" (Lear). Thinking of trees: for three or four years now, a barn owl beats up the corridor of maple and butternut trees, his axis, finally roosting in a big maple across the road from my house. There it sits, "the owl's presence deepens the light" (Lear). From that tree it telescopes in on mice, frogs, toads,

whatever ventures out on the dirt road. The moon, or starlight, perhaps even the light from living-room lamps, the natural light of the
night, illuminates the road, more or less, depending. This owl once
flew so close that it had to be on purpose, considering it had the
entire sky at its disposal. When she was five, my daughter gave a
report on owls to her kindergarten class. It consisted of ten sentences, the first of which was, "The barn owl is pretty big, the saw-
whet owl isn't." / The three maples directly in front of the house
were named after each of the daughters of Will Peck, who, in 1848,
built my house. They were born in the "birthing room," now a
library. The second summer of our ownership, Charlotte Peck, age
eighty, came from Peacham for a look-see, as she put it. It happened
to be her birthday; I suppose seeing her childhood house was a birthday request. Pretty soon the neighbors had been notified; we had a
little impromptu birthday party, a candle in a cupcake, and video-
taped her memory tour of the house. We learned so much it would
take pages to reiterate. Finally, she noticed that one of the maple
trees was missing. I informed her that lightning had struck it, and it
had befallen other natural disasters, and large limbs were suddenly

cracking off, children played beneath it, and so on. "Plant another one, why don't you?" Charlotte said, looking at Emma. It felt something like an inheritance; in the least, a provenance. What a lovely day, captured on grainy film, a day developed slowly and taking its sweet time, a daguerreotype come to life. I felt we were walking in sepia light. I mentioned barn owls; Charlotte said, "Oh, you build a barn, a barn owl sees it a mile away and sets up house." Lear: "The owl's arrivals and departures are memorable incidents." / Merwin: "These woods are one of my great lies."

6. JAKE: Lear wrote, "After my purchases at the stationer's, my pens, my parchments, I sat beneath the wide oaks and prayed blessed gratefulness to trees for allowing the epistolary life, my drawing life, and so forth." / These titles arrived in an old-fashioned telegram from a bibliographer in Ottawa: "The Flame Trees of the Savannah," "A Swinger of Birches," "The Trees in My Life," "All Day Spent in Trees," "Tree House," "Tree Swing, Home and Hearth," "Trees Commemorated in Quilt & Painting," "Across the River and into the Trees," "Tree Farm," "The Christmas Trees," "Tree of Life," "Trees," "The Dignity of Trees," "Trees and Shrubs, Weed and Flower: A Memoir," "Bird Nests in Trees," "Basic Tree Identification," "Photographing Trees," "Trees in Photographs," "Barbara and the Lightning-Struck Tree," "The Solace: Trees and Their Shade," "Branching and Leafing in Lithographs," "Tree Farming in Canada," "The Owl and the Oak," "Elaborate Tree Houses of the Victorian Era," "Trees and Flowers on Chinese Vases," "The Buzzard and the Buzzard Tree: (My Life Studying an Ugly but Lovable Bird)," "Adventures of a Tree Surgeon," "Tree Surgeon in England," "Tree Damage During WWI (a study of violent change in European landscape)," "One Hundred Questions & Answers about Trees," "The Botany of Redwoods," "Quite a Tree in Your Front Yard, There, Mr. Rhodes," "Might I Sit Beneath Your Trees and Rest Awhile: Conversations with My Ohio Neighbors," "Harmful Tree Beetles: A Monograph," "Breathe Deep What the Tree Gives," "The Giving Tree," "Lazy Days and River Trees: A Memoir," "The Rain in the Trees," "Metaphor of Trees and Last Poems." / The semiretarded young man, Randolph, just appeared one morning out in the field near the house. He had an air rifle and a plastic bag full of pellets. He was wearing army fatigues, an entire camouflage outfit. I'd seen him walking briskly along Route 14 at all hours. He was out in the field,

shooting at birds, aiming toward a stand of trees atop a hill, firing away, loading, firing. I called from the road, "Hey, Randolph, whattaya doing there, my friend?" "The birds are driving me nuts!" he called back. He was overweight, with scraggly brown hair, wearing jeans, a T-shirt, sandals, and a cowboy hat. I'd heard that on occasion he'd walk all the way into Montpelier, about twenty miles. It's a fine line between confrontation and neighborliness, between patience and impatience, between legal and illegal, between a random visit and trespass, between sane and not sane. It was just an air rifle, but it was still a rifle; it did damage. It tore up leaves. It tore up bark. "When you run out of pellets, there, Randolph, I'd like you to walk back down to the highway. And be sure you take the road that way— not past my house, you understand?" "Yes, sir, I understand." "I don't like you shooting at trees on my property, Randolph. You didn't ask permission. If you'd asked permission, I would've said no. Do you understand that?" "Yes, sir, I do. I do understand that. I understand no." "All right, then, Randolph—finish shooting and go home or wherever you're going. And please don't come back here with that rifle. OK?" "OK, yes, sir, OK. Are you going to call the police?" "Not unless you come back." "I won't—are you going to call my father and mother?" "Yes, I am. To tell the truth, I am." "I know you're supposed to—everyone around here does, don't they?" "Yes, they do." "Go ahead, then, call them up. I'll finish up here." "I don't like you shooting at birds, Randolph. It's stupid." "I don't hit anything." "You might hit a bird by accident, that's the problem." "I'm going to finish up here, then." "Finish up right away, Randolph, and don't walk past my house." Village life.

7. JAKE: My problem is, I cling to my regrets, once I discover what they are. (Therapist) "Well, you ought to stop that." / I'm glad you weren't cross that I'd named the cook in *The Haunting of L* Berthot. I didn't intend it as a cameo, rather a turning point. Thanks for your letter to that effect. I have twenty-eight enlargements from slides of your trees on the wall. I am thinking of your "transition" from city to country, urban to rural, how to put it? I suspect you'd "all along dreamed trees" (Emerson) no matter where you lived. I don't mean to suggest that your tree drawings and tree paintings are "waking dreams." No, more, it's as if they were always fully resident in your psyche, and now are featured in the work. They haunt; some seem capable of engendering storms. / "Insomnia designated me its fond-

est partner" (Edward Lear), four consecutive nights: how to put this time to best use? How to use the night hours? Write letters; watch Kurosawa movies; reread *Montauk* for the umpteenth time; read strange *Doctor Glas*, by Hjalmar Soderberg; the hours pass. The nightjars and owls in the trees. The moon-illumined field. The barn owl returns to the barn and it's morning. Read "Anecdotes and Incidents of Reincarnation," a travelogue by Bernard Heuvelmans, 1850. "I asked to see the local cemetery," he writes, "and a child no more than nine or ten led me to an orchard. I saw right away what he meant. Ah, to be reincarnated as a plum tree, amongst friends and acquaintances, family, all the rest in the plum orchard surround."

8. JAKE: All at once a few of your trees remind me of the Scotch-Irish word mallalorking. It means "restlessness before a journey." The wild, agitated density, even within their rooted fixedness, of your trees evoked this. The human correspondence might be a form of anxiety. "The misalignment of emotions," Edward Lear wrote, "before sailing to Corfu. The eternal battle of TWO KINGDOMS: staying, departing; home, casting memory back to home." In 1977, on a ferry, Nova Scotia to Newfoundland, I heard it actually put to use, by a man in his eighties, I guess. I had always thought of the word as a verb. However, he used it as a noun, a malady. "I had the mallalorking on dry land, before our transport left for France. Into the war, eh? I just could not keep still. I was the oldest man in my unit, and I'd volunteered. I was a surgeon's assistant. I remember, I bit the corners off a detective novel I'd been reading. To this day, I remember the title, *The Case of the Poison Pen Letter*. (I forgot who wrote it. I tasted printer's ink. I bit the corners off the pages, just for some reason, the effects of mallalorking. I left *The Case of the Poison Pen Letter* on board ship, too. I didn't take it into France. Whoever found it, if they read it, must've wondered, 'What the hell happened to these pages?' I should write my life story. Do you know anyone who could teach me to use a typewriter?"

9. JAKE: In a dream I heard myself say, "I know I'm difficult, but I'm so often in pain; I apologize." Five kidney stones in three months; I'm "producing" them. The vocabulary is largely geological. "Gravel," "stones," "alluvial movement down the tract," which may be the only reward of this condition, except introspection about what I might be being punished for (so many possibilities!). / Yesterday at about four P.M., on my dirt road, I met two neighborhood girls, age eleven and nine. The youngest said, "We spent all day in a tree." It's raining. I'm sitting in my cabin thinking of unpleasant things. Why didn't I have a father who taught me the names of trees? Then, at about six P.M., the sky darkened and the trees along the stone wall began to gyrate in unison; it was as if they were producing crows. Crows flying every which-way "out of their hidden conferences" (Edward Lear). / Last evening I picked up a friend at the little train depot in Montpelier. A young woman got on the train. Her parents were seeing her off. It was the first time I ever witnessed an actual tear-streaked window. Her face, her palm against the glass, and reflected on the window was a tree (situated behind her parents

across the parking lot) full of wind, in which resided the woman's face. / Startled awake at four A.M., from an absurd dream of dizziness and complications. Three of your tree drawings on the guest-room wall come directly into focus. One sees the trees inside first, then up comes the shade, the outside trees.

10. JAKE: (Overheard) "Did you ever see a ghost?"—"Yes, sure I did. I'm no different than anyone else." / Once, from a train car, I saw, under an enormous maple tree across a creek, a man kissing a woman upward from her knee. She had on a summer dress out of Chekhov. / In "Anecdotes and Incidents of Reincarnation," Heuvel-mans is shown to a plum tree. "You see," a woman says, "it is especially gnarled, the branches seem in agony, don't they? It is my uncle. Even so, I am happy to see that his life has improved from the last life." / In that train compartment was a man who had fought in the Great War. His name was Serge. He first brought my attention to the man and woman under the tree. He had done this by tapping his pencil against the glass until I looked. "So, you see," he said, "some things are eternal." I thought then of Lear. "A philosophical tonic," he wrote in a letter of some scene or other, "but, upon seeing such a thing, one must immediately flee, lest the moment be ruined by mundane postscript."

11. JAKE: Percocet, tea, Percocet, tea, hospital waiting room, "gun-shot wound" and "kidney stone" sitting side by side, both reading magazines, not speaking. It felt like I'd died and this was hell. Night in the city. Now, gratefully, just a few days later, I'm in Vermont. In my cabin. Still, there's Percocet, tea, and pain—but I'M SUR-ROUNDED BY TREES. There's more oxygen to breathe. Read of a morning *Fellow-Townsmen,* by Thomas Hardy, and found myself, oddly enough, sobbing at the end. "Fellow burgesses Barnet and Downe are old and good friends in the Wessex town of Port Bredy, yet fate has treated them differently. Barnet, a prosperous man, has been unlucky in love, and now lives with the consequences of a judicious but loveless marriage. Downe, a poor solicitor, is radiantly happy in his small family home, surrounded by his doting wife and adoring children. A chance meeting one night causes them to reflect on their different lots in life, and sets in motion a train of events that will change their lives forever. As he chronicles the cruel twists and turns

of human fate, Hardy offers a compassionate portrayal of the trials of the human heart." How do you like that for my flap copy? Brevity of human happiness, whatever the definition of it, seems always to have been Hardy's subject. / When I think of Hardy, I always think of trees. He writes with great dedication about trees: "Trees about

the harbour road had increased its circumference or disappeared under the saw, while the church had had such a tremendous practical joke played upon it by some facetious restorer or other as to be scarce recognizable by its dearest old friends." A forest is the older cathedral to Hardy; he often mentions trees in relation to church, or walking to church, or staring out the window from church. / Last summer, during a tremendous storm in northern Vermont, lightning struck an oak tree in the village of Craftsbury Common. The oak split and part of it toppled against a smaller tree, which in turn fell against a wooden fence. Chain saws were out by morning. The wood was distributed to fireplaces in the new library, a few neighbors, a few stacks for sale at the general store. A length of the tree remained in the common for a few days. One morning I saw a woodpecker foraging it; I wondered about its evolutionary gyroscope; did it think it was moving vertically, up and down, despite the fact it was tapping along horizontally? "I walked amongst the trees and was fully restored—and, yes, dear one, I do mean my soul" (Hardy).

12. The light in the butternut trees was so beautiful this morning, JAKE. It's been a night of sobbing in my house. Weeping. A lovely, beautiful poet, living in our house in the city, has taken her small son's life, then her own. Unimaginable. Eerie. "To join a procession of ghosts going somewhere to take the mystical waters" (Lear). Her mother, from India: "She was blessed with a peaceful place to begin her journey." The grandmother did not, however, mention the grandson. There was a vast black cloud in the moonlit night sky last night; it literally took the shape of a flying crow, or raven. It took no imagination to see this. It was just there. Each person in the car, it felt, had the same thought, or almost, to come out later in speech—: "Perhaps they are riding on it. Perhaps this is their guardian angel, this great bird." Or: "That is the kind of darkness that fills the brain, chokes out all light at such a moment of plummeting despair." These are just initial responses. / Heuvelmans, in "Anecdotes and Incidents of Reincarnation," writes: "Years of travel, I have come to a conclusion about myself, which is that I believe the human mind is basically generous in its ability to comprehend beliefs other than the ones we were brought up with; however, still and all, when believing, finally, in a plum-tree orchard whose trees are comprised of former men, women, children—an orchard of reincarnations— now, truly, that does require exacting, poetic and rather unusual strategies and agreements with one's own otherwise censorial mind, doesn't it?" / I set your tree drawings out at four A.M. on the kitchen table. To sit with them. To have a cup of coffee. Scarcely dawn now; to sit, to just look one after the next, these trees, these solitudes, this "melancholy botany" (Lear), this sadness, this beauty.

13. JAKE: "To take a son's life—." I sat up suddenly awake hearing these words, but from whom? Some snippet of a nineteenth-century sermon, in a Vermont church, floating in the wind all these years? The police, the FBI, the forensic vocabulary. One feels diminished. This has been a "waking nightmare." Shusaku Endo, the Catholic Japanese novelist, wrote, "The world is ugly; the children beautiful within it." (He was speaking of a dingy oil-drilling village, when

367

sixty percent of the citizens died of tuberculosis.) Late this morning, I stopped briefly along the road near an open field to watch an "ecologically correct" play, *The Story of Johnny Appleseed*. Of course, Johnny was traipsing about the land, planting apple seeds, as was his modus operandi; in this particular play, in a field ringed by birches,

he was, I think, supposed to be not only an early environmentalist, but a kind of immigrant, too. He spoke in a strange, polyglot accent meant to represent perhaps all exploited farmworkers. Following in his footsteps were children dressed as trees, who, at the word "apple," stopped—or planted themselves where seeds had fallen. At the end of the play, which was primarily a disquisition on the paradox of ugly circumstances resulting in transcendent beauty (i.e., backbreaking labor / the pastoral), it all had a rather grim inevitability about it. Then it started to rain. The play ended. Since only four people were in the audience, most of the applause came from the actors and director, who was himself Johnny Appleseed. Apples were distributed. / The world is ugly, the trees beautiful within it. Jake, your good letter arrived today. In which you said you were "working well." / While driving late at night, I saw, through a living-room window on a back road, a television, on which was the scene in *Lord of the Rings* where the trees take revenge, wreaking havoc, confronting human evil, and—all the while, shouting across the apocalyptic flooding landscape.

14. All of this, JAKE, is of such a personal matter. (I keep seeing the little boy's face; it is he who requires a separate ethics of thought.) / I threw out my essay on a photograph of an iceberg; I threw out my essay on the books David Mamet has given me over the years; I threw out my essay about a stanza of a poem by Robert Hass; I threw out my essay about following Max Frisch around in New York City in the 1970s; I threw out my essay about seeing, out of the window of a bookmobile, my own father, whom I hadn't seen in three years, step into an apothecary; I threw out my essay about buying a fraudulent letter (supposedly) written by Victor Hugo's daughter, Adele, in Halifax. That has been my summer; 238 pages in the bin. I'll start in on each again. / Very early Sept. last year, a friend, Charlotte, had a "housewarming" party on a hill here in Vt. Her house was only the foundation. She had a blueprint available for everyone to see, a sense of the future. Including which new trees would be planted, and where. Friends of twenty-five years attended. At dusk, people started to drift off down the dirt drive, in pairs, singly, in small groups. It was a long way out to the main hill road. Crepuscular light. In the distance, house lights on far hills were coming on. Like campfires in ancient Italy, it struck me; are legions marching, are shepherds settling for the night—Charlotte is a potter, and her "foundation" could be mistaken, in a certain light, for an archaeological dig, rather than a beginning. Sections were marked off with twine, sacred to the memory, as if not to be disturbed. Magnificent view. Last light gathering in the trees. And standing there, I noticed that when they reached halfway down the drive, or nearly halfway, people raised

their hands to wave or gesture "goodbye," often without turning to look back. It seemed an unconscious gesture, a farewell. I could not help feel they were walking into the afterlife. It was haunting and beautiful, not at all morbid, or even melancholy. In fact, none were dead in the next year, though several quite diminished. I was the last to leave; even Charlotte left before I did. I cannot describe the dusk-resonances of the closest trees, the trees along the old lumber road around the nearest farmhouse. You could have drawn it.

15. JAKE: Jacques Dupin about Giacometti: "Drawing is another breathing." Bruce Chatwin, travel writer, flaneur, novelist, told the London audience of a certain tree he'd seen in a Chinese gorge which was "a veritable eleventh-century ink drawing of a classic sort. Bare, gnarled branches, and two crows facing the same direction. And nothing else. The philosophy of spareness and restraint; and yet, an exacting sense of isolation and despair. The powerful brush stroke; the delicate brush stroke. I walked directly beneath it and nothing moved. Perhaps it was not even I who was moving." Apocryphal or not, it certainly was fine writing, and delivered with somber nostalgia, as if he should never have left that place in the world, because, quite simply, knowledge was to be gained there that could not be gained elsewhere. / It occurred to me, in my stupid single-minded purpose in keeping a journal, that when, finally, I look out my cabin window, I'm looking at six Japanese crab apple trees sorely in need of care. (I write this; but I should be attending to them, and will.) The grass and weeds have grown up around their slim trunks. As my gardener friend Gary Katz said, "It competes with the crab apple trees for water and nutrients. It can choke them out." I believe I have, via reading and just thinking about it, and possibly dreaming, adopted to some extent the persona of Bernard Heuvelmans—or possibly this is a kind of vicariousness, as in "researching" a character—and have come to think of this modest orchard of Japanese crab apple trees as where former Japanese travelers, as in ink drawings, now reside, bearing up in the heat and cold, rain, sleet, snow of this climate. / Insomnia-wracked, caffeine-zagged, I met my friend David for breakfast in the village of Cabot. Challah French toast—David ordered eggs and toast. He quoted for me a Jewish proverb or saying: "Walking along, if you see smoke rising from a house in the distance, you are not allowed to pray that it isn't your house." I felt momentarily calm. I understand why David offered this. It means, despair of the

despairing incident, the gathered black cloud in the mind, the murder of a son; but that it happened in—to—your house is merely fate
and happenstance, not the house's predisposition. In *The Anatomy
of Melancholy*, it says (of suicide): "Don't try to find a way to
comprehend this; in turn, expect all manner of distress, bewilder-
ment, and no small measure of regard for the sanctity of life." Every
wise thing helps; nothing does. / I hope you drew trees today.

Late 1940s, photographer unknown.

WILLIAM GADDIS
A Portfolio

Paul Auster and Siri Hustvedt
David Grubbs
Russell Banks
Susan Cheever
Ben Marcus
Mary Caponegro
Steven Moore
Sven Birkerts
Robert Coover
Don DeLillo
Bradford Morrow
Joanna Scott
Rodrigo Fresán
Cynthia Ozick
Maureen Howard
Jonathem Lethem
Edie Meidav
Joseph McElroy
Stewart O'Nan
Carter Scholz
David Shields
Christopher Sorrentino
Joseph Tabbi
William H. Gass

Edited by Rick Moody

William Gaddis: A Portfolio
Edited by Rick Moody

THE TEN YEARS AFTER a writer's death are crucial to the reputation of his work. And the fates are capricious during this important decade. Writers who have the veneer of durability can dwindle into obscurity. Writers of little more than mediocrity can linger inexplicably. In such a period, any critical perception trumpeted with the necessary brio can doom or rescue. Think of Melville in the decades of his wilderness.

The remarks that follow here are assembled near to the fifth anniversary of the death of one of the last century's most influential voices, William Gaddis. Gaddis, during his lifetime, attracted passionate responses. He was a writer eagerly castigated in some quarters, even as he accomplished the considerable feat of winning the National Book Award not once, but twice (for *J R* and *A Frolic of His Own*). He wasn't a celebrity; he was, more likely, an enemy of literary celebrity, a writer who rarely gave interviews, never read aloud from his work, didn't blurb, wouldn't turn up at book parties. His work was gigantically ambitious, demanding, especially in his first two novels, but it was also hugely entertaining. He lived and worked from the ferment of the fifties, through the experimental upheavals of the sixties and seventies, the minimalism of the eighties, into the go-go digital culture of the nineties, and yet he was never allied with the literary fashion of any of these periods. He was an adherent of no particular literary movement. He was neither modernist nor postmodernist; neither realist nor fabulist. In fact, any attempt to arrive at an exhaustive critical analysis of Gaddis's output seems doomed to little more than provisional usefulness. The scale of his work always exceeds small-minded taxonomies.

As many of the writers who contribute below also observe, what gets lost in the debate about Gaddis, however, is how much *delight* there is in him, both on the surface of his novels and in their subcutaneous pulsations. When we lost the voice of William Gaddis, we lost one of very few American writers who could produce genuine comedy without sacrificing literary values. All of Gaddis's novels (with the exception, arguably, of the posthumous published work) were laugh-out-loud funny, full of the characters who surround us every day—the unredeemed frauds, quacks, artists, and con men—but who too rarely turn up in the naturalist fiction of the present moment. Gaddis wrote as a ghost inside the machine of late-model capitalism, with a dark understanding of its costs, and he did so without yielding to the seductions of the literary demimonde. Along the way, he magnified language and imagination, making the tapestry of literature that much more glorious to behold. His passing has robbed us of a sensibility that enriched the world of books. But perhaps by assembling some of the people who knew him or found value in his project, we can reignite his bright candle for readers of the next generation.

PAUL AUSTER AND SIRI HUSTVEDT

—I REMEMBER WHEN we met Gaddis. It was 1984, at a dinner party in New York given by Bud and Cecil. Bud Bazelon was a composer, and Cecil Gray, his wife, was a painter. We had met them because Cecil was the cousin of someone we knew in Brooklyn. Also at that dinner was Don DeLillo. And Muriel. She was a pistol. Was that the dinner when the dog ate her shoe?

—No, I think that was the second dinner—the surreal dinner. But the first dinner was very jovial, everyone liked each other.

—Gaddis struck me as someone who was very comfortable in his skin. Very calm. And very droll. Nearly everything he said was funny. He genuinely engaged himself with the young people who were there.

—Yes. And as a woman I have to say I found him very handsome and very charming. I mean, extremely charming. You wanted to sit beside him. And to keep up with him, too. To say things that weren't dull.

—One of the nice things that came out at that first dinner, I remember, was how much he loved his children. His son was working on a film at the time. I can't remember the details, but Donald Sutherland was in it, and we got into this long talk about Donald Sutherland. I remember saying that I thought Sutherland was rather a lugubrious presence, and Gaddis said, "Exactly. That's the word. That's precisely the word."

—*Lugubrious!* Right, but there's a famous event that we have to get to. That thing on Long Island. We have to talk about that.

—Absolutely.

—We were staying with—

—Norman Bluhm. You know Norman? A terrific painter. He's dead now, but he was a great friend of mine, for years. We did a book together back in the seventies, published by John Bernard Myers. For some crazy reason, he and his wife, Carrie, had moved out to East Hampton. Norman hated it, and after a couple of years they left for Vermont. Bud and Cecil, the people who had originally introduced us to Gaddis, were renting a place out there too, and they got in touch. They were organizing a picnic and invited us. And we thought, great, we'll go to a picnic. And at this picnic—

—You can't imagine.

—Not only was Gaddis there with Muriel, but Benny Goodman.

—*Benny Goodman!* Benny Goodman and his . . . paramour—

—Carol Phillips.

—She had been the editor of *Vogue.* And now she was the CEO or something at Clinique makeup.

—Benny Goodman stared at Siri's legs the whole time. She was wearing shorts. She has the most beautiful legs in the world, and this man, who no doubt appreciated fine things, was like, like this . . . like this. (*Stares at Siri's legs.*)

—It was agapē, agape. I kept thinking: Benny Goodman likes my legs. And because it was Benny Goodman, that somehow made it good. It made it special. We were all at the beach, and because we were so much younger than everyone else—and so much less sophisticated—I felt like a heroine in a Henry James novel. You know, the young woman who goes off to Europe and is presented with a collection of dazzling, worldly people. The American innocent.

—And then, out of nowhere, Bud whacked Siri on the ass.

—I turned around, and he said to me, "I've been wanting to do that for a couple of years!"

—But he was a rascal. An imp. There was nothing malicious about it.

—No, not at all. I forgave him.

—But anyway, Gaddis and Muriel were at the beach with us. And you had this talk with him. You tell the story.

—He had just won a MacArthur. Not a surprising thing, considering that it was Gaddis. But I said to him, "I think it's great that you got it, you know, and the money's terrific and everything, but I kind of wish that these prizes were given to people when they were young and really needed them." And he just looked at me, and there was a big pause—he was kind of a comedian, he knew just what he was doing—and he said, "Baby, you just dialed my number."

—At some point during that weekend, we stopped by the house where Muriel and Gaddis were living. He and I were standing by the window together, and he said a very touching and funny thing. We were having cocktails, and he lifted his glass and looked at the Scotch in it for a moment and said, "This is the one friend who's never let me down." He half meant it, and he was half joking, but he said it in such a deadpan way that it became extremely poignant. Then he started talking about wealth, the world of the New York WASPs, and a kind of comical bitterness came pouring out of him. "These people with money," he said, "they have no idea how to live. They eat the worst food. They wear the worst clothes, they have the worst lawyers." Again he was very funny. But he really meant it. He felt that world was contemptible, utterly degraded.

—The last time we saw him was at that party in New York. The one given by Brad Morrow—right before the Gulf War.

—Yes. I remember it well. It was quite an evening.

—Gaddis, Coover, Hawkes, Abish—they were all there.

—I wound up going into the kitchen for a drink. They were all standing around, and I listened in on the conversation. And what they were talking about was . . .

—Reviews.

—All the bad reviews they had ever gotten. Saying, "In 1961 that sonofabitch in the *Boston Globe* said this about me." You know. "In 1958 that asshole in Philadelphia . . ." They all remembered them. Every attack, every bad word that had ever been written about them. I was amazed. Just amazed.

David Grubbs

TO BEGIN WITH, here are two things that *Agapē Agape*, William Gaddis's final novel, is not. It is neither modernist distillation nor is it a summation of Gaddis's art.

In Thomas Bernhard's *Correction*, Roithamer's manuscript begins as an eight-hundred-page draft, then is rewritten at a length of three hundred pages; further corrections shorten it to eighty, and finally to twenty or so pages. The slim, hundred-page *Agapē Agape* has a curious prehistory that elicits comparisons to Roithamer's shrinking manuscript. Don't be fooled. The novel *Agapē Agape* shares its title with Gaddis's broadly researched and never-completed history of mechanization and the arts that took the player piano as its luminous example. In *J R*, *Agapē Agape* is the book that Jack Gibbs can't finish. Gaddis collected material for the nonfiction *Agapē Agape* for over half a century, and much of this research is cast into the novel, which presents a narrator's frustration in struggling simultaneously with illness and with unruly piles of accumulated research. The fruits of? It's hard to say. Over time, Gaddis saw his project rendered increasingly obsolete, and obsolescence has zero recuperative force in either version of *Agapē Agape.* Bernhard's ghost is summoned by the fact of *Agapē Agape* consisting of a lone paragraph stretched over the book's length. The kinship between Gaddis's and Bernhard's outraged narrators only deepens as excerpts from Bernhard's *Concrete* and *The Loser* are dropped into *Agapē Agape* with nary a quotation mark—and nary a trace. It's possible to read the book and not spot the lengthy excerpts from Bernhard. I can't help but take pleasure in the pointedness and the small perfections of phrase in this single, sustained screed: "[T]hat's what it's about, that's what my work is about, the collapse of everything, of meaning, of language, of values, of art, disorder and dislocation wherever you look, entropy drowning everything in sight, entertainment and technology and every four year old with a computer, everybody his own artist . . ." But how much more of this can a person take? Which is to say, would it really have been better to see the nonfiction work completed? As you can guess, in railing against discord and disorder, Gaddis proves himself a master of representing these conditions. Where Bernhard's Roithamer corrects his manuscript nearly out of existence, *Agapē Agape* succeeds in finding a form not only with which to make use of Gaddis's research, but also to play out the dark comedy and the mere darkness of writing in the nearer shadow of death. I say this in spite of the narrator's conclusions: "[S]haky uncertain like every wrong decision I've ever made never made any other kind, never came through for anybody, why I end up here with a hopeless project like this one . . ." The most painful element of *Agapē Agape* has nothing to do with whether the critical study is going to be completed. It won't. There's disarray in the final push, tremendous sadness—far from a mathematical winnowing out. Instead, the most heartrending aspect of the book is the narrator's inability to live in peace with his younger self: "Age withering arrogant youth and worse, the works of arrogant youth and the book I wrote then, my first book, it's become my enemy, o Dio, odium, the rage and energy and boundless excitement the only reality where the work that's become my enemy got done . . ." Awful. Boundless excitement, no; energy falters, returns, falters; but *Agapē Agape*—which did indeed get done—doesn't lack for rage. Movingly, it lacks not the slightest for rage.

RUSSELL BANKS

WILLIAM GADDIS'S PROJECT was noble and exemplary. Those books, the first three, especially, are like icebergs calved off a gigantic glacier. As a young writer, I mainly steered around them as they floated into my more southerly latitudes, knowing that if I hit one straight on, I'd sink. So I admired their colossal size and whiteness from a safe distance, mostly.

There are certain twentieth-century American literary projects, like Olson's Maximus cycle or Pound's *Cantos,* that we need because of their gigantism, their absurdly vast scale, if only to take an accurate measure of our own feeble attempts. Gaddis is like that in prose fiction. Dahlberg. Paul Metcalf. Harold Brodkey. Writers like that, without whose work American literature would be a much diminished thing. Their existence enables the rest of us to be both more reckless and more ambitious than we'd ever dare to be otherwise.

He was to me a true deep modernist, only a little late for the party (we didn't know postmodernism back then), so he seemed almost anachronistic. His influence on me, such as it was, came early, in my twenties and, as I said, was about scale. I tried to marry him to Dreiser, which clearly would not have been a happy marriage for either, but it's one I try to live with myself and would not have dared to try without his example.

I have a theory, not very original, that postmodernism is mainly an intellectually nostalgic holding action against the death of modernism. Gaddis might be a case in point. If literature is, or was, a church and Joyce in the 1920s and '30s its pope, then Gaddis in the 1950s and '60s was its American cardinal. Possibly the last one. The shadow cast by the High Modernists was so long that, after they'd stepped out of the sun and were gone, it was hard in the 1950s and '60s, except perhaps for the Beats, to write anything not conceived in terms of that preceding generation's High Priestly ambition. Gaddis looms larger, casting a longer shadow of his own, than all the others of his ilk and kin, Barthelme, Hawkes, etc., in that term mainly, ambition, but it was an important one, and he helped keep it alive.

His ilk and kin, more wise than he, or shrewd, may have backed away from it—too transparently oedipal, perhaps, or simply too risky to put so many eggs in one enormous basket. But when Gaddis went to market, he brought home the whole pig, and I love him for that.

SUSAN CHEEVER

I'VE ALWAYS BEEN FASCINATED by Gaddis, the man and the work. I read *The Recognitions*—although I probably couldn't pass a quiz on it. Because I'm not so smart, I like *Carpenter's Gothic* the best of all the books. I thought it was an astonishing, moving tour de force.

When I knew him, he was living happily with a woman I also loved, named Muriel. Muriel was a herring princess. That's what we called her, "the herring princess," and Gaddis lived in her house in East Hampton. It was the house you would have wanted to have there, very understated and on the water. A kind of island of class in an ocean of flamboyance. They also stayed at her apartment on East Seventy-first Street. We had dinner there once. Muriel had a mail-order steak with which she disappeared into the kitchen. Soon there was the smell of burning and clouds of smoke. Gaddis got wittier and wittier to cover up the disaster. Why aren't dinner parties like that anymore?

Also when he and Muriel were living in East Hampton I used to see them. The last time they took me and the kids out for ice cream.

He was also one of the funniest men in the world to talk with. I miss him.

BEN MARCUS

ON THE OCCASION of his posthumous publications, Gaddis faced new accusations of difficulty, unreadability, unworthiness. Instead of actually reviewing these publications, an attack was launched, from a writer concerned to seal the limits of literary art, to insure that if the art is to advance, or to be accorded status, whatever that means, even by someone now dead, it will do so only under his own terms. The subtext, to misquote Cormac McCarthy (another writer who fled his own difficulty): a complexity that exists without my comprehension exists without my permission. If I cannot understand it (contain it, make it safe, dispel its force), it is not worth my time.

The identity of Gaddis's attacker is significant, since he has concerned himself with outing, and trouncing, an unarmed minority that seems essentially ignored by the dominant culture: artists of language who may not be entertaining large numbers of people, true, but who nevertheless still matter to a very small group of readers. He is killing the dead, with a very big stick. The attack is additionally an attack on Gaddis's readers, by a writer who once notably complained that it was hard to compete with the Internet (and then did! And won!).

What a relief, when this literary grandmaster, ratified by sales and accolade, admits that he finds some kinds of supposedly serious reading an unrewarding chore. The grandmaster establishes himself as the absolute ceiling of difficulty, beyond whom no writer, or reader, need go. Not content with fluent populism, he wants to operate at the last rewarding level of difficulty. He has divined the height of that ceiling and written his balls out to a hair's inch of it. The result: the new difficulty, which is simplicity itself. Beguilement, ambiguity, linguistic complexity? No more. If, God forbid, there exists writing beyond that ceiling, in the joists, it will operate at a difficulty that is, trust the master, not worthwhile. He has done the math for us.

MARY CAPONEGRO

HE WAS ELEGANT, urbane, unassuming: a gentleman of unostentatious refinement. One could not imagine him without his tweed jacket, just as one could not imagine calling him by other than his surname. As Joy Williams incisively described in her memorial eulogy, he was always "Mr. Gaddis." Not William, certainly not Bill. He was not an academic, but toting his impeccable leather briefcase he surely looked the part. He was a writer who taught, though seldom. Thus it was all the more my great fortune to be in the right place at the right time, that place being Bard College, midseventies, which he visited, on a weekly basis, to teach two classes and to confer one-on-one with students in his assigned office in ivy-covered Aspinwall. The Bard literature division had a predominantly tweedy cast to it, but as Bard's liberal arts were emphatically liberal, and as it had already a history of harboring esteemed and audacious authors, in and out of the mainstream, it was a perfect marriage of author and institution.

But let me back up a bit, because William Gaddis was the agent of epiphany for me not once but twice, well thrice in fact, during my college years: the first two on the page and the third in the flesh. At seventeen, I went to school to "become a writer" with little sense of the magnitude of such an undertaking. My wish was to be a poet, but I was hungry for good novels, vast, demanding, original fiction. In my freshman dorm (an unsavory cinderblock structure, Bard's least appealing abode), I met an economics major from Chicago named Sue Baughman, and discovered she possessed extraordinary literary taste. Likewise ravenous for good fiction, she had already devoured quite a bit of it. It just so happened that she was reading *The Recognitions*. I recall her explaining to me that it captivated her to such a degree that after she finished the thousand and twenty-first page (of that cream-colored Bard/Avon edition with the huge-lettered title, diced in three, and the tiny print inside), she turned back immediately to the first to commence rereading. I knew her recommendation should be taken seriously. My winter "field period" was like a crash course in masterpieces. After *Ulysses* and *The Magic Mountain* and the collected Kafka stories, I began the book; lost myself in it, but the mystical experience that resulted was so immense I felt it might cause me to explode were I to attempt to relive it. Its difficulty and brilliance and ambition, its erudition and scope, its subtle yet utter originality overwhelmed me. He was as austere a chronicler of social relations as James—equally at home with American and European milieus, though with a more elaborate political agenda—and as masterful a manipulator of syntax. The comparisons to *Ulysses* were utterly cogent, as Gaddis had single-handedly developed a technique I'll dub stream of *societal* consciousness. He combined an infallible ear with infinite mind and inexhaustible vision. Master synthesist, he married Apollonian to Dionysian magnificently. He is to be blamed, I suspect, for my tendency thereafter to assume that from a single random sentence I could extrapolate to judge the merit of an entire literary work, because in his work the complexity of the macrocosm was perfectly mirrored in the microcosm. His vision was a breathtakingly broad aerial view that happened also to have the breathtaking beauty and intricacy of a Persian miniature. One could never in one's wildest dreams exceed, not even match, yet how could such an achievement not make fiction feel . . . *necessary?* Though I did not manage, as Susan Baughman did, to repeat the feast on the heels of the last bite, I did ever after imagine the fullest possible literary life would take the form of a perpetual rereading of *The Recognitions:* a Borgesian experience: to be perpetually immersed in a book that contained the world.

And then, no sooner had I begun to digest the first masterpiece than *J R* appeared. There was something even more thrilling about being able to read a master's work just after it was published, and to reflect on the fact that this was being written in *my* lifetime; may you live in interesting times indeed! Surely for a writer there could be no more interesting time than one in which these two novels emerged. (It was fashionable when I was a child that women fib about their age, moving up their date of birth a year or two or more, but I thought if only I could move back the year of my birth by one year to coincide with the publication of *The Recognitions;* wouldn't that be auspicious!) What a heady time to be a reader and aspiring writer. *J R* was equally brilliant, and incredibly funny, and again a world's worth of vision. The whole world of commerce crammed into more or less the same number of pages, this time, and this audacious move was to shape a narrative almost entirely of dialogue. He proved himself again a clear-eyed, shrewd, uncompromising observer of humanity, and of the bluster and frailty of human institutions. He balanced clarity and cacophony, chaos and control. Who could call such synthesis incoherent? Only those philistines, it seemed to me, who shuddered with revulsion rather than delight before the late Beethoven quarters, or the last sonatas, or for that matter, the Bartók quarters, all of the above having provided mystical experiences as well during that period of my life, and analogous to these magnificent tomes. Extended passages so wild as to appear improvisatory— but within the form, or rather, becoming form! How did he do it? This writer from the extraordinary Harvard bunch that boasted Creeley, Hawkes, Ashbery, and company, this man whose lab was the social world with all its wheeling/dealing/lusting/failing was himself no card-carrying experimentalist. He took modernism to the next level but not by post-ing it! The confluence of speech and depiction in his novels was something wondrous to behold, like a beautiful shape-shifting creature, ungraspable, inimitable. The verisimilitude was so striking and the dialogue so unstylizedly pitch-perfect within this master stylist's supple prose that you couldn't necessarily identify, moment to moment, where the hyperbolic quality lay. But it was in the fullness, the density of experience and speech, that he transcribed, conjured, synthesized. Because he was indeed the master synthesist. And he never had to go inside a character's head, he did it from outside. How could someone who had, in his first novel, fashioned, through the conceit of forgery, the most profound novelistic statement on authenticity, then turn inside out the conventions of narrative proportion to create a kind of *pan-dialogos* (recovering from Plato the literary truth that emerges from sculpted conversation), all centered around a junior-high entrepreneur protagonist? One from Long Island to boot! (This seemed to me, as a fringe benefit, to redeem the place in which I had spent the majority of my disaffected adolescence. Brilliance could be made of the geographically mediocre!)

It was at the end of my sophomore year that I learned he was actually coming to teach at Bard. What aspiring writer's angel/muse could have choreographed this custom-made miracle? And I—so pathologically timid that I might flee manna falling from the sky lest it hit me in the head—resolved not to blow the opportunity to study with the greatest American novelist of our time. He taught a fiction workshop and a Literature of Failure course, the syllabus for which now stands in the Joe Tabbi–edited book of his essays, *The Rush for Second Place,* informed by his intimate knowledge of the business world: fruit of the "day-job" speech writing and such that had given him access to the absurdity he would later transform. His second class was to be a fiction workshop. It seemed I would have to become a fiction writer. I fumbled my way through his workshop, risking little, as trying *on* fiction was risk enough, and he was kind—the authentic kindness that made the "with kindest wishes" he inscribed in such elegant penmanship in both my treasured Gaddis masterpieces feel not just polite but real. He challenged in the gentlest way, and the following year he was generous enough to direct the first semester of my senior project.

In the classroom, he was no showman, no hocus-pocus prof. He preferred to come weekly to Bard than to do the local library gigs characterized by the pedestrian questions of those who hadn't read him: the audiences who asked the predictable, *How do I become a writer?, Where do you get your ideas?* kind of questions. Not to say that I wasn't in that league myself, wanting to know how, through osmosis, to absorb those very ideas, and know not only how he got but how he executed what would seem reductive to term mere ideas! His dignity was such that one would consider it unseemly to share one's personal traumas or inquire of his; he was not the kind of teacher who doubled as a therapist. I do, however, recall his joke—more an anecdote—about a therapist (delivered in classic Gaddis understated drollery) involving a man studying with Jung, who flew to Switzerland and packed in his suitcase a single shoe—and when asked why he had done so, replied, "to throw it away." I loved how this amused him: how the author whose vast vision assimilated the broadest absurdities of our existence and our society reveled in the tiny absurdities of life. I was stunned that the man who had raised American Literature to the nth power would bother to make small talk with an utterly inchoate writer, discuss the most mundane trivialities such as how the Long Island Railroad stopped at Jamaica to change for Brooklyn even though the majority of the passengers were going to Penn Station. But any bond to him was precious. I was honored that he too was mortal, capable of generic writer anxiety, and that he would share this vulnerability: disclose that while trying to write—Mr. Gaddis was one of the last of the two-fingered typists—he would, in the course of numerous pauses, be disconcerted to hear his then eleven-year-old daughter typing away uninterrupted! (His mild-mannered black humor was so gentle from his mouth, and oh-so-scathing on the page, while no less elegant.)

If I asked if he would give a reading, he would in his typical modesty express a quite pragmatic reservation: "How would I read all the voices?" A reasonable question in fact. He'd need an entire cast. I remember scrutinizing the playful image of his self-portrait: a headless, glass-holding, jacketed torso (in a book of author self-portraits by Jill Krementz, I believe, a birthday gift from my sister) that now adorns *The Rush for Second Place*. Mr. Gaddis, self-depicted, going through the social motions. But above the collar of that headless, jacketed torso, were, left to the viewer's imagination, the *contents* of his head: those two vast fictive compendiums, those nearly two thousand pages of sheer erudition and originality. His patrician countenance likewise omitted. He flaunted nothing. Nor evinced bitterness for the lack of readership. Rather, he effortlessly maintained his respectful, dignified reserve and modesty, a formality that, on one level, went hand in hand with the fiction. He was not stiff or standoffish; rather, a gentleman who was naturally, graciously formal, whose self-effacement was somehow replete with dignity instead of awkwardness, and with considerable wit, as demonstrated by the self-portrait. Such a subtle ironist, he was all nuance. He mentioned the player piano project once or twice, I believe, and its rejection by the *New Yorker* in that same witty, understated way.

His prescription for the novel of another thesis advisee, a more accomplished writer, Liza Wherry, was to include more dialogue, having just proved that novels needed nothing else—as heretical as Copernicus! In my student pseudonovel, heavily under the influence of Kafka, and not much engaged with any social reality, he recognized this was not appropriate. He treated every unsophisticated sentence with respect and seriousness. *A mind becoming unhinged* was his synopsis of my plot (such as I ever used plots), and he deemed it worthy. He recommended Abe's *Woman in the Dunes,* which he admired and thought relevant to my particular pursuits. And then his favorites, *Play It as It Lays,* Joan Didion; *A Handful of Dust,* Evelyn Waugh; the etiquette depicted therein seemed akin to his own. I had found the world of another hero: William Gass's *Willie Masters' Lonesome Wife* at the used bookstore in Rhinebeck, which he praised highly when I brought it in for show-and-tell. But on the whole he could not read contemporary fiction while writing, he said, having to keep those voices at bay as he was manipulating so many voices in his own head, and as his writing stints were obviously protracted, he felt out of the stream. A fact of life, one which makes it more admirable still that he could be bothered to write up "crite sheets," a Bard evaluation vehicle, to urge us on and guide our progress. "Gone is almost all the self-indulgence," one of those sheets said, and how accomplished it made me feel. I'm afraid the *almost all* was too generous a measure, but that was typical of his ability to honor effort and potential, to work from what you had, no matter how ostensibly slight a talent. I can still hear the slightly muffly quality of his voice—it reminded me when I first heard it of—of all people—Dick Cavett! Hard to imagine it ever raised—his diction always refined, politely reserved. I remember the quality of its benignity when he would, years later after grad school, honor me by calling me his only student who'd gone on to publish. That he'd kept track of my modest career touched me deeply. His Nobel-worthy career, on the other hand, was never a topic for boasting, nor for condescension. He sought no glory. All the books of his career were milestones; each furthered his unparalleled vision. To find his subsequent fiction as I myself matured as a writer was yet more special: the *Gothic* (whose comparative brevity was initially a shock, but why shouldn't the master prove he too could write a "normal-sized" novel); then the *Frolic,* which had ingested a play as it brought law to its knees—and now, posthumously, even more riches. He could have ceased after the immensity of his early contributions, and still known he'd had enormous impact, but his inventiveness could never rest. It's been, for me, unceasingly inspiring to follow each audacious foray, frolic, feast.

STEVEN MOORE

THE FOUR CARDINAL POINTS of any civilization are its art, economics, religion, and law. William Gaddis's great achievement was to apply cutting-edge fiction to a stringent analysis of these very points to define "what America is all about": art, both sacred and profane, in *The Recognitions*, a Gothic cathedral of a novel that still casts an enormous shadow over contemporary fiction; economics in the acoustic collage *J R*, which satirized the abuses of capitalism in its day and even predicted the rot at the core of the junk-bond eighties, the dot-com nineties, and the corporate scandals of our day; religion in *Carpenter's Gothic*, exposing "true believers" as the most dangerous and deluded people on earth; and law in *A Frolic of His Own*, a code for conduct subverted to cover every form of misconduct. And as a coda, an opinion like those written by his own Judge Crease, *Agapē Agape*, a final, impassioned outburst summing up his half-century inquisition of American civilization.

The breadth of his material, the depth of his reading, and the range of his technique make Gaddis the greatest American novelist of the twentieth century, in my opinion. It's a minority opinion, and probably always will be, but it belongs with the same minority Gaddis rightly claims kinship with in *Agapē Agape* (quoting Flaubert to George Sand): "Nothing is important save a small group of minds, ever the same, which pass on the torch."

SVEN BIRKERTS

WHEN RICK MOODY SUGGESTED in a recent review of *Agapē Agape* that the best way to "get" William Gaddis, especially the Gaddis of the daunting longer novels, *The Recognitions* and *J R*, was to read quickly, I blinked and shook my head. In all the time I had put in struggling with these brilliant monstrosities, this had never occurred to me, but I see how it might indeed be the answer. Speeding a text lowers inner resistance and allows a larger, looser frame of reference, which might be just what's needed to apprehend these particular works. Alas, it feels like it's too late for me. I don't think I can now change the amalgam of habit and self-excoriating conscience that is my reading self. But Moody's insight helps me grasp what is both my Gaddis problem and the source of his particular emblematic stature for me. It seems that I am wired in such a way that I cannot proceed with a book—a novel, say—so long as I feel that there are things I should be getting but am not. I cannot move to *C* until I've absolutely nailed *A* and *B*. Long before Gaddis it was Joyce—the Joyce of *Ulysses*—who tied me into knots. But the cruxes of *Ulysses* could be gotten eventually—they could be looked up and patiently deciphered. I had no such luck with *J R*, however. Pulled into its density, its sharp comedic rhythms, certainly enough to recognize that I was in the hands of a master, I soon began to bark my nose on its experimental referentiality. I was intrigued, then stymied, then driven crazy. The fact that for pages at a time I had no idea of who was speaking to whom was more than I could tolerate. And no matter how often I wound my way back, no matter how much care I took to mark the verbal trail, I invariably got lost. It was my problem—I'll own it. I don't know how many hours I spent living with the simultaneous awareness that I was in the presence of the highest artistic craft—maybe greatness—and that I could not grasp it to my satisfaction. I should have read faster. I should have used the time I spent getting all balled up doing the other thing—speed-reading the work several times through, and then going back. But I couldn't, and can't.

I have read and written about other works by Gaddis, but in fact it is on the basis of my experience with *J R* that the author has become one of my private reckoning figures, a polestar, or, if that's too finite an image, my idea of a horizon. For years now, I've let the attractive difficulty of that one novel get tangled up with the more general question of literary ambitiousness. I don't mean personal ambition—ambition for the self—but for the expression. Gaddis undertook to write the novel as summa, and in asserting the possibility, he held open the door for others. He was one of the few who gave us the dream of scale and consequence, and for me the work is almost as important as a sign of faith in the enterprise as an artistic statement in itself. What doesn't kill us makes us stronger, said Nietzsche. And what outstrips us, I would add, both quickens our yearning and fortifies our will (until we give up, of course, at which point the arrow points to depletion). I feel fortunate. Gaddis remains for me an emblem of ultimate authorial ambition, and *J R* one of the books—there is a small shelf of them—I will someday read as they deserve to be read. Whether the novel is finally great or not is almost beside the point. The point is that I long ago allowed it to daunt me in the deepest way, and for that reason it has chafed and charged my inner life as much as any work I've read and "gotten."

1960s, photographer unknown.

Robert Coover

It was the grad-school summer of '60, I was lingering in Chicago past quarter's end to edit the university calendar, earn some pennies to help pay the obstetrician who would deliver our firstborn in August, subletting a friend's basement flat, and using the downtime to do a lot of reading, which that summer of occasional light-fingered forays into bookstores (I have done penance through the years since, buying more than I can possibly read) included, simultaneously, two big fat novels: Saul Bellow's *Adventures of Augie March* (Bellow was already a Chicago legend and I was a fan of *Dangling Man* and *Victim*) and William Gaddis's *The Recognitions* (he was unknown to me, recommended by some forgotten person), with the immediate consequence that I found Bellow's Chicago saga of Augie humping the old fellow to the local whorehouses a boisterous treat, a tale I felt as if my own (just look out the window, there they go), whereas the Gaddis book was difficult to get into (all that talk, I kept losing my place); but as the month wore on, Augie's tale paled even as it moved south into the sun and soon the book got tossed in disappointment across the room, while in Gaddis's great universal satire the characters behind the voices (all that talk!) had come vividly alive, and the likes of Basil Valentine and Esther and Wyatt, Stanley, Esme and Otto, and Recktall Brown (Recktall Brown!) and Agnes Deigh and the Town Carpenter had moved into the basement flat with me, companions for life, far from noble though they mostly were and failing even to last the book out, their lives eclipsed by chatter's echoey art.

Don DeLillo

I remember the bookstore, long gone now, on Forty-second Street. I stood in the narrow aisle reading the first paragraph of *The Recognitions*. It was a revelation, a piece of writing with the beauty and texture of a Shakespearean monologue—or, maybe more apt, a work of Renaissance art impossibly transformed from image to words. And they were the words of a contemporary American. This, to me, was the wonder of it.

Years later, when I was a writer myself, I read *J R*, and it seemed to me, at first, that Gaddis was working against his own gifts for narration and physical description, leaving the great world behind to enter the pigeon-coop clutter of minds intent on deal-making and soul-swindling. This was not self-denial, I began to understand, but a writer of uncommon courage and insight discovering a method that would allow him to realize his sense of what the great world had become.

J R in fact is a realistic novel—so unforgivingly real that we may fail to recognize it as such. It is the real world on its own terms, without the perceptual scrim that we tend to erect (novelists and others) in order to live and work safely within it.

Two tremendous novels. And the author maneuvering his car out of a dark and cramped driveway, the last time I saw him, with four or five friends and acquaintances calling out instructions as the car backed onto the country road, headlights shining on our waved good nights.

BRADFORD MORROW

GADDIS. EVEN WHEN, during our dozen or so conversations, he brought his mind to bear on such repugnant spectacles as the publication of *Millie's Book: As Dictated to Barbara Bush* (Millie being the former first lady's springer spaniel), or the fallen preacher Jimmy Swaggart's tearful televised mea culpa after he was caught with a prostitute (Swaggart's brimstone sermons were brilliantly mad— "The man scares me to death," Gaddis told me on the phone), there was combined an intrinsic satirical sense of humor and a true ethical gravity.

Many personal moments come to mind. Moments seemingly insignificant in themselves but which accrue, much as the ostensibly tiny narrative and dialogic gestures accrue in the novels, toward such a larger image I have of Gaddis the man. At an American Academy reception in May 1985, he confessed he was worried that Vietnam veterans were going to come after him for his depiction of the sodden, pestilent, charlatan vet Paul Booth in *Carpenter's Gothic*. I tried to assure him not to bother thinking about it—this was William Gaddis, after all, standing there in an elegant gray suit, sipping Scotch from a plastic glass, looking at me with his formidably assessing, somehow never-not-severe but also mischievous blue eyes. The night, over a decade later, when I had dinner in a French restaurant on the Upper East Side (evening arranged with typical, charming obsessiveness by John Hawkes), with William Kennedy, John Barth, the Hawkeses and—he came late, for dessert—Gaddis. I remember Barth talking about his days as a jazz drummer; Hawkes about the foie gras,

391

the Bordeaux, and equally sensual literary matters; and then Gaddis rolling in, wanting wine but given he was trying to cut back, saying over and again, "Cuppa tea, cup o' tea, cupatea," as if testing out the possibilities of a detail for one of his thousands of detailed pages. When he came to a party at my walk-up apartment near Washington Square—Hawkes was there, Ashbery, Coover, Saul Steinberg, even Deborah Winger, of all people, with her then-boyfriend Senator Bob Kerrey—his emphysema kept Gaddis from making it to the third floor without a rest on the landing of the second. We brought him down a chair, a drink, and an ashtray, and there he sat for a few minutes, simply impishly enjoying the minor transgressiveness of the moment. He then made the last flight and found himself the quietest place he could amid the mob, where he did his dignified best to disappear into the wallpaper, cutting up with old friends, snarling yet always a bit removed. Once, when visiting him at the house he shared with Muriel Oxenberg Murphy in the Hamptons, deep in the afternoon on an autumn day in the late eighties, I saw his worktable. He had left me alone while he went to search for either, yes, tea, or, yes, gin, I forget which now, and the notes he was making toward *A Frolic of His Own* were there by a bank of windows that looked out over Georgica Pond. The pages, tidily stacked, were covered with Gaddis's angular, meticulous handwriting. Scene notes, dialogue, lists in dark blue, as I remember, pitching up and down like the seismographic log of a serious earthquake.

It is nothing new to criticize Gaddis for difficulties he choreographed for his reader to negotiate. The uncompromising narrative terrains he created were natural and necessary to the harsh cultural terrains he wished to explore. Why should a journey through hell be a cakewalk? Gaddis once remarked, in one of the few moments he willingly discussed his work with me, that the idea behind suppressing speaker indicators—*he said, she said*—as well as adverbial garnish—*she said bitterly*—is that he wanted to break down as much distance as possible between the voices on the page and the reader. A simple enough idea, one that led to inherent discomforts for the reader, yet an honest aesthetic put into place by an honest practitioner.

It was, in part, the very difficulties I encountered when first reading *The Recognitions* that drew me to his work. *J R* confirmed for me what I had learned from the first book. Here was a master, a writer unafraid of what words on a page could do to readers who were willing to engage. *Carpenter's Gothic*, the runt of the litter and sometimes unfairly overlooked, is a masterpiece of subtextual intricacies (look again at that first sentence, its hopscotch syllabic structure). *A Frolic of His Own* is one of the funniest books I have ever read. Like other Promethean moments in literary art—*The Waves, Ulysses, The Golden Bowl, Moby Dick, Tristram Shandy*—Gaddis's novels present the sorts of perplexities, weirdnesses, mysteries, dilemmas, unpredictabilities of form and use of language that have always struck me as the real "realism." At the end of the day, Gaddis wrote the truth.

Joanna Scott

To TELL THE TRUTH is to tell a lie, he persuades us. More importantly, he suggests, to tell a lie is to tell a truth, if the listener knows how to hear what isn't said. Within the words, between them, because of them, there are complex implications. Nothing is simple because the simplest word in context is bursting with possible meanings:

> —That's not what it was.
> —What what was, the . . .
> —I said that's not what it was!

Through the action of his prose, Gaddis demonstrates the investigative potential of imaginative thought. He shows us how we can think beyond what we know if we think hard. He makes us think about the potential for reaction. He makes us think about the consequence of doing nothing.

I met him only once, at a dinner in Washington, D.C. On that occasion he invited all of us at the table to touch the bulge of his pacemaker beneath the skin of his chest. He ate his meal mostly in silence. He seemed admirably cautious about giving his opinion but proved himself to be the most decisive among us when action needed to be taken. There was, I recall, a fat, happy cockroach climbing up the wall beside our table in that fancy restaurant. A cockroach on its way home from its own good dinner. First one of us stared at the bug. Then another in our group noticed that the other was staring. Soon five out of six of us were staring. Then the sixth member of our party, the gentleman with the pacemaker, the best-dressed among us, Mr. William Gaddis, noticed that something on the wall behind him had caught our attention. He pivoted in his chair to see it for himself. Without hesitation, he thumped his fist against the wall, leaving a stain in place of the cockroach. Then he wiped his hand on his napkin and returned to his meal.

"What what was, the." Suggesting with every intricate phrase that those who pay attention to language are the ones who will know best how to respond.

RODRIGO FRESÁN

"JUSTICE!—YOU GET JUSTICE in the next world, in this world you have the law" is the first line of the last novel William Gaddis published during his lifetime. Once again Gaddis was right and the problem is that the law is usually in the hands of bastards you can't fire. And once again we march into the same old-new dark ages where the less than fine art of public burning of William Gaddis is the imperfect strategy of *this* world to cope with all that *this* world is not qualified to understand. A world where *difficult* equals *bad*. A world without justice.

The "trouble" with Gaddis—I always considered him a writer *and* an inventor—is the same trouble that usually comes with unique and definitive genius: it makes you feel so small. And there are people out there who don't understand the subtle pleasure of being in the presence of greatness, and they feel so great, and it's such a nuisance to have to look at themselves in a mirror so big. So they smash or try to smash what they don't look like, what they can't and never will do. It's better that way. Let's keep on with simple things. Let's take it easy, easier. Difficult is suspicious and Gaddis—as Melville before him—committed the unforgivable sin of writing about the Absolute in an Absolute style. Melville—as Gaddis after him—thought that literature was the only way to portray our wayward world. Both of them dealt with Chaos as one of the most disciplined and holy incarnations of Art. Both of them wrote something and about something that looked and sounded impossible to write. And still . . .

In brief: you don't explain—or understand—a great writer as you don't explain or understand the pyramids. You just stand there, under their huge shining shadows, with eyes and mouth open. You say the only educated and grateful thing to say. You say *thank you.* It's the least you can do. And you keep on reading. You get to the last page, yes, but you have never really finished reading a book by William Gaddis. So you start all over. I'm doing it now, and that's the good part of all this rotten affair: it makes you want to reread Gaddis. Again. Thank all of *you* for this.

There's a big big big difference between recognitions and corrections. Please, allow me to choose, one more time, as ever, as always, the first ones.

Let me choose justice.

In this world.

CYNTHIA OZICK

NEARLY TWO DECADES AGO, in a review of *Carpenter's Gothic*—an atypically short work; short, at any rate, for William Gaddis—I wrote of him with the kind of contagious fury that his novels evoke, turning readers into mazy-minded simulacra of Gaddis's own inventions. Gaddis, I said, has been

> prodigious, gargantuan, exhaustive, subsuming fates and conditions under a hungry logic. His novels are great vaults or storehouses of crafty encyclopedic scandal—omniscience thrown into the hottest furnaces of metaphor. Gaddis knows almost everything: not only how the world works—the pragmatic business-machine that we call worldliness—but also how myth flies into being out of the primeval clouds of art and death and money.

> He is a possessed receiver of voices, a maniacal eavesdropper, a secret prophet and moralizer. His method is pure voice, relentless dialogue, preceded by the serenely poised Joycean dash and melting off into the panning of a camera in the speaker's head. Speech is fragmented, piecemeal, halting and stunted, finally headlong—into telephones continually, out of radio and television. Through all these throats and machines the foul world spills.

> Gaddis is a preternatural technician and engineer: whatever turns, turns out to turn again; things recur, allusions multiply, pretexts accrete, duplicities merge, greed proliferates, nuances breed and repeat.

Well, all that was method—"merely" method, skill heightened to the most innovative coinage on the literary/technique scene. The substance, however, was nearly always rage, mostly rage about false belief. You could say that Gaddis was a sublime Kantian (note that I did call him a secret prophet) who harvested his morals out of atheism: his hatred for all varieties of fakery—the thousand faces of the counterfeit—was incandescent, and for Gaddis nothing was faker than religion. This made him love the devil, or at least love watching him at work. He loved agreeing with the devil's relentlessly precise assessment of humankind. (The chief scalawag of *Carpenter's Gothic*, for instance, is a heavy smoker slyly named McCandless, readily parsed as Scion of Darkness.)

Gaddis in person, the man who lived, or at least pretended to live, outside of his books, suggested none of this. He was what people call "retiring" when what I suppose they mean is publicly reserved. For a long time I stupidly imagined he had begun as some sort of businessman: he was so well acquainted with the inside maneuverings of rotted-out corporations. He eventually made it plain that he had worked in business as a *writer,* and that he had never been anything other than a writer. Since our conversations were infrequent and casual, it took me some time to learn this. For me Gaddis was his books. When *The Recognitions* first appeared, I was lost in an early novel that underwent spontaneous abortion; I was deeply lost. But I kept *The Recognitions* on my desk as a talisman, and kept it there for years, and read it to tatters. Sometimes I would open it and read around in it at random, for sustenance, for hope, for its penumbra of ingenuity, of mind, of genius.

In 1994 Gaddis surprised me. I knew him, after all, only from this-and-that and now-and-then; I could not count him as a friend; I did not have that privilege. That summer Sidney Lumet was directing a play of mine at the Bay Street Theater in Sag Harbor. Suddenly a magical invitation arrived from Gaddis: come to dinner. He drove to where my husband and I were billeted, picked us up, and sped us to his house, buried in greenery. The (to me) formidable Lumet was there, across the table, and more accessible and jokey than I had ever seen him (I hadn't realized he and Gaddis were friends); the late Saul Steinberg was at my left, recounting the ferocities of Europe; and other luminaries all around. What I remember mostly about that evening of spilling stories and contentious laughter were its two overriding elements: first, our host's limitless kindness, his going-out-of-his-way kindness; and the astonishingly unexpected conversation that preoccupied the dinner—God. God, in Gaddis's house? Where was McCandless? But the air that lifted from that dazzling table had nothing of the devil in it. It was all sweet.

396

Maureen Howard

MONEY. THE FIRST WORD OF *J R*, but what a line it launches: *Money . . . ! in a voice that rustled.* Followed by: *Paper, yes.* So the big book is launched with a question, an almost impossibly naive question in a scene of vaudevillian comedy—who's on first? Who's listening? William Gaddis's urgent voices have been coming at us since the fifties. On paper, on the pages to be honored in the art of his novels which never deal in false currency, though his characters do in their schemes, nickel-and-dime whoever is at their mercy, often dealing themselves a rotten deal. The victims of monetary calculations are endless: perhaps that girl in the Hong Kong factory *who'd like a free ride to New York, give her a handful of quarters how much are the sweaters worth at retail. . . . Fine just insure her for a quarter of a million write in the company as beneficiary. . . .* Or the distraught heiress in *Carpenter's Gothic* who is called into account for thirty bucks she pays the Haitian maid. She is no king's daughter, no golden girl, her voice not full of money. Gaddis moves beyond any romantic reference, any recoverable past, to the insistent present tense of our getting and spending.

Money, beginning to end, has been a pressing theme in the American novel. Ishmael—*having little or no money in my purse. . . .* Huck's got six thousand dollars at the beginning and end of his adventures. Is it Twain's joke that the interest has never accumulated? At the end of *Sister Carrie* Hurstwood bums a quarter: fifteen cents will buy a room in which he can kill himself. In the opening of *The House of Mirth*, Lily Bart—she *cost a great deal to make.* Dos Passos's *USA, In the Money.* Gaddis understands, not for the post-WWII generation alone, but for the present in which all great work continues to live (and for the moment in which I write with the National Debt soaring to unaccountable fantasy), that somewhere along the way we lost the gold standard, went to paper which he so often describes as torn, crumbled trash. On the page, many sturdy, enlivening pages, he performs the act of redressing our moral debt.

Jonathan Lethem

HOW LONG DID *The Recognitions* sit on your shelf before you plunged in? For me, three years. I bought it at nineteen, at college in Vermont, a used copy offered at another student's jumble sale in the student commons. I didn't read it until I was twenty-two, in Berkeley. For three years I circled the artifact like a Kubrickian ape, daring myself to touch it, letting it make me more intelligent by implication. Did I wish to evolve? Did I want it to demolish my primitive religion? What entity, what arrogance, had brought such a conundrum into the world? The weight of Gaddis's idea of himself and his novel is communicated before anything else, is itself the first layer of art, and contemplating that veiled self-declaration is like gazing into a darkened doorway—a stubborn portal into a lonely kingdom. Then, when you touch the monolith, when you drink the long poison, Gaddis is a bit less lonely, and you a bit more so.

Sweating actors in ape suits pretty much describes the initial reviewers of *The Recognitions*, whose shrieks and grunts are compiled and excoriated in Jack Green's *Fire the Bastards*, a thrilling rant in six broadsides, written and mimeographed on the spot, then retailed in hardcovers by Dalkey Archive a decade ago. (Does any hippopotamus of a book have an odder and more delightful bird sitting in its mouth, cleaning its teeth, than *Recognitions* does in *Bastards*?) Really, though, *The Recognitions* makes apes of us all. It's only a matter of whether your shrieks are those of pleasure. How strange and faintly embarrassing that a human life had to be lived during, then after the writing of that book—how awkward for us all that the deed was done by *some guy*. Except that in *J R* he had another monolith to plop on our turf.

Nietzsche: "The thinker or artist whose better self has fled into his works feels an almost malicious joy when he sees his body and spirit slowly broken into and destroyed by time; it is as if he were in a corner, watching a thief at work on his safe, all the while knowing that it is empty and that all his treasures have been rescued."

Maybe we'll find another Gaddis manuscript buried on the moon.

EDIE MEIDAV

IT WAS THIS IMPULSE to extend his boundaries which had finally given chance the field necessary to its operation. For those made timid by the cultural frenzy surrounding the man, William the Mysterious now five years off in some realm of his own imagining, we offer this guide:

1) How to enter Gaddis

Read the seductive, somewhat atypical first paragraph of *The Recognitions*, his first sally. This (apart from *Carpenter's Gothic*) has been called his most reader-friendly book. Note how it is not impossible that the weight of the book could scare a person. The heft itself a rhetorical gesture, making a simultaneous promise and demand: this book will request your participation! It is mad with life and modernism. Though generally the pilgrim must, by nature, lack an absolute image of the destination, here an important exception should be made. You might prefer first viewing the promised land miniaturized into a small amulet? Respectfully, therefore, an additional suggestion:

2) Read the last paragraph of *The Recognitions*

If that reassures, read any semblance of a paragraph, chosen at random, from the dense heart of the book (or of *Frolic*, or of *J R*. Even of *Carpenter's Gothic*). See whether you do not have the sensation of enormity winking back at you. A giant eye, both sapient and bright with the world's absurdity. Perhaps this will induce you to begin your own journey. Succor and rest stops promised along the way. You'll see. If all goes well, you may end by winking back, succumbing to folie à Gaddis believing the book was written to your consciousness alone. A common pathology, arising from the very narcissism of our culture, one of WG's favored subjects. And consider: of all the literary arts, *ventriloquism* may be the most American, simultaneously populist and flattering, elitist and utilitarian.

3) How to gain empathy for Gaddis

If all this Dale Carnegie–like advertising rhetoric sets you off, think what it did to the man in his long life as a public relations man. Hence, perhaps, the result we see before us: the difficulty of his literary execution. Please be kind enough to verify for yourself the worth of difficulty as contrasted to mere, potentially object-free opacity. In difficulty you actually do find something worthwhile behind the curtain. William himself, speaking in Albany: "What I want is a collaboration, really, with the reader on the page where the reader is also making an effort." The reader of Gaddis must decide on his or her own relation to society: this is how his irony and play lure you into the very opposite of laziness. *Torschlüsspanik* is the

In New Zealand while on a United States Information Agency tour, 1987.
Courtesy of Christchurch Press.

German for *fear of a missed opportunity* (literally, fear of a closing door) and is also the German title of Gaddis's last posthumous publication. Isn't it the case that you might end up leading a better life if you can just let your *Torschlüsspanik* get you to read the man?

4) If all else fails, no one will penalize you: you can always come home to that pesky and inviting first paragraph. Or the last. *Everything moved, and even falling, soared in atonement.* It all may be tough to memorize, but at least you'll find yourself humming the tune to this most ambiguous of anthems.

Joseph McElroy

A HABIT, NO MORE THAN his acute ear maybe, yet it stays with me in my sense of the great Gaddis creations: people not completing a reply, a thought, breaking off (Edward, Jack, Agnes Deigh, Amy, others), these chronic ellipses . . . intimate, uncertain, a self hung up in its parts, falling short, doubt's pause, second thoughts. This cadence in Wyatt, too: though once at least to Esther's question What's he been *doing* all this time they've been apart? a blunt *Nothing.* Just one no doubt minor sign, these moments, of that other intimacy the exponential scale of *The Recognitions* and *J R*, taking on the whole culture, embracing the cheap or not cheap imitation as a very material of life—failure of gift, quest, concentration, love; that awful joke, that tragicomic waste though with never a spilled word in the prose.

A work adequate to our underground history and pretension, carried through no matter how long it takes: this is the Gaddis example, an idea of a book itself, what it could hold. Worth writing, worth reading, it will be a book to be *in,* not just to pass through. His first somehow I waited to read, and it for me, its rumored art forging my image of it for seven years before I bought a copy in London in '62 and even compulsively tracked some of Gaddis's Clementine texts at the British Museum: though consumed by then with the smuggling trope of my own first book, so that I was mysteriously confirmed to find in Gaddis that bottle of schnapps Guyon hides like contraband "in the cavity cut ruthlessly out of *The Dark Night of the Soul.*"

The hole so overflows with voices twenty years later when Gaddis comes to unprecedentedly dismantle and deconstruct our capitalist-totalled, both abstract and stacked-with-junk, shuddering-out-of-control system—the wasteland up for grabs so who better than a kid (here heard but not much seen) to make it work?—that the reader, a riveted central operator of an ultimate conference call, could be in the dark groping for the furniture, the bathwater, the novel's so-called world; but somehow the talk when it does not imply all of that displaces my need for it. Difficult? The only problem is that *J R* is so unremittingly entertaining we might just forget to examine a premise here and there—that someone, composer, writer, abandoned son, failed because of circumstances. Gaddis difficult? A difficult act to follow in a market where distinction is difficult for some people to swallow.

STEWART O'NAN

I'M NOT SURE when I came across the name and reputation of William Gaddis for the first time, but I was impressionable enough that when I spotted a fat old hardback of *The Recognitions* at a used bookstore, I slipped it from the shelf and blew the dust off the top. The front cover had come loose from the binding, but the ear apparent in the language and the heft of the paragraphs and of the book itself sold me—and shoot, it was only two bucks. At a hefty three pounds, it was a great buy, pagewise. It was—the book's a first edition, filmy Bible-like pages, dust jacket and everything. I'm not sure if Mr. Gaddis would be aghast at my stupid fortune or just laugh. When I finally did meet him, many years later on a couch in a hotel lobby in Cologne, he seemed to me a cantankerous old cuss, very much the author of his work, a bit miffed at his public reception, but wry about it as well. He was bony by then, and wore a beige suit and carried a walking stick like some down-at-heels country count, a deflated Buddy Ebsen. As the fawning German interviewer lobbed soft ones, he reared back and scourged the American reader, comparing himself to Melville with a crabbed laugh. And then twinkled, Grinchlike, and gave me a wink. He knew the artist's outrage was an old softshoe too, a routine he'd played before bigger houses than this. Made me like the guy.

CARTER SCHOLZ

AS LOU HARRISON SAYS in his *Music Primer*, "The composer himself subsidizes the art of music." Despite the thriving of book clubs and the generosity of Hollywood, this unwelcome truth also informs and bedevils the lives of writers. Samuel Butler knew it, having published all his own work at his own expense, pursuing nothing but his own satisfaction and "the battering down of falsehood to the utmost of my poor ability." William Gaddis certainly learned it. He came of age in perhaps the last historical moment when literature seemed to matter. Now the word can hardly be said without quotes. In a late speech, Gaddis preferred to say "something that will last," adding, "And everything seems to be against that."

The young Gaddis believed that conscientious work would meet with a just and conscientious appraisal. This falsehood was promptly battered down. His critics seemed to pride themselves, then and for the next fifty years, on not reading the work before them, on misreading it, on overlooking its achievement to disdain its very effort to rise up from a morass of ease and corruption.

The one good thing to come from this hostile reception was the clearing of "the writer's perennially naive notion that through calling attention to inequities and abuses, hypocrises and patent frauds, self-deceiving attitudes and self-defeating policies, these will be promptly corrected by a grateful public." From this hard-won clarity Gaddis produced *J R*, a masterpiece that expects no gratitude and leaves no illusion standing.

Justice is not in this world, which may be why some insist on bearing the cost of making something that lasts, not as consolation or corrective, but as compelled testimony of that absence. The cost is their lives; and their gift, so difficult to make, is easy to spurn.

DAVID SHIELDS

NEARLY TWENTY YEARS AGO, I listened to a tour guide at the National Gallery ask his group what made Rothko "great." Someone said, "The colors are beautiful." Someone else pointed out how much people paid for his paintings. A third person mentioned how many books and articles had been written about him. The tour guide shook his head and said, "Rothko is great because he forced artists who came after him to change how they thought about painting." This is the single most useful definition of artistic greatness I've ever encountered.

In 1984, Cynthia Ozick said, "I recently did a review of William Gaddis and talked about his ambition—his coming on the scene when it was already too late to be ambitious in that huge way with a vast modernist novel." She reviewed *Carpenter's Gothic*. The "vast modernist novel" to which she referred was, of course, *The Recognitions*. It's difficult to overemphasize how misguided this heroic (antiheroic) way of thinking is.

In 1976, I was a sophomore at Brown, trying to figure out how I wanted to write. One of my teachers was John Hawkes, who wrote, "Beyond the edge of town, past tar-covered poor houses and a low hill bare except for fallen electric poles, was the institution and it sent its delicate and isolated buildings trembling over the gravel and cinder floor of the valley." Hawkes was an inspiring teacher, but I had no instinct for the symbolist surrealism of which he was a master; his work offered no guideposts for me. My other teacher at Brown was R. V. Cassill, who wrote, "Cory Johnson was shelling corn in the crib on his farm. He had a rattletrap old sheller that he was rather proud of. Some of its parts—the gears and the rust-pitted flywheel bored for a hand crank—had come from a machine in use on this farm for longer than Cory had lived." I wasn't in any way connected to place in the way Cassill was—I knew virtually nothing and cared less about the San Francisco suburb in which I grew up—and though he was also an exceptionally fine teacher, his work (as beautifully crafted as it was) didn't trigger anything particularly crucial for me, either.

One snowy night, lying on a couch at Pembroke Library, I picked up Gaddis's *J R*, which had recently been published:

> —Money . . . ? in a voice that rustled.
> —Paper, yes.
> —And we'd never seen it. Paper money.
> —We never saw paper money till we came east.
> —It looked so strange the first time we saw it. Lifeless.
> —You couldn't believe it was worth a thing.
> —Not after Father jingling his change.
> —Those were silver dollars.
> —And silver halves, yes and quarters, Julia. The ones from his pupils. I can hear him now. . . .
> Sunlight, pocketed in a cloud, spilled suddenly broken across the floor through the leaves on the trees outside.

For the next week I did no schoolwork. I read *J R*. The way, as in all of Gaddis's work, form reads as content; his obsession with miscommunication as our only communication; his ability to render with amazing exactitude the widest variety of American voices; the luxurious, intensely palpable abundance of his work; and, especially, perhaps, his fusing of the banal and the baroque—all of this enthralled me, utterly. He provided a road map (many different road maps) to follow; I've stumbled along ever since. He is, inarguably, a great writer. He changed the terrain for every serious writer after him.

> I told him this morning I don't have to anymore I don't have to try to write music. . . . —I never had to, it was just something I'd questioned before I thought it was all I was here for and he, everybody thought that that they thought I was doing something worth doing he did too but he, nothing's worth doing he told me nothing's worth doing till you've done it and then it was worth doing even if it wasn't because that's all you. . . .

CHRISTOPHER SORRENTINO

I'VE ALWAYS BEEN PARTIAL to writers to whom you couldn't go for the felicitous phrase; who abjure their alleged obligation to "fine writing." My first encounter with William Gaddis's work served simultaneously as a reassurance of the primacy of style—a welcome corroboration of my suspicion that perhaps the need to appear smart, to remain quotable, was for the bushers after all—and a jaw-dropping experience all of its own. To the apprentice writer, this was work that revealed the arduousness of its construction (and by extension the arduousness of all such construction); to the inveterate reader, it was work whose arduousness had effaced all evidence of itself to simply flow, inexhaustible and inimitable.

Roland Barthes anticipated Gaddis's detractors in a wonderful little essay entitled "Blind and Dumb Criticism." Such detractors have a case, I suppose, if you hold innovation, difficulty, length, and erudition against a novel. I would have trouble copping to this and, apparently, so do the detractors; and so you have the Snobby Book thesis, which suggests that a complex novel is out to make a fool of you. Stoke your dislike of it to the point where you surrender to the urge to make ludicrous public statements (a tendency shared, I've noticed, among Gaddis detractors past and present) and it just might.

JOSEPH TABBI

I CAN'T BE THE ONLY one to have noticed that the ideas Jonathan Franzen uses against Gaddis were all lifted *from* Gaddis's work. Franzen is entitled to his opinion concerning "serious" fiction, even if he starts off talking pretty seriously about Status and Contract in American culture. Gaddis and writers of his generation have the status, apparently; Franzen wants to enter into contracts with readers. Nowhere does he mention, however, that Gaddis himself works with that very distinction on page 393 of *J R*—well before Franzen, by his own admission, stopped reading: "whole God damned problem's the decline from Status to Contract right . . . ?"

Franzen says Gaddis worried that he would be perceived as a cartoon. "But a cartoon," Franzen concludes, "is what *Agapē Agape* is." Here is what Gaddis wrote: "I can't even go into it, you see that's what I have to go into before all my work is misunderstood and distorted and, and turned into a cartoon because it is a cartoon."

We hear about the death of Franzen's father; elsewhere Franzen mentions being accused of plagiarism. He likes to lay bare his open wounds—but when Gaddis does the same (posthumously, and frankly), Franzen's right on him. "We" really don't like to see an author in this state, says Franzen, as if personal, physical suffering were less suitable than confession as a subject for narrative.

Passive aggression was well understood by Gaddis—"worst God damned thing you can do," says one character about an estranged wife in *J R*, "bunch of God damned open wounds lay them in her lap what the hell do you expect. First time she has to get the God damned knives out she can't resist them, laid them all out for her she knows right where they are can't resist them. . . ."

Franzen wants to convince readers that Gaddis's fiction after *The Recognitions* is difficult. He says that Gaddis was incapable of constructing an argument. But the books aren't nearly so hard that readers will miss in them the source of ideas, arguments, and attitudes that Franzen wants to pass off as his own.

WILLIAM H. GASS

"OUR IMMORTALITY IS made of memories and lies," Gaddis whispered to me as our group struggled up tenement stairs toward the door to Raskolnikov's room. The air was cold, the stairs were old, and Willi had the collar of his camel-hair coat up around the muffler he also wore. I knew how to say "Willy" but not how to spell it—certainly not "Willie," nothing about "ie" seemed right; wasn't it "Willi Brandt"? yes, "Willi" was more appropriately European, and where else were we? Leningrad in winter, at the frozen edge of Asia—consequently I said, "Willy, do you remember what Rilke wrote to open his piece on Rodin?"

We could step up two abreast but only if we sidled, so we were facing one another. Gaddis's silence told me that he never indulged in smartass references and didn't take tests. Which wasn't fair, because his books, his carpers said, were full of arcanity and longer than the bar exams. "Fame is but the sum of the many misunderstandings that have gathered about a new name." I recited my reconstituted quote through a cloud of aspiration. He put the red tip of his nose between the soft paws of his mittens and groaned. He put his nose between his mittens. "Pity poor Dostoevsky," I said, sotto voce. Now of course cured, I could be fatuous in my middle age. "These guys can't even leave the man's characters alone," he said upon removing his nose from his mittens. The draft, basement-born, wasn't warmth rising, but it was nevertheless filling me like an arm through a sleeve. At yet another landing, in front of a boarded door, stood a sickly green bucket, its lid thrust out like a lower lip, its wire handle flipped up the other way as if soliciting a lift. Mary's red scarf was much admired but, during the darkness of the afternoon, admiration for everything had died away. Except for Bakhtin, of course, who was now more important than Dostoevsky. Ginsberg wore a flapped hat, Gaddis an inadequate gray cap, Auchincloss was in a dark stocking. "This is it," the professor who was serving as our guide announced, allowing his arms to leave the chest they had been hugging. "The murderer's apartment." Comrade Granin had become reverence itself, like a bust on a pedestal, and now he waited for us to take it all in. "From here it is exactly mumbled steps to the spot of the crime." I was bareheaded because I am hardy and brave, eschewing stock, cap, and hat. I scorned cover because nothing could ever replace the aviator headgear I was given when ten. I was so proud of. After a time the flaps no longer fastened under my chin. But I sported. I was Raoul Lufberry, French air ace. In snapshots, I grinned. "Is the bucket a historical marker?" Gaddis asked our guide, who gave no answer. He was, I suspect, furious with both of us. We had been disrespectful for three quarters of an hour.

Or had I misunderstood the nature of our journey? Was this the old woman's room and had we been retracing the murderer's skittish course across the courtyard below and up these windy stairs? Had we managed to pick up an ax from beneath some handy porter's bench on the way? "And here was the fourth story, here was the door, here was the flat opposite, the empty one." (I have just now looked up the passage.) I was certain that Gaddis understood our situation because, for him, Dostoevsky was as near to God as nature got. He would have been as disdainful of our guide's confusion of fiction with reality as I was, but he would have listened to every unclear word like a mole for a footstep. Then it was that our proctor, according to his guidelines, began to read the appropriate passage out of some authorized Soviet translation. My wife, Mary, standing with Adele Auchincloss a step above me, reached back a restraining hand and took my arm. Shut up, it said, with a squeeze for please. Gaddis had disappeared into a roll of wool. These Russians were not my idols. Well, perhaps André Bely was a bit golden toed and his pseudonym properly accented, otherwise my daily devotions were in Flaubert's French and Rilke's German. But the Russians spelled his first name Andrei, I remembered in the nick of time. On account of his accent, Professor Granin had turned the reading over to Mischa, one of our young translators. "Don't you think," I said to Gaddis, "that when a new character is introduced the reader should be given more information than a long unpronounceable name?" "Just say he comes from the provinces." We stood, our feet as fixed as our expressions, in a faint urine-yellow light. It was going to be a long read. Mischa held the book close to his face. His accent was excellent.

I had teased Willy a bit about his English-aping bourgeois enthusiasms early in our journey and before I realized how serious and full his appreciation was. So he might not relish my popping off even though his gorge was also rising through this well of iced air. The muffler concealed his chin but not his opinions. Which I wanted to be the same as mine despite indelible differences. Though I had lost sight of the set of his jaw. How much of his youth was he carrying around now under his camel-hair coat? Remembering, as he was supposed to, while Mischa recited, his own youthful reading. The tensions of the first time. Wasn't Muriel, his beautiful companion, Russian as well? Which accounted for just what, exactly?

Gaddis's love for the Russian novel—and for the predictable Russians at that—had surprised me, though in hindsight it shouldn't have, if I'd kept *The Recognitions* fully in front of me, because these works were nothing if not epic, with a reach as extended as their own steppes, with borders as far off as their frozen mountains. "Loose and baggy monsters," my treasured *cher maître* had said of them, a description too enviously mean-spirited to be forgotten yet memorably on the mark. In sum, they wore plus fours though not for golf. But if loose and baggy, *The Recognitions* was nevertheless knit. These Russian tomes were broody books too, fundamentally melancholy, especially when, as Gogol was, they were funny. Above all, as Bakhtin had finally made us aware (bless his sainted name),

Dostoevsky at least was demonically polyvocal. He had been infernalized at an early age. Novels jam-packed with passionate ideas half-understood but as motivational as money. Every one evincing major moral concerns. Moreover, their authors were majestically indifferent to their mistakes, confident that any error would be but a beauty mark on a work of genius. Novels made of issues as well as innumerable details, richly peopled, penned in brash and innocent confidence, and written from outrage as much as ego. Worse yet, bedbugged and flea-bagged by proper names. "Just say he wore a dusty overcoat and checked trousers, and came out hatless onto the low porch of the posting station at X," Gaddis said. "There is a bucket marking the spot where Mr. Hatless stood."

It was kind of Gaddis to give me my Turgenev at this juncture. "Bely was a bloody mystic," he said, withdrawing his offer of *Fathers and Children*. "Which one of them wasn't cuckoo?" I was standing on a creaky tread. "Doc Chekhov."

Though he had crossed oceans in his youth, and run around nations in pursuit of girls, I felt Gaddis would have turned down a similar invitation to visit almost any other country now. However, the Russians would be an irresistible draw. I did remember how Raskolnikov had hung the ax head from a noose concealed beneath his coat. Present custom would advise a sawed-off shotgun. Or a malicious self-serving review. Neath his fulsome robe Phaedrus concealed someone else's speech which he planned to deliver as his own. And I've noted since how cleverly Dostoevsky lets the ax hang, as if swung by Damocles, over the old woman's figure while he describes her "thin, light hair, streaked with gray and thickly smeared with grease," before its blunt end arrives to bloody her head just a bit above that broken comb the author has deftly put there, as well as the rat's tail in which the wretched woman's hair was plaited. Beautifully done, no doubt about it. An ax murder by a master.

Gaddis had bade the quad a pissy goodbye during the sad senior year of his Harvard career, so he was largely self-taught and would not be disabused of his youthful enthusiasms as I suspected most of us were who went on through the levels of snobbery one's momentary peers deemed necessary to an education. I remember having to leave Spengler and Tchaikovsky, Emerson and Nietzsche, e. e. cummings and Thomas Wolfe behind on my journey to more elevated realms—as much as I had loved them once. And the higher one rose in the ranks of the System the greater the sacrifice the System asked for: eventually Verdi was dumped for Monteverdi, Tolstoy for

Flaubert, and everybody for Cézanne. It took twenty years for me to return to Nietzsche, Emerson required even more self-discipline, while Dickens was recovered the day I believed I had at last learned to read.

Yet even when I was aware I had shaken off my bad ideological habits, and was actually paying attention to the words as they miraculously ran from Cap to Period, I never felt so special that I could call myself a Dickens reader or want to hold him to account for faults I may have feared I had. I could have complained: "Hey, don't get so soggy, and leave melodrama for the movies," but aren't we always grateful for the sins of others? His readers loved him for his weaknesses because they shared them. Gaddis's critics hated him for the strengths they didn't have.

Stendhal wrote, he said, for the happy few a hundred years ahead. It's true that the happy are always in the minority. But if you wrote for the happy few a hundred years ahead you would certainly be scorned by the miserable many presently in dire need of fun and absorbing story. It was pitch dark at three in the afternoon and there was snow everywhere in the city that lay always under an alias. It was a habit of postrevolutionary countries to buy new street signs for every regime change—so the Esplanade of Friday the Thirteenth could become the Plaza of Fallen Heroes. In a wink the Highway of High Hopes got renamed Sellout Strasse. Regally titled Königsberg was now a plebeian Kaliningrad. Kant, the city's most distinguished citizen, remained *der Allzermahler*, even if there was no moral law *within* to build *without* the universal kingdom of ends.

Starless, moonless as it was on Neva's banks, you could still see by the snow's sheen where to go in search of Raskolnikov's lodgings. No. I was out of step again. Now we were hunting for Dostoevsky's digs. His furniture would be at home even if he wasn't. I prefer movies in which people cars planes and buildings are blown up and gasoline abused, because I don't have to think, then, about people cars planes and buildings blowing up and dreams being misused. Could I count myself one of Andrei Bely's happy few in that case? 'Fraid not. Merciless man. Bely called his novels "cerebral play." No one reaches visceral velocity. Early in our visit, one of the bullies who called himself a host asked me whom I took to be Russian literature's most important character. Mr. Shishnarfne, I said, who enters *St. Petersburg* as a hallucination and dwindles to a dot.

Gaddis's god had never risen from the dead as so many of mine had, and I could see his youthful love glowing plainly when our group visited Dostoevsky's apartment. The sight of the master's desk actually wet Willy's eyes. I envied him. When my eyes moistened it was only for Bette Davis, and such a shallow show of weakness made me angry with my soul. I fancied that he was feeling the same sort of exalted state of nostalgia for an imaginary past that I had felt a few days before when our party had left Moscow in a midnight snowfall for Leningrad on the legendary Red Arrow Express. The train moved slowly from the station through a whitened landscape more literary and historical than railed, while I cooled my glass of weedy tea against the compartment window, and wondered if it could really be little ole me at midnight on this train tracking a perfect Russian snow, leaving my beloved Anna, Katya, or Marfa Petrovna behind, on my way to relieve Leningrad from its one-hundred-day siege by the huns. Dostoevsky's room contained a table whose cloth covered all but its corners with red leaves cut into velvet. A lamp that bore a shade resembling a beaded-glass crown shone on a casually opened cigarette box so directly the case's golden bottom glowed. Gaddis allowed a forefinger to rest upon the corner of a desk where the most ordinary of objects lay—letter opener, penholder, inkwell. This— *this*—is Dostoevsky's desk, his finger said. Or more likely: this is where those remarkable pages were made. Willy had taken his cap off as he entered, said nothing, but looked at everything as one looks at a lover at long last unclad.

I am an irreverent person because I believe reverence is usually misplaced when it isn't faked, but I felt reverence for his reverence then.

Mischa asked of some small box: "What's that?" Mary was shaking her hair out of her hat and had no hand to restrain me. "A bomb in a sardine tin," I said. Mischa was a nice young man. He laughed. Such a showoff, I said of myself to myself, but was it showing off when no one but a nice young man was shone? Maybe it was art.

Another of Willy's admirations was Samuel Butler's *The Way of All Flesh*, a work Theodore Dreiser also prized, perhaps because it gave parents a bad time, dissed marriage, was scornful of religion, and exposed Victorian institutions as guardians of privilege and power. Or because it was as pointlessly plotless as our hunt for a fictional murderer's bedroom. Or because it was fundamentally philosophical, as Dostoevsky always tried to be. And dealt with money and property as though they were cards. Well, a book in which the Bible gets kicked across a room into a forlorn corner certainly has merit, I thought, but these reasons did not account for the supremely

411

William Gaddis

Key West, Florida, February 1998. Photograph by Benjamin Swett.

high regard in which Gaddis held it. I felt happier in my conclusion that Butler himself was part owner of Willy's praise since he had kept the manuscript locked up till his death, and even if he were protecting the relatives it savages by waiting for their deaths, he could never be accused of writing this book for money, fame, or sex with a faithful reader.

For Willy, writing was a serious matter. How serious? Beckett serious. It was serious in the sense that any aim disgraced it that wasn't utmost. He never toured, read in circles, rode the circuit. He rarely gave interviews or published opinions. He didn't cultivate the cultivated, nose around the newsworthy, network or glad-hand, sign books or blurb. He didn't teach, prognosticate, distribute awards. He was suspicious of wanna-bes, wary of flatterers, he guarded his gates. He didn't write the way he did to prove how smart he was, to create a clique that would clack at his every move. Or to get reviewed. Or to receive the plaudits of some crowd. Or to be well paid and bathe in a tub of butter. Or to be feared or sneered at or put down by pipsqueaks. He wrote as well as he could and as he felt the art required, and he knew he would not be thanked for it. Nor would he have an ass available for posterity to kiss.

Willy followed no false gods for he believed in none. Mankind's most universal habit was hypocrisy; its true and enduring love was money, its favorite avocation litigation, its drug of choice amusement, and the fullest expression of its fears to be found in the dogmas, trappings, and hierarchies of organized religion. He would have liked to have been an *Allzermahler.*

Gaddis knew the realities so worshipped by readers were fakes. Instead he created realities fashioned from their lies, their superstitions, their fatuous remarks, their pretensions, their envy, their guilty excuses and habitual bad faith. His chuckle was the chuckle of someone whose business was "seeing through." He knew that entertainers ate the survivors of their shows. He knew what it was like to be distasteful to tastemakers. He knew when and for whom he should doff his cap.

How Russian was he? Had Viktor Shklovsky read him he'd have said that Gaddis's novels practiced *ostranenie* in its purest form, i.e., defamiliarization, placing inanities, like urinals, in hallowed places, grocery lists in museum cases; consequently *zatrudnyonnaya forma,* or defacilitation, as well, by forcing the reader to pay attention and puzzle over meanings; then *zamedlenie* or retardation, too, sacrificing easy enjoyments to demanding strategies.

William Gaddis

J R did for money what Butler did, but *J R* was also a music box, a Bely-organized symphonia. You only had to open it. Then it would start its tunes—tunes that ranged from hymns to hurdy-gurdy. How could you not hear? It's what the Englished Dostoevsky doesn't have. Listen to the guy I call the God damn man:

> Sixteen years like living with a God damned invalid sixteen years every time you come in sitting there waiting just like you left him wave his stick at you, plump up his pillow cut a paragraph add a sentence hold his God damned hand little warm milk add a comma slip out for some air pack of cigarettes come back in right where you left him, eyes follow you around the room wave his God damned stick figure out what the hell he wants, plump the God damned pillow bandage read aloud move a clause around wipe his chin new paragraph God damned eyes follow you out stay a week, stay a month whole God damned year think about something else, God damned friends asking how he's coming along all expect him out any day don't want bad news no news rather hear lies, big smile out any day now, walk down the street God damned sunshine begin to think maybe you'll meet him maybe cleared things up got out by himself come back open the God damned door right there where you left him . . .

Maria Callas can remain enshrined in her shellac. Willy was a metasinger because he was a metaman. The world suffered, he said, from metapsychosis.

We made our way down the stairs. They wouldn't pass the fire code, these worn wooden sticks. I put my hand on Gaddis's shoulder, not to steady either of us, but to soothe what I felt was a shared exasperation. Though muffled by his muffler, Willy snorted on my behalf. He wore the wrong kind of cap for this cold. His ears glowed like Fyodor's cigarette box would when we got there. "Sentimentality should be one of the deadly sins," I said to no one in particular, still stuck in my fatuous phase. It was especially mortifying when one's tears ran from the contemplation of a pregnant Bette Davis. "Faith is bad, bad faith is deadly," Gaddis answered to no one's question. For folks our age, Sartre was unavoidable. And during our brief span of effort and exclusion, excellence as an ideal became romantic.

Well, excellence is inconveniently difficult. Moreover, as Aristotle argued concerning virtue, it is neither guaranteed nor rewarded by any external sign. We shall all go to our graves in ignorance of our

414

work's worth. Our aims may be as perverse as our group's search for Raskolnikov's room was that dark afternoon, and our comfort as cold as a Leningrad winter, but perhaps we can say with some honestly earned pride that during our most minor and marginal lives we did not dishonor our gods.

NOTES ON CONTRIBUTORS

JULIE AGOOS is the author of *Above the Land*, selected for the Yale Series of Younger Poets and winner of the Towson State University Award for Literature (Yale University), and *Calendar Year* (Sheep Meadow).

DAVID ANTIN is a poet, performer, and critic. His most recent book (with Charles Bernstein) is *A Conversation with David Antin* (Gramercy). His last book of talk pieces, *what it means to be avant-garde*, was published by New Directions. He has just completed a book of talk pieces called *i never knew what time it was*.

RAE ARMANTROUT's latest books are *Veil: New and Selected Poems* (Wesleyan) and *The Pretext* (Green Integer). *Up to Speed*, a new collection of her poetry, is forthcoming next year from Wesleyan.

ELIZABETH ARNOLD is the author of *The Reef* (University of Chicago).

PAUL AUSTER's eleventh novel, *Oracle Night*, is forthcoming from Henry Holt in December.

RUSSELL BANKS has written fourteen books of fiction, including the novels *Continental Drift*, *Rule of the Bone*, and *Cloudsplitter*, and five collections of short stories, including *The Angel on the Roof: New and Selected Stories* (all Harper-Collins). He is president of the International Parliament of Writers.

MADISON SMARTT BELL's eleven novels include *Anything Goes* (Pantheon), *Master of the Crossroads*, *Ten Indians*, *All Soul's Rising*, and *Soldier's Joy* (all Penguin), which received the Lillian Smith Award in 1989. He has also published two collections of short stories, *Zero db* (Macdonald & Company) and *Barking Man* (Penguin).

MARTINE BELLEN is the author of six collections of poetry, the most recent of which is *The Vulnerability of Order* (Copper Canyon). Forthcoming is the bilingual (German/English) *Magic Musée* (Verlag im Walgut).

DONALD BERGER is the author of *Quality Hill* (Lost Roads). He administers and teaches in the Creative Writing Program at the University of Maryland.

MICHAEL BERGSTEIN is managing editor of *Conjunctions*, and is currently working on a novel and short story collection.

JAKE BERTHOT's work is included in numerous major collections in the United States and abroad. He teaches at the School of Visual Arts in New York.

SVEN BIRKERTS recently wrote the introduction to the paperback edition of William Gaddis's *Agapē Agape* (Penguin).

MARY CAPONEGRO has recently been anthologized in the *Italian American Reader*, edited by Bill Torelli (William Morrow), and in Italy, in a collection of works about 9/11, edited by Daniela Daniele (Einaudi).

HAYDEN CARRUTH is the author of twenty-nine books, among them *Scrambled Eggs and Whiskey* (Copper Canyon), which won the National Book Award for Poetry.

SUSAN CHEEVER is the author of ten books, including *Home Before Dark, Note Found in a Bottle,* and *Treetops* (all Washington Square). Her biography of Bill Wilson, co-founder of Alcoholics Anonymous, is forthcoming in February 2004.

MERLE COLLINS's books include two novels, *Angel* (Seal) and *The Colour of Forgetting* (Virago), a collection of short stories, *Rain Darling* (The Women's Press), and two poetry collections. A third collection, *Lady in a Boat,* was published this fall by Peepal Tree Press. She is presently finishing a novel entitled *Streams of Water.*

ROBERT COOVER's latest books are *The Grand Hotels (of Joseph Cornell),* by Burning Deck, and *The Adventures of Lucky Pierre* (Grove).

WILLIAM CORBETT is editing *Just the Thing: The Selected Letters of James Schuyler,* forthcoming from Turtle Point Press. He lives in Boston and teaches writing in MIT's Program of Writing and Humanistic Studies.

SEAN COTTER is the translator of three books of Romanian poetry, the newest of which, *Goldsmith Market* by Liliana Ursu, was published this fall by Zephyr Press.

The most recent of DON DeLILLO's thirteen novels are *Underworld, The Body Artist,* and *Cosmopolis* (all Scribner). He is also the author of two stage plays, *The Day Room* and *Valparaiso.* He was born and raised in New York City.

RIKKI DUCORNET's seventh novel, *Gazelle,* was published this year by Knopf.

STEVE ERICKSON is the author of seven novels, including the latest, *Our Ecstatic Day*—from which "Zed Lake" is an excerpt—to be published in 2004 by Simon & Schuster. He is also the editor of *Black Clock,* a literary magazine published semiannually by CalArts beginning next spring.

BRIAN EVENSON is the author of six books of fiction, most recently *Dark Property* (Four Walls Eight Windows). He teaches in the Creative Writing Program at Brown University.

417

Among RODRIGO FRESÁN's books are *Historia Argentina* (Autrement), *Vidas de Santos, Trabajos Manuales* (both Planeta), *Esperanto, La Velocidad de las Cosas, Mantra,* and *Kensington Gardens* (all Mondadori). He lives and works as a journalist and translator in Barcelona.

WILLIAM H. GASS's latest book is *Tests of Time* (Knopf).

RENEE GLADMAN's newest collection of prose, *The Activist,* was published this year by Krupskaya. Her previous books are *Juice* (Kelsey Street), *Not Right Now* (Second Story Books), and *Arlem* (Idiom). "Untitled" is from a new work, *Newcomer Can't Swim.*

DAVID GRUBBS is a Brooklyn-based recording artist and writer. His newest release is *The World Brushed Aside* (Fatcat, United Kingdom).

ANSELM HOLLO's latest book, *Notes on the Possibilities and Attractions of Existence: Selected Poems 1965–2002* (Coffee House), received the San Francisco Poetry Center Book Award for 2001. "Guests of Space (II)" continues the work begun in "Guests of Space" (which appeared in *Conjunctions:35, American Poetry: States of the Art*).

Among MAUREEN HOWARD's many books are *A Lover's Almanac, Big As Life: Three Tales for Spring* (both Penguin), and *Natural History* (Carroll & Graf). She is working on the next season, summer, the subject of the third novel in her quartet. She is a fellow this year at the New York Public Library Center for Scholars and Writers.

FANNY HOWE's new collection of poems is *Gone* (University of California). Her book of stories, *Economics,* was published last year by Flood Editions.

SUSAN HOWE's books of poetry include *The Europe of Trusts: Selected Poems, Pierce-Arrow,* and, most recently, *The Midnight* (all New Directions). She is also the author of two books of literary criticism, *My Emily Dickinson* (North Atlantic Books) and *The Birth-mark: unsettling the wilderness in American literary history* (Wesleyan).

SIRI HUSTVEDT's third novel, *What I Loved,* was published by Henry Holt this spring.

CATHERINE IMBRIGLIO has new work appearing or forthcoming in *Pleiades, Denver Quarterly, First Intensity, American Letters & Commentary,* and *No: A Journal of the Arts.*

ROBERT KELLY is completing a novel, from which the chapter appearing in this issue is taken. His next collection of poems, *Lapis,* is forthcoming from Godine next spring.

JONATHAN LETHEM is the author of six novels, most recently *The Fortress of Solitude* (Doubleday).

Among JACKSON MAC LOW's most recent books are *20 Forties* (Zasterle), *Struggle Through* (Tsunami Editions), and *Doings: Assorted Performance Pieces 1955–2002*, selections from a half-century of Mac Low's verbal, graphic, and musical scores (Granary Books).

CLARENCE MAJOR was a finalist for the National Book Award in 1999 for *Configurations: New and Selected Poems.*

NORMAN MANEA is the Francis Flournoy Professor of European Culture and writer in residence at Bard College. His most recent book, *The Hooligan's Return*, was published by Farrar, Straus & Giroux in August 2003.

BEN MARCUS's latest book is *The Father Costume* (Artspace Books). Forthcoming is a collaborative book with the painter Terry Winters.

CAROLE MASO is the author of nine books, including *Beauty Is Convulsive: The Passion of Frida Kahlo* (Counterpoint). She teaches at Brown University.

JOSEPH McELROY is the author of eight novels, including *Actress in the House* (Overlook), which came out earlier this year.

EDIE MEIDAV is the author of *The Far Field: A Novel of Ceylon* and the forthcoming *Crawl Space* (both Houghton Mifflin). She directs the M.F.A. Program in Writing and Consciousness at New College of California in San Francisco.

W. S. MERWIN's most recent book of poetry is *The Pupil* (Knopf).

This year RICK MOODY's *The Black Veil* (Little Brown) received the PEN/Martha Albrand award for excellence in the memoir. He is currently at work on a new novel.

HONOR MOORE's newest books are *Darling* (Grove) and a biography, *The White Blackbird, A Life of the Painter Margarett Sargent by Her Granddaughter* (Viking).

STEVEN MOORE is the author of several books and essays on the work of William Gaddis.

BRADFORD MORROW's latest novel, *Ariel's Crossing*, was published this summer in paperback by Penguin. His short story "Lush" won an O. Henry Prize for 2003. He is founding editor of *Conjunctions* and teaches at Bard College.

HOWARD NORMAN's forthcoming books are the memoirs *My Famous Evening* and *Don't Forget Me*. His novels include *The Northern Lights, The Bird Artist*, and *The Haunting of L.* (Farrar, Straus & Giroux).

JOYCE CAROL OATES is the author, most recently, of the novel *The Tattooed Girl* (Ecco) and the story collection *Small Avalanches* (Harper Tempest). Her play *Dr. Magic* premiered at Bard College in 2002 and has since been adapted as a chamber opera. She is professor of humanities at Princeton.

419

STEWART O'NAN's latest novel is *The Night Country* (Farrar, Straus & Giroux).

CYNTHIA OZICK's latest novel is *The Puttermesser Papers;* her newest collection of essays is *Quarrel & Quandary* (both Vintage). She is currently completing *Lights and Watchtowers,* a novel.

RON PADGETT's newest books include a collection of poems, *You Never Know* (Coffee House), and a memoir/biography, *Oklahoma Tough: My Father, King of the Tulsa Bootleggers* (University of Oklahoma).

MICHAEL PALMER's most recent collections of poetry are *The Promises of Glass* and *Codes Appearing (Poems 1979–1988),* both by New Directions. His contribution to a multiple collaboration with the painter Gerhard Richter was published by the San Francisco Museum of Modern Art as *Richter 858.* A new book of poems, *Company of Moths,* is in preparation.

STANLEY PLUMLY's latest book is *Argument & Song: Sources & Silences in Poetry,* a selection of essays (Handsel Books/Other Press). "Spirit Birds" is from a new collection entitled *White Bruise.*

ELIZABETH ROBINSON is the author of *Pure Descent* (Sun & Moon), winner of the National Poetry Series in 2001, and *Apprehend* (University Press of New England), winner of the Fence Modern Poets Series in 2002.

A Book of Witness, JEROME ROTHENBERG's eleventh book of poems from New Directions, appeared earlier this year. Other books include selected poems from 1980–2000 in French and Spanish versions, two volumes of the anthology *Poems for the Millennium* (University of California), and *Writing Through: Translations and Variations,* forthcoming next year from Wesleyan.

MARK RUDMAN's poetic trilogy, published by Wesleyan, includes *The Millennium Hotel, Provoked in Venice,* and *Rider,* which received the National Book Critics Circle Award. His latest book is *The Couple,* also by Wesleyan. "Birthday Call" is from his recently completed book-length poem *Sunday's on the Phone.*

LESLIE SCALAPINO's newest books include *Zither & Autobiography* (Wesleyan) and *Dahlia's Iris—Secret Autobiography and Fiction* (a novel from FC₂).

CARTER SCHOLZ's books include *Radiance* and *The Amount to Carry* (both Picador USA). He is a member of Frog Peak Music, a composers' collective.

JOANNA SCOTT is the author of six novels, including *Arrogance* (W. W. Norton), *The Manikin* (Henry Holt), and, most recently, *Tourmaline* (Little Brown), and a collection of short fiction, *Various Antidotes* (Henry Holt).

REBECCA SEIFERLE's third poetry collection, *Bitter* (Copper Canyon), won the Western States Book Award and a Pushcart Prize. Her translation of César Vallejo's *The Black Heralds* is forthcoming this fall from Copper Canyon.

REGINALD SHEPHERD's fourth collection, *Otherhood,* was published this past spring by the University of Pittsburgh Press. Several poems in that book first appeared in *Conjunctions.*

DAVID SHIELDS's *Remote: Reflections on Life in the Shadow of Celebrity*, winner of the PEN/Revson Award, has recently been published in paperback (University of Wisconsin).

CHRISTOPHER SORRENTINO is completing his new novel, to be published by Farrar, Straus & Giroux.

JOSEPH TABBI is the author of *Cognitive Fictions* (Minnesota) and *Postmodern Sublime* (Cornell). He edited and introduced the last fiction and collected non-fiction of William Gaddis.

JAMES TATE's most recent books are *Memoir of the Hawk* (Ecco) and *Dreams of a Robot Dance Bee* (Verse).

REETIKA VAZIRANI (1962–2003) taught in the *Callaloo* Creative Writing Work-shops at Emory University and at the Bennington Writing Seminars. She au-thored the books *White Elephants* (Beacon) and *World Hotel* (Copper Canyon), which won an Anisfield-Wolf award.

ELIOT WEINBERGER's most recent books are *9/12*, a collection of political articles; *The New Directions Anthology of Classical Chinese Poetry*, which he edited; and a new edition of his translation of Vicente Huidobro's *Altazor*.

PAUL WEST's new novel is *The Immensity of the Here and Now*, a passage from which won a Pushcart Prize this year. A book of essays, *Sheer Fiction IV*, will be published in 2004. He is now working on *Prisoners of War*, about his soldier father, excerpts from which have recently appeared in *Harper's*.

NEW DIRECTIONS
Fall 2003/Winter 2004

NOON

A LITERARY ANNUAL

1369 MADISON AVENUE   PMB 298
NEW YORK   NEW YORK   10128-0711

EDITION PRICE $9 DOMESTIC $14 FOREIGN

Indiana, Indiana
Novel by Laird Hunt
ISBN 1-56689-144-2 $20.00
"Faulknerian . . . vivid (and heartbreaking)."
—*Kirkus Reviews*

Echo Tree
The Collected Short Fiction of Henry Dumas
ISBN 1-56689-149-3 $15.95
"Each sentence a revelation of experience. . . .
Actual black art, real, man, and stunning."
—AMIRI BARAKA

The Grasshopper King
Debut Novel by Jordan Ellenberg
ISBN 1-56689-139-6 $14.00
"A brilliant debut: Jordan Ellenberg's *The Grass-
hopper King* is perhaps the funniest and best-
written 'college' novel I've read since *Pale Fire*."
—JOHN BARTH

In the Room of Never Grieve
New and Selected Poems 1985-2003
by Anne Waldman
ISBN 1-56689-145-0 $30.00
The essential collection and companion CD.

The Cloud of Knowable Things
New Poems by Elaine Equi
ISBN 1-56689-142-6 $15.00
"You've heard of 'smart drinks' or 'smart drugs,'
said to chemically boost intellect? These are truly
smart poems." —*L.A. Weekly*

A Handmade Museum
New Poems by Brenda Coultas
ISBN 1-56689-143-4 $15.00
"In these five sets of poems, Coultas unearths an
entire America." —*Publishers Weekly*

Coffee House Press

Fiction & Poetry

Available at fine bookstores everywhere.
Good books are brewing at coffeehousepress.org

the false sun recordings

new poetry by James Wagner available from 3rd bed & SPD
104 Pleasant St. Lincoln, Rhode Island 02865   3rdbed.com

At a time of extraordinary displacement and global confusion,
these insistently sane poems manage a remarkable interaction of viable
realities, of multiple twists, turns and provisions of language's singular
instrument, syntax, and the words which it puts in order. Each turn here
is a possibility, an endlessly refracting multiplicity of instances.
Each word takes its own step, as it must, toward recognition.
—*Robert Creeley*

Pegasus Descending: a Book of the Best Bad Verse
edited by James Camp, X. J. Kennedy, & Keith Waldrop

Out of print for thirty years, this hilarious and disgusting anthology is again available, complete and unexpurgated. The editors have rummaged the arsenal of English poetry for its most spectacular fizzles. They have been no respecters of persons: Sarah Taylor Shatford rubs shoulders here with Milton, Keats and Wordsworth. The poems presented are absolutely sincere; no failure is faked. All infelicities are unintended. Here there is—as James Wright declared after hearing these poems—"nothing mediocre!"

Anthology, 240 pages, offset, smyth-sewn, ISBN 1-886224-68-4, original paperback $10

Dallas Wiebe: The Vox Populi Street Stories
A satirical novel, narrated by Gottlieb Otto Liebgott, a retired German doctor who lives in Cincinnati. It centers on the life and career of Dallasandro Vibini, a private investigator of petty crimes that are emblematic of the inanities of our absurd world. It hilariously blends the shaggy dog story with mock-detective fiction and, finally, mock-romance as Vibini (over 50) marries an eighteen year old girl and finds salvation in becoming a father.

By the author of *Going to the Mountain, Skyblue's Essays,* and *Our Asian Journey.*

Fiction, 312 pages, offset, smyth-sewn, ISBN 1-886224-64-1 original paperback $15

Marie Borel: Close Quote
[Série d'Ecriture Supplement, Nr. 4; trans. Keith Waldrop]

Borel forces "other people's sentences" into a dialogue with each other, the spirit of irony ruling the space between. Simple sentences, everybody's sentences form something like *Everybody's Autobiography:* "A simple man, he loves the lake, money also somewhat..."

Beside *Fin de citation,* Borel's books include *Le léopard est mort avec ses taches* and *Trompe Loup.* She lives in Paris.

Prose poems, 40 pages, offset, saddle-stitched, ISBN 1-886224-67-6, $5

Ludwig Harig: The Trip to Bordeaux
[Dichten=, Nr. 6; trans. Susan Bernofsky]

Four adults, a child and a cat. Harig tells their adventures in humorous permutations, Baroque word-games, confrontations, catalogs, and snippets of philosophical discourse lifted from Montaigne, the some-time mayor of Bordeaux. A riotous tale.

Harig, born in 1927, was part of the experimental Stuttgart School. He is author of many novels. This is the first translation into English.

Novella, 104 pp., offset, smyth-sewn, ISBN 1-886224-53-6 original paperback $10

www.burningdeck.com
Order from: Small Press Distribution, 1341 Seventh St.,
Berkeley, CA 94710 1-800/869-7553 orders@spdbooks.org

DAHLIA'S IRIS
Secret Autobiography and Fiction

LESLIE SCALAPINO

FICTION COLLECTIVE TWO
HTTP://FC2.ORG

2003
World Fantasy Award Finalist

CONJUNCTIONS:39

THE
NEW WAVE
FABULISTS

Guest-Edited by
Peter Straub

This anthology features eighteen previously unpublished stories and two essays by leading science fiction, fantasy, and horror writers who simultaneously explore and erase the boundaries of those genres. Contributors are Jonathan Carroll, John Crowley, Andy Duncan, Karen Joy Fowler, Neil Gaiman, Joe Haldeman, Elizabeth Hand, M. John Harrison, Nalo Hopkinson, John Kessel, Jonathan Lethem, Kelly Link, China Miéville, James Morrow, Patrick O'Leary, Paul Park, Peter Straub, Gene Wolfe, John Clute, and Gary K. Wolfe.

The issue also features eighteen specially commissioned original drawings and a color cover by master cartoonist Gahan Wilson.

448 pages. $15.00, shipping included.

"... unfailingly well-written."

—*Philadelphia Inquirer*

"Read them all and let your imagination out for a romp."
—*The New Mexican*

CONJUNCTIONS:40

40 x 40

Edited by
Bradford Morrow

New fiction, poetry, plays, and creative essays by forty of our favorite contemporary writers. Contributors include Can Xue, Robert Coover, Lyn Hejinian, Robert Creeley, Martine Bellen, Joyce Carol Oates, John Ashbery, Ann Lauterbach, William T. Vollmann, Rick Moody, Eliot Weinberger, Lois-Ann Yamanaka, Han Ong, Christopher Sorrentino, Angela Carter, Robert Kelly, Frederic Tuten, William H. Gass, among others.

The issue also features a sixteen-page color portfolio of paintings and text by Ilya Kabakov.

408 pages. $15.00, shipping included.

To order, please send payment to:

Conjunctions
Bard College
Annandale-on-Hudson, NY 12504
Phone: 845-758-1539
Email: Conjunctions@bard.edu